TRAPPED!

I looked over to the door, which was now moving back and forth. Someone was jiggling it. That same someone was using a knife to try and get the lock open.

Suddenly the knife withdrew. I heard a very faint, metallic noise that sounded distinctly like someone slotting a bullet into the chamber of a gun.

I froze for just a second, and then decided I was not willing to wait to find out whether I was right. I looked for someplace to hide, and unless I thought the shower curtain in the bathroom was going to shield me, I was out of luck. I tried the door at the back, but it was locked tighter than the door from the hallway.

I had to get out of here.

As quickly as I could, I went to the window. The lock was stuck, the window swollen with moisture. The wind belted another flock of icy pellets against the glass. In a moment I was going to be on the receiving end of all nature's fury. Still a better option than a gun.

I started bashing the lock on the window.

Books by Dana Cameron

MORE BITTER THAN DEATH
A FUGITIVE TRUTH
PAST MALICE
GRAVE CONSEQUENCES
SITE UNSEEN

MORE BITTER THAN DEATH

AN EMMA FIELDING MYSTERY

DANA CAMERON

AVON BOOKS

An Imprint of HarperCollinsPublishers

AVON BOOKS
An Imprint of HarperCollins*Publishers*
10 East 53rd Street
New York, New York 10022-5299

Copyright © 2005 by Dana Cameron
ISBN: 0-06-055463-0
www.avonmystery.com

First Avon Books paperback printing: June 2005

Avon Trademark Reg. U.S. Pat. Off. and in Other Countries, Marca Registrada, Hecho en U.S.A.
HarperCollins® is a registered trademark of HarperCollins Publishers Inc.

Printed in the U.S.A.

10 9 8 7 6 5 4 3 2 1

For my parents,
Joyce and Al,
on the occasion of their fortieth anniversary

Acknowledgments

I'D LIKE TO THANK THE GOOD FOLKS WHO cheered me on through the process of writing this book, kept Emma true to herself, offered their expertise, and were in so many ways helpful: Ann Barbier, Susan Buffum, Pam Crane, Toni Kelner, Beth Krueger, and Anne Wilder. Christina Ward, my agent, and Sarah Durand, my editor at Avon, are always there with a safety net when I try something new; I'm also grateful that they continue to push me out onto new, higher, and more interesting tight-ropes. James, as always, you rock.

Emma J. Fielding   is scheduled for the following events at
the January meetings of ASAA, Green Bank, NH

Brrrr! ☺

Wednesday: Moderator, Tour of Site, Fort Providence, Penitence Point, Maine
Note the following additions:

Duncan Thayer — *Evil! Why him?*

Meg rules!   Meg Garrity   ☠

Wednesday PM: Panelist, Plenary Session. Papers in Honor of Julius Garrison

Our fearless leader!   Scott Tomberg, Moderating

Jerk   Julius Garrison   *Petra W. must be wrangling him...*

"Larry" rules the old timers!   Frank Lawrence

Thomas Roche   *old coot!*

Bone Lady = voice of reason   Carla Sandfield
                                here...

~~Opening Cocktail Reception and Dance~~   *THE POKER GAME!!* ♡♢♧♤
Scott and Carla say these guys are in:

Brad DuBois   Chris Hensley   Jay Whitaker   Lissa Vance   Sue Ayers

Thursday: Participant, Artifact Comparison Roundtable.   Note the following additions:
ARA ··· THE GOODY GRAPE! ☕

Misha — sweetie!   Michelle Lima

Beatrice Carter   *absolutely barmy...*

New kid?   Kelly Booker

Noreen McAllister   *Witch. Tramp. Whiner!*

No clue who he is → William S. Widmark *??*

Your paper presentation is on   Thursday   *So, what do we all do* __after__ *Thurs.?* ☺

Saturday PM: Banquet   *Rubber chicken and speeches — yawn.* ☺
*Must check on students: Meg + Neal, Dian, Katie Bell.
Also — Alex, Jordan, Hedia?*

★ *Look for Laurel Fairchild! She knows everyone!!* ★

MORE
BITTER
THAN
DEATH

Chapter 1

I WAS BACK AT PENITENCE POINT. THEY SAY THAT every criminal returns to the scene of the crime, and I sure felt guilty, but I wasn't sure about what. I had a lot to choose from, at the moment.

Although we were all stamping and shivering, walking on paths that were carved out of the knee-deep early January snow, I was knocking almost everyone dead with my tour of the site. Nearly everyone had paid attention when I warned them to dress sensibly, and the good thing about the gray afternoon was that it was perfect for imagining what it must have been like here four hundred years ago when the English colonists were wondering what the hell they were doing stuck in Maine. And frankly, being on the Atlantic coast when a storm was brewing, you had to want to be there for some reason. The snow that was already on the ground damped out the ambient noise of the twenty-first century, the dull light warning of the promised storm made you pause to think about life when you couldn't just flick a switch for light and heat, and the sound of the water brushing the beach and rolling the cobbles lent you a little of the sense of isolation that must have characterized the days of the first English settlers on this shore. I made good use of these points as I walked the group over to where we believed the buildings of Fort Providence once were, and to judge from the responses—oohs, ahhs, questions, and laughter in the right places—I was doing a great job.

This was one of my favorite things: talking about my archaeological work with my colleagues from up and down the East Coast. The conference we were all gathered for was one thing—a yearly archaeological jamboree of hundreds of kindred spirits—but actually being on the ground, at the site, in the environment, with a group of people who spoke your language, should have been sheer bliss.

What was really pissing me off was the two men who were tuned out, each in his own little world, at opposite ends of the site. The way I see it, if you're not going to pay attention, you shouldn't really take up someone else's space on the bus. More than that, I couldn't stand how childishly angry I felt with them—each for separate reasons—and struggled to focus on what was important.

I kept my talk brief and to the point, however, because the wind whipped right off the water to bite right through to the bone, no matter how many layers of wool or fleece or Gore-Tex you wore. And every time I looked over, they were the only two not paying attention. I tried funny, I tried serious replete with jargon, I tried romance and pathos. The rest of the group was right there following along with me, but no matter what I did, those two just wouldn't react.

I hate when that happens. I hate how petulant I felt, no matter how well I was hiding it.

What do you want, guys? Archaeology not enough for you? I can do murder and mayhem, if that's more to your taste.

Ah, to hell with them, I thought, and concentrated on the people who knew enough to pay attention, strutted and shimmied for them all the harder: archaeology as performance art. Knowing the older guy was just looking off to the water, and the younger, red-headed guy off to the right was looking around like he was waiting for a bus, impatient and bored, just gnawed at me. I had enough on my plate dealing with the past—my own personal past in this place—without them making it worse.

It was time to go.

The skies were darkening, low clouds heavy with snow as I finished off the spiel and began to herd everyone up the slope toward the bus, promising coffee and hot chocolate and a warm ride back to the conference hotel in New Hampshire. We'd been lucky so far, but the weather was looking nastier by the minute and the news had been promising a good solid storm by nightfall. I counted off the folks as they climbed on board, accepting praise from some, offers of data from others, making sure I didn't strand anyone at the site: that would have been a little too realistic a historical reenactment for anyone's liking. Stuck alone, miles from help, with winter's wrath about to unload on them . . . Actually, it struck me as a sound punishment for some.

I felt my smile fade as the last person in the line reached me. I knew why he was last in line, the same way I knew why he hadn't been all that interested in my talk. What I couldn't understand was how quiet he'd been; that was unlike him. He looked just the same as I remembered from our undergraduate days. If he was a little more lined about the face, or a little more gray in his beard, the red hair and cocky attitude I knew so well was still there.

At first I didn't think he was actually going to make eye contact, was hoping he wouldn't, but he surprised me. Not for the first time. Damn his eyes.

"Good stuff, Em," he said, pausing a little before he climbed into the bus.

"Thanks." I couldn't bring myself to say his name and

coughed to cover my surprise. He didn't look nearly as bad as I'd hoped, a little puffy—tired perhaps. But the horns and sores I'd wished on him years ago were surprisingly absent.

I fussed with the clipboard; I was still one body short. "I've gotta go find Garrison," I said, nodding too briskly. I stepped back and around him, too obviously. Still not fast enough for me.

My graduate student Meg Garrity was waiting off to the side, probably for a quick postmortem of the tour and last-minute instructions. She probably saw me acting jumpy, but knew me well enough not to ask what was wrong. She herself was shuffling from side to side, which was also unlike her, but it was so cold it was probably a good idea for anyone to keep moving. Her hat, a colorful Andean woolen thing with earflaps and an improbable peak, was also well warranted. It covered all of her short, usually spiked hair and most of the piercings I knew about. There was one in her left eyebrow that I had never seen before, but I wasn't surprised by it.

"That went well," she said.

"Yeah, I was pleased. Remind me to thank the state park people for getting the snowblower out here for the paths, would you? And thanks again for coming out early and getting the building outlines set up—I know you had to work on your presentation. I was glad that you were available. Neal was supposed to, but he's running behind on his paper. But I don't need to tell you that."

"Yeah, I know." And there came the sort of pause that, with no other warning, instantly tells you that something big is coming. "So. We got engaged over the break."

"Hey . . . wow." I felt the smile freeze on my face and my eyes widen for a split second before my better socialized superego took over and did the correct thing: I wouldn't let my own past color her good news. "That's fabulous! You guys are great together. Congratulations!"

"You seem . . . surprised." Meg didn't mean it in a good way; she was instantly defensive.

I rushed in to repair the damage, cursing my inability to hide my reactions, no matter how transient, no matter how outdated. Despite my own experiences, intradepartmental romances could work out, and no one could deny that Meg and Neal belonged together. "I *am* surprised. It's big news, but it isn't exactly out of the blue, is it? You guys have been living together for a couple of years."

"No. Well, we'd talked about it, but he did surprise me." She smiled, a little shyly, and looked impossibly young. "New Year's Eve. It was really nice."

And I'd have never taken Meg for a romantic. "Do you have a ring?"

"Yep." She pulled her left mitten off—also colorful and South American—and showed me a round diamond, flanked by two smaller ones in an old-fashioned gold setting. It was very traditional and it struck me just how traditional Meg could be, though you had to look hard past her piercings and demeanor to see it. "It was his great-grandmother's. He had the two little stones put in on either side, so it would be really mine."

"It's beautiful," I said, and meant it. "Look, I want to find out all about the rest of it, but I've got to get this show back on the road." The first snowflakes were starting to fly, and it looked as though it would get thick and heavy in a hurry. "Let me buy you both a drink later?"

She nodded enthusiastically. "Sure. Is everyone on the bus?"

"Nope, I've got to fetch Garrison."

"Want me to?"

"No, that's okay. I'll get him." No point in throwing Meg to Garrison; she had her whole professional life ahead of her and didn't need to get on his bad side. That could have a deleterious effect.

"Okay." She bounded back onto the bus, which was on the driveway of a house I had loved, but that was no longer there.

I paused at the top of the slope. It didn't take me long to locate Garrison, the older man who wasn't riveted to my talk; the site isn't all that big, just about an acre. Trudging past the place where the wrought-iron fence had stood, it was hard to believe that just a few years ago there had been a fire that not only wiped out the big gray Victorian that had been here but killed a person I dearly loved. Now there was nothing but too many memories, too much open space, and an almost unnoticeable depression in the ground where the foundation had been. A rustic wooden shelter protecting a map and a sign describing historic Fort Providence was all that marked the site now, crowded with memories and ghosts.

Garrison had wandered over to the edge of the property, close to the nearly new fence that kept people from getting too close to the eroding cliff. He was staring out over the water, as though personally in charge of overseeing the play of the wind and the whitecaps. As I followed the unevenly plowed path, away from the main part of the site, wondering what drove him out here, the air seemed a little warmer and the wind was picking up; the weather was turning sooner than I'd hoped. He was leaning against the fence, concentrating on the horizon, and it was as though the old man was calling the storm down on himself.

The traffic was backed up as we cut across Maine into central New Hampshire—everyone seemed to be leaving work early on the threat of the incoming storm front, even though it was slated to hit inland later than the coast. We were running more than an hour late as we traveled over hilly highways past innumerable snow-covered chalet-styled resort buildings and motels that marked the approach to our destination, the General Bartlett Hotel. By the time we pulled up to the pillared front porch, still decorated with pine branches and white Christmas lights, I realized I had just enough time to take a good warm shower and get my wits together before my second big task of the ASAAs, or more formally, the Association for the Study of American Archaeology conference. After I was done with this, I just had the card game, which was something I was looking forward to, the Goody Grope, which was always amusing, and then the presentation of my paper, which, compared with the excruciating task of writing this plenary essay, would be a walk in the park.

But having to speak to the big redheaded guy by the bus out there on the site had rattled me sufficiently that it took the whole ride back to the conference hotel to get myself under control. I'd known since before the conference that he would be there, but when I first caught sight of him, it was like a body blow. The name "Duncan Thayer" hadn't been on my list; he was a last-minute addition to the tour. Talking to him had been worse. I'd been less prepared than I imagined I would be.

The shower took a little more work than such things should. The outside of the hotel told the whole story. Once there had been a large farmhouse that evolved into a tavern that serviced travelers on the lake and the northern-running roads. After that had burned down, the original part of the hotel, which still housed the lobby and offices, had been constructed in the 1880s. The 1950s had seen a much larger addition constructed that not only extended the porch and façade but also wrapped halfway around the original inn, providing many more rooms. Although the hotel had never truly been close enough to the mountains for skiing, more recently there had been a renovation in an attempt to draw conference business.

Many of the rooms had been recently remodeled, as advertised. The plumbing, alas, had not enjoyed a completely successful upgrade. I found myself playing "raise you one" with some other unknown denizen, cranking up the hot water every time he or she turned it up, causing me to freeze. A very unsatisfactory five minutes later, I worked on drying my hair and getting ready for the plenary session paper I was to present. It took me maybe twenty minutes to get my act together, which is five minutes more than usual, but since I knew *he* was here, anything I could do to boost my confidence I was going to attempt, up to and including matching my bra and panties and wearing stupidly high heels, heretofore reserved for weddings and the occasional date night with my husband, Brian Chang.

I checked the clock and swore. I grabbed the sheaf of papers that comprised my presentation, checked my bag for my room key, purse, name tag, and miniature flashlight—you never could tell what the lighting situation was going to be in these places—and legged it down to the elevator. Carla was waiting there as well, for which I was glad; she and I had been part of the same conference scene since we were new graduates, and it was a relief to see her. The ends of her hair were still damp, and I wondered if she'd been the one competing for the hot water with me.

She jabbed at the elevator button repeatedly. "Come on, you no-good, useless, motherless—."

I edged up behind her and nudged her. "Hey lady, don't take it out on the architecture."

"And why don't you take a flying—" then she turned and saw it was me. We hugged warmly, briefly. "Good. Someone else with sense, here at last. Come on, we're taking the stairs."

I didn't say anything about my shoes; if I was dumb enough to wear them, I was dumb enough to be macho about it too. Besides, Carla's skirt was a good five inches shorter than mine, just shy of indecency, and if she was going to take the stairs in her rig, then so would I. Despite being a good four inches shorter, about five foot five, and twenty pounds heavier, Carla gave me a run for my money.

"You know," I said as we found the staircase, "they can't really start the plenary session without us."

Carla didn't answer but hustled down the stairs, which were dimly lit with nothing but bare utility lightbulbs that seemed to draw warmth from the space rather than add light. The dust, gum wrappers, and cigarette butts told just how often the hotel staff expected the stairs would be used: It was more of a de facto lounging area than a working exit.

We stopped abruptly at the door to the second-floor mezzanine. Carla smoothed down her skirt, adjusted her shirt, then tilted her head back so I could see straight up her nose.

"Any Buicks in the garage?"

"No Buicks, nor bats in the belfry, and neither are you in need of a hankie."

Carla nodded thanks, then shot me a look that was a question that she wasn't asking, yet. "Great. Let's get ourselves to the ballroom. Thank God we only had to come down the one floor. My feet are killing me already."

As we strode down the hallway, we passed clumps of our colleagues who called out with promises to catch up later. We paused in the ladies' room just outside the ballroom, which we had all to ourselves. Carla hogged the mirror, trying to tame her frizzy ash-blond curls back into a respectable knot. I made a pit stop; an hour and a half can be a surprisingly long time if you're not prepared for it, especially if you're trapped up onstage for all the world to see.

"You know," she said. "You know" came out more like "ooo oww;" Carla was making a mouth, messing with her lipstick. "I was looking out my hotel window this morning when I see this little red car pull up in the parking lot. Someone's running late, I thought, then I realized: Emma's local. She didn't need to come until today, when things get started.

Zipping around with all that panache, I couldn't believe it was you. That can't be Emma, I told myself, but no one could miss that red hair of yours, even from the third floor— the short hair looks cute by the way. It's even shorter than last time, but you can carry it off. Anyway. Pretty snazzy car. Not what I picture you in, usually."

My faithful Civic had finally given out last year, and I treated myself to my first brand-new car. "I like the Jetta; red was the only color the dealer had left." I didn't tell her that rather than wait for a more sedate model, I had also agreed to take the sports package for a reduced price, secretly antic- ipating a little oomph in my driving. It was a good deal, I had reasoned aloud to Brian. I think he knew better; he can usually see right through me.

"Yeah, well, whatever; the attitude, it was great to see. Made me want to cheer whoever it was, and I was delighted that it was you. Not like that other schmuck who pulled in, right after you did."

Something was going on here, but I wasn't certain what. Carla looked, well, uneasy. Unsure, and that wasn't like her. She fiddled with mascara, ignoring the time constraints that she'd cited in dragging us down that dusty stairwell. Every time she added makeup, she always went a step further than I would have, applied it a little more brashly. She pulled out brushes and mechanisms that reminded me of medieval tor- ture devices. One of these she used to curl her eyelashes.

I had less to do. I combed my hair, but since it was only about three inches long now, it actually looked better a little tousled. Eyes, nose, still there, still inoffensive. I tried a lip- stick that my friend Marty had made me buy, just to keep with the spirit of the moment, and checked my teeth for food.

Carla opened eyes wide while she used another brush to touch up her eyebrows—I wasn't even aware such a step ex- isted. "No, ma'am," she continued, "that other guy, he was a turd bag. I could tell by the way he tore around the parking lot—"

"You just got done telling me that I was zipping around like I owned the world." I watched her fussing over her appearance: Carla fusses with things when she's nervous.

"Emma, you followed traffic lanes. You had both hands on the steering wheel, at ten o'clock and two. Shit, you signaled before you pulled into the parking space, and there wasn't anyone else in the lot! Not like this dickweed—"

Why was Carla getting so wound up about this guy?

"Nope, he obviously cut across the parking spaces because he couldn't be bothered to steer any harder with only one hand, the other being firmly clamped to his cell phone. And he wasn't going the speed limit, not even just a little bit above. He was tearing around like he was the only driver in the universe. Until he got to a pothole, and then he slowed down, so he wouldn't hurt the suspension of his SUV." She paused. "And you know how I feel about vanity plates, right? I mean, if you have to announce your presence to the world on your car, then how sad must you be? Well, this was the worst: XCAV8. Get it?"

That's when I knew what she was saying, because *I* was the one who'd come up with that particular plate, back when I was an undergraduate, back when I thought announcing my presence to the world seemed like a fine idea, the only logical thing to do. You needed to give the world a head's up, right? I felt my mouth go dry, a reflex, even though I knew what she was trying to do.

"And you know that joke about the difference between porcupines and SUVs? About the pricks being on the inside? Well, this jerk was the living embodiment, in his big old Suburban Assault Vehicle—"

Carla drives an SUV too, but at last I knew what was going on. I put my hand on her arm. "Carla, it's okay. I knew he'd be here. He was out at the site today. God knows why."

"No sir, I didn't like the look of him a bit. He probably ran over a few baby fur seals on his way here. Ran them over and backed over them once or twice." But Carla looked relieved, now that I understood what she was trying to tell me.

It was kind of her to be concerned, after so many years, but it also made me wonder what people, the ones who knew about my past with Duncan, really thought of me, that I might be that fragile or had behaved that badly about it. Well, I had been fragile and I had behaved badly, once upon a time, but it had been years ago and a lot of water under a bridge that had been burned long since. Maybe that was why, because it had been so long since that last, bad time. Thing was, there were only a few people at this conference who were there for that last one, so many years ago, and I was thankful for that. I wouldn't have nearly the same audience, and not everyone would remember, and of those who did, very few would be expecting me to freak out. That was the good news.

"He's here. So what? I haven't thought about him for a long time, not until recently, so don't you think about it either." I put on a braver face than I felt and infused enough enthusiasm into my words to be convincing, and then slung my bag over my shoulder. "You ready there, gorgeous, or what?"

"Or what." She packed up her makeup, which she'd been able to spread far over the vanity in a remarkably short period of time. "Come on, let's get this eulogy over with."

I had to pause there. "Doesn't it seem a little hypocritical of us? Presenting these papers when we don't even *like* Garrison?"

Carla shrugged and threw the lipstick in last. "It's tradition. Bastard gets old enough, you have a party for him."

I frowned at my reflection. "Yeah, well, nothing says we have to perpetuate it. I finally decided that I could do the presentation because he's made genuine contributions to the field. But I can't stand him."

"No one says you have to kiss him, Em. Now if you're done rationalizing . . . ?"

"Let's go."

We met up with the rest of the panel backstage. Carla had a quick look around. "Where the hell is Garrison? The man is late for his own party."

I spied Scott Tomberg, who was shaking a pen like it was an old-fashioned mercury thermometer. Carla fussed and organized things when she was upset, but pen abuse was Scott's barometer. "Dr. Tomberg." I gave him a hug, and though he was about my age, addressed him by his formal title just to give him a cheap thrill. What are old friends for?

"Dr. Fielding." Scott was a small caveman with big hands, wide shoulders, and a square head on a thick, muscled neck; when he hugged me back, it was like being hugged by a tank. Old-fashioned glasses, black plastic over the brow with silver earpieces, helped jazz up his look, which was also modernized with a crew cut, mostly pepper and lots of salt at the temples. He was still pretty fit, and wearing what he always wore, jeans and a button-down shirt, but had added a navy blazer for the occasion.

"And how are we today?" I asked.

"We are sucky," he said, frowning hugely. "Our guest of honor is nowhere to be seen—he got in late last night, like most of us. He went on the tour out to your site?"

I nodded. "I bundled him back onto the bus myself, so he's somewhere around here."

He flicked the pen button a couple more times. "Well, there's that. Now that you and Carla are here, we just have to hunt him down. I sent someone up to his room—he wasn't answering the phone. To top it off, the airline lost my luggage yesterday. I've been wearing the same pair of shorts for two days now, since I left home yesterday."

I made a face. "And that is officially more information than I needed. Did you ask someone if they could spare a pair for you?"

"I'm not going to wear someone else's underwear!" Then he looked sheepish. "No one here's going to have anything that wouldn't look like a thong on me. There wasn't a pair that might fit to be had, for love or money."

"And with whom have you been trying the love?" I said.

Scott's face lightened up. "There he is now!"

I looked where Scott was looking. "You tried to borrow underpants from Garrison? You're a better man than I—"

But I didn't get to finish the line because Scott had all but fled in his haste to greet his tardy guest of honor.

Garrison was looking a bit dazed, a stewing chicken of a man whose suit hung off him. He had a nose so sharp you could cut cake with it. Petra Williams, who brought him down, lingered by his side. She and Scott conferred for a moment and nodded. Garrison seemed to be shaking off his confusion, and he put his hands up in protest—no, he was fine, he would go on, I imagined he was saying.

I stiffened when he batted at Petra, a stout little porcelain doll with Dorothy Parker bangs and a bun. She had to stand on tiptoe to take off his ever-present black beret and smooth his hair. She batted back at him, an ex-wife's prerogative. He said something heated, and she handed a retort right back to him, no less angrily, taking her time to get him just so, and only then let him go. Garrison walked past us, not saying hello to anyone. He grunted at Scott when he showed him the way to his seat. He sat and flipped through a pile of index cards that he took from his pocket.

Scott came back for the rest of us—me, Carla, and the others—and showed us up to the stage.

"Ladies," he said with a flourish, showing Carla and me where to sit.

"Where?" Carla asked, whipping her head around.

I shook my head; it was time to play grown-up and get down to business.

As president of the East Coast chapter of the ASAA, it was Scott's party, so he was moderating and introducing the panelists as well as presenting.

He began his own paper, "Julius Garrison and American Archaeology," the big biographical paper. Scott had slaved under Garrison for too many years as a graduate student and then research assistant. He was perhaps the only person I knew who could have done it and survived with his sense of humor and humanity intact. Having put up with that much scurrilous abuse, he had dedicated the rest of his career, when he was appointed to a department in Georgia, to being as laid-back as possible while still remaining in the field. Nothing could faze him anymore; he was settled into life with his Savannahian wife and their three Southern children.

I always liked listening to Scott; he has that great way of giving you a lot of high-level information in a casual way that doesn't feel like you're being talked down to. It was a painless history of our branch of the field, as shaped by Garrison, and I couldn't wait to see a copy of it in print. It would be a great research tool for the students, for anyone. Much as I disliked Garrison, you had to give the devil his due. He was officially retiring and was essentially doing a victory lap around the region, collecting lifetime achievement awards. This was just one stop among many.

After Scott's introduction, he brought on Professor Thomas Roche, a colleague of Garrison's who was covering Garrison's prehistoric contributions in the northeast. If it had been ten years earlier, I bet they would have had my grandfather Oscar up there, which would have been interesting to watch, if he'd agreed to do it. Oscar and Garrison had hated each other with a white-hot passion, professionally and personally.

Roche laid it on thick, proposing that Garrison's office be

donated to the Smithsonian, and after Carla discussed the
early osteological studies, it was my turn to talk about the
early historic-sites work he'd done. Then it was an old friend
of mine and Garrison's both, Frank Lawrence. The last
speaker was Garrison himself.

"Thank you, Frank." Then Scott introduced Garrison,
who coughed, paused to shuffle through his cards, and then,
it seemed to me, simply put them aside.

"In the course of a lifetime—and apparently, it's been a
little too long, to judge by the length of the papers given here
tonight . . ." He shot a sharp look at those of us sitting on the
stage.

There were nervous titters in the audience; I frowned. We
hadn't gone over long enough to warrant a crack like that.

"But I've managed to do a lot, and perhaps it wouldn't be
immodest of me to think that I've made a few contributions
along the way. I've had the pleasure of working with some fine
archaeologists. I've made a few friends, and more than likely, a
number of enemies. I'm content with that. That's all anyone
can ask of this life; and that's what we're talking about here,
isn't it? When people start doling out the lifetime achievement
awards, it's usually because they expect you to die soon."

There was a reaction of distaste from the crowd at Garrison's words; they struck a little too close to the mark. Typical of him, I thought.

He continued. "Well, maybe. Maybe. The important thing
is I can say I've learned a fair amount, in the course of my
career, and even some of it had to do with archaeology."

More laughter now from the audience, and I saw my fellow panelists relax a little bit. This was closer to what we'd
all been expecting.

"One of those things I'll share with you this evening,
since you've been nice enough to suggest that I'm worth listening to and silly enough to give me the opportunity to exploit that fact. And that is: keep fighting."

There was some polite clapping, at this point, but Garrison just kept going.

"That's why I went to Washington to comment on the U.N.'s issues of cultural patrimony and illicit trade of looted materials."

More clapping here; this was something that everyone could get behind.

"Keep fighting for what you believe is right. That's why I am still here, still dragging my old bones through the cold to do the work. That's why I told my friends on the New Hampshire state legislature to veto the proposed state historic village, because it doesn't make good sense. It's taking money away from other work that is starving for it, and if you want a damn carnival, a tourist trap, go to the private money. In the end, it's just providing a lot of pork for a lot of people who want to call themselves archaeologists. Let's not confuse the difference between education and entertainment."

Now there was a gasp from the audience, and muttering. I couldn't see beyond the lights that were on us on the stage, but I didn't need to, I knew who it was. My friend Sue Ayers had been working her guts out to push that project through, and now she'd just learned all her hard work had very probably gone up in smoke. Such was the power of Garrison's opinion.

"Keep fighting for what's important about the past, it's worth the effort, for as long as you've got. Don't let anyone push you around, push you into thinking about superfluous trappings rather than what you're really supposed to be serving."

He looked around at the audience, he looked at the panelists one by one, coming to me last, and then shrugged. "Well, that's it, I guess. That's all I've got to say."

And he shuffled off. Didn't go back to his chair, he headed right off the stage and didn't come back. Left the lot of us staring after him, even as the ill-fitted door slammed shut behind him.

Chapter 2

THERE WAS SCATTERED APPLAUSE AND A LOT OF muttering in the audience and some up on stage. Scott ran offstage to see what was going on. He came right back, alone.

"I guess Professor Garrison wanted to get started on the serious drinking," he said into the mike, with a conspiratorial DJ's voice. There was a little laughter, but much more concern and buzzing still over the strange performance. "In any case, I'd like once again to thank our speakers and invite the rest of you to the main ballroom, where we can get this party started!"

He sold the line; everyone laughed, but I could tell that there was going to be a lot of talk about Garrison's little performance for a long time to come.

"Damn, Scott's still cleaning up after Garrison after all these years," Carla muttered to me. She stretched, her shirt riding up and showing the waistband of her pantyhose, but she didn't care in the least. "Quick turn about the floor of the reception and then off to the game?"

"Sounds good. Hey, Scott, what's up with Garrison?"

Scott had just got done shaking the hands of the more senior members of the panel and reassuring some of the audience who were concerned about Garrison.

"I think he's just tired, he was complaining of fatigue when Petra caught up with him. And when Julius Gilbert Garrison has decided he's done, you know he's not the kind of guy to stand around. He thinks that everything's been said and there's no point."

With the plenary session abruptly completed, everyone was herded out into the hallway and into the next ballroom for the reception. This is where I got to finally say hello to a lot of old friends and start the perennial catching up, but typically enough, the lines for the cash bars instantly jammed things up. The line I was in stalled by a glassed-in case containing a few artifacts associated with the hotel's construction and history. There was a silver-plated trowel and spade, both inscribed with the dates of the hotel's refurbishment in the nineteen fifties. There were a few fragments of pottery that had been collected by some curious observer of that period, and a series of maps showed the location of the hotel over time. One plan from the early nineteenth century showed a series of outbuildings around the old structure, as well as the post road and other towns on the lake that caused the inn to grow from a large farmhouse into a tavern and, eventually, a hotel.

"Could be a piece of a hinge, maybe," a woman's voice said a few bodies down from where I was standing. I saw a well-manicured hand pointing toward a strip of rusted metal.

"No, I don't think so," I said absently. "It looks like a piece of a pair of ice tongs. You can see in that second map, there's a little block that says 'ice house' underneath it."

I pointed to the clue I'd seen. I glanced over at the woman and found myself on the wrong end of a venomous stare. Oh crap, Noreen McAllister. Just my luck.

A loud "tch" was her reply. Noreen flipped that big mess

of blue-black hair—she never bothered tying up her pride and joy—and pursed her lips, but fortunately for me, the line shifted forward and took Noreen away. Someone had wised up and got another bartender on duty.

Once I got my drink, I said hello to a few more folks, but I wasn't sticking around for long. I caught my friend Chris's eye and he nodded; then he jerked his head over to where another fellow conspirator, Lissa Vance, was talking to someone. I caught her eye and raised my eyebrows. She nodded and began to extricate herself from her conversation with Bea Carter, which if history was any indication, would be an involved process. The Bat Signal had been lit and it was time to go. I put down my empty glass and surveyed the scene.

The hotel had a little combo playing in the reception area, and the lights came down when they went on. This was obviously meant as a treat, but the musicians were more enthusiastic than talented, and those who were grooving to them did so with a pronounced sense of irony. Though most of the older folks left the floor in a hurry, some remained and cut a fair enough rug, but then the younger cadres came out, graduate students, some ABDs, a smattering each of new PhDs and undergraduates snaking their way onto the floor, laying claim to the one place this weekend where they might have some authority. One Gypsy-clad young lady slinked onto the floor, taking a willing guy by the hand; I could see a pint bottle of vodka stuck in his back pocket. Their skins were tribally pierced and colorfully illustrated. Ties and skirts were still in suitcases waiting for paper presentation time; now it was either hyperbaggy pants or skin-tight jeans hovering three inches and more south of where I thought they should properly rest. Others were scrounging the "free" food at the buffet, squirreling some away for later. Standard operating procedure.

I didn't know many of them and realized that as much as I might feel it, I was no longer a part of the puppy crowd. At their age, for us, it had been a single pierced ear or maybe long hair for the guys, big, bad hair for the girls. I wasn't even an aging puppy, I was a big dog now, and the thought made me sad as I watched the dancing.

The game, our game, was scheduled during the dance reception. I wasn't much for dancing, myself, and the music was usually pretty wretched. The other folks in the game would stick around for a few minutes, sometimes, but we always ended up in someone's room, with the same nasty sticky deck of cards we'd been using to cut for years— featuring the shaved and slicked charms of the Chippendale dancers—and a new deck for the game itself.

The game had started out as a reaction by me and my friends when we were the puppies. We got tired of trying to meet up with the people we were trying to imitate, trying to accost for whatever reason. We decided that if they could withdraw, pointedly excluding us, to their rooms for private drink, and who knows what else, then we could jolly well do the same. So we instituted the poker game and kept it to ourselves, fifteen years ago or so, with all the vindictiveness of snubbed mid-twenty-somethings. There hadn't been much variation over the years—everyone brought something to drink, ordered something to eat, and left their attitude at the door, as much as humanly possible—but the rules were strict: no discussion of professional news, only catching up with each other. No telling others outside the group about what went on in the room, save to say that it was a card game, nothing more. No television, and no radio either, because it only distracted and caused fuss. Bring cash and no whining, about anything.

I picked my way through the crowds toward the exit. Over the years the game had devolved from a rebellion into a retreat, a counter to the overstimulation that characterized most conferences. For many of the attendees, the attraction of being at a conference was the chance to slip the leash, behave badly in the company of their understanding professional peers, or find a little extracurricular sexual activity. I had been naively shocked when I realized this, early on, and it only tired me to think of it now. Drinking too much and dancing too late were one thing, but I just didn't understand how, morals quite apart, anyone could possibly have the time or the energy for an affair.

So the game was a chance to catch up with friends who'd known each other for, well, almost two decades now; the longevity, a shock in itself. We'd passed the age in our lives when a wave across the room was enough to hold us until the next conference, because there'd always be another event. Now, however, we wanted to spend some time with each other.

I guess I shouldn't have been so surprised when my graduate student Meg Garrity appeared in my path.

"I was wondering if you needed another hand at the table," she said. I saw her flushing red to her roots, which were now what I assumed was her natural brown, for about two inches, then to another three-inch fringe of platinum. It looked interesting, but I couldn't tell whether she was doing it on purpose or just getting sloppy about color maintenance.

I blinked. "Well, I—"

"I mean, only if it's cool," she hastily added, when she saw my surprise. I realized she'd been watching me, waiting for this moment.

"Well, we're actually pretty full." I saw her face go carefully blank, and she nodded. "It's just cards, Meg. It's just a bunch of us getting together, you know, to catch up and all. It's nothing special."

"You don't have to explain," she said quickly. But if the look on her face was any indication, I did have to explain.

"Honestly, Meg, it's not like it's the hot ticket of the social season. It's just . . . friends . . . no big deal. I mean, we don't even talk about work, all that much. If it was only up to me,

I'd say yes, but it's not. You understand. Maybe you and Neal will be free later for that drink?"

She nodded, but she turned away, her jaw set. "Sure, no problem. I'll catch you later." Meg hurried off, even before I could say another word. I saw her find her fiancé Neal and lead him to the dance floor. He complied with a fair competence and I wondered why I should be at all surprised he could dance.

She didn't understand, I realized, she even thought that I was trying to keep her out of something. Well, I was, but not the way she thought. This was not some kind of Star Chamber, a sanctum sanctorum where important and discipline-changing decisions were made. It was a room of friends in their late thirties and forties trying to act like human beings.

Shit. Well, I would have thought exactly the same thing at her age. I didn't even know whether I'd have had the guts to ask to join the game, if I'd been in her place. But it wasn't my decision, and it was over now.

With a sigh, I turned and headed for the elevator banks.

"Hike up your skirts, ladies, we're entering the gates of hell," I said, as I finished dealing the cards. Brad DuBois removed the emptied plates. "Who's in? Carla?"

"Wait a minute, don't change· the subject!" Scott said. "Never mind skirts! You were in your *underwear*?"

Jay Whitaker furrowed his brow. "Never mind that. Are we here to play cards or what? Chris, man, lend me twenty?" Jay ran his hand through thinning brown hair; at least he'd had the sense to cut off the damned ponytail he'd been clinging to for years, leaving the last of his misspent youth behind him. He'd been partying hard since he arrived the night before and needed a shave and a change of chinos, but that was understandable as this was as much of a vacation as he ever got: The struggling contract company he'd founded kept him digging all summer, and in the lab all winter.

"Of course I was in my underwear," I said. "That's what makes the story embarrassing. What about it, Chris?" I was only asking to keep Jay on tenterhooks; it was just so funny to watch, and plus, it kept him off his game. He and I played hard in our competitions over the years.

"I'm folding." Chris threw down his cards in disgust. "I might as well still be at home, snowed in with Nell and the herd. Here," he said, handing some bills to Jay, "make these last awhile this time, Jay-Bird."

"I'm sure that Nell would love to hear that," I said. "Looks like lots of folks got hit by the storm on the way in last night; I noticed the crowd seemed pretty thin. What about it, Brad?"

Bradford DuBois, occasionally known to his intimates as "Brad the Boy," stood up, which didn't take long. He was short, thin, brown hair curled as tight as his uptight attitude. He was one of the most phenomenally lucky archaeologists I ever met, which counts almost as much as being good, which he also was. "I'm out. Anyone want a beer? I brought low-carb."

"Thank God!" Carla said. "Now we can get down to the serious partying." She snorted in disgust, whether at her cards or the notion of Brad's fake beer, no one could tell.

"I'm sorry, but can you please tell me the point of low-carb beer?" Lissa, known only to her parents as Elizabeth Bell Vance, wiped the last of the crumbs from her place at the table onto her empty plate. "Isn't that water? Bring me a Bass. And a glass, would you? Thanks." Lissa was a poster child for the perfectly turned-out blond sorority sister, never a hair out of place, even when she chases bulldozers across battlefield sites in her hard hat.

"Don't tell me you're going all carnivorous and carbo-phobic on us?" Chris asked. "Weren't you a vegetarian this time last year?"

"Now we're totally vegan," Brad said. "Still am. And occasionally, we go uncooked, just for good measure. I'm just watching my weight. Some of us could stand to." He glanced meaningfully at Chris's straining shirt buttons.

"And by doing so, with one stroke, you've eliminated two of man's finest achievements: the invention of fire-on-demand and animal domestication." Chris remained happily unconcerned with his diet and his thickening waistline. "Bring me a beer, boy!" he called in his best imitation of Hagar the Horrible. "Make it two! Real ones, none of your pallid *Schweinwasser!*"

The rest of us put in our orders and Brad was kept busy for a few minutes ferrying beers to us. Carla, of course, changed her mind three times about brands, and he actually obliged her twice, then finally told her to go to hell when she complained about the label coming off the last bottle.

"And may I say thank you again for rescuing me, Em?" Lissa said. "I swear, Bea Carter's just like a big, obnoxious octopus, and once she gets you trapped, she sucks the life out of you."

"Kinda mixing your metaphors there, aren't ya, Lissa?" Carla said.

"You know what I mean. And Brad, thank *you* so much for finally, finally shaving that darn porn-star mustache of yours. You look ten years younger."

Brad bowed, on his way back with the beers. "Francine likes me clean shaven too."

"Anyway, who's got dirt?" Lissa asked, after she opened her bottle and carefully poured it into a glass. As if we hadn't heard that hoary old line a thousand times.

"No, you're not going to do this to me!" Jay said. "Let's play the damned game!"

Scott was right there with him: "I'm out, too, but Emma, tell me what happened! There was underwear, you left off with underwear!"

"Okay, okay," I said. Carla and I exchanged raised eyebrows: something was up with Jay's hand. "So I was in there cleaning the bathroom—"

"You clean the bathroom in your underwear?" Scott said.

"Naturally; how do you do it?"

"I don't clean the bathroom," he announced stiffly.

"Figures," Lissa said. "Makes his poor wife Cathy do it."

"But I'm sure she doesn't take off . . ." he started, confused. Was it possible? Had he missed it? You could practically see the questions running through his mind.

"You don't want to drag your shirt over a wet tub or toilet," I explained, "and you just end up splashing yourself anyway, and since you're probably going to just shower after you get done with the housework—"

"And if you strip down to your birthday suit," Lissa added, "you're giving up important support and protection, and trust me, if you don't want to have your shirt slapping against a wet tub, you sure don't want your boobs to either."

Trust Lissa not only to have made the experiment, but also to come back and report on it.

"In any case," I interjected firmly, "since it was cleaning day, it also meant that it was laundry day. So my garb was of a somewhat eclectic nature. It had been a couple of weeks since the laundry mound had actually moved closer to the washer so . . ." I paused to reshuffle my cards, not because I didn't know what I had, but to see Jay's reaction. He watched me like a dog tracking a steak, and then he sat back and looked at his own cards in disgust. So his was that good a hand? I thought.

I continued out loud. "So when I leaned out the window to wave to Brian, you know, give him a little thrill while he was working in the backyard?—I was wearing a more festive variation on my usual undergarments. Recreational, shall we say?"

"You were wearing your date bra," Carla said.

"Alas, yes. I was wearing my lucky leopard-print bra—"

"Lucky Brian, more like. A matching ensemble, perhaps?"

"No, more's the pity. Not that that would have helped anything, because as I was leaning out to wave, I did not realize that Brian's friend Roddy had dropped by to pick up some reports. No, it was Roddy who got my blinding smile and animal-printed cleavage."

"What did you do?" Lissa asked.

"What could I do? I faced it out. I just kept waving and said, 'Hi, Roddy, tell Brian to take out the trash when he comes back, would you'? Then I quietly collapsed under the window in a fit of mortification."

Jay was torn between what was clearly a fabulous hand and getting the lowdown on this heretofore unsuspected element of housecleaning. "But what were you wearing below the wai—below the windowsill?"

"Ah, that's where I was glad that we don't have a balcony with French doors or anything that posh. I told you it was laundry day; I was wearing a pair of Brian's plaid flannel boxers. It was quite a rig, let me tell you."

Carla took a swig of beer. "Sounds comfortable."

"It is," I said. "Why do they always make men's clothing so much more comfortable and durable than women's clothing?"

"Don't forget cheaper," Chris added.

"It's a conspiracy," I said.

"I can't believe you'd wear any men's clothing," Lissa said primly. "I mean, yeah, maybe for kicks in bed, but it's just . . . I don't know . . . weird to wear it in public."

"I'm still dealing with the fact that she was half naked in front of a man," Scott said.

"Oh, come off it. I wear less on the beach," Lissa said.

"You wear less to the supermarket," Scott retorted.

"The beach is a different context," Brad said. "You don't just hang out at home naked, do you?"

We all exchanged looks. "Not naked, but not always dressed for company," I conceded. The rest of them nodded: that sounded about right.

"It's different when you have kids. Don't get me wrong," Chris said. "I don't want mine to be prudes, but I don't want them in therapy either, seeing dear old dad scratching and grinning in the altogether."

"Can we please get back to playing cards!" Jay was ready to blow a gasket.

"Sure," I said. "Coming around. How many you want?"

I dealt cards to Lissa and Carla. Jay made a reluctant show of holding; I held my breath and took one.

"Man, can you get over Roche, with his 'Julius Gilbert Garrisons'?" Lissa said. "Talk about your constant refrain! Julius Gilbert Garrison this, Julius Gilbert Garrison that, we are here today to honor a man who—"

"Who has caused more shrinks to retire early," Chris filled in, "fat on the pickings of desperate archaeology students—"

"Who has been a bigger setback to women's self-images than airbrushing—" I added.

"Who is more steadfastly evil a villain than Darth Vader, Hannibal Lector, and Hitler all rolled into one," Carla finished.

I glanced over at Scott; he was doing his best to keep his head down and was noticeably quiet.

"I mean, don't get me wrong," Lissa said. "I like the guy, I just thought Roche's butt-kissing was a bit florid."

I looked at her sharply. "You like which guy? Not old Roche?"

"He's all right, but I was talking about Garrison," Lissa said.

"The man's a dickhead!" Carla said.

Lissa shrugged. "He's always been nice to me."

"Was he hitting on you?" I asked.

"No, he was getting me some data from the nineteen forties on forts that he knew about."

"And he wasn't a jerk to you?" I said.

"Not a bit. He's an awful oenophiliac, but I can forgive that in most people."

"You can forgive someone for having a blood-clotting disorder? That's big of you, Liss," Scott said.

"Actually, it's blood thinners he's on, I heard," Lissa said. "And I said 'oenophiliac,' not 'hemophiliac,' you dope. As in, if you cut him, he'd hemorrhage wine."

"Not lately, I've heard. He's been on the wagon."

"Then you're behind the times," Jay said. "I saw him lapping it up earlier. And yeah, he's not a bad guy. Bit opinionated, maybe."

"He shouldn't be drinking, not with that ticker of his," Scott muttered. "Petra says he's on a boatload of new prescriptions."

"Well, I've never minded him either," Brad chimed in.

"Who asked you?" Carla was really annoyed now. She liked consensus in her loathing. I have to admit, I was surprised at Brad as well.

Brad ignored Carla. "I don't have a problem with him. He's not a friendly guy, but he's usually been decent to me. And look what he's done for the field. Practically established the field in the Northeast, one of the founding members of ASAA, authored some of the most important artifact studies of the early years. You can't deny that."

"Fine. By any standards, yes, he's achieved a lot, but it's like admiring the pyramids without asking who suffered to get it done. Runs roughshod over people, uses and abuses them." Carla looked to Scott. "Help me out, man. Tell us some horror stories from your days as his lackey."

"Nope." He fiddled with his beer bottle, giving it all his

focus. "I don't live in the past. It was tough, it's over now. That's it."

"You're an archaeologist; of course you live in the past."

"Not me. It's over, I don't worry about it now."

Carla snorted with disgust.

I got the bidding started and watched Jay get more and more excited. His bet—and potential raise—would tell me whether I could get away with what I planned. I mentally crossed my fingers.

Carla said, "So did everyone see Emma's new car? Quite the sporty little number. Jetta."

"How do you like it, Em?" Chris asked.

"I like it a lot, so far. Peppy," I said, feigning concentration.

"Yeah, and it's just the car for her too," Carla said. "Heaps plenty of abuse on her, just the way Emma likes it. Little Miss Control Freak."

"Oh?" I said. This was a well-worn path we were traveling.

"Yeah. You're so uptight that when the ABS light comes on, you think it's time to go to the gym and work on your gut."

"Very funny, Carla," I said, feeling unreasonably nettled.

Lissa was caught drinking, and ended up gargling some of her beer, not quite a nostril purge. "Yeah, and when she sees the airbag logo, she thinks the car is telling her she's talking too much!" She almost choked again, laughing at her own joke.

"You're all a riot," I said, shuffling my cards around one more time. I couldn't understand why these retread jokes, as much a tradition as the game itself, should bother me so. "Don't we ever talk about archaeology anymore?"

"Jeez, Em, all we do here is talk about archaeology. This is for fun, this is us hanging out. Talking about your uptight-itude, Jay's familiarity with every croupier in every casino on the planet, Lissa's sex life—"

"Well, if we're not talking shop, let's go back to discussing Lissa's sex life. And leave me and my foibles out of it."

"Fine with me," she said, wiping the last of the beer off her chin. "Did I tell you—?"

We heard a strangled noise come from across the table. "Emma! Play the frigging game!"

We all turned to Jay, who had turned bright red. His heel was no longer wagging, but he was spastically tapping his cards on the table. His OvenStuffer timer had popped and he was done to a turn, I thought, as I admired my handiwork. If he'd been a turkey instead of a pigeon, that is.

"Gotta pay to find out, I guess, huh, Jay? So what are you so excited about?"

Jay shrugged. "You'll see."

I threw in a couple more bills to call, then dramatically raised Jay's raise. Everyone looked at me in surprise. "I don't know," I said, "I guess I've had too much beer."

"Ha!" Lissa announced. "That'll be the day. Too rich for me."

"Me, too," said Carla, throwing in her cards.

"Horseshit!" Jay frowned. "You're bluffing."

I smiled and batted my eyes. "Pay up and find out."

He saw me and raised again. "Take that." By the way he was wagging his heel under his chair, he had a whopper of a hand. Moby Dick, Jaws, Behemoth.

"Okay, then you take *that*." I saw him. The pot was very plump now, thanks to our table rules on betting.

"You can't scare me, Fielding."

"Then let's see 'em, Whitaker."

"I'm sorry, Em," he said, grinning hugely as he put his cards down. "Flush."

"Wow," I responded. "Oh, man, Jay, you kill me! How often do you see a hand like that? Just look at that, a flush. Damn."

"Yankees just can't play cards," he said smugly. He reached over to high-five Lissa, who ignored his hand and gave him a stony look.

"Who are *you* calling a Yankee?" she said caustically. Lissa's family had got to North Carolina just after Virginia Dare. "Like Maryland is the South, anyway."

Jay took the rebuff in good stride. "It's all relative, babe; maybe it's just chicks who can't play cards, then. You guys are fun, but I usually hang out with *serious* players." He stuck out his tongue at Lissa, who seemed to study it for possibilities, and then he rubbed his hands together and reached over to scoop the kitty toward his pile.

"Hang on there a second, friend." I put down a queen-high straight flush. "Sorry Jay. Just call me the queen of spades."

A phone rang, and while everyone else checked their cell phones, I took the opportunity to scoop all the cash over to my side of the table. It was my phone that kept ringing. Even after a couple of years, I'm still surprised when it happens. I left the table, where Jay was still staring at the cards dumbly, jaw dropped to his chest. Carla reached over to feel his pulse and got her hand slapped away for her trouble.

I cleared my throat. "Hey, Brian!"

Everyone around the table dutifully called out "Hello, Brian." I stuck my finger in my free ear.

"How'd the presentation go?" he said.

"Good. I'm glad it's done."

"I just wanted to make sure that you got in from the site before the storm caught you."

"It's not here yet, and yes, we're all fine."

"I'm about to head to Kam's. Marty's off to her parents' with the baby and I told him I'd keep him company." Kamil Shah was Brian's friend and his boss at United Pharmaceuticals, and Marty—Mariam—had been my undergraduate roommate, and a spectacularly perceptive bit of matchmaking on my part had got them married. Their daughter Sophia is my goddaughter, and I feel particularly responsible for her, as she is perfect.

"You be careful out there. And don't forget to check the furnace, okay?"

"I will. And already done."

"And did you put down the cat feeder and extra water?"

"Just did that."

"And did you get a chance to—?"

"Come on, Emma. In the first place, I'm a reasonably intelligent guy and I don't want to come home to a couple of frozen and starved cats or a burned-out shell of a house any more than you would."

I looked out the window at the flying snow and wished I was home. "Aren't you the one who was following me around, asking me if I packed clean socks and my toothbrush and my paper and slides? I know, I know you've got a handle on the small things."

"Exactly. I was just being helpful. And speaking of which, I also had to deal with that sink full of ladylike unmentionables you left for me."

"What ladylike unmentionables?" I could practically feel heads swiveling behind me. "What are you talking about?"

"You know. Your moon pies, your jockstrap."

"It's not a jockstrap," I said. "It's a female groin protector. There's a big difference. And you should just call them breast shields. Sorry about that—and thanks. I meant to get to it, but I just didn't get a chance." By the curious glances of my colleagues, it was more than time to change subjects. "What are you two up to while Marty's in New York?"

"Movies. Lots of explosions, gunplay, and semi-naked women. Meat, cheese, beer. We've been planning for two weeks now. Kam's desperate for male company, someone over the age of two. He's had enough of play dates for Sophia, this one's for him."

"Well, you can help there. Okay, have fun. Careful out driving."

"Yep, you too. Good luck with your paper. And did you have a chance to take care of you-know-who yet?"

I turned away from the table. "Yep. Just did."

"Good. Wouldn't want to ruin a tradition."

We said our I-love-yous and goodbyes and I returned to the table.

"Trouble in paradise?" said Brad.

I looked at him, surprised. "No. Why?"

"Little spat over domestic duties." He smirked.

I shrugged, annoyed with him. "Please. That was a discussion. Brian and I are both lead dog–types, and sometimes, without anyone else around, we start both trying to lead at the same time. We know what's up."

"I'm surprised with your enlightened view of the world, you'd be so unsympathetic," Carla said to Brad.

"Not at all," he replied. "It's just that we schedule everything out so there is no distraction from what's important in life."

"Well, if you all aren't going to ask her, I am," Lissa said to the table at large. "What the heck are you doing, wearing a jockstrap?"

"Like I said, it's a female groin protector."

"Groin protection. Breast shields." Lissa chewed that over. "What are you and Brian up to? I'll give you credit, you're into some advanced stuff. Most of us just muddle along with nubbly condoms and vibrators."

"Ha. Ha." I looked over my cards. "It's for my Krav Maga, to keep from getting kicked or punched somewhere fragile."

"Krav Maga like Kama Sutra?"

"Do you always have to take the low road, Liss?" Carla asked. "It's E's fancy self-defense class, Israeli martial arts."

Brad shuddered. "You're going to ruin your joints with all that violent stuff. You should try yoga. More yin, less yang."

"Right." I made a face. "In my abundant spare time."

Brad was insistent. "It would help with your stress. And by the way, you were late tonight, Emma. It's not like you to keep us waiting."

I wasn't about to tell him what I'd actually been up to; Carla and I had a thing about playing practical jokes on each other. "I ran into a student of mine," I said as casually as I could; it was true anyway. I just made a detour after that. "She wanted to ask me something before her paper. Besides, Jay was here only a minute before me and Sue's later than both of us."

Carla was eyeing me hard, and I worried she smelled a rat. She made a rude noise. "And Jay? Where were you?"

"Oh, I was talking with our illustrious guest of honor," he said, stacking his chips. "Garrison had some questions for me. More like demands."

"Ha!" Carla snorted. "I hear that."

Jay continued. "But where's Sue anyway? She trying to save money by not showing up to let me take it?"

A knock at the door answered her before we could, and I got up to find it was the woman herself. Her eyes were red, her fair skin was blotchy under the freckles, and while nothing could shift her fan of strawberry-blond hair—shellacked into looking permanently windblown—her clothes were rumpled.

"Where've you been?" I said. "You ducked out of there pretty quick." When she didn't say anything, I tried to joke. "And you missed me trouncing Jay. It was beautiful."

Jay glared at me. "Evening's young yet. Not even near over."

"After I got done in the ladies' room, I got caught in the bar," Sue explained. "Took me a while to get free. Lots of sympathy to deal with."

"I'm sorry." I handed her a beer. "Everyone knew that Garrison was talking about your project."

"And he's two seconds away from permanently retiring!" Her words came in a rush. "It all comes down to a difference of opinion, and he's got to screw five years worth of work. Bastard."

"You had to know it was coming," Chris said.

"Yeah, well, as far as I knew, it was a go until *he* got tapped for the advisory board. They all suck up to him. Then . . . phhht."

The news I'd heard about the project didn't give me exactly the same vibe, and I thought that Sue was working toward an extreme long shot, but I wouldn't have said so for the world.

She sat down, put her head down between her knees.

"You okay, hon?" Lissa asked, patting her on the back.

"Yeah," came the muffled reply. A long shuddering sigh followed. "Just give me a minute, okay?"

We exchanged looks; there was nothing more we could do. I opened my mouth to say we didn't need to play cards tonight, this was too important, but with a determined shake, Sue sat up and immediately changed the subject.

"Gimme some damned cards. Did you know this place is haunted?"

"Get out of here," Chris said, dealing.

"Yes," said the rest of us. We all looked at him. He stopped dealing.

"Well, clearly I didn't get the chance to study up on the hotel, like the rest of you. I didn't schedule, clearly, Brad, and I spend my free time enjoying my family life. Besides, it's in New Hampshire and it's after eighteen fifty, so why should I care?" Chris had his own priorities, running a small historical district visitors center in western Massachusetts. He resumed dealing the cards.

"Anyway," Sue said, after a moment, "it's this whole thing about a bride on her wedding night. Found out her groom was unfaithful, beat him to death with a poker."

"Cool," Carla said.

"So let me guess, he wanders the halls trying to make it up to her?" Jay asked. He was chewing on his bottom lip this time, and I figured once he straightened up that his hand wasn't all that great.

"No, she wanders the halls with the fireplace poker, looking for him in case he comes back. I guess she died a month later. She had the room so she stayed there. Died of a broken heart."

"So why wasn't she hauled off to prison?"

"I think it was rumored that she killed him; the plaque says that he probably fell down the stairs and broke his neck."

"See, ghost stories never make any sense," Scott said. "Waste of time."

"I think they're great," Lissa said. "Really fascinating."

"You would. All spooky and romantic and all that horseshit." He threw his cards down in disgust. "I'm out."

"No, it's because these stories tell you what people *wanted* to believe," she replied hotly. "Give me another card."

Betting followed; Lissa, Carla, Scott, and I were out and it was left to Brad, Jay, and Sue. The stakes got pretty high, well, high for us, and there might have been forty dollars in the pot at point.

The remaining players sized each other up. Brad glared at the other two, breathing in through his nose and out through his mouth like he was invoking his yogic calm and it wasn't coming. Jay and Sue stared at each other, small smiles playing around their lips. Finally, in the last round, Jay and Brad folded, and Sue scooped the pot over to her pile.

"Come to mama. Well, at least one good thing came out of this evil night."

Brad was picking up the cards that Sue had discarded. "Hey! You were bluffing. You had two threes, that's all!"

"You jackass, since when do you get to look after the fact?"

Carla slapped at Brad, but he'd already backed out of range.

"Look, she was bluffing," he said, showing the cards to Jay, who scowled.

"You have to pay to find out, Brad. That's the rules. No snooping around after the fact," Sue said.

"Don't be such a pussy," Jay said. "Suck it up, man."

"But she was bluffing! And you bought it too!"

"Yeah, man, you always bet too much at the wrong times," Chris said to Jay.

He shrugged. "You gotta have faith in the cards."

"No, I have faith in beer. I always know exactly what beer will do for me in any given situation," Chris said. "Cards are too unpredictable, or have you forgotten the strip poker game that gave you your nickname, Jay-Bird?"

"As in nekkid-as-a?" Carla said. "Huh. I always thought it was because he was noisy and pooped all over the place."

"Well, that too," Chris assured her. "This particular event was sometime during that extended holiday Jay took after high school. Undergrad shouldn't take six years, dude."

Jay shrugged. "You go with your strengths, Chris. I was good at spring break."

"Speaking of strengths," I said, "if you can't tell when Sue's bluffing, then you shouldn't be betting, *Brad*."

Brad made a face. "But I had a *good* hand!"

"So you should have stuck with it."

"Whatever."

The game shut down soon after that and Brad, perhaps still miffed by his loss, bullied me into meeting him in the gym the next morning.

"But my session's first thing," Carla complained. "Aren't you guys coming?"

We seldom made it to each other's panels.

"I don't want to get up that early," I said to both of them. "Why do you want to work out anyway?"

"Didn't you bring your stuff?"

"Yes, but I didn't expect—"

"Meet me down there at seven, no better make it six-thirty. We can catch up." Brad raised his eyebrows in what I suppose was meant to be a meaningful fashion, and I reluctantly agreed. He usually didn't bother with subterfuge, and I was curious.

"Fine, but you're going to get what you deserve," I muttered, throwing my cards away. My luck had run out for the night. "And since I'll be getting up at the crack of dawn, Carla, I'll be sure to catch your paper."

Scott said he had to wash out his underwear or go commando the rest of the weekend. Brad, of course, had his schedule to keep and wanted to make sure he got enough sleep to counteract his present sleep deficit. Jay was going to another room to catch the basketball game, on which he claimed to have a sure bet. Lissa announced she was going back downstairs, and hit the bar. I had figured to go back to my room, but said I'd go with her, because Sue was going too and looked like she could use some friendly faces at the moment.

Carla yawned, fit to swallow a pig. "Well, I'm going to sleep, if my room's warmed up any. It was as cold as hell when I left for the plenary, and they said they were going to work on it."

"Funny," I said. "Mine was as hot as hell. Must be Château Dante we're staying in here."

We walked down to the bar, and it was packed: The conference bar is like the watering hole on the veldt, with everyone stalking everyone else. I noticed Duncan over in one corner, holding court with the same effortless magnetism I remembered from years ago. He caught my eye, but didn't do anything else, so I just followed Lissa and Sue to where they were going and hoped that the service would be a little better than it was this evening after the plenary. Sure enough, there were three waitresses pushing their way through the crowd. I hoped they were getting well tipped; the bar was nearly as hot as my room was.

We got a seat with Laurel Fairchild, who always seemed to occupy the same spot in every bar at every conference she went to. As far as I knew, she left only to present her own papers; she believed that she would run into everyone she wanted to simply by staying put and letting the world come to her. This time we lucked out, and got seats during a lull in her evening.

From a distance, Laurel resembled someone who'd been frozen in time at the last heyday of the hotel: black turtleneck, black cardigan, black Capri pants, a brunette bobbed Beatnik with cat's-eye glasses. Closer up, you realized that she was maybe in her late forties or fifties, but it seemed like she'd always been at the conference and would always be. She swore like a trooper and would still be chain-smoking unfiltered Camels, if it hadn't been for the fact that cigarettes were prohibited almost everywhere she had a reason to be.

Lissa said, "Good Lord, Laurel. Don't you ever get bored of just sitting there, like a lump?"

"Christ, no. Not when I've got entertainment like the floorshow that's been going on here for the past hour." She gestured over to the corner, where Duncan was telling a joke, an energetic pantomime. I noticed that there were brownish spots on her hands now, something I didn't recall from previous years. Yikes. It didn't seem right that she should be showing signs of age.

She continued. "And my feet are killing me. I shouldn't have worn shoes that weren't broken in."

I looked down and saw that she'd taken off her new pumps—pointy-toed, achingly narrow, and far too fashionable for me—and was rolling an unopened beer bottle with her stockinged foot. It was an old trick I knew from the field, but I usually saved it for more private venues. She was drinking a glass of wine, so I didn't know what she was going to do with that beer when it warmed up . . .

"You could wear sensible shoes," I said.

Laurel agreed so politely that I knew that my suggestion had been dismissed out of hand. "How you doing, Sue?" she asked, looking down past her glasses to the other woman. The effect made her look even more avian than ever, with her beaky nose and sharp, dark eyes. "Garrison unloaded a real shit-storm, huh?"

Sue nodded. "I'm okay, now. You always think you can deal with this better than you do, you get the rug pulled out from under you like that. I felt like I was going to throw up for a while there."

Laurel nodded, looking sympathetic, and somehow at the same time gestured to the waitress as she passed with a tray of loaded drinks. Laurel had better bar karma than almost anyone I knew, and that was on top of her propensity for giving large tips. We'd be well looked after tonight, as long as we could stand the noise and the heat.

"Let me get this. Happy New Year," she said. "Or to a better year after this, I should say."

"Amen to that."

There was no talking among us after that. Sue sat and drank steadily, but although her shoulders were slumped with obvious fatigue, it didn't seem as though she was getting destructive about it. I sipped at a bourbon, more for something to have in my hands than any real interest in the drink. Laurel held court from her chair, keeping track of a ridiculous number of meetings with apparent effortlessness, all arranged at the top of her voice to be heard over the din. Lissa went up to the bar for some popcorn and had never made it back; someone had waylaid her and the pair of them were talking animatedly, unheard over the racket. Somewhere in the background the bar's sound system thumped and provided not so much a soundtrack as an underlying percussive structure to the cacophony. I was just glad that there was no smoking, else it would have been pretty nigh unbearable. As it was, it was only my friends who were keeping me there, and they were all in their own little worlds.

I glanced across the room through a temporary gap in the bodies and saw Duncan holding forth, expressively and charismatically, alternating humor and seriousness. People were clustered around him, either because they were truly interested in what he had to say—his information was usually interesting and useful, if nothing else, and he had influence in the field as a professor at an important department in New Hampshire—or to bask in his reflected glow. Larger and larger concentric circles formed around him, satellites gravitating toward a bright star. At one point he leaned in, as if speaking confidentially, and the people around him leaned in too; then he exploded up, nailing whatever punch line or conclusion to a shout of laughter.

I looked away and took another sip of my drink; I wasn't so curious about the story as I was about my feelings, now that I'd seen him, testing them gingerly, the way you step on ice that you know is probably too thin to support you. When I got done being fascinated by the melting ice floating and clinking unheard in the glass, I looked up and saw that Laurel was watching me.

She did a little chin jerk and eyebrow thing, asking me wordlessly if I was okay; I just rolled my eyes and nodded. There was no reason for me not to be okay, I just found myself going over a long-buried past and wishing I didn't need to. I'd successfully avoided it for over a decade; I didn't see why I should bother digging it out now. Laurel nodded and turned, immediately caught up in another round of where-can-we-meet-and-talk with yet another passerby.

"Hey."

Meg and Neal had come into the bar. I hooked Lissa's abandoned chair by the stretcher and pulled it over for them.

They sat down, one butt-cheek each on the chair. "Not inter-rupting anything, are we?" Meg asked.

I couldn't detect any layer of hurt in her voice, but I was acutely aware enough of having been less than gracious in my dealings with her all day. "Nothing at all," I said. I had just been about to excuse myself, but this seemed like a good time to make sure Meg and I were cool. "You guys got time for that congratulatory round I promised?"

"Always," Neal said. "Meg's told you, then?"

"Word's been getting around." I leaned over to Sue and Laurel and shouted, "Meg and Neal just got engaged. Two of my best students!"

"Well, I know what we need to do, then!" Laurel once again easily caught the attention of the harried waitress, who came right over. Other tables might go dry and pine for a sup of beer, but those who sat with Laurel never would. "Got any champagne?" she shouted. "We've got an engagement to celebrate!"

"I wouldn't call it champagne," the waitress said, shaking her head, looking alarmed. She glanced around her, and see-ing none of the other staff, said confidentially, "I'd stick with the hard liquor and beer, if I were you."

"Thanks for the warning," she said. "Emma?"

I looked around. "Whiskey's okay with everyone?"

Everyone nodded. "Whiskeys all around, then," I said. "Single malt, if you've got it."

By the time she came back with our drinks, Lissa had made it back with the popcorn and her colleague. I ex-plained to them what was going on and lifted my glass. The others fell silent for a moment.

"To Meg and Neal!"

"To Meg and Neal," the others chorused. One of their friends—the Gypsy-clad woman—already in the know, wandered over and added, "And all the babies to come!"

"Go to hell, Jordan!" Meg said.

Quick as lightning, she flicked a piece of popcorn and landed it squarely on Jordan's chin. The young woman clearly knew to expect it, and her laughter infected the rest of the party.

Suddenly it seemed that everyone was swarming around our table, and the energy of the bar changed, shifting to our side of the room. Meg and Neal answered all the usual questions—no, they didn't have a date set, but probably after Neal defended his dissertation successfully; yes, they would probably stay in Maine for the time being; honeymoon destinations were limited by a graduate income, but there was a chance they could borrow a friend's family's condo in the Caribbean for a week. Pretty soon the conversation switched back to our work at Fort Providence and then early sites in general, and then everyone started to splinter off again, group energy renewed.

My energy, however, was gone for the day, and my head was starting to pound with the noise and excitement. After a decent interval and the second round, which for me was a quick soda, I excused myself, hugged the happy couple, and made my way toward my room. Leaving the bar was a good start, but my room was still an oven, and I knew that even if I sat up long enough to drink some water to stave off dehydration, it would still be an hour before I had any chance of getting to sleep in there.

I got the water and cracked the window, but I knew I couldn't stay in there to roast until it cooled off. Checking the thermometer, I saw that it had gone down ten degrees since my complaints, and was probably repaired for the night, but I decided to pull on my boots, jeans, and parka and go out to look at the moon in the snow. By the time I got bored and cold, it might be possible to get some sleep.

I actually made it outside without getting caught by anyone in the lobby or the bar, which was something miraculous, even considering the conference attendance was lower because of the canceled flights. Although our group was often close to five hundred or more, I heard we were down to about four hundred today. There's always someone wandering around at conferences, and it's always a pick of the draw to see whose floor you'll be on, what famous person you'll run into in the restroom, or who'll be sharing your table at the boxed lunch.

The cold air shocked me as I stepped out of the revolving door on the side of the lobby. The wind had died down somewhat, but it was still snowing like fury, and the moon was nowhere to be found, of course, behind the clouds. There was plenty of ambient light from the Christmas-lit hotel and the parking lot, and I figured that I could follow the walks around to the back and maybe even down to the lake, if the outside lights were still on there.

The walks weren't shoveled out, but it still wasn't deep enough to be a nuisance yet: The storm was swinging up the coast and we were still inland from it. The walking was easy, through the light fluffy stuff, and was actually easier than it had been earlier, as the slush had frozen solid, into an uneven surface. Now the new snow made it easier to keep from sliding. As long as I brushed myself off good before it melted on me when I returned inside, I wouldn't even get all that wet.

I love walking through snow, if only for the acoustical tricks that it plays on you, deadening sound, distorting the sonic impression of distance, and giving you a sense of solitude that is altogether too difficult to come by in the crowded Northeast. One of the benefits of doing archaeology out of cities, or traveling to places off the beaten path, was the comparative quiet. Or rather, there was a different, quieter set of sounds that weren't purely human in origin. But there weren't even any animal sounds now—everyone but me was safely snugged away for the duration of the storm—and the creak of branches overhead, the wind coming across the frozen lake, and the feathery soft sound of landing snow-flakes were worth escaping the cacophony inside. The noise of my crunching boots made very little impression on the woods surrounding the hotel.

The long, shallow path that led down to the lake was not only lit, it was pristine. The landscapers had created a series of many short steps punctuated by longer, level landings, so the trip down was designed to be inviting and gentle. I decided that I felt warm enough to continue to the bottom, and then would head back to my room, pleasantly worn out.

I got the cadence of the staircase quickly: five regular stairs followed by three to ten regular paces of flat landing, then the next set of steps. Bump, bedumpt, bedumpt, swish, swish, swish. There was the occasional turn, so that it wasn't a straight shot down to the lake, and I assumed that during the day, the walker would be treated to various vistas or landscaped intervals. I counted about twenty of the steps-and-strides combinations, and made it down to the bottom after several minutes of hard work. I wasn't worried about getting lost, even though the snow was heavier now, as the railing would lead me back to the top of the stairs and the back of the hotel.

There was a little beach down by the lake at the bottom of the steps, where the pines fell away into a circle. Maybe when it wasn't covered by an even layer of snow that seemed to flatten and compress the difference between shapes and heights, you could identify boulders, chairs, perhaps outdoor grills and chimneys for lakeside gatherings. There was a raised area to the right, which was a gazebo or covered deck, which might have been ideal for small wedding parties, maybe a buffet or the bandstand for larger affairs. With the blanket of snow, it was impossible to tell but imagination filled in the spaces. Trees spread out to both sides beyond the clearing, and it looked as though paths followed the circumference of the lake to the left and right. Mountains rose up into the clouds across the lake, lit and shadowed by the snow. On the left-hand side of the clearing, I could see the dock, all closed down for the winter, and the ice spread across nearly half of the lake.

I didn't dare go down off the stairs to explore, though if the weather cleared up, I promised myself a walk around when it was a little easier to navigate. I looked out across the lake, through the veil of falling snow, and was rewarded with a glimpse of the moon, through a break in the wispy clouds. The vision lasted no more than two seconds, and it was quickly covered up again.

I had just turned around to go back when I heard a tremendous thud, followed by a sharp noise like the crack of a rifle. That surprised me, but I immediately attributed it to snow falling off weakened branches and a branch cracking under the weight. It didn't end there, though; I heard rustling/crunching noises that were too large to be scattering squirrels or birds and too small and consistent to be branches settling or rebounding.

It sounded human.

I felt my mouth go dry again. "Hello? Is someone out there?"

The noises ceased suddenly, only to be replaced by what sounded like gargantuan moaning. That definitely sounded like something alive, in the animal-not-tree sense.

"Hello?" I tried again, feeling nervous and vastly stupid, all at once.

Nothing was to be heard but the wind, the snow, and the sound of my blood pounding in my ears. In the two minutes I'd stopped at the bottom of the stairs, the cold had driven its way through my parka and into my bones. In the long ten seconds during which I'd heard the not-quite-natural noises, it froze the heart of me as well. I wanted to be out of there, now.

Sue's ghost story in my head, I turned and ran up the stairs, stumbling over the roughness of the terrain, grateful for the handrail and the fact that I could see no other foot-prints but mine as I ascended, as hastily as I could. Whatever was out there, hadn't come from the hotel, and so therefore was probably not human. My movements were clumsy, and I knew that I was probably just scaring myself, but that didn't keep me from slogging as fast as I could until I got to the top and ran around the front to the doors of the hotel.

I don't care how dumb I might have looked: You don't go wandering out by yourself in the middle of a snowstorm and then go off to investigate unearthly noises when instinct is telling you to run the hell out of there as fast as you can.

Chapter 3

I GOT BACK TO MY ROOM AND WAS IN A COLD SWEAT. The heat had gone down rapidly, and the room was now habitable. I took a shower to calm down. My heart rate slowed, but I was by no means relaxed. I checked the clock: It was just past one. Too late for company, though it would be easily found if I wanted it; too early to go to bed, as I was less inclined to sleep than before I went for my nerve-wracking walk. At home I would just be thinking about whether there was anything else to do before I hit the sack, but conference time and energy is never the same as at home, and I knew I needed to do something to unwind before I went to bed. I could check on my slides, that would burn a few minutes. The mundane task of reviewing the images and my forthcoming talk would calm me down enough to sleep.

I found my tray, checked the location of the preview room, and found my way down to the second-floor mezzanine. As I wandered over to the rail, I could see the desk across from the main doors, several lounge areas scattered around, and the restaurants off to either side. Outside the coffee shop was a pinball machine, now silent, and I promised myself a game later.

I was lucky, and the room wasn't locked; I found the light and the projectors were all out and waiting for use. Pretty soon I was immersed in scanning through my paper, reconsidering one image over another for a greater impact; the little plastic tack-tack of the slides being inserted into the carousel the only noise. It calmed me like nothing else could.

The door opened. I glanced over.

It was Duncan.

I would have gnawed off my leg, like an animal in a trap, to get away from there. I very nearly turned and ran when I saw that we were going to be alone in there, but pride wouldn't let me do that, and since I was already halfway done, I kept on going, stomach churning. Duncan paused by me, then went to work on his own slides. Maybe he would see that I wasn't interested in talking. I would run through my slides as quickly as I could and get the hell out, pride intact, boundaries maintained, and no messy interactions.

It was a good plan, but it went awry right away. I have a fifty-fifty chance of having the kind of carousel that doesn't work on the projectors at any given conference, and I'd come up short this time. I kept promising myself that I was going to go to one of those computerized presentation programs, but I always worry about other, more pressing things and never got around to it. Now I was paying the price for it. I turned the carousel over to make sure that the little metal flange was in the right place, and then the plastic circle that keeps the slides in place fell off and my slides tumbled to the carpet, some of them cartwheeling clear across the room.

"Fuck!" The word came unbidden and was pure acid; my emotions were getting the better of me. It had nothing to do with the possibility of getting lint on my slides.

I got most of them and then paused as I crouched; there

were three over by Duncan's chair. Correction, there had been three. He'd picked them up and come over to where I was. I stood up slowly, and took them by the white plastic frames, careful not to touch the film or his hand.

"Thanks." I didn't really meet his gaze, just gave him a casual flip of the head and an unconvincing imitation smile as I turned back to the carousel on the table.

I could practically feel him hesitate behind me, and sighed with relief as he moved toward the door. I heard it shut and relaxed, just then noticing how my fingers were trembling as I tried to replace my slides in order.

Then I heard soft footsteps on the carpet behind me.

"Emma, can't we talk?" He had a riveting voice, low, a little husky, very sure.

Shit. Shit. Shit.

"Sure. What do you want to talk about?" I kept my eyes on my work, carefully blowing a hair from the dark square of the image. Nice picture, artifacts from Fort Providence, very early seventeenth-century, the photographer did a good job on them . . .

"No, I mean, really talk. About . . . about what's bothering you."

I kept focusing on the slides, each tinny little click as they fit into the slots a small victory for me and my composure. "What's bothering me." I shook my head. "What do you want, Duncan?"

That was a mistake. "I want you to talk to me like I'm a person. We can't go on this way forever, can we?"

I shrugged. "It's worked okay so far." Even as I spoke, I could feel my face growing hotter and hotter.

He shrugged. "We don't run into each other all that often. The big conferences are so big we don't meet. The little ones . . . I'm not usually at."

Duncan never bothered with the regional meetings. Not a big enough audience for him.

"But I don't want it to be like that," he was saying. "I mean, doesn't this feel bad to you?"

"It's small potatoes compared to how I felt when you dumped me on my ass!" I hadn't meant for it to come out like that—I hadn't meant for it to come out at all.

He moved back, surprised by my anger. "That was a long time ago. Can't we even talk to each other? Can't we be civil?"

I sat back and looked at him closely for the first time: Yes, he had aged, but the lines in his face added character. He was tanned, but not the same way I remembered: this was more an expensive winter vacation tan than a fieldwork brown. He'd always been a little proud of his hair, and so he still hadn't cut it short, though I noticed there was a skillful part that might just disguise a receding hairline. A little bit of grey in the beard, now carefully and closely trimmed. Gray eyes, still no need of glasses. Damn his eyes.

"Hmmm. I say hello, I nod, I keep out of your way. No firearms, no knives. Civility city."

"Not my definition of civility, but I can see that it's been an effort for you."

There was the first sign of his temper. Good—why? Why does he care?

I took a deep breath, and the words came out like soda rushing from a shaken bottle. "Yeah, an effort. Why shouldn't it be? We had a lot of plans and you changed your mind all of a sudden, and I was left looking like an idiot."

There was the faintest flicker of satisfaction across Duncan's face: I'd revealed a weakness. "And you've always hated looking like—"

My face went warm again and I tried to unclench my teeth. "You don't have the right to psychoanalyze me, Duncan. You never said goodbye, you never had anything to say for yourself, so don't start now. You don't have the right."

He was quiet for a moment. "Okay, I'm going about this

the wrong way. I didn't handle things well when we ended. Then it was, what . . . another two years before we saw each other? Not much had changed, I was still figuring things out. Then another five years, and then you were married, and I was married and we never sorted it all out, the way I should have when we broke up."

"Let's get the semantics right, shall we?" I jabbed a finger at him. "You split."

"Fine, okay," he said quickly. "I apologize for not being a better human being then, for not knowing better how to do things."

I looked at him, disbelieving. If there were words I'd ever wanted to hear, it was these, but they were nearly twenty years too late.

"I'm serious, I mean it. But I'm glad I did it; it worked out better in the long run. I'm just sorry you're still hurt." Duncan shifted and sighed. "I miss you—!"

I threw the slide carousel down onto the table.

"Wait! I don't mean it like that! Jesus, I forgot what your temper could be like!"

"Well, it's a good thing you didn't stick around then, isn't it?" My temper's only getting worse as I get older. He didn't do anything to improve it. I never let myself go like this. I could barely contain myself and I hated it.

"Emma, it would have been a mistake! I thought it was then, and I was right! I knew I wasn't ready—what kid is when he's twenty-three?"

I took deep breaths, working to calm myself. "I knew. At least, I was pretty sure." And I was a year younger than you, I added to myself.

He shrugged. "Maybe you were. Can't you forgive me for not being ready? For being scared?"

It was my turn to shrug. "I don't have a problem with people being scared. I have a problem when they don't handle it well."

"I apologized for that already."

We both knew there was a big, nasty elephant still standing in the middle of the room. "And the other thing?" There were a lot of "other things," and I was curious to see which one he'd pick.

"Yeah, and you know that lasted about ten minutes, same as my next half-dozen 'relationships.' It's taken me a long time to sort out my act."

I said, "I just want to keep the story straight. You were seeing her long before you walked out on me." Christ, why couldn't I keep from sounding so shrill? "If we're going to discuss it. Civilly." As soon as I said it, I realized that I didn't want to discuss it, I was too tired and had too much else I'd rather do. Get a Brazilian wax, clean a septic tank, shove splinters under my nails . . .

"Okay." He turned to the door, then paused. What would it take him to get all the way through that door and close it behind him? "My mother really appreciated the note that you sent. When Dad died."

Damn it, that was low. And just when I had been working up a really good head of steam. "Your dad was a great guy," I said simply. "And your mother . . . I really liked her a lot. It was the least I could do."

"She misses you. A lot. She likes Cindy—my wife, now—but she really liked you. She wouldn't mind hearing from you."

I snorted. "You don't ask for much, do you?"

"It's for Mom. That's all."

"I'll see you, Duncan."

He finally left. I waited, then picked up my slides, finished placing them back in order, and left the slide room. I ducked back into the doorway when I saw Jay was also heading for the elevators. Thank God; I was pretty sure he didn't see me. I just didn't want to see anyone, didn't want to talk to anyone.

No such luck. "Emma! Get your ass in here!" Lissa called from the bar.

Much of our poker group had coalesced around Laurel's table by this time; I was reminded of the old computer game, Life, when groups of cells formed, moved, broke off, reformed. I shook my head; I was way too tired.

"Now, Fielding!" Chris bellowed: He was deep into the beer and I went over to keep him from shouting again.

"I'm heading up to my room," I said, shaking my head. "I'm beat!"

"What! It's only Wednesday! You can't crap out on us so soon!" he said. "Let me get you a drink."

"I'm serious, man. I've had a rough night."

"Why, what's wrong, Emma?"

"Oh, I . . . I went for a walk and got the stuffing scared out of me. Noises outside spooked me. I ran all the way from the beach to my room. I was just checking my slides to try and calm down, but I'm going to go to sleep now."

"Hey, Emma got scared by Sue's ghost," Lissa yelled, laughing hysterically.

"Emma needs to lay off work, if she's seeing ghosts," Scott said. "C'mon, have another drink!"

"Tomorrow, I promise," I said. "G'night everyone."

After a few more protests, I escaped. Once I got up to my room, I glanced at the clock but went straight for the phone anyway.

A sleepy, grumpy voice answered. "Hello?"

I didn't let it bother me. My younger sister, Charlotte—and while she might be Carrie to her few friends and veterinarian colleagues, she'd always be my kid sister Bucky to me—is always either sleepy or grumpy. "It's me, Bucks."

"Hey, Em." I heard muffled voices, the television being muted in the background. "What's up?"

"I can't just call you to say hi?"

"Not when you're at a conference. Not at this time of night.

If you have the time for calling, it's usually Brian." There was a pause. "So how's the weather in New Hampshire?"

Damn. She knew. "Cold. Started snowing like mad."

"It's already dumped more than a foot here. Duncan's there, isn't he?"

"Yep."

"Seen him, have you?"

"Yep. Today at the tour I gave of the site." I paused. "He just cornered me in the slide room."

"Talk to him?"

"Some. Not much." Not well, I added to myself.

"Good. He's a shithead and I hope he burns in hell, the fat lump of pig vomit."

"Bucky . . ." I don't know why I felt compelled to defend Duncan, as I felt pretty much the same as my sister. I was just more able, or willing, to compartmentalize my feelings and leave them—I hoped—to fade over the years.

"He left you a letter, a note on your bureau, for when you came back from break and . . . poof! That was it."

"It was a selfish thing to do," I agreed carefully.

"Selfish? Selfish! You're kidding me! Goddamned pretty boy, *mama's* boy, son of a bitch, tail-chasing, monkey-humping, loser, suck-up—"

I let her go on for a while, knowing that it was pretty much useless to break in before she'd gotten some of the poison out of her system.

"Hey, kiddo—?"

"—and whatever happily lives in a diseased weasel's lower intestine would cross the street rather than run into him!"

She drew a breath and I tried again. "Okay, Bucks? Feel better?"

"You know my opinion on the subject, Em. Why else would you bring it up, unless you wanted some sisterly support?"

"Ah . . . good question. I don't know what I want." I suddenly felt exhausted. Bed. I wanted bed.

"Well, I know what you need, and I have just the baseball bat for you to use. Aluminum, bought just for the purpose, kept safe and shiny all these years—"

"Bucky, lay off."

"I've always hated him, Emma. I'm just glad you got out of it before it was too late."

"He was the one who got out of it. I would have married him."

"No, you wouldn't. You would have come to your senses before anything drastic happened."

"Bucky." I took a deep breath, ashamed at how much effort it took to say the next words. "I loved him."

"Like you love Brian?"

"God, no," I said, without thinking. "I mean, no, of course not, *now*. But I was happy with him at the time, you know?"

"No, you weren't. You two never stopped fighting. You were always arguing."

"No . . . I mean, yes, we argued a lot." I shook my head, trying to remember clearly. "We were young. Competitive, you know how it is." Or maybe she didn't; charges of laziness or performing at sub-ability levels had always been levied at my brilliant sister. Where any such comment would have driven me mad, she paid no attention and did exactly what she wanted. "We were undergraduates with a mission, ready to take the world by storm. You couldn't not argue, not the way we were."

"Right. Because you were both exactly the same, that's all. That's not love, that's narcissism. Maybe even masturbation. You felt the same way about enough things that it seemed like you had a lot in common. And it was probably the sex, too. I never asked, but I assume it was at least acceptable—"

I looked away, even though there was no one to make eye

contact with, and felt my face burn. I wished I could blank it all out, I hated knowing that other people knew how young and weak and stupid I'd been. I hated how it could still affect me, that it wouldn't just go away.

"—and I am certain that was the extent of it. There, that help?"

I stared at the numbers on the phone for room service and the concierge. "Oh, sure, as much as having my nearest and dearest tell me what an idiot I am ever helps."

"I was dumping on him, not you. There's a difference."

"Oh, okay, sure, right. So, how're things with you?"

"Good. Busy."

I heard a muffled voice in the background saying "Carrie? What is it?"

A suspicion struck me. "And Joel?"

"What about him?"

The wariness in my sister's voice told the whole story. She'd gotten back together with a perfectly decent guy she'd been scared enough to ditch, and still didn't have the guts to admit that I'd been right about him, and about her, and how good he was for her. It took a sister's perspective, I suppose, to cut through the ego and get to the real story. I didn't mind; it was good for her to be challenged once in a while.

"How's he doing?"

"Good." She paused then admitted it. "He's right here."

"Oh, jeez, if I'm interrupting something—"

"No. He lives here now."

I lost interest in the hotel phone numbers. "He lives— what? What do you—?"

"He moved in. Two weeks ago."

"And just when were you going to tell me?" I could barely keep the disbelief out of my voice.

"Don't get all huffy with me! I'm telling you now. Why, did you plan on stalking him at his old address or something?"

"No, you know what I mean! Well, I'm glad. Congratulations."

"Why? For what?"

"It's nice, that's why. Don't act so suspicious. He's a good guy."

"It's nice, okay. It's also late. I want to get to sleep."

"Yeah, but—"

"I'll talk to you later, okay, Em? Bye."

She didn't give me a chance to say goodbye. I hung up, thought about calling Brian at Kam's, but I didn't want to disturb them; it really was too late for anyone but a Fielding. All I wanted was my bed; I was grateful for the exhaustion and the cooler room. I brushed my teeth, undressed, and climbed between the sheets. Luckily for me, I fell asleep almost immediately and I wasn't subjected to an endless playback of my every personal interaction, past and present.

Chapter 4

THERE WAS A BLURRED BUZZING IN MY HEAD THAT wouldn't go away. I began to realize that it wasn't just a part of some vague dream and found myself being dragged from sleep by the alarm clock. It took me three or four tries to focus my eyes: the burning red numerals spelled out the horrible truth. It was six fifteen A.M., Thursday morning.

You've got to be kidding.

With a moan, I rolled over and burrowed under my pillow, but I didn't turn off the alarm, and eventually the country music and static that was playing instead of the NPR station I thought I'd found last night wore its way insistently into my brain until I was convinced that I really wasn't going to go back to sleep again. Why did I tell Brad that I would meet him so damn early? And in the gym? For God's sake, Emma . . .

I threw the blanket back and, with a yelp, pulled it back over me again in a hurry. The room had gone from being subtropical to arctic frigidity overnight. I summoned up my courage, dove out of bed, grabbed my parka, and stood in front of the thermostat. It was now fifty degrees in my room.

I'd set it for sixty-five. I fiddled with the controls but never heard any indication that more heat was heading my way. I went to the bathroom and saw the coffee maker, but there were no coffee packets to be found.

I stared. No, God. You can't be serious.

I looked in the closet by the iron, I pawed through the little bottles of conditioner that I never used, but there was no coffee in my room. Disgusted, I threw on my workout gear, made sure I had my room key, and went downstairs to the hospitality suite. Passing the mezzanine, I saw that there was no one in the lobby yet.

My heart leapt—the door to the hospitality suite was open. There was, however, nothing on the tables besides empty coffee urns.

I went to the lobby, where at least it was warmer than my room on the third floor.

There was no one at the front desk, and no one appeared when I rang the little bell. I cursed and headed behind the desk and past the offices for the fitness room.

There, at least, was heat, and so far seemed to be one of the only parts of the hotel that had actually been renovated. That was nice, but not nearly enough to make up for the ghastly hour and the debilitating coffee deficiency I was now forced to cope with.

After I did fifty jumping jacks, I began to work on my shadow boxing. It's great for keeping yourself warm, and I always need the practice, since I am terribly self-conscious about pretending to hit and kick someone who isn't there. It's a whole lot easier when there's actually someone to provide the target for you.

I felt better than I deserved, late night and emotional turmoil considered. For a while, I'd thought about letting my training with my instructor Nolan go—it took up an awful lot of time and just saying the words "martial arts" felt overdramatic—but was glad that I decided to stick it out.

The workout I got with Krav Maga was great, and I realized that not only had my posture and energy improved, my attitude had changed for the better as well, and you couldn't beat that with a stick. Plus, it was more fun than running. When I let too much time go between our sessions, I even miss how much I ache after. I didn't know what missing pain indicated about one's psyche, but so far, it was working for me. Go figure.

Brad gets five more minutes, I thought grumpily. I hated returning from that happy place that distraction takes you when you're working out. Two more minutes, just to polish my form, and then I'm out of here. He should know better than to mess with—

"Ah, good morning, Emma!"

I kept staring at myself in the mirror, trying to keep my stance correct. I threw a very nice left hook, followed by a rather impressive, fully loaded right uppercut. Too bad all my best moves were always made out of the sight of my instructor, Nolan. Can I help it if my native modesty keeps me from doing my best when someone is watching?

And he knows full well that cheery crap is *exactly* the wrong tack to take with me, I thought, sighing. "Yeah, morning, Brad." I glanced at the clock: six forty-eight. "You're late. What's up?"

"Still not a morning person, Em." He shook his head and slung his towel over a chair. He was wearing loose drawstring trousers and a T-shirt with a Chinese dragon on it. "I wouldn't have asked to meet you so early if it wasn't important."

I personally couldn't think of anything important enough to warrant being out of bed at this hour. Or even in bed, not asleep. Brian and I had an agreement: I wouldn't try anything when *American Chopper* was on, and he didn't make a pass at me before ten or eleven in the morning, if we had the opportunity to sleep in. I nodded, but I also pretended that it was Brad's head I was smashing with my knee, before I finally stopped and got a drink from the water cooler. "No. What's up?"

Instead of answering me, though, Brad started doing yoga stretches. He made some interesting breathing noises, but sticking his butt out in the air like that was extremely ill-advised considering my present state of mind. I'm pretty good at kicking, especially when someone offers me a target like that. I drank some of my water and tried to think past my burgeoning headache.

A few moments later, he looked up, dreamy-faced. "Sorry, I needed to get some good, deep breathing in. Breathing is so important."

"Yeah, I'm fond of it myself. What's up?" And if you don't answer me this time, I'm leaving.

He sat up and twisted to one side, exhaling deeply before he answered. "It's really important, and a bit personal. I didn't want to talk in front of the others."

I nodded, trying not to cross my eyes with impatience. I also attempted one of his poses, the one I recognized as "the tree." I made it, barely getting my right foot against my left knee as I stayed balanced, but it was harder than it looked. As I sat down, I revised my opinion of Brad's perpetual look of anxious malnutrition; he was stronger and more flexible than I thought.

"I'm thinking about making some changes in my life, Emma. I was wondering whether you would be willing— Hey, Carla!"

Carla stuck her head inside the door; she was dressed in another abbreviated suitlet and already had makeup on. "Hey, Brad, Emma. Em, you look like shit."

"Don't start with me, Carla, I've already got Brad over here picking on me and he—"

"What can we do you for, Carla?" Brad interjected hastily. I couldn't help rolling my eyes this time. He was worried I would reveal what we were talking about, and he hadn't even told me yet.

"Either of you seen Scott?"

"Hell, no," I began, but Carla looked really serious, even more so than she usually did before a session. For which she was also up too early. "Why would he be up yet? What's wrong?"

"I just gotta find him, in a hurry. Tell him I'm looking for him, if you see him, okay?"

"Yeah, sure. Anything we can do?" I asked.

"Just let him know I need him." And she vanished.

"She needs to relax a little," Brad said absently. "I wonder if she's getting enough fiber."

"Brad, if you don't tell me what you called me down here for, at this ungodly hour, I will scream. Then I will hit you repeatedly until I feel better about us both."

He was foolish enough to think that was hyperbole, and did more painful-looking stretches and deep breathing. Thing was, I could tell he was trying to get himself screwed up to deal with something important. "Emma, it's hard for me, okay? But I appreciate your eagerness to help."

"Let's not confuse it with an eagerness to get out of here and get some coffee." As soon as I said it, I felt bad. Brad's face fell. He wasn't the dearest of friends, and his earnestness was excruciating at times, but that didn't mean I could treat him so casually. "I'm sorry, Brad. I'm a jerk. I'm not really up yet. What is it?"

He took another deep breath, and the door burst open again. This time, it was Lissa. Her eyes were barely open. "Scott?"

"Not here," I said. "What's wrong?"

"Carla's looking for him" was all she muttered, and turned around to leave, walking straight into the doorjamb. "Aaoow." She found her way out, but clearly not by sight. The door clicked behind her, and I looked expectantly at Brad.

"Okay, now, quick."

"This isn't going the way I wanted," he muttered. "I'm usually much more together than this."

That much was true: If Brad were any more together, he would collapse in upon himself and implode. "You had a favor you wanted to ask me?" I tried.

"Yes." Relief on his face was palpable. "It's just that I was hoping I could get you to—"

The door opened a crack, and Chris stuck his head in. "Emma, have you—?"

"No, I have no idea where Scott is," I said. "Look, if you could just give us—"

"I don't care where Scott is," he interrupted back. "I was going to ask if you had anything going during the first session. Something's come up, and we need a moderator, post haste."

I did have something, but it was recreational and not nearly as important as whatever was making Chris look so worried. "Yeah, sure I can do it. What session is it?"

"It's the session on early sites assemblages, eight-thirty. It's first thing, over in the Manchester Ballroom A."

I frowned, trying to recall the schedule. "So where's Garrison, that he can't moderate like he was supposed to?"

Chris shook his head. "No one can find him. Scott went round to get him for the breakfast meeting—past presidents and board—and he wasn't in his room. We have no idea where Garrison is."

Garrison was missing? That wasn't so unusual—like his performance last night, he pretty much came and went as he liked—but it was strange for Scott to be concerned about it. "Okay, I'll go get dressed," I told Chris. He nodded, a look of relief on his face.

"Thanks, Em," he said, slipping back through the doorway.

I turned back to Brad. "Okay, I've got to get going. Is it something you can tell me real quick?"

He hesitated, weighing the unsatisfying choices, then he blurted, "Yes. I want a letter of recommendation from you. I'm thinking of moving from Pennsylvania to Connecticut, and I don't want it to get around. I'd appreciate your discretion in this, Emma."

I wasn't surprised that he wanted to be discreet; this would be a big move, from one tenured position, presumably to another. "Where to?"

"The Connecticut University job."

"Lot of competition, I'll bet." I wondered why I hadn't heard about the opening there yet. Not that I was particularly interested in moving from Caldwell College in Maine—it had the advantage of being close to my areas of study and I'd recently gotten tenure—but one always liked to keep an ear to the ground. What did surprise me was that Brad was willing to uproot his perfect family from their perfect home and resettle them in a different state. Still, it was good money, I'd bet, and a lot of prestige. It had been Garrison's first tenured position. "Wow. How's Francine feel about it?"

He wobbled a bit as he moved through a "moon salute." "I haven't said anything to her yet. I don't want to, until I know I've got a chance."

Well, he's going to have to tell his wife when he starts flying off for interviews, I thought. I'd be nervous if I had to spring something like that on Brian, too, but Brad was good at what he did, and the job would be a good fit. "Okay, I'll do it," I said. "We can talk about this later, okay? I guess I have to hustle, if I'm going to help out with the session."

"Sure, thanks, no problem. I'll catch you later." And Brad went back to happily tying himself up in knots, smiling sincerely for the first time that morning.

I ran back upstairs, took a brisk shower—it started out okay, but the water came in cold bursts as more people woke up and caused competition. I got dressed as quickly as I could because it was still freezing in my room. I called down to the desk while I toweled my hair, and this time, got an answer and reassurances that they were working on the problem with the schizophrenic thermometer and would have it fixed soon. A few more minutes of preening, and it was just past seven-thirty. I had time for a cup of coffee and a muffin before it was time to go on, if they still needed me. That was good, as I wouldn't be doing anyone any favors if I went down to the session sans caffeine.

The General Bartlett Hotel had two restaurants, one a diner-themed coffee shop that did quick breakfast and lunch items. The other was a fancier sit-down affair, all dark greens and heavy wood, that seemed to be having a breakfast buffet at the moment and was packed to the rafters. I didn't care about anything so much as coffee now, and found that the coffee shop was full, too. Luck was with me in the guise of Lissa. I forced my way through the crowd as politely as I could—which was straining it, by this time—and found she'd saved me a seat at her table for two.

Whatever else we did not agree on—and sometimes that seemed to be almost everything—Lissa and I understood that there were some things that were sacred. For both of us morning coffee and its worship was one of them. Lissa nodded at the chair, and I nodded back as I took it. I turned over the mug and poured from the carafe on the table, sniffing at the coffee before I sipped. So far, I'd been unimpressed with the workings of the hotel, however great it might have looked on the outside and in the public spaces. To my surprise, the coffee was great: hot, strong, flavorful. I didn't focus on the exact nature of the flavors because I was functioning only on lizard brain; gourmet identifications came only after more basic functions were up and running.

Lissa waited until I'd got through the first cup, and then didn't bother with the preliminaries. "I still haven't seen the waitress since she dropped that off. We'll have to stand on the chairs and scream if she doesn't show up soon."

I nodded. Drastic times called for drastic measures. More coffee flooded into my system and I began to acknowledge my extremities.

I'd made my way through the second cup when our server shuffled over.

"HiI'mEleni." She said it all as one word, looking away from us to the cashier, who seemed to be of far more interest to her. "I'll be your server. What can I get you?"

"More coffee," I said.

"Me too," said Lissa.

"And a bagel, toasted, with cream cheese," I said. "Please."

But Eleni did not seem to be registering our presence, much less our needs. She was looking at the cook, a young man frenetically wielding a spatula by the grill.

"Busy today," I observed, trying to get her attention back to us and our order.

She sighed. "I had a helluva night last night."

Eleni didn't strike me as having a lot on the ball, so I asked her to bring my check, too, when she returned with the food. She nodded, distracted again, and shambled away. Her feet scuffed along the ground like she was wearing bedroom slippers.

"She had a helluva night last night," I informed Lissa.

Lissa put down her cup and glared at Eleni's back. She drew a deep breath, as if she was going to tell me exactly what she thought of Eleni's late night, then found the effort too much, and settled for another sip of coffee.

Ten long minutes later, we got another carafe of coffee, and I got my bagel. The coffee was again surprisingly good, and Lissa and I had eventually worked our way up to communicating with meaningful grunts and squeaks.

"Eve didn't eat an apple," Lissa said, at last.

"Huh?"

"She ate coffee beans. That was what was on the tree of knowledge."

"Ah." I wiped my mouth and pushed my chair back.

"Emma, mind if I take your place?" Jay had materialized behind me; he looked like he'd been up way too late last night.

"Knock yourself out," I said, throwing my napkin down.

"Lissa says you saw the ghost last night," he said, sitting down and shoving my cup out of his way.

"Lissa's a drama queen and a damned gossip," I replied. "I didn't see anything, I heard a noise. There was no ghost."

She stuck her tongue out at me, then said, "Someone's got to keep things from getting too serious around here."

"Like that's a problem. I've gotta run, I want to get down to the session a little early to introduce myself," I said. "Later, guys."

"Knock 'em dead, Em," Lissa called after me.

I waved and headed for the partitioned ballroom where I found Scott pacing once again at the back of the meeting space. He was so big and the space so small that he could have used a tug boat.

"Good, Chris found you?" he said. He was wearing a blue rosette that said "President." It might as well have been a target.

"Yep. No sign of Garrison?" I asked.

"Nope." Scott's pen was clicking away like mad. "He's always done this, decides that he's not bothered, or uninterested, or that this is all beneath him, or is off staring at dust motes or something. But you'd think this once, he'd cut it out."

I shrugged. "If he shows up, I'll hand it over to him."

Suddenly, a burden had tumbled off his back and the sun broke through the clouds. "Thanks, Em. I appreciate it. I'll get you a drink later."

"You can get me two drinks later; I was supposed to be taking it easy this weekend," I groused. "Half the reason I worked so hard to get off the board was to get out of getting up so early."

He smiled broadly, knowing that I was only kidding, and I remembered why we were friends. "Okay, two drinks. The good stuff. You're a peach."

I find it absurdly sweet when Scott calls me a peach, for some reason. Maybe it's the novelty of the name, which is so old-fashioned, maybe it's Scott himself, who really did work hard to make things come out right for everyone. Scott left to see if he could locate Garrison—again—and I introduced myself to the members of the session. Since I was just there to keep time and introduce folks, I didn't have to say anything particularly clever, which was good, because the session was on European tobacco pipe manufacturers. While, like every good archaeologist, I have a set of drill bits in my bag—to measure the diameter of the pipe stem bores to get an idea of the manufacturing date—any further expertise was limited to where to get started looking in the library. Maybe I'd pick up something edifying today.

After I checked in with the presenters and made sure they were all ready and accounted for, I explained to the audience that I'd be moderating instead of Dr. Garrison, who was presently unavailable, and got right down to the business of introducing the first thirty-minute paper.

Instead of sitting down in the front row, I hung out over by the side of the room, near the light switches, to keep that end of things running smoothly at least. Standing up kept me from falling asleep, and it gave me a good view of the audience as they settled in for the talks. A few latecomers straggled in, glancing nervously around to make sure they weren't disturbing anyone, but the last stayed by the door, holding it open to finish a whispered conversation with someone outside the room. I frowned, and was just about to sneak back and ask whomever it was to come in or go out, when the door quietly shut, and I realized I was glaring at Duncan Thayer. That jerked me out of the sleepiness that was stealing over me.

Unlike the others, he didn't seem to mind whether he was disrupting anyone, and he stepped into room, but stood to the side of the door, as if he wouldn't be staying long. He eventually glanced around, an old trick of his, to see who was here, and saw me staring at him. He gave me a casual nod of the head, a you-know-how-it-is-at-these-things gesture, and I raised an eyebrow, and pointedly returned my attention to the speaker, who was going on about the change in marks over time in a pipe factory in southwest England. Nothing drove Duncan crazier than the idea that someone could resist him.

The next two papers rounded out the first ninety minutes, and in the middle of the fourth, there was another, louder disturbance by the door. Again I could see that Duncan was involved, and now faces—including that of the speaker—were turning toward them and back to me. I rushed to the back of the room while the speaker continued hesitantly, not knowing whether he should stop.

"Could you please keep it down," I hissed. I looked from Duncan to the person he'd been speaking with and saw to my surprise that it was Scott, who looked pale as a sheet of paper and slick with sweat. "What's wrong?"

He took my arm and pulled me out of the room. Duncan followed.

"We found Garrison, Em." Scott swallowed a couple of times. "He's . . . he's dead."

"Oh, jeez," I said, shoulders slumping. "What was it, his heart or something?"

"They found him outside. They think it was exposure, but it might have been his head."

"What do you mean? Like a stroke?"

"I dunno, it could be." Scott looked off, then straight at me. "He was out on the pond behind the hotel. Out on the ice. There was a hell of a lot of blood. His head was split open."

Chapter 5

"THEY SAID IT LOOKED LIKE HE FELL ON THE ICE, and cracked his head open," Scott continued. He was shaking like a leaf, and it scared me to see him so. He exchanged a look with Duncan, and I found myself suppressing an urge to shoo Duncan away.

But of course he was looking at Duncan; they were at New Hampshire College at the same time. Under Garrison.

"Okay, do you want me to make an announcement?" I asked. "What are we supposed to do in this situation?"

"I don't know. What I want to do is wait until the authorities can make their way here and take care of the body. I don't want to make any formal announcements until we hear from them, and that's going to take a while because of the weather. I'm hoping it won't get around too much, but you know how gossip moves."

"Who found him anyway?" I said.

"One of the hotel people gave me the news. One of their people went to get a snowblower out of the utility shed down by the lake."

I looked at Scott closely; he was still sweating and his face was now gray. "Are you going to be okay?"

He shook his head. "Yeah, but I think I want to sit down for a bit."

"Let's go over there." I indicated a couch flanked by two end tables with ghastly, oversized silk floral arrangements badly in need of dusting. As I put my arm around his shoulders, I bumped into Duncan's hand. Although my first instinct was to pull away, I wasn't about to make a scene in front of Scott.

"It's okay," I said. "I've got it."

"No, that's all right, Emma," Duncan replied. "Why don't you go back to the session?"

"Why don't you go and—" I took a breath. "Scott was looking for me. I'm fine here."

"Actually I was looking for—" Scott began, then sat heavily onto the couch. "I was looking for Dunk. But I'm glad you're here too, Em. I'll need all the help I can get."

"Right, sure, anything," I said, nodding quickly. "Do you want some water?"

"That'd be great."

"I'll get it," Duncan said before I could answer.

I sat next to Scott, whose head was in his hands. I put my hand on his back, and waited for him.

"It's just so strange," he kept saying to the carpet. "The man was a force of nature. Not that he was Superman or anything, he was old, and was feeling his years. Healthwise, I mean. But his personality, for whatever faults you might have seen in him, was just huge."

I chose to take Scott's "you" as the general one, and not me personally. Duncan had returned with a glass of ice water from the coffee table.

"I just can't believe that he's . . . that he won't ever . . . ever again."

"It's the end of an era," Duncan said.

I wanted to tell him to shut up, and I almost did, but then I saw Scott nodding again. I bristled, thinking it wrong that Duncan should also have history with Scott, who was *my* friend; territoriality, especially under these circumstances, is not my best look.

"Yep. Now we need a plan. I want to wait until the business meeting tonight, to make a general announcement. That will give me a chance to talk to the board and to call his family; I think that would be best, even if the authorities contact them too. If we address it tonight, we can get that over with, maybe have a few speeches and a moment of silence, or something, and carry on with things tomorrow."

I opened my mouth to protest, we couldn't possibly carry on, and then realized that of course we could. We should. "Right."

"He always said that there was no excuse for not handing in work, and even a death certificate wouldn't be sufficient, as you should have anticipated it and planned your work accordingly," Duncan said.

Automatically I checked for whether he was being sincere, but I didn't see any of the telltale signs that would indicate otherwise. Scott cut me off in my thoughts.

"Yeah, you're right." Scott turned and smiled ruefully at Duncan, then gave himself a shake. "Right, thanks guys, I'm feeling better. Let's say if I need you to do anything, I'll leave a message in your rooms or on the message board. Okay?"

I nodded and glanced at my watch. "Sounds good. I've got to get back in there and finish up this session. With any luck, the paper hasn't ended early. As if that ever happens. I'm really sorry, Scott."

He nodded. "Me too. Figures it happens when I'm the one running the show. Old bastard."

But he said it fondly, not with any of the real ire that I'd always heard from Grandpa Oscar and sometimes used myself. Duncan nodded, of course, and said to Scott, "Walk and talk with me."

I got up and left abruptly, hearing him say "Good-bye, Emma," from behind me. I waved my hand without looking back.

As I suspected, I got back to my post just in time to give the "one minute, wrap it up" signal. To my relief, no one much noticed my hasty departure, and things seemed quite as usual. The reader obligingly finished, fairly smoothly, and I got up to announce my own student, Katie Bell, whose paper I was planning to see in any case.

Several things happened at once. As I announced Katie's name and her paper title, I heard a roar of laughter from the session right next door to us. That meant that they were running over, but it also meant that my little surprise for Carla had been discovered, just about on time. I also noticed that Katie kept looking around, disappointment evident on her features. As she fiddled with her scrunchie, which was too big for the ponytail it held, I realized that she hoped that Garrison would appear in time for her paper. I couldn't tell her that wasn't going to happen, but I did give an extra flourish to my introduction, which brought a smile to her long narrow face.

I don't know why I should have been nervous for Katie, except that she was young, just a senior, and this was her first paper. All on her own, she was showing enough nervous energy to power a small factory, but I had vetted her paper at her request, made some suggestions, and she swore that she'd practiced reading it out loud to her roommates. It was good experience, and I didn't think it would do her any harm, but she was high-strung as a new tightrope and as jittery as the first person to try it out. I guess I just felt for her.

She started off okay—she'd managed to clear her throat away from the mike and didn't go three octaves higher than her normal voice—and was actually doing well reading the paper, which was on the smoking pipes from the Fort Providence assemblages. I actually found myself leaning forward, eager to hear her next words about a site I'd researched and excavated myself, until she went disastrously off script.

She lost her place, which led to several seconds of stuttering. Then she took a deep breath and a drink of water, just like I'd told her to do if she got hung up somewhere. Then, for some reason, she started talking about the slide that was showing a preliminary overview of the site with the location of the units superimposed over it. She was starting to repeat what she'd already said at the beginning, and worse, seemed to be spiraling downward into needless detail. I sat on my hands and tried to find the right moment to correct her course, biting my lip in anxious sympathy.

"—and the crew used trowels—not the roundy, gardening kind, but flat mason's trowels—to dig. They followed the existing stratigraphy, the layers of soil that were deposited by wind, water, or human landscaping, until they hit the glacially deposited sand, which meant there would be no human artifacts below that, because there were no people around here before the glaciers. As far as we know."

Aw, hell, Katie, I thought, you don't need to go into this basic stuff, not with this crowd. Grandma doesn't like being taught how to suck eggs. I considered clearing my throat, trying to get her to go back to her discussion of the site and the goodies, but imagined it would throw her off balance even more, and then she'd be explaining about how the Europeans had actually started regularly visiting this side of the ocean in the fifteenth and sixteenth centuries, but that the Indians had been here a good long stretch before that.

Her extemporaneous ramblings seemed to peter out and she faltered, looking around the darkened room nervously. She caught my eye and I just about strained something, simultaneously trying to look reassuring, urge her on, and indicate that she should get back to the substance of her paper. She nodded, found her place, and began to read again, moving through the text smoothly, once in a while looking out to the audience, and pausing occasionally to point out something in one of her slides. She didn't go too fast, she read the paper as if she was familiar with its contents, and she remembered to breathe normally. I began to relax as she did, and found myself nodding as she hit the right beats about the pottery and the military artifacts. When she showed the slide of the tiny early pipe-bowl fragment, which was our present pride and joy, unearthed during the last field season, there was an appreciative murmur through the crowd that made her flush with pride.

At last she finished, just a minute ahead of schedule.

"Thanks, Katie, well done," I said.

Katie'd done a good job overall, but she again looked like a deer in the headlights. For an instant, I thought she was going to stay frozen up there as the polite clapping for her petered out; I moved to announce the final speaker, thinking I would have to nudge her back to her seat, when a louder ovation, more raucous than the rest of the audience, came from the back of the room. I peered through the lights and saw a cadre of graduate students, led by Meg Garrity, standing at the back, clapping and shouting for Katie. She flushed and smiled, collected up her paper and her water, and ducked her head, giving them an embarrassed little hand flick as she found her way back to her seat.

"Our last speaker, Michelle Lima, will be presenting her paper entitled 'English and Dutch Pipes in the Mid-Atlantic Colonies Before Seventeen Fifty.' Michelle?"

Michelle was right on cue, coming up the stairs as I was going down. I stopped to let her pass, and she leaned over to speak in my ear.

"You going to be at the Grope later, honeycakes?" she whispered.

"But of course, my darling Misha-lima. Wouldn't miss it for the world."

"And it wouldn't be a party without you." She got to the lectern and in a much different, fully professional voice, said, "Thank you, Emma," and began her paper.

After the questions at the end of the session, I found Katie out in the hallway, and congratulated her, moving her out of the crowd intent on finding their ways to the next papers. "That was great! And look, you were able to walk away! Very far from what you were predicting back on campus."

She twisted her presentation pages into a tube. "I got nervous. Could you tell? I just lost my place for a minute, and then I started thinking about who was out there, listening to me, and I just started babbling. I looked like an idiot."

"Naw. I think people knew that you were a little nervous, but that's okay, and you recovered really well, and that's the name of the game, right? And then you finished up like a pro, so that was more than ninety percent that went smoother than silk."

"Yeah, I guess so." She stuck the tube between her knees, trying to recapture the escaping scrunchie. "I was kinda disappointed that Professor Garrison didn't show up. I really wanted to meet him, today. I mean, especially since I got into his session rather than the general one on pipe studies."

I thought, please don't ask me to introduce you later, please don't ask me to introduce you later, please don't ask me—

Katie hesitated, then looked up. "If we see him later, would you introduce me to him? I'd really like that, because I wanted to ask him about some of the stuff in his book on West Devon factories."

I really wanted to tell her, but I also wanted to respect Scott's wishes about how he announced the news of Garrison's death. "Look, he's kind of hard to pin down sometimes. We'll see what we can do, okay?"

When I saw the eager look on her face, I couldn't resist adding, "I wouldn't get your hopes up, is all."

She nodded. "That's okay, that's fine. I gotta go, I wanted to catch another paper at twelve and I don't want to be late."

"Okay, see you later, Katie."

She practically sprang away and loped off to her next session, her slide carousel left forgotten by the projector. I went to retrieve it, and found Meg waiting for me outside after.

"Nice of you guys to come by to support Katie," I said. "I think she really appreciated it."

"Yeah, well, she's not a bad kid," Meg replied. "And we all knew that she was wicked nervous. She kept going on and on about it, so Neal and I figured we'd let her get it out of her system and then get her good and drunk tonight."

Wicked? I thought. More of Neal's New England speech patterns must be rubbing off on our transplanted Ms. Garrity than I imagined; although Meg had traveled all over as part of a military family, most of her accent seemed to have been developed in the western United States. "Of course, you've all taken into consideration that she is actually of legal drinking age? That she in fact imbibes?"

"Katie? Oh God, yes. Why do you think the other undergrads call her 'Sandbag'? Because the morning after a party is the one time that she isn't rocketing around like a spaz." She looked at me, conceding the point. "And she turned twenty-one over the Thanksgiving break."

Was spaz back into the common parlance? It never took more than a few moments with any of my students to plumb the exact depths of the generation gap that separated us.

"She's eager," I said. "I'm sure you were exactly the same way, when you were younger."

Meg gave me a cool and long-practiced glance.

I shrugged. "Okay, maybe you weren't."

"Were you?"

"I don't know that I was as hyper as Katie, but I had a lot of practice in how to behave at conferences. Not everyone grows up with this coming to them like second nature, right?

But the thing is I remember how Katie feels. Perhaps you can recall some similar—though not, of course, identically expressed—feeling?"

Meg rolled her eyes. "Maybe."

I wasn't letting her off the hook that easy. "And the great thing about being young and immature is that you eventually outgrow it, right?" I insisted.

Meg snorted; apparently Katie was beyond hope of salvation. "If you're lucky. Where are you off to now?"

"Artifact Comparison Roundtable."

"Ah, well, maybe you'll let me go next year? With the stuff from the second season at the Chandler house? Once we get it cleaned up."

"Sure, if you want to. I didn't know you were so inclined."

"Can't hurt."

Her career, she meant. "Okay, well just list anything we come across that is particularly nice or unidentifiable, and we'll pull it for you next year."

"Good enough. See you later?"

"Absolutely."

And my second student flew off. I found my way up to the room reserved for those of us who made it a point of getting together every year to show off our best stuff and try to identify the things that were seemingly unidentifiable. It eventually was formalized into the roundtable, limited to a dozen people or so, but we just always called it the Goody Grope. It was porn for archaeologists, a chance to touch the stuff, grok it in fullness, and maybe learn a little something new. The great thing was that, no matter what period you were interested in and no matter what artifacts were actually present, you ended up building up a pretty good awareness of who had what, and from what site.

I glanced in the room before I got in there, and the good news was that for once, it was a good-sized space. I mean, you can sit there in the lobby or the bar and look at artifacts, but what you really want is a nice big table, plenty of chairs, light, and a bit of elbow room to pass the stuff around. The bad news was that Noreen McAllister was first in there, and she'd already seen me. Crapshitpoop.

I raised a hand, not quite a wave, and walked in, grabbing the chair that was nearest the door and farthest from Noreen, who immediately pulled out a notebook and became engrossed in it. My watch told me that I was just a few minutes early, but other folks should have been here by now, shouldn't they?

"Pretty good papers so far," I hazarded.

"I thought they were better in Chicago," she said, not looking up; her dark hair made a curtain between her face and sight of me.

"Oh." I pulled up my briefcase and rummaged around inside until I found the small box of goodies that I'd brought. "How was your summer?"

"Rotten. Never made near the numbers for our field school, so we had to cancel it. Didn't get a tenth of the work done I wanted to."

Little Miss Mary Sunshine. "Bad luck."

She grunted, and flipped a page of her notebook.

I heard a rustling in the hall and looked up just in time to see Lissa look in and see that it was just the two of us. A look of horror crossed her face, and despite my pleading glance, she scurried right past the door and down the hallway. Thanks a lot, Lissa; see if I ever talk to you again, you wretch.

Carla came in right after, and she was followed by Chris.

"Hey, Carla, Chris," I said, not about to let them get away. Carla hesitated by the door, but, God bless her, came through and sat down next to me. Chris, oblivious to it all, came in, said hi to me, and sat down heavily at the middle of the table.

"How you doing, Noreen?" he said.

"Hi, Chris!" She gave him the first smile I'd seen out of

her, and she called him over to her end of the table. "I got something you might be interested in."

Fat chance, I thought. Slut.

"Glad I got here when I did," Carla whispered while she settled in. "I can call the trauma team ahead of time so that they can come in and clean up the gore before it hardens and sticks to the walls."

Carla rummaged through her bag and pulled out a couple of small, brown, acid-free boxes. "That's disgusting," I whispered back. "It's not that bad."

"What channel are you watching? I'm just glad Chris was here to throw himself on the grenade."

"Chris is too nice a guy to realize he's a diversion."

By this point, several others had come in, including Lissa, who strode in and took a neutral seat, smirking, her eyes bright with concealed merriment. I mouthed the word "bitch" to her, and she put her hand up to her throat in feigned surprise. She could barely conceal her giggling.

"What's wrong with you?" Carla demanded. "You choking on something?"

Lissa tried without much luck to compose herself. "Me? No."

"Then why is your face all screwed up like that?"

"Excuse me," Lissa said, and bolted from the room. I heard the ladies room door open, and gales of laughter gradually suffocating as it closed.

"Well, she can talk and run, so she's not going to choke to death," Carla said. "Sometimes I think Lissa's crazier than a shithouse rat."

I introduced myself to the only person who was new to me, a middle-aged guy who looked like the caricature of an accountant—receding hairline, on the tall, slightish side, bad suit. The very picture of a pensive, butt-puckered corporate bean-counter.

"William S. Widmark," he said, shaking my hand. "I'm

not here because I've got something, but because my engineering company has just acquired Northeastern Consulting and my colleague is presenting a paper right now. Dr. DuBois was kind enough to let me sit in."

"You'll find it's a lot of fun, very informative," I said, trying to think of what I could say that would give him a good impression of archaeologists and what we do. You never could tell what was going to happen to the archaeologists when a bigger company swallowed up theirs. The seats were filling up, so I returned to my chair.

Michelle came in and slid into the seat next to me. "You're saving this for me, aren't you, love?"

"And no one else," I replied.

Brad walked in and overheard us, and gave a startled double take. "You got something you want to tell me, Em? Michelle?"

"No, Brad," Michelle replied. "You got something you want to tell me?"

He shook his head, took his place, and looked around the table, counting to himself. Brad was the de facto moderator because he'd assumed the role the first time, six years ago, and we needed one. He was good enough at it, but certainly did make a big deal out of a small occasion. I had to admit, though, it helped to have someone do the dirty work of keeping us all in order.

"I think we're short two," he said. "I'm expecting Jay Whitaker. And Bea Carter responded to my email and said she was going to join us." He shrugged, and we all exchanged glances; Bea was perennially late and notorious for being a flake of galactic proportions. "Well, we'll get started and they can jump in when they get here. As usual, we will start to my left and go clockwise. Chris, what have you got for us?"

Chris brought out a piece of pottery.

"Looks like redware, Chris," Michelle said. "Local? New England?"

"Yeah, it is, but have a look at the inclusions." He pointed to the tiny bits of pebble and shell that were incorporated into the paste of the fragment. "My idea is that the inclusions are a little different from the other stuff we've found locally, and since I think we might actually have some Native people working in the neighborhood we're exploring now, I was wondering whether they might be using some Indian techniques and applying them in making the Anglo-American forms that their neighbors would have been used to."

"Umm, sounds a little dicey," Brad said skeptically, "unless you've got hard proof they were actually Indians. I mean, you get all kinds of variation of temper and inclusions, depending where you are—"

"See what they're doing?" I whispered to Widmark. "They start off with what they know, and try to expand from there, based on other evidence. It's kind of like how detectives work."

He shot me a startled, puzzled look. "Oh. Okay."

I turned back to the discussion; if he wasn't interested, he shouldn't have bothered coming.

Then Kelly Booker brought out a small lump of metal; it seemed to be brass to judge from the corrosion: there were still traces of greenish corrosion, though she'd cleaned it up nicely enough. After a moment, it was obvious that it was a button and that there was lettering and a date on it, some of which read: "638" and then "ourable Art."

"If we could see it better, it would say sixteen thirty-eight, and 'Ancient and Honourable Artillery,' " Lissa said promptly.

"But it's from a farm that dates to the middle part of the eighteen hundreds," Kelly said doubtfully. "The context is probably eighteen sixty, but I suppose it could have been an heirloom someone lost."

"It was, but it's a nineteenth-century button," Lissa explained. "The U.S. Army issued them right at the beginning of the nineteenth century, to commemorate their roots in the seventeenth century."

"You could try looking it up in a text, Kelly. Any text," Noreen said. She was looking out the window. "You would have seen it's not four hundred years old."

Kelly nodded. "Well, yeah, I didn't think it looked that early—the shape is all wrong—but I was cleaning the bag with this in it right as I was leaving, and it was so cool, I figured I'd bring it with the other stuff Dr. Marlatt sent with me."

Noreen pursed her lips, irritated to be troubled with so obvious a problem.

I couldn't resist poking at her a little. "The great thing about the roundtable is that it is easy for someone else to identify what you've got right away, and then the problem is solved."

"Moving on," Brad said hastily. "Michelle, what have you got for us?"

Jay came in then, flushed, and apologetic. He grabbed a seat and tried to make himself as unobtrusive as possible, but that just made things worse, and he took a while to catch his breath. Still, it was good seeing him try to make an effort with the professional aspects of the conference, rather than chasing parties the whole weekend.

Michelle had a textile fragment from a National Park Service site; none of us could identify it, but a couple of people suggested contacts. I had some pottery from Fort Providence that Brad confirmed was French; Carla suggested a book that had illustrations of the forms. And so it went, until everyone had had a turn, everyone a little better informed, a little more enlightened.

As we packed up, Noreen approached me. "Hell, Emma, why do you have to encourage them with that small stuff? We're here to get some serious work done."

"Kelly seemed pretty serious to me," I said, my hackles rising. "And it solved her problem, made her happy, and didn't cost anyone anything. Except maybe a little patience."

Noreen remained unconvinced. "Speaking of which, I'm starting to lose mine with that other little *noodge* of yours. She keeps trying to get me to talk about a project that was over years ago. I keep trying to tell her it's not something I can remember offhand, but she won't stop pestering me. And I'm not the only one—Duncan Thayer actually lost his temper with her. Would you speak to her?"

"Which little *noodge* are you talking about?" I asked, but I suspected I knew. And I really would kill Duncan if he'd been mean to Katie.

"Katie something. I just keep thinking of her as Katie Car Alarm, the way she keeps harping and harping on the Pelletier site. Do me a favor, do us all a favor. Tell her to calm down."

"Katie Bell. I'll have a word with her. Don't worry, I've got a copy of the Pelletier report. I'll lend her my copy, so she won't bother you anymore."

"Good." She brushed past me, and I had just enough self-restraint left to wait until she was out of the room before I stuck out my tongue.

"She gives us Canucks a bad name," Carla muttered. "What's the hair across her ass?"

"She and I just hate each other," I said. "Always have."

"Why is that?"

I thought about it for a minute. "You know, I can't even remember. But I suspect her warm and obliging personality has something to do with it." I turned to Lissa, who'd just finished with packing up a piece of creamware with a spectacularly ugly overglaze painted pattern. "And you, thanks a lot for leaving me to the wolves."

"There was just one wolf. Is it better to have two of us miserable, instead of one?"

"I could have used a little cover there."

"Hey, it's women and children first, as far as I'm concerned. You see those giant front teeth of hers? They're used to shear the heads off her peons. I'm not getting anywhere within striking range. You guys want to get a drink?"

I checked my watch; it was barely one, but what with conference time—brought on by being closed off from the rest of the world, with no natural light and irregular sleeping and eating—it felt much later. "Little early for me. What about some lunch?"

"We signed up for the boxed lunches. Oh, lord, there's Bea. And would you look at what she's wearing? Bless her heart."

"Oh, there you all are!"

Bea Carter was striding toward us, as if she'd finally caught us doing something illicit. Lissa was right; Bea was clad in complicated swaths of blue and green, over billowing trousers of the same material. Imagine a teal and turquoise tornado with red shoes. A walking hangover.

She stopped in front of us, panting. "I suppose everything is done, is it?"

"Well, yeah, Bea. The Grope is from twelve to one," Carla said.

"I would have been here on time, except that someone stole my artifacts!"

She said this with such satisfaction, as if convinced of something she'd been claiming all along, that I did a double take.

"Someone stole your artifacts?" I said. "How could that have happened?"

"It could have been anyone in the hotel. It could have been any of . . . us."

"Heck, Bea, who'd want *your* artifacts?" Lissa said. "Who cares about some early twentieth-century kiln furniture anyway?"

Carla and I scowled at her, but she didn't back down. "Well? I'm serious. Who'd want broken bits of pottery?"

"You mean besides archaeologists?" Carla said.

"You know what I mean," Lissa retorted.

"Was anything else stolen?" I asked Bea.

"What do you mean?" She'd danced around to the side, as if my question was an attack.

"I mean, was your room broken into? Or was your luggage ripped off at the airport?"

"No, I mean, not any more than the usual rifling they give your stuff these days. I had them here, with me. I was showing them around last night, Wednesday, after I got in, to other people working on pottery manufactories." She glared at Lissa. "It was shortly after that."

"And your room, nothing else was touched," I said.

"No, Emma, nothing else was touched. In my room, that is. I guess you all haven't heard about the book room."

"What about the book room?" Lissa demanded.

"One of the poster exhibits was broken into. A bunch of the stuff was taken, some of it was broken." She gave me a significant look. "Also last night."

"Which one was it? Was it only one?"

Again, Bea took the defensive with me. "It was the one on the Florida underwater project."

"That doesn't make any sense," I said, and Lissa nodded. "Why would anyone mess with that? Wasn't it mostly reproductions? All the stuff that was taken was fake; the only real things—the broken fragments—were left behind."

"What do you call the reproductions?" Bea asked. "Everything made by humans is—"

"I know, everything manufactured or altered is an artifact," I said, barely able to suppress my annoyance—she had no capacity for sticking to the important points. "I mean old artifacts, things that were made a long time ago, archaeologically recovered."

"Well, there was nothing else taken or bothered. Except for my stuff. I'm trying to find Brad to let him know what's going on."

"What's he going to do about it?" Lissa said.

"He's got to help me find them. It's his fault; I wouldn't have brought them if he hadn't organized the roundtable again. Now, if you'll excuse me." She bustled off, and Carla and I exchanged glances.

Lissa made a face. "Ooh, Brad! The great-big-pieces-of-crap thief found me! Oooh!"

"We seem to be suffering a logic shortage around here," I agreed.

"Oh, don't worry about her. Her rubbish will show up, it always does. She'd lose her head if it wasn't stitched on by some well-meaning but ill-inspired medical student."

"You think so?" I said.

Lissa shrugged. "She's got the brains of refrigerator mold and she's always blaming it on someone else. Her brain only serves to keep her soft little skull from collapsing altogether. Don't worry about her. She just drives me crazy, latching on to me all the time. I'm too polite to blow her off."

"Ha!" Carla said.

"What about the underwater exhibit?" I asked. "Who'd mess with that?"

"I saw that exhibit yesterday." She shook her head and her hair fell back perfectly into place. "Emma, chill out: it's *Bea*. There were fragments in there already, so I doubt anything was really broken, or taken, even. Probably they were pulling it to show someone, or something. Maybe it was a practical joke, who knows?"

I shot her a warning look, but Carla didn't respond to Lissa's pointed remark. Worse than that, she had made no mention of the surprise I'd left for her this morning. Worrying.

"We'll catch up at the business meeting tonight?" Carla said.

"Sure," I said, thinking about the announcement that was going to floor everyone. "What are you going to see before then?"

"I've got to read over my paper. I might stop in to hear the feminist theory papers, if I have time. How about you?"

"There's a megasession on battlefield archaeology that I'm catching. And yours of course."

"Carla? You're coming to mine?" I wanted to see whether she thought she could nail me with her practical joke then.

"Nope, it conflicts with the one I really want to see. On human remains."

I nodded. "But if you're that interested, I'll send you a copy, but don't worry about just being polite."

"That's one thing she's never been worried about," Lissa announced. "Come on, Carla. Let's go get our dried-out tuna sandwiches, bruised apples, and warm sodas."

I stopped by the message board on my way to lunch and saw there was the usual array of invitations to meet for job interviews at contract companies, the reminders about the various specialty group meetings and cocktail parties, and, now that we were into the first official day of papers, the first crop of notes for my colleagues were thumbtacked to the too-small bulletin board. Pieces of hotel stationery, small pieces of wire-bound notebook paper, their torn edges lacy, and even a few cocktail napkins, their pen marks bleeding through, fluttered festively as I approached. I checked for notes for me—funny how it always made me feel so particularly wanted to see one of these unofficial missives waiting for me—and found two, neither of which were from Scott. One was the one I was expecting, reminding me that I'd promised to meet with a colleague from Rhode Island to talk about doing a guest lecture for his class on colonial artifacts. The other was in an unfamiliar hand—not that that was anything unusual—and I flipped it up to read what it was about. It was from a potential student wanting the chance to talk with me about coming to Caldwell to join my program. But it was the note that was next to mine that really caught my attention. When I pocketed my notes—I was by now immune to the temptation to leave them on the board, to show how very in demand I was—another fell down, having been supported only by virtue of having been wedged behind mine. I couldn't help reading it as I picked it up: "I'll see you tonight, after the reception and business meeting. Don't make me come looking for you again."

Wow—strong words. It was unsigned and it was addressed to Dr. Garrison.

As I replaced it, I noticed that it had been pierced through three times. I did a little analysis of the arrangement of the notes: Okay, say it was posted before mine—that was one. Someone came along and used its tack to hold both mine and his up—or had Garrison read it and replaced it for some reason? That would be two. I had no idea why it should be pierced a third time, and tiredly realized that I needed to stop doing taphonomic studies of the bulletin board. When you start attempting to identify just how and in what order the notes were placed on the board, it's more than time to take a break.

Just about the moment that I put the note back, a flood of people exited the rooms where the one o'clock sessions were held, all of them heading toward the restaurants and the boxed-lunch concession. Just a few steps ahead of them, I hurried toward the coffee shop, and with a bit of luck that had nothing to do with the affection that Eleni had developed for me at breakfast time, got the last deuce in the corner, an ideal spot for people-watching while still keeping my own back covered. Although I was actually getting to eat earlier than I usually would, I was ravenous and already exhausted. Again, the conference effect came into play, and I was convinced that the low pressure from the storm presumably still raging outside wasn't doing anything to help it. I ordered a cheeseburger and a chocolate shake, watching

Eleni's enormous sigh of despair as she observed the line, full of impatient, hungry academics forming outside the coffee shop.

Noreen was at the head of the line, and I kept my head down, hoping she wouldn't ask to share my table. Not that I was expecting a conciliatory overture, but I sure as hell wasn't going to invite her. If she wanted the seat, she could do the asking.

But the gods of restaurant seating smiled on me for once, and a stool at the counter was freed up almost as soon as she started into the coffee shop. I could have sworn that a look of relief crossed her face as she seized it, probably mirroring my own.

Eleni scuffed over with my shake. "You mind sharing the table with another customer? You don't have to, but . . ."

"I don't mind," I said, happy to repay the restaurant gods for not being visited by Noreen.

The new guy from the artifact roundtable came over. "Thanks for sharing."

"No problem . . ." I searched my memory for his name—we'd just been introduced at the Grope and I still had to resort to his name tag; he was that forgettable. "Mr. Widmark. No one will ever get to eat, otherwise."

He sat down. "Call me Will." Any hopes I had of having a quiet lunch were dashed. Widmark was a talker. Worse than that, it seemed as though he had brushed his teeth with crushed garlic and week-old sushi that morning, because he had the worst breath of anyone I'd met in a long time. That was the most outstanding thing about him. He was built like a pregnant lollipop stick, brown hair badly cut, brown eyes, completely unremarkable features, and nondescript plastic-framed glasses.

"I'm pretty new to these things. Seems pretty ordinary, though," he said. He suddenly straightened his spine, seeming to grow in height, as he craned to get a look at someone.

He didn't appear to recognize whomever it was, however, as he relaxed into his chair with a slump.

"I suppose. I get the impression that archaeology conferences are a little low-tech, compared to some." I tried to ease myself back in my chair as surreptitiously as I could to escape the range of his bottom-of-the-komodo-dragon's-cage breath. "You know, other professions."

"Oh?" he said sharply.

"Well, like high-tech, or bio-chem," I said. "The ones my husband goes to are a lot flashier than these—more celebrity speakers, more giveaways, more high-tech presentations."

For some reason, Widmark seemed to relax a little. "Yeah, I suppose now that you mention it, the engineering events I've been to were a little more . . . uh . . ."

"Upscale?"

He nodded as he flipped through the menu. Again, he bobbed up, looked around, then settled back down. "Thanks for not making me say it. As I mentioned before, we've just acquired a small contract archaeology company, Northeastern Consulting. I've always been fascinated by archaeology, so I volunteered to get the lay of the land."

"Oh." Seemed a little strange to me; why would they send one of the bigwigs over if they were going to acquire someone who'd be coming to these anyway? Who knew, with business, these days.

"So, I take it this isn't your first conference?" He put his menu down.

I laughed. "I started coming to these when I was fifteen. That's about twenty years worth of them now."

"Well, I guess I just got lucky."

"Excuse me?"

"I've been trying to get familiar with some of the bigger names around here, and it sounds like you'd be the person to tell me whether I'm on the right track."

I chewed on my straw, trying not to get drawn into this.

"Uh, well, I guess it depends on what you're trying to figure out. If there's a specialty, for example, like a certain kind of artifact or a time period, you're going to find that they're different folks you need to talk to."

"What about a geographical area? We're going to be expanding in the Midwest, Michigan to Minnesota, down to Iowa and Missouri. Who'd be good to meet who knows those areas?"

"Oh, well, you're actually better off going to one of the central-area meetings then. Right up your geographical alley. They're scheduled in three months—"

"Oh, we'll get some people there, of course, it's just that I'll be away and I wanted to try and make the most of the opportunity here. Anyway, I also heard that Duncan Thayer would be a good person to talk to. Is he here?"

I knew it was coming, but just the sound of his name made me go stiff as a plank. "Yes, he's here. You can't miss him, big guy, used to have lots of red hair, getting a little thick around the middle, I guess. Still, some people age better than others—"

"Right. Recently he's worked on the New Hampshire-Vermont border, is that right? And New York State, before that?"

"I guess. You'd have to ask him. He's giving a paper this afternoon, but I don't know what on."

"Okay, I'll check it out. Is there anyone else who specializes in that geographical area, particularly with artifact expertise? As I understand it, we're going to need a lab supervisor, and I guess it wouldn't be a bad idea to see if there's anyone in the area who's looking."

"Trust me, all you have to do is put up a notice and they'll come flocking to you." What was with this guy, that he had nothing better to do but come out to a conference and blunder around like this? Oh God, a hobby for his financially comfortable middle age, I realized. The archaeology section would be his pet, heaven help them all. "And besides, if you're acquiring—was it Northeastern Consulting you said? I'm not familiar with them."

"Oh, it's a very small operation in Vermont—I think there were only ever three permanent hires and they relied heavily on seasonal recruiting. Lots of department-of-public-works work. Do you know Jake Sherman?"

I shook my head, wishing there hadn't been so much of the name to exhale. Mr. Widmark needed to discover Listerine and possibly the name of a good dentist. I was surprised that his own eyes weren't watering.

"Well, no matter, we're going to be expanding considerably anyway. And you'll hear all about us then. We've got a lot of very big—"

Fortunately, Eleni came rushing over with my cheeseburger, interrupting Widmark and his paean to his very big plans. She dumped it on the table so hard that it nearly slid off the plate into my lap, and dashed off before I could even ask for any water. I retrieved a couple of stray French fries and pushed the burger back onto the plate. Widmark handed me the catsup before I could ask for it.

"Thanks. I hope you don't mind if I start."

"Please, go ahead."

I started eating as fast as I could. It wasn't that he was a bad guy, it was that every time he breathed, you could see the veneer on the table begin to peel up.

Eleni ran over and took his order for an omelet; I took the opportunity to ask for a cup of coffee. It was going to be a long afternoon, and I wanted to stay on top of things. Eleni grunted and ran off, and I figured I had about a fifty-fifty chance that she'd heard me.

"So who else should I talk to?"

I gave him a few more names, then suggested he go to the receptions and university parties, which would be held throughout the weekend.

He nodded. "Okay, I'll do that. So are you going to Dr. Thayer's paper today?"

"Um, probably not. I've got one of my own to present, and I think there's a conflict." I didn't tell him that I thought the conflict was one that had more to with my never wanting to see Duncan again unless it was to see him one last time, as he slid into quicksand with his anvil collection.

"What time is your paper? Maybe I'll stop by and see that."

Man, this guy was like dog poop on a boot tread. "It's at two-thirty. In fact, I should be off to look over my notes as soon as I can get my coffee and ask for the check."

Eleni appeared at that moment like a sour genie and deposited Widmark's eggs and my coffee. I asked for my bill, and she took it out of a fan of at least fifteen of them and slapped it down on the table, scuffling off before I could even say thanks. The thing was that the coffee was great, again. It didn't make sense. I'd read *Like Water for Chocolate,* I knew what could happen if you cooked with the wrong attitude. I'd seen Eleni make the coffee herself, and if temperament was any indication, the coffee should have tasted like lighter fluid, or at least no better than fast-food coffee. This was almost as good as at home.

And that's why I stuck around a little longer than I meant to. I did want to go over my notes, but I sure didn't need an hour. I just wanted to get away from the table and his breath before I pointed out that "Bonito Breath" was not a term of endearment. At least the meal was helping damp down the reek from across the table, and Widmark was well-behaved enough to chew with his mouth closed, which counted for big points with me. It was while I was engrossed with the coffee that I noticed something about Widmark that took me aback. While he was eating, he was listening to the conversations around him. Not that anyone was trying to keep their voices down—with the lunch rush in the coffee shop, you now had to shout if you wanted to be heard at all—but it was just strange that he should be so engrossed, intent even. I watched him from behind my cup, and saw that his face changed slightly, not enough to do anything but make me curious. Before he'd seemed amiable, if a bit overfriendly and underprepared, but now there was a sharpness that hadn't been present before.

As I signed my name and room number to the bill, I heard what he was listening to. It was a couple of guys going on and on with the venerable debate over whether archaeologists had rights over the general public when it came to the use of sites for research and recreation. How to reconcile tourism, diving, and the protection of underwater sites, which often had the potential of great preservation of fragile materials. Does the recovery of a site and its information take precedence over the income states could get from tourism, that sort of thing.

It was so interesting watching him eat so absently and listen so avidly that when he suddenly looked up at me, he caught me staring.

"Sorry, I'm being awfully rude, I know," he said before I could fashion an excuse for my own bad manners. "It's just . . . well, it's rather embarrassing. I'm getting close to taking an early retirement, and I'm indulging in another one of my hobbies a little early."

"Oh?" I hate the word hobby, as well as the word hubby; they sound like the fat, silly cousins of the things they represent.

"Everyone always says that you should pay attention to how people talk, if you want to write good dialogue, so I'm making the most of my time here. Lots of different kinds of people."

"You've been writing something? A book?"

"Yes. You know, I think an archaeologist would make a wonderful character for a book. You, for example, with your experiences and everything, why you'd be perfect—"

And now I was going to be perfectly sick. The guy was hitting on me, and it was only lunchtime. He didn't even have the decency to be drunk or wait until I was, which was the way one could either proceed or reject the offer and everyone could get out of it without losing face. Widmark really didn't know anything at all about conferences.

"—and so I've been really paying attention to people, and I think it's working out. It's just a little difficult, because it looks strange, when I record it on paper. It doesn't look correct, if you know what I mean."

Then he noticed that I'd finished my coffee and had left the signed check sticking out of the folder, so Eleni could come and collect it. "Oh, rats, you shouldn't have to pay for your lunch, not when you've been good enough to share your table and answer all my questions, and everything! I was going to get it."

I scratched my chin with my left hand, trying to show off my wedding band and engagement ring, just to get the point across. "Thanks anyway. Please don't worry about it. I've just got to get going."

"Well, maybe you'll let me buy you a drink tonight, at the reception before the business meeting. Please, it's not like it's coming out of my wallet, and the guys at home will think I haven't been working if I don't spend some entertainment money."

I switched to rubbing my eyebrow, wiggling my rings just a little bit. I just wanted the guy to get the idea. "Hey, like I said, it was no problem, I'm happy to help."

And when I saw he was about to protest again, I said hurriedly, "But if we run into each other tonight, you can buy me a beer. That's the common currency among archaeologists."

"Great, talk to you later!" he said brightly. This time it was garlic and onions, but that was far better than aging bait fish. I was glad to have made him happy, but jeez, the guy was like a leech, and I was eager to get away.

I brushed past the line of hungry, cranky conferees and all but ran for the elevators. Although I had plenty of time, something in me just wanted to be away from the throng for a moment. I checked the messages on my room's phone and was disappointed not to have one from Scott. The rest were confirmations of dinner arrangements, and one that seemed like a wrong number, asking whether I was "up for a little crawling tonight?" Graduate students crawling the halls, looking for important parties to crash, no doubt.

I deleted the messages and went through my slides. Good: they were still in the order I'd left them last night. You never could be sure that they mightn't have gotten rearranged at some point. I read through the paper again, only halfheartedly, more eager for it to be done with and get the fresh rush from questions rather than getting off on hearing my own voice or reading my own conclusions on the excavation of Fort Providence so far. When I'd first started reading papers, long, long ago, I lived in fear that anyone would have anything to say about my work. Now, good commentary was the best part of any session.

I called Scott's room and left him a message, telling him where I'd be for the next couple of hours, and that he could also leave a message on my cell phone, although it would be turned off. Then I found the room for the session on first-period sites and took a seat in the front row. The volunteer who was handling the slides came in to set up, and I left my carousel with him, letting him know I would be the last speaker and giving him a few other instructions.

The room filled up quickly, and we got underway. We were almost through with the presentation before mine when a young woman came up to me and introduced herself in a whisper. "I just wanted to get the chance to say hello. I'd like to talk to you about some of the—"

"Look, I don't want to be rude, but this isn't the best

time," I said. "I'm about three seconds from having to go up there and give my paper. Do you have a card?"

She nodded; it was already in her hands.

"Write what you want to discuss on the back of your card. If I get a chance to see you later, great, otherwise I'll email you when I get back to campus, okay? And here's one of my cards; if I don't get back to you in two weeks, drop me a line."

She nodded, scribbling on the back of the card. She handed it to me, apologized profusely in a hushed tone, and scuttled away.

I collected myself, got my game face on, and prepared to wrap up the session with my paper. Things were going smoothly, and I was about twenty minutes into my paper, when the audience broke out in a gale of laughter. I looked up, startled, and reread my last sentence, convinced that I'd inadvertently written something rude, an accidental double entendre, but the sentence was fine. I was about to resume, still puzzled, when I realized what had happened and looked at the slide screen next to me.

There, instead of the last slide I was showing, and much, much larger than life, was Kermit the Frog. Someone had taken a puppet, dressed it in a smoking jacket and fez, given him a scaled-down martini glass and what looked like a hand-rolled cigarette, and set him next to a balk from a site that had nothing to do with the barrack building of Fort Providence I was discussing. Carla had struck back in retaliation for my switching her slide of French pottery for a movie still of a Tarzan knockoff, with an extremely buff young man in a very small loincloth. That had been the cause of the uproar from her paper this morning.

Although Carla had said she'd be elsewhere, I saw her at the back of the room and waved, acknowledging that she'd got me in spite of my instructions to the slide wrangler. I finished up my talk without the last slide, which was more of scenery rather than information, and suggested that if certain other people put down their drinks long enough, they might also come to the same conclusions.

A few questions followed, and as I answered, I noted a couple of points to clear up in my paper, if I reused any of it in a report. I looked up, and the last person with a hand up was in the back, obscured by the lights in my eyes. I pointed. "Right, in the back."

"I'm wondering about your use of polychrome tin-glazed earthenware to date that particular feature." It took only three syllables before I recognized it was Duncan asking the question. "If the only other artifacts you've got in the unit can only be dated to within twenty years or so, what makes you think that something that ubiquitous can support your assertions? I'm not trying to be picky, but it's the lynchpin of your entire argument and it seems somewhat tenuous to me."

Duncan, how freaking obvious of you. But it was trying to sound reasonable that gives you away; you still try to cover up an attempt to nail someone with politeness and it still doesn't fool me, though you've gotten better at it. "I guess I should have emphasized this more strongly in the paper, considering how exciting this information really is. I'm looking at the color of the glazes. I got the data from a European source, as yet unpublished, but it's coming from a good, sealed context, backed up with a recently discovered set of factory documents—"

"And this European publication?" He sounded doubtful.

"Right, Compton and Ashford, *Proceedings of the Marchester Archaeological Society*. The title is . . ." I spoke slowly, as if I was concerned that he might not be able to copy it down accurately otherwise. Duncan only nodded. "And it should be out next year."

The moderator stood up, directed the last few questions to the appropriate presenters, and then thanked everyone for coming. As I collected cards from people who wanted copies of the paper, I saw Duncan watching me. He leaned over still looking at me, and whispered something into Noreen McAllister's ear. She threw her head back and laughed.

I was hoping to collect my carousel and leave before they could catch me, but Duncan made a point of loudly congratulating me on my paper. Shit-heel.

"You know I have to bust your chops," he said in a lower voice, like we were both in on the joke, but still loud enough for anyone to hear. "You know, now that you've got tenure, someone's got to keep an eye on you."

"And you think you're the one to do it?" I couldn't stand the way I sounded, the way I wanted to react. The greedy look on Noreen's face was the icing on the cake, and I all but ran out of there.

I noticed a few startled faces—usually hanging around to chat afterward was the best part—and I knew I'd have to do some explaining later on. I didn't care.

I stopped by the desk, checked for messages, then looked over the bulletin board. Nothing. I went up to my room, called Scott's number and got nothing. There were no new messages for me there or on my cell phone either. I wasn't about to go back downstairs, but I sure as hell wasn't going to hide out in my room.

The red light bubble on the phone got me thinking, and I called down to the desk, identifying myself. "I'm trying to find Dr. Scott Tomberg," I said. "He's been sorting out the issues with the, uh, with Dr. Garrison's decease."

"Just a moment."

I heard Muzak—apparently one of the things that was updated at the General Bartlett Hotel was the phone system—until another voice, this one male and even more businesslike, picked up the line.

"I'm the day manager. I don't know where Dr. Tomberg is, but if you'd care to leave him a message?"

"No thanks, I've done that," I said.

"It's possible he's been speaking with the police. They arrived here about an hour ago, along with the ambulance. There's been a lot of delays with the storm."

"I see. Thanks for your help." I didn't wait for his response, and all but slammed down the phone. I grabbed my coat, gloves, and hat, pulled on my boots, and shot out of the room. I didn't wait for the elevator, but ran down the stairs and down the side of the lobby to the side entrance, zipping up as I went plowing through the snow.

I was glad for all my heavy gear, for although it had warmed up since yesterday, the snow was still flying and had mounted up considerably through the night. Wet snowflakes had replaced the light fluff, and if I kept standing there, I was going to get soaked through. I kept moving, slogging along a path that had been made by a herd of anonymous officials who'd been by this way not too long before me. If I didn't keep moving, keep following that path, if I stopped where I was, I would begin to blend in with the rest of the landscape, just another indistinct shape that wouldn't regain its identity until spring or a premature melt.

The well-trodden path led out around back and down the stairs to the lake. I hesitated at the top of the hill for a moment. Snowflakes had begun to fill the footsteps, blurring them, yet the pathway was marked out in front of me as clearly as a sign. The wind buffeted me, and I clung to the railing, almost giving myself enough time to think about what it was I was really doing. What are you waiting for, Emma? What do you want?

I was just about to answer myself, was on the verge of turning around and going back into the hotel, when a gust of wind kicked up and all but shoved me forward down the staircase. I slid a ways, the stairs never where I expected them to be, the path iced over by compacted snow. When I regained my footing, I continued to follow the steps and path down to the lake.

I was glad of the twists and turns in the staircase, which gave me occasional glimpses of the frozen lake—and the tableau that was displayed out there now—while still concealing my own progress. I knew that Scott was nowhere near out here, and I knew that I would be shooed away as soon as I appeared. I wanted to postpone that moment as long as possible.

I could see a gurney and some dark-green uniformed officers busying themselves about near the base of the stairs. Frowning, I continued down, wondering why they would be working so close by the stairs. Perhaps Garrison had taken his walk later than I had; maybe he'd gone this morning, I thought, and that's when he kicked it. A stroke, maybe, or perhaps his heart just wasn't up to all those stairs. Something like that.

The sound of voices muffled by the snow grew louder as I descended, and branches swayed slowly under their burdens; a wet flake of snow hit my neck where my longer hair used to be. I could just about make out that people were starting to take notice of my arrival, and I made use of the switchbacks through the trees to make my way as far down as possible before I was stopped. I actually made it down to the beach when the four men near the stairs realized I wasn't another officer or EMT. There were an awful lot of folks here for an accident . . .

One of them was just zipping up a body bag. "Would you mind staying where you are? In fact, if you could just turn around and—"

"I'm looking for Scott Tomberg," I said. "I was told he might be here and he wanted my assistance in dealing with . . . well, I'm assuming that's Professor Garrison."

"Mr. Tomberg isn't here right now. I think you'll probably find him back in the lobby."

"He wasn't there, and they sent me out here." I tried to put as much authority into my voice as possible. The snow-covered ice on the lake was no longer pristine; an irregular

rectangle almost thirty feet on its long sides had been trod-
den. A dark red stain ringed with diffusing pink was near
one edge of the space. Must have been where he fell, I
thought, the way the blood had . . . bled into the snow. "Do
you know when Professor Garrison died? Mr.—?"

"Officer. Walton. He's been out here a while." Walton
shrugged. "Hard to tell with the temperature."

"What about the snow?" I pressed. "Was there a lot on top
of him?"

He wasn't giving any more away, however, and said with
an annoyed look, "Who are you?" He was joined by a second officer, who looked no more helpful and less friendly.

I introduced myself, noticing a distinct lack of enthusiasm
in the officers. "I thought I could help. You see, I was out
here last night, just before one o'clock, and this was all fresh
snow then. No tracks that I could see." No body either, I continued to myself.

"Well, they're going to take a look at him and see what it
was that did him in," Walton said. "Shouldn't have been out
here at all, man of his age. Constitutional or no. Probably
wasn't too bright of you to be out here either, in a storm. You
take constitutionals too?"

"I just wanted to get some air before I slept," I said, realizing that Walton hadn't said so directly, but suggested that
Garrison was out during the night. "My room was too hot
and the crowds were too loud."

"Well, if you wouldn't mind, we'd like to get out of the
snow now," he said, with mock courtesy.

"Sure."

I stepped back as they hoisted the gurney up the stairs. It
was going to be a long trip for them. I let them pass, and then
tagged along, not too far behind.

"This is all a shock," I said, scrambling to keep a foot in
the door, so to speak. Crunching up the stairs, our breath
came in gasps as we stumbled over the patches made icy

from compaction. "I mean, he was a colleague of my grand-father's. He used to come to our sites, my grandfather's sites, all the time." Which wasn't quite stretching it past truthfulness; just a matter of contextual timing.

That bait seemed to work. "Sites?"

"Archaeological sites."

"So you've known him for a long time?"

"Seems like forever." Sometimes, it really felt like for-ever, too. "I know he was old, but I didn't think he was par-ticularly frail or anything."

"We'd heard from Dr. Tomberg that he was a little unsteady. And that other one, the older woman, Petra Williams? She said that his medications had been bother-ing him."

"I didn't know he was on any medications." No reason I should have, but I was on a roll here.

"Anticoagulants, among other things. I guess they were making him a little dizzy, but even if he hadn't been on them, he shouldn't have been out here in that weather. What time did you come out here again?"

"It was before one, I think." As I said it, I remembered the noises that had ultimately driven me back into the hotel. I told him about the noise I'd heard, the sharp crack and muf-fled thud in the woods I'd attributed to breaking branches.

Officer Walton was interested for real now. "And he wasn't there when you were out?"

"No. It seemed like I was the first one out here then. I mean the snow was still pristine, still in drifts, if you know what I mean."

"No footsteps that might have been filled in? No cleared-off railings, nothing like that?"

I thought back, and all I could come up with was just how untouched everything was. "I really don't think that there was anything like that. I would have noticed. If someone had been out there ahead of me, he would either have had to come a different way or been out there so much earlier that all the traces were reburied by the snow. And there was no . . . Garrison was not out on the ice when I got there, that much is for sure."

He sucked his teeth, unconvinced. "You would have noticed?"

"Yeah."

"Why?"

It was on the tip of my tongue to say: Because I'm an archaeologist, damn it! Don't you ever watch the Discovery Channel? Right next door to a forensic investigator, hell, I'm doing it a few hundred or thousand years after the fact, instead of hours or minutes or days, and that makes me better at it, to my mind! Because I'm paranoid as hell. Because I've been through this before . . .

"It's sort of a thing with me," I said. "You know, seeing how sites get formed. I practice at home, identifying what my husband's been eating based on the crumbs and plates; what he's been doing when I'm not there. Noticing that the cats have been fighting while I'm gone, that sort of thing."

He raised an eyebrow. "And how can you tell the cats have been fighting if you're not there? They get scratched?"

"No. Tufts of hair on the carpet or couch."

"Oh. You must be a lot of fun to live with."

I shrugged. "But I'm pretty sure about what I saw last night."

Walton barked a laugh. "If you had any idea of how sketchy eyewitness accounts can be . . ."

"But I do have an idea," I said, thinking of the hundreds of documents I'd evaluated for what was said and what was left unsaid. "And this isn't like I was observing the color of someone's eyes or what football team shirt they were wearing. This was whether someone had come down the steps before me or not."

"Gotcha." He smiled, maybe at my earnestness, maybe

my naïveté, and I noticed how photographically cute he was, snowflakes on eyebrows.

We were coming to the top of the stairs. The gurney was being loaded into the ambulance, and I noticed that there was a growing crowd gathering outside the side doors, wide-eyed and whispering. So much for Scott trying to keep things quiet until the official announcement. I didn't want to be a part of the show, not with this audience, so I made as if to leave.

Walton put his hand out. "You wait right here, a minute." He turned his head and hollered. "Hey, Mark? Detective Church? Over here."

The two conferred for an instant, but before I could blink, I was being handed over to the second officer. I would have passed him by in any crowd: just below medium height, not-quite-stocky frame, short blond hair that was just barely visible beneath a navy blue baseball cap, he looked like any number of junior corporate types up in New Hampshire for the skiing.

"Hi there, how're you doing?" he asked me with an unexpected smile that knocked me for a loop. "I'm Mark Church."

I found myself smiling back, and then he launched into the questions. They were the same that Walton had asked me, and he went over them like he already knew what was going on here.

"I don't know what it was," I said as I finished telling him about the loud cracking noise I'd heard, "but now I wonder if it mightn't be significant."

"That's good, that's real good, thank you," he said, beaming, and I felt like I'd won a ribbon.

By the time he was done, there was quite the crowd by the side door. I cast about desperately and caught Walton's eye.

I hurried over to him. "Maybe you could do me a favor? Maybe you could let me know when you find out whether it was a heart attack, or something? I'd just feel better knowing, you know—" Here I stopped because I didn't know why I'd feel better knowing, or even how I could plausibly lie about what earthly reason I might have for wanting to know.

"Because of your grandfather," Officer Walton filled in.

"Yeah." I shrugged and smiled a little. Jesus, Emma, what is your problem? Why are you doing this?

"I'll see what I can do. You staying here?"

"Yes. Well, I gave you my room number, but here's my card too." I wrote my cell phone number on it in ballpoint, so it wouldn't run.

He looked at it, nodding slowly, then handed me one of his own. "You don't hear from me in a couple of days, give me a call. If I can help, I will."

"Thanks, I appreciate that."

And then there was nothing else for me to do but go back into the hotel. I didn't really fancy answering a lot of questions from those waiting there—I didn't know anything about what had happened, after all—but I decided I couldn't very well wait outside until everyone left. It was just too cold, and, well, there was no reason for me to be here really. I just felt protective of . . . I didn't know what.

Luckily I didn't know too many of the people there. Widmark had been by the doorway, but he ducked out of the way as the cops and stretcher went by. The only two I knew there were Noreen, who I ignored, and Sue Ayers, who was pale under her freckles.

"Damn, Emma, what happened? Are you okay?"

"Am I okay?" Why wouldn't I be okay? "I was just getting some air, and they were there."

"Oh, how horrible for you! Are you sure you're okay?"

"Really, I'm fine." What was her problem? She kept patting at me and trying to look in my eyes. Maybe she was afraid that I was contaminated somehow.

"It was Garrison, wasn't it?"

"I'm afraid so."

Her eyes were suddenly filled. "Emma, I'm so sorry." She patted me on the arm.

I was still puzzled. "I'm just going to go up to my room."

"Of course, come through this way."

I could feel some of the eyes from the group on me, and just managed to catch a familiar voice saying "—making a scene, first in the session and now here. Can't stand not being the center of attention."

Screw you, Noreen. Center of attention, my eye.

Chapter 6

I GOT UPSTAIRS AND THEN WONDERED WHAT I HAD been doing all afternoon, avoiding my friends and real work, getting into stuff that didn't really have anything to do with me. Why was I drawn to go to where Garrison had died? Was I coming to some sort of decision about how I wanted to fit into these investigations? Or was I just indulging in a world-class morbid streak?

I guess I wasn't willing to come to any real conclusion yet, but neither was I about to go down and resume life as a normal person either. There was no way I wanted to run into anyone downstairs in the common rooms, so I got another load of gym stuff out and went back to the fitness center. It wasn't a great solution, but I told myself it would do for the moment.

It was empty, as I'd hoped. I hopped up onto the treadmill and started to beat it. After about ten minutes, I could feel my muscles loosening up, and I was getting to that place where if I'm not actually enjoying an endorphin rush, I am able to pretend that I'm not bothered by the things that are on my mind. The door opened and I saw that it was Petra Williams, Garrison's ex. I immediately caught myself; I *had* to stop thinking of her as that; she'd had a career of her own, as overshadowed as it was, and it was just plain ignorant and unfair of me to use the shorthand that everyone used. She pulled back, and I noticed that she was wearing her business suit, but was also sporting tennis shoes—not sneakers, not running shoes, real live tennis shoes—instead of her low heels.

"I'm done here," I said quickly, in case she was after the treadmill. "Or are you looking for someone?"

"No, I just wanted to get a little exercise. But only if you're sure?"

"I'm going to stretch now. I just wanted to warm up. Please." I sprayed a paper towel with the disinfectant and wiped off the handrails and control board. "It's all yours."

"Thank you. My doctor is always after me . . ." She trailed off, lost in considering the controls. I was just about to offer to help, when she found the setting she wanted and set off at a gentle, walking pace.

I suddenly realized that I wanted to offer her my condolences, but what if she didn't actually know herself? I realized I didn't know who knew about Garrison and who didn't. I scanned her face, looking for signs of grief, and didn't see anything obvious. If she did know, however, she wouldn't know that Scott had told me too, and so I decided to keep my mouth shut.

I sat down on the mat at the far side of the room, and began working out the kinks. Five minutes later, I'd just managed to convince my back that it could in fact uncurl a little more, that I could just about put my chin on the outstretched legs in front of me, when Scott came in. His hair was askew and his pen was in rapid motion, waggling to beat the band. He looked as though he hadn't slept in a long while, and the overhead lighting wasn't doing him any favors. His clothes were starting to crease, becoming shiny with constant wear. He looked at me and looked at Petra, who was puffing slightly as she slowly but steadily moved along. I mouthed, do you want me to leave, with a jerk of my head toward the door, but he waved me off, forgetting about me just as soon as Petra looked up and saw him.

"So?" was all she said.

"They're done now. We should know something soon."

"Thank you for letting me know. The business meeting tonight—?"

"I've already spoken to the board about it. We'll make the announcement then. You're sure you don't want to . . . do something more? Call things off? I'm sure it's not up to me, but . . ."

"Not in the least. Not what he would have wanted either." This last she said firmly, as though Garrison's wishes were still paramount.

"Okay." Scott looked around, distracted, then shrugged. "I can't think of anything else, at the moment."

"Then, please, don't worry about it." She reached into her sleeve and pulled out a small, plain linen handkerchief, and pressed it carefully to first one eye, then the other.

"Okay." He nodded, but hesitated a moment longer when he saw the handkerchief. "Is there anything—?"

"Thank you, Scott." The handkerchief vanished back up her sleeve and Petra moved steadily along.

"Okay." Scott shook himself and left without another glance at me.

I decided I should just keep stretching back there, let everything I'd heard sort of fade away before I made my presence known again.

"Presumably you know? About Garrison?" She didn't even turn around to ask me, but rather asked the reflection in the mirror, looking back to where I was trying to be invisible. Her voice started off shakily, then firmed up.

"Yes. I'm sorry. I didn't know whether you'd heard the news yet." I got up and moved down so that she could look at me directly. "I'm sorry for your loss."

"Thank you. Even when it's not unexpected, it still takes one unawares. Scott wouldn't have said anything, if you hadn't known. He worries about that kind of thing, though he pretends not to." A businesslike sniff, then a pause. "I suspect many people are learning, now. How did you hear?"

"By accident. I thought Scott was looking for me, but he was actually passing it along to someone else. We're old friends," I finished, as if that explained everything.

"Who was he telling?" she asked, suddenly switching off the machine.

I took a breath. "Duncan Thayer."

"Of course he was. Partners of old." She nodded her head. "It's natural to turn to your friends at such a time." Then she regarded me sharply in the mirror. "But then, perhaps that's how you know him. You're Oscar Fielding's granddaughter, aren't you? Didn't recognize you, at first, with your hair short like that, but you'd been seeing Mr. Thayer before he came to us, hadn't you? Garrison told me." A small smile crossed her face, and it gave me the shivers. "Quite the affair, as I understand it."

Then Garrison was better informed than most of our colleagues, I thought. "It was a very long time ago" was all I could manage safely. Anything more and I would have begun explaining too much.

"Oh-o," Petra said. It sounded like a thousand other things more condescending and complex, though, to my ears, and I suddenly felt like a fourteen-year-old. My face burned.

"Well, we'll make the announcement tonight," she said. "I don't want them to be too formal or too grief-stricken. It wouldn't have been what Garrison would have wanted."

"Oh?"

"Well, I knew him as well as anyone, having been married to him, as long ago as *that* was. In fact, we were both in this very spot last night. About nine." She frowned and her words became sharper, almost accusatory. "He didn't like not being able to go outside, but his balance has been so bad, recently. I tried to get him to use the treadmill up here, I tried, but the old . . . grump was too upset at not being able to get his constitutional as he wanted. He just sat here with me while I walked. There was no *need* for him to go out there, he could just as easily have used the . . ."

She took a breath, calming herself. "I walked him back to his room, made sure he could get into bed all right. He hated it, but he would have hated being found in a heap someplace even worse." She looked at my reflection straight in the eye. "I never could talk him out of anything he'd decided. I guess he decided he was going outside anyway, stubborn old man."

"I guess." It seemed to me that Petra needed to believe that she'd done everything she could to look after Garrison. Divorce or no, she cared about him.

Maybe Petra felt she'd showed me too much of herself. As the machine slowed and turned itself off, she announced, "Well, now that I've satisfied the letter of the law, maybe I'll violate the spirit of it by having an early Bloody Mary as a reward."

She stepped off the belt with care, but marched briskly out of the room without a glance back at me.

I rested my head on my knees, letting the tension that had built up during our talk dissipate. Hard enough, to offer someone condolences, worse to watch her struggle between the desire to talk about it and the urge to maintain composure before a total stranger.

Not a total stranger, I reminded myself. And she certainly didn't mind chewing over my discomfort over Duncan.

Shoot, Emma, you can't even let the woman have that

much distraction? It didn't cost you anything. A lot of folks of that generation don't like to talk about personal things, emotional things, even as they're trying to deal with them. Imagine what you'd feel if you'd done everything you thought you could to look after someone, and they still . . .

But . . . Garrison had told her he was going to bed, had actually gone to bed, but then got back up? Sometime close to nine-thirty? It made no sense to me, for all Petra was willing to chalk it up to his stubbornness.

I turned around, and seeing the dopey, puzzled face that stared back at me from the mirror, scowled. Then I composed myself and put on my best game face, the neutral one that Nolan, my trainer, was trying to get me to wear, even when I got hit or hurt during sparring. It took some effort, because surprise is a strong reflex, but I was getting better at it.

Following the lead my face was setting me, I began to shadow box, throwing lefts and rights, then working in a couple of combinations of threes and fours. Slipping imaginary punches, bobbing, weaving, I was starting to lose my self-consciousness and began to throw in some kicks as well. Then I really let myself go for a minute, paying attention to my footwork, trying to keep loose, and trying to form planned combinations and then execute them, all at once.

Duncan was there, in the doorway.

I saw him as I laid out a sidekick. I've learned, the hard way, to always look at your target when you are attacking, and although my balance was pretty good, the sight of him watching me—how long had he been there?—threw me for a loop. I fumbled a little, but thought, hell with him, and managed to follow through with a fairly convincing back kick. I decided I wasn't up to ignoring him while I did more, and cooled down again with simpler combinations. I caught sight of my face and was impressed by the serious lack of humor. Now *that* was a game face.

"That's new. Lotta stuff new, about you. Looks good on you."

I wasn't getting dragged into this, but I also bit my tongue before I asked him whether he wasn't keeping an eye on me full-time now. I wasn't going to give him the satisfaction. Why didn't he just go away? If I could have wiped him away, along with all the memories of our relationship, I would have.

"Scott just left, if you were looking for him." I didn't stop my boxing, and used all my focus to ignore him.

"I am looking for Scott. I meant it, though. It suits you."

I kept working. "I'm pretty much the same as ever." But that was mostly a lie: I was changing. I was just contradicting him for the sake of it.

He nodded and left. I kept throwing punches, but my heart wasn't in it anymore; I wanted to go up to my room and hide under the covers, but I didn't.

The cocktail party had already started and, as usual, was a mob scene. The drinks were ridiculously overpriced, filled with weak liquor, and there were only four harassed bartenders to cater to the ever-increasingly desperate needs of over four hundred thirsty archaeologists who were let off the leash, and that included the ones hunting for data, jobs, gossip, references, or connections. Still, I noticed that the usual frenzy was tempered: word about Garrison was getting around. I got my drink and tried to find some of my friends to hang out with. Instead I got rushed by people who wanted a copy of my paper and a couple of students who were asking about my classes in the Caldwell College archaeology program. That was fine, and got finer still when I saw that my tall friend with the bad breath was craning his neck, peering over the crowd, his hands hanging straight down at his sides like a meercat. Dear God, a meercat with halitosis.

Looking for me. I kept my head down, leaning into my own conversation more intimately than I was used to.

But the last student had other schools to investigate, and he flitted off sooner than I would have liked. I looked around and instantly made accidental eye contact with Widmark, but he only waved offhandedly and kept peering around. I began to worry that I'd offended him, by trying to duck out on him earlier, and then decided that I was willing to pay the price of that guilt. Someone bumped into me, and if I had been drinking from a glass, it would have spilled all over the place. Drinking beer from a bottle is not merely a matter of machismo.

"Jay, take it easy, huh?" I said. Jay, my recent poker victim, was plastered, well ahead of schedule, and mumbling into his cell phone.

"Sorry, Em," he mumbled. Stepping away from me, he knocked into Laurel.

"Watch it, asshole," she barked. Maybe recognizing him stemmed the flow of profanity I expected to follow. "Oh, it's you, Whitaker. Learn how to walk, would you?"

"Sorry. I guess I'm just tired."

"Well, put the damn cell phone down, this is a social event."

He swayed slightly, beet red and not just from the press of the room. "You don't really think I'm an asshole, do you, Laurel? I'm sorry, I'm sorry . . ."

"No." She flicked at Jay, who was trying to brush at her to wipe the martini off her jacket. "Just . . . just take it easy."

"But you still love me, don't you Laurel?"

"Of course I still love you, but now you're becoming a lachrymose and fuckwitted nuisance."

"Lachrymose?" He turned to me, his eyes welling, confused.

"She means you're getting maudlin," I answered.

"Oh, okay. I'm all right now," he said, and lurched away, still clutching his cell phone.

"I very much doubt it," Laurel mumbled, as she tried to mop up. She turned to me. "Em."

"Hey, Laurel. Where'd you get the martini? Didn't think they were getting that fancy in here."

"They're not. I brought it from the bar. I refuse to drink the shit they serve at these things. Self-preservation."

I raised one eyebrow. "Drinking vodka is self-preservation?"

She shrugged. "Well, you know. Besides, it's good vodka, if that's not a contradiction in terms. How's it going?"

"Not too bad, I'm just trying to avoid someone. But I think he's found another target."

"Who's that?"

"Tall guy, skinny, gormless, some kind of archaeologist wannabe. Boring, boring, and if I include his breath, boringer still. As in, it would bore a hole through you." I looked around apprehensively, trying to find him.

Laurel did the same, much less obviously than I. "Sounds scary. Oh, I got him. Someone needs a visit from the Fab Five, don't they? He's looking over here."

"Just don't make eye contact. Pretend we're talking."

"We are talk—ooph!" Laurel lurched again, and this time lost most of her drink. "Jay! God damn it! Now you are officially an asshole!" she called to Jay's retreating back. "Walking around with that freaking phone! If you can't handle your liquor, do it in your room where you won't spoil it for the rest of us, you useless sot."

But by the time she'd got to the word *phone*, Laurel's anger had dissipated, and she was on autopilot. "I thought he was supposed to be getting his act together," she said to me. "Business has been picking up after a dry spell, or so I heard."

"Beats me. I haven't had a chance to catch up with him about work. But I'm glad to hear it."

By now Scott had made his way to the front to make a few

announcements, but he was accompanied by a couple of uniformed officers. At the same time, my friend Widmark had suddenly found a need to depart, rapidly. Again, he snaked through the crowd, and something about the way he moved struck me as oddly familiar, and not at all in character with what I'd observed of him at lunch. I couldn't place it, so by the time he left, I turned to hear the official announcement. People began to quiet and turn toward the front of the room.

"Ordinarily now's the time when we'd move into the ballroom for a brief business meeting. I've met with the board and we've decided that we need to make an announcement while I've . . . we've still got you all here."

Someone whooped, to a small pocket of laughter—someone who didn't know, apparently—but Scott wasn't smiling. "I'm afraid it's bad news. We learned this morning that our guest of honor, Julius Garrison, passed away during the night."

Dead silence was followed by a murmur of distress, which quickly grew. I frowned. Surely, this shouldn't be so great a shock to everyone? He was about six hundred years old, and as he said himself, they don't start giving you lifetime achievement awards unless they think you're going to kick off soon. A surprise, certainly, but an anticipated fact of life as well.

"We are still looking into the details and trying to fix the time of his death. If everyone who saw him last night will come forward so that we can get a statement, well, I'm sure that his family will be very glad to hear whatever we can put together of his last evening. After all, he was among those he loved best."

Oh, please, Scott. That's a bit much.

"Hear, hear," someone called out. It was echoed strongly across the room, riding the budding crest of whispered exchanges.

I looked around, puzzled. This was not what I was expecting.

"So, I don't know, maybe we can all lift our glasses and say goodbye to a fine scholar, a righteous man, and a hell of an archaeologist. To Julius Garrison."

"Julius Garrison!" came the overwhelming reply.

I turned around to see what was going on, still frowning, then sipped automatically.

"Em, you okay?" Laurel asked. She was sipping from her glass, drinking the toast herself.

"Yeah, I'm fine. I'm just not . . ." I shrugged. "Toasts? This is Garrison we're talking about, right? Am I losing my mind, or what?"

Laurel looked around then shrugged. "A lot of people thought he was really important."

"Yeah, sure, but this?" All around us people were somber, some looked shocked, and a few had handkerchiefs out, visibly upset. "What's with all the crocodile tears?"

"Maybe not crocodilian, Em. Lots of people liked him."

"Lots of people were *afraid* of him. He messed with people, bad. And, 'righteous man'? I don't know what Scott is thinking." I couldn't stop shaking my head. "Doesn't sound like the man I knew."

She sipped her drink. "Emma, I doubt very much that these people knew him the way you did."

I turned on her. "And what does that mean?"

"Just what I said. I think that—"

At that moment, an uproar broke out near the door. A crackle of radio static and words that were loud but barely audible broke over the muted hubbub like an unwelcome drunk at a wake: shots had been fired outside.

People turned toward the noise and the announcement, and then turned toward me. I looked behind me, only to see everyone looking in my direction as well. A uniformed officer and a man in a red parka—Detective Church—spoke to some folks, the only one I could make out was Noreen—and they all pointed toward me. I turned around again, but this time it was unmistakable: The police were coming for me. I was still surprised when they stopped a few feet away from me.

"Emma Fielding? We'd like you to step outside with us for a few moments."

"Why, what—?"

Detective Church said, "We have a few questions about where you were last night."

The words carried across the now-silent ballroom, filling my ears until there was nothing else in my head. Numbly, I followed the cops out of the room, feeling every set of eyes in the place on me.

Chapter 7

"CAN YOU TELL ME WHAT THIS IS ALL ABOUT?" I asked Church. We were walking across the lobby now, and though he was perhaps an inch shorter than I, close to five-eight, he matched my stride. "Have you found out anything new? Officer Walton said he'd give me a call—"

"Did he?" This was with humor. "Actually we've got a few questions for you, if you don't mind."

"No, of course not, but I'm pretty sure that I told you everything that I saw when I was out on the stairs—"

He stopped. "Why *were* you out on the stairs?"

"I told you. I was looking for Dr. Tomberg."

"Actually, I meant last night."

"Like I told Officer Walton. I was taking a walk. I needed some air."

He flipped through a notebook. "So you did. And earlier today? You seemed interested in what was going on. You seemed really curious about the deceased."

"Well, yeah." Then it occurred to me that my interest might not be as self-explanatory as it seemed to me. The tone of his voice was deceptively neutral. "You're right. I was curious. It's just . . . it's just . . ."

I realized that I was about to say the words out loud for the first time, and I was a little reluctant, as if saying them would seal my fate forever. "I'm thinking that maybe . . . I'm going to look into forensics, maybe forensic anthropology. I mean, I'm an archaeologist now, and I've become . . . I've seen . . ." I took a deep breath. "I've been considering getting training so I could work with the state police crime lab, or coroner, or something like that. Stuart Feldman—he's with the Massachusetts State Police Crime Lab? He's been trying to get me to look into it."

Detective Church nodded slowly, like this seemed logical to him. "Lot of people here are archaeologists. They don't seem like they are all rushing down the stairs to see a corpse. A corpse that looks like it died by accident."

If was an accident, then why the continued police presence here? Why is everyone rushing around like it wasn't an accident? I was at least smart enough to keep all this to myself. "Like I said, I knew the deceased. So I had a couple of reasons."

"Plenty of people here knew him, from what I can see. How did you?"

"I knew him through my grandfather. He used to come visit our sites, years ago."

"Seen him much since then?" Again came the ready smile, the one that made me want to answer him just as smartly as I could. I realized he had a talent for getting people to talk.

"No, not much. Occasionally, at professional things like this."

"So he wasn't really an old friend of the family?"

"Well, he was, but—"

"A lot of folks saw the two of you alone, yesterday. Arguing, it looked like."

"What? They couldn't have—" The bus had been up by the road, and you couldn't really see down to the site so well—could you? Well, yes, you could, now that the house was gone.

Church smiled encouragingly. "Out on the field trip? The tour of the site?"

"Oh . . . but we weren't . . . arguing. He was just . . . telling me some things about Oscar. Oscar was my grandfather."

"People said you looked flustered. Was that 'friendly'?"

"I, well, not—" I could feel myself getting confused, my thoughts tripping over themselves before they could make it to my tongue.

Suddenly Duncan was there. "She knew him about as well as I did, Mark. Which is to say, a little professionally, a little socially."

If I thought Church was smiling before, when he saw Duncan his face lit up with genuine pleasure. "Mr. Thayer! Excellent to see you."

Church shook hands with Duncan, the kind with claps on the back that speaks of more than passing acquaintance.

"Mr. Church. You're looking very fit."

This banter sounded like it dated back a long ways. I was so taken aback that Duncan had inserted himself into the situation, at once sticking up for me and doing the old-boy glad-hand stuff, that I was momentarily speechless. Rage, confusion, and envy—how come a jerk like Duncan got to be at ease, got to slide through this kind of situation as if he'd been born to it? Of course he had been born to it: We were in his territory, it was no surprise that he should know people—male authority figures—and be at home with them. He *was* at home. I bit my tongue and waited for things to play out before I added anything. Like kerosene to a fire.

"And you know Miss—er . . ." he flipped through his notebook. Somehow I knew he didn't need to.

"I've known Dr. Emma Fielding for years," Duncan said. "Since college. Best kind of people."

I hated that he was sticking up for me. I couldn't stand that he used my title. I didn't want to be beholden to him for any reason, and I didn't want him bruiting about our past—why couldn't he let it lie decently buried? I hated that he was helping me. And I knew he knew it.

"Well, we're just asking her about her interest in the deceased. Why she was out trying to get a look at the body."

He beamed expansively. "Then I'm sure she'll give you all the help you need. I'll be seeing you."

Church put his hand on Duncan's shoulder. "Look, Dunk, we need to talk to everyone who might have seen Mr. Garrison before he died. So I'll be seeing you a lot sooner than we might otherwise."

"No problem." Duncan shook his head. "It's been too long. Time gets away from you, Mark."

"Sure does."

Duncan was all business again. "When would be convenient? Just say the word, man."

Officer Church settled back comfortably. "I'll give you a call when we're ready for you."

"Great. Here's my room number. If you need anything, any help with anything, let me know. I'll do what I can to see you get everything you need."

The way he said it was as though he was modestly understating his importance, while letting it be known just how big a fish he was. As if the cops would need his help with anything. I looked at Church quickly, but was disappointed.

He nodded, pleased. "Thanks, Dunk, I appreciate it."

The two men shook hands again, and Duncan touched me on the shoulder as if to reassure me or to assert some sort of proprietary rights. I managed to nod, not bite his finger. What was all this about? He knew how I hated to have other people help me.

Whatever it was, Officer Church's demeanor toward me changed significantly, though I could tell he went to pains to disguise it. He relaxed more, was more sure of what he was going to get now that I had been validated by Duncan. A pause in his gum chewing, and I realized that he could see I was tensed up. I tried to relax.

"So, can you tell me where you were last night? Before your walk."

"Card game with friends, from about eight to eleven. Then I was in the bar, with Laurel and Sue, and some others. Then I went for a walk. Then I went to my room, then to the slide room. Duncan . . . saw me there. In the bar again, briefly, after that. Then I called my sister. That was after one."

He wrote all of this down, noting the names and times especially.

"And you last saw Professor Garrison—when?"

"I think it was at the presentation, and that was before everything else. But I know that Petra Williams saw him later, walked him up to his room," I said. "You might check with her about the time there, I think she said about nine, so some time after that. And there was a note for him, someone left on the board. They were supposed to meet last night, I guess, and the writer, whoever that was, seemed angry, like he'd been blown off. Maybe you should check that out too."

"Maybe I already have." Again came the smile, and it could have sold everything from toothpaste to foreign policy. "And we've spoken to Dr. Petra Williams."

"Oh." There were no flies on this guy. "So, what's with the shots that were fired? You know, what we heard on the radios at the reception?"

He tensed, the smile faltered. "Probably some misguided hunter, nothing to worry about."

I looked at him, waiting.

"That's my opinion, but we're looking into it. But other than that, all's I can tell you so far, is no one thinks you fired them. We need to take a count of who was where, so your friends back there in the ballroom are going to be mighty jealous that you got done so quickly."

I'll bet, I thought. "Do you need to know anything else?"

He laughed, and I felt absurdly pleased with myself. "I need to know almost everything, but . . . why don't you tell me about the words you had with Garrison."

Hell, I walked straight into that one. I took a deep breath. "He was asking about my grandfather Oscar's involvement with the site. Oscar introduced me to the owner—Pauline Westlake—when I was very young, and we'd been good friends. Pauline . . . Pauline was killed, murdered, a few years ago. He was asking me about that."

"And that made you angry."

I held up a braking hand. "I just didn't want to talk to him about Pauline, or Oscar either. I . . . I didn't think he had the right, the way he'd behaved toward Oscar. And I didn't like him asking me about how my friend died."

"Really."

"If he knew that Pauline was murdered, he should have known well enough that it might be a source of pain for me still. That's why I might have been 'flustered,' as you put it."

As I spoke, I felt myself getting stiffer and stiffer—posture, demeanor, everything. I could feel my face shutting down, banking down my emotions. As much as I wanted to be forthcoming about Garrison and what I knew about him, this was off limits.

Church nodded, once, twice, and resumed chewing his gum. "Right. Well, you can leave. Oh, hang on one more second." He pulled a piece of paper out of his pocket. "We were talking about notes, before. This one was left for you on the bulletin board. Can you tell me anything about it?"

He handed me a photocopy, and I looked at it, puzzled, expecting that it was a note from Scott, or maybe another student. It was a copy of both sides of a smaller piece of paper. One side had my name on it, handwritten. The other read, "Stay out of it. It's not worth your life."

I felt the hairs on the back of my neck prickle and my hands went cold. "Where . . . when . . . what is this?"

"You can't tell me?"

"No, of course not! I had no idea—you said you got it on the notice board?"

"Yes. You don't recognize the handwriting?"

"No, I don't. What . . . what have I been talking to you about? I mean, that would get anyone so . . . would make someone write this?"

"I surely don't know. At conferences—isn't there a lot of fooling around? Drinking, jokes, that kind of thing?"

I didn't buy it and he knew it.

"But just in case it isn't, you might want to keep in sight of crowds, this weekend, in case this isn't some kind of joke. Better to stick to archaeology than criminal investigation, right?"

"That's what I'm here for," I said absently. The note didn't feel like a joke, and if it was, it certainly wasn't Carla's style.

He took down my room number, again confirming things I'd already told the other officer, and then sent me on my way.

I wanted to go up to my room, and once again I found myself wishing to avoid my colleagues, but I knew it would only feel worse, that it would look bad, for whatever reason, if I hid myself away. The bar was emptier than I'd seen it yet that weekend. It was filling up slowly, as people exited the police interviews in the ballroom, and everyone who came in was subdued. Eyes flickered watchfully, a little fearfully, and a lot of glances lingered on me a little longer than I liked. Drinks were clutched, ignored, or swallowed too quickly.

I found Sue there, sitting on a stool off to one side, her head nearly bowed to her lap, elbows on her knees, her hands clutched to her mouth. A drink sat mostly drained before her on the table. She squared her shoulders and shook herself when I greeted her.

She looked up. "I'm sorry? What was that? I'm still out of it, hon."

"No problem. I was just asking if I could get you a drink or something. Orange juice, a Coke?" *Just in case you wanted to stop the hard stuff.*

She thought for a moment, then grimaced, shaking her head. "Not unless you can rustle up a vernal cocktail."

"Huh?" Was this something new, from *Sex in the City*, maybe?

"I need a little spring in my life, Em. I've had it with feeling like I'm setting my teeth, hunkering down, *enduring* all the time. You know, when the fall starts turning really cold, and you have to start thinking about storm windows and raking and firewood and whether you've got deicer and sand in the car? I'm sick of it."

She paused and reached into her glass, popped a couple of ice cubes into her mouth. I assumed she was drinking water and lime, as I couldn't smell gin or rum, but I didn't know for sure.

When she got done crunching, she said, "I want . . . I want to remember what it feels like when a warm breeze runs across your face and your shoulders unknot and you start to feel hopeful again. Daffodils and early tulips, flowering buds on the trees, wild birdsong. New grass breaking through the hard soil. I need that, Emma. I can't stand this other feeling anymore."

She sighed so deeply that I thought she would cry. I followed her glance to the window, where the world outside was shrouded in white, buried in snow, and all hope of spring had to come from memory, because we were about as far from it as you could possibly be. The frost-rimed glass let in a bluish black light from the outside lamps, but blocked out any more distinct images. The exception was a single black and skeletal branch, evenly draped in a snowy mantle with icy fringe, as it tapped like a bony finger against the window.

I shivered, glad to be inside, but the feeling of being trapped inside—not only in the hotel, but too near Sue's depressed state of mind—was total.

"I don't know," I said slowly. "Sometimes the snow is nice. Covers up the dead grass and leaves. Makes you feel secure, all cozy indoors." But I was far from feeling any of that now; I just felt stranded.

In spite of that, Sue's next words surprised me.

"I'm done. I'm not going to do this anymore. I can't keep bashing myself against walls I didn't create, keep working for something I don't feel I can really change. Last night decided me. I'm done."

"What do you mean?" I could hear the stupidity of my question even as I said it, but what she was proposing was so extraordinary that I couldn't help it. "You're leaving archaeology?"

"Yep." Sue looked at me, half defensive, half hopeful.

I immediately discarded the first things that sprang to my mind—you'll get over it, you've put so much of your life into it, you just need to get some sleep—and tried to really think before I spoke again. "You've been thinking about this for a while."

She nodded. "Like I said, last night decided it, though."

I squelched the automatic responses again, and something like a band snapped off my heart, and I could breathe again. I hadn't even realized that I had been holding my breath, for what seemed like months. "What will you do?"

"I've been doing a lot of thinking. I've even spoken to a career counselor, and I've been talking to some friends. I think I'm going to look into business. I'm looking at some management positions in a software company."

The surprise must have shown on my face, because she scowled.

"I've never wanted to teach and the state job is killing me. I want something that I can leave at work when I'm done for the day—well, leave more than I could archaeology. If I take this job, I'll get to use my skills, I'll get to work with people, and there'll be some research. I'll get benefits, I'll get a decent paycheck. I don't need it to be my life, I just need something to pay the bills and I'll find my fulfillment after hours."

"I'm sorry," I said quickly. "The corporate world, well, it doesn't seem like a natural fit, but I see how it can work, now. I'm surprised, of course, but it sounds like you've got a good plan. Most people aren't capable of identifying what will make them happy."

She nodded hurriedly. "I'm sorry, I don't mean to be so . . . prickly. You're the first person I've said this to, here, I mean, and I guess I expect people to . . . not to . . . react well. I mean, we spend so much of our time bitching that it seems like the natural state of things. It's radical, I know, but I just can't do this anymore."

Now she really did seem like she was going to cry. It occurred to me that if Sue had already been looking for new jobs, then maybe . . . what if the grand project she'd proposed, the historic village, was more of a heroic gesture, a swan song? Maybe she was looking for someone to make the decision to leave for her.

"Hey, you don't have to apologize to me. You don't have to apologize to anyone. It's none of their damned business, is it?"

"Spoken like a true New Englander." She managed a rueful grin. "Avoid emotions and keep your business to yourself."

"No, it's not like that—" And then I realized she was kidding me. "Hey—you learn fast."

She looked at me. "You know, I was kind of dreading telling you, most of all."

"Why?" I knew, or suspected, and tried to conceal the hurt I felt.

"I dunno. I just . . . I dunno." She suddenly retreated to the ice in her glass again.

I leaned in to her. "Yes, you do. Why?"

"I thought . . . well, you've just always been so into this. I thought you'd try to talk me out of it."

I looked at her, horrified. "Sue, please tell me I'm not as bad as that." At least she'd had the guts not to hesitate too long.

"No, no, not really. It's just you've always been so . . . sure."

I laughed. "Kiddo, it's a big act. No one is that sure of anything." And least of all me, these days, I added to myself. I thought about telling Sue what I'd been thinking, and decided maybe it would be good for both of us. "And besides, I've been thinking of making some changes myself."

She crunched more ice, maybe a little lifted by her confession. "Oh yeah? Like what?"

"Well." Now that it came time to say it out loud, I again felt strangely reluctant. "I've been thinking of . . . changing directions. Just a bit, nothing extreme. Just . . . maybe looking into . . . the . . . you know. Forensic side of things." I couldn't believe how difficult it was for me to say the words.

"Fuck me, Emma." She stared at me with frank shock.

I thought Sue would be more understanding, considering. I thought she'd get it.

"Don't you think that's kind of . . . ?" She spread her hands wide apart, shook her head. "Extreme?"

"Maybe. But I think it's something I need to check out for myself."

"That's some midlife crisis." She hastily signed her bill. "But you've always been precocious."

What was going on here? "I think it may be more than that. We'll see."

"God, you know, I'm beat." She collected her things, dropped the pen in her haste.

"Where are you off to?" In such a hurry, that you haven't got two minutes to listen to *my* big crises? Sue had always been so much better at this stuff than so many others, and I was really feeling hurt.

She fished on the floor for the pen. "You know, I was thinking of going up to my room just when you came in, so I'll see you later, okay?" She didn't even look at me as she walked quickly from the bar.

I was so angry, so hurt, that I almost threw my glass at her. Well, I guess that's what I get for exposing those rusty New England emotions, I thought. There's a good reason, apparently, for keeping your business to yourself, especially when old friends can't even spare the time to nod and pat your hand, even if they don't get it. Even if they don't approve.

To hell with you, I thought. I stared for a minute, then sat down, wondering what had just happened. Then I berated myself: Come on, Emma. Sue's having a hell of a time of things right now. She probably can't handle someone's issues on top of her own.

But among all the things that were currently distressing, Sue, I thought, never once mentioned Garrison's death, or the police, or the gunshots.

Huh.

More for camouflage than anything else, I took out my phone and checked for messages. Brian had left one, and I dialed in to get it.

"Hi, I just wanted to let you know that I made it fine to Kam's, and I'm glad we'll be going to work from here rather than coming from home—the last part of the drive was a killer. I guess if this snow keeps up, we might not be going to work tomorrow either, if there's a snow emergency or whatever."

There was a pause. "And since they got hit in New York

before they got hit here, all the flights were canceled. So Marty's stuck here with us."

Another pause, then Brian soldiered on. "So I guess she and Princess Sophia will be staying with us. It was good, that they canceled the flight before she got to Logan, but she's really, really not happy about it. I think she was really counting on seeing her folks—hang on a sec."

There was a muffled sound of the phone being moved and I heard Brian say, "Yeah, thanks, Marty. I'm just on the phone to Emma. Yeah, I'll tell her hi. Popcorn? Great. I'll be right there."

When Brian got back to the phone, he sounded even more deflated. "Okay, I gotta go before the no-salt fat-free popcorn gets cold. Marty's feeling fat and trying to watch her eating, so we're kinda toning down the whole snacking thing."

I thought about the elaborate plans that he and Kam had made so joyfully, involving prepackaged salty meats, cheese, and alcohol.

He continued with the message. "She says she hopes you're having fun, up in New Hampshire with your friends."

Ha! I thought. Everyone always thinks these conferences are for fun.

". . . and all I can say is, Kam owes me for this, big time. Okay, you don't have to call here when you get in, I don't want you to wake Sophia, but if you want to leave a message on my phone, that would be cool, 'cause I'll leave it off. I love you, pork chop."

I hung up, trying not to think about how depressed he was, and how bad off Kam must be, when they'd been so looking forward to being guys together, as they had been when they were roommates. At least Brian was safe, and Marty, and that was the important thing. But it was sure not the fun they had planned.

Jay and Chris came in about ten minutes later, and Brad a

few minutes after that. Jay had calmed down or sobered up since the events in the ballroom, and Brad was ashen. Chris looked troubled.

"I'm going up to bed," Brad announced suddenly. "I'm not feeling very well, I think I'm coming down with something."

"Hey man, I haven't seen you all day almost, Braddy-boy" Chris said. "I've got some NyQuil if you want it. Take it prophylactically, get you some sleep anyway."

"What am I supposed to do, rub it on my dick?" Brad said.

We all looked up; it was unlike him to make rude jokes.

He shook his head. "I'm sorry, no thanks, Chris, I've got some echinacea and goldenseal I can take. I really am feeling poorly, though, so I'll say good night." He lifted a hand vaguely and moved to the elevators.

"That was strange," Jay said. His phone was out of sight now, and he seemed to be drinking a coke. "But what happened to you? What did the cops say?"

"They were just asking about the last time I saw Garrison, where I was last night," I said.

"Holy shit," Chris said. "I wonder if it had anything to do with the artifacts that were stolen?"

"Or the shots that were fired," Jay added.

"They didn't say anything useful about them," I said. "Chris, are you talking about Bea's artifacts, or the repros from the book room?"

"Either. There's a hell of a lot going on here, now," he answered. "The cops talked to you, huh?"

I exchanged a look with Chris; he knew that I'd had experience talking to the police from a nasty little event that took place near his place of work in western Massachusetts. I guessed it was his way of asking how I was doing.

"What were they talking to you about?" Jay asked.

"It wasn't anything special," I said, after a moment. "They weren't accusing me of anything. Though they did make a meal of the fact that Garrison and I spent time alone out at the site yesterday. He and I spoke for maybe two minutes on the way up the hill to the bus."

"Damn, Em," Jay said. "That's messed up."

I spread my hands. "Tell me about it. But that's all it was, really."

"Quite the news about Garrison, huh? And after we were all just talking about him last night?" Carla had joined us. "It's enough to make me want to start smoking again."

We greeted her, but we were all really wrapped up in our own thoughts.

"Hey, you." She nudged me. "Serious weirdness going on, huh?"

I nodded. "You can say that again. Say," I asked her, keeping my voice low, "the slide with the frog in the fez—that was the only thing you left for me, right?"

"Whatever do you mean?" she said, batting her eyes at me. Something in my face must have clued her in, because she stopped fooling around right away. "Yeah. Why do you ask? What's wrong?"

"Someone left me a nasty note," I said. "Real nasty. The cops tried to make out like it was a joke, but at the same time, they suggested I don't go wandering off on my own, you know what I mean?"

She shook her head. "No way, it wasn't me. I wouldn't—"

"Yeah, I know," I said. "I just thought I'd make sure, you know."

The bar was filling up now, and maybe it was the drinks, maybe it was the density of souls that was bringing a little more life to the gathering. Liveliness went straight into a kind of high-tension frenzy, as people put a little too much effort into putting the evening behind them or into perspective.

Jay went up to the bar to buy drinks. I watched him order, then his attention was drawn to the fight on the television. I glanced at it briefly—it was a heavyweight match, and so a little slow-going for me; those big guys don't often have the speed to keep moving for very long. Jay, still watching the television, motioned for the bartender, asked him a question; the bartender scowled, shook his head, held up his hands. Jay took out his phone, eyes glued to the match, and made a quick call.

Another archaeologist in a name badge accosted him. When his order came, Jay and his friend both looked over at me, briefly. Jay shrugged, came back with the round of drinks, but even before I got my bourbon to my mouth, I saw his friend go over to his own party, all of whom immediately swiveled their heads my way before leaning into each other to talk.

I picked up my drink and thought: that's how rumors start. God only knew where they would take me from here.

Chapter 8

IT WAS STILL SNOWING WHEN I LOOKED OUT THE WIN-
dow the next morning, Friday. After a round of shower
combat, followed by coffee and a muffin wolfed down in the
lobby—the restaurants were just too crowded this late in the
morning—I pulled out my phone. I was really not looking
forward to telling Brian what was going on here, afraid of his
reaction to what was a perfectly normal situation. Well, if not
normal, then not unusual. For us. For me, anyway. But after
we said good morning and I told him about the events of the
previous evening, explaining that, so far, the cops were
telling people that the gunshots were probably from hunters
and that, so far, despite the fact that Garrison was found outside, they had no reason to suspect that he hadn't died of natural causes. I had, however, omitted the note that Church had
showed me. No need to get him excited over nothing, yet.

Brian was uncharacteristically inattentive. "Well, let me
know when you hear anything definite, okay? And look after
yourself, whatever the case" was all he said.

And then I was aware of another pause, a hesitation that
was hanging particularly awkwardly on the other end of the

line. It was the kind of hesitation that every person in a long-term relationship learns to recognize, the one where you can practically hear the nervousness on the other side, the sort where you just somehow know that the next words that come are not going to be good news.

For once it was Brian who was hesitating with the impending doom-laden silence. If it had been anything truly awful, he would have said it up front, so it was a second-tier disaster or less. I found myself almost eager to hear his story even as I felt the apprehension building.

"Brian, what is it?"

Brian's words came out in a rush. "So. If you talk to Marty, don't believe her. She's got all those hormones and everything, and it makes her exaggerate and you know how she's given to dramatics anyway—"

"What's Marty going to tell me? And what shouldn't I believe?" Marty's hormones weren't part of the issue; Sophia was nearly a year old and Marty'd pretty much evened out after the first few weeks. Dramatics, on the other hand, were another story.

"I'm perfectly fine. It's not nearly as bad as she says and you can ask Kam too, he'll tell you—"

"What happened, Brian? Tell me *right* now."

"My nose isn't even broken, and there wasn't *that* much blood."

"Holy crow, Brian! Will you tell me!"

"Okay, so you know how things haven't exactly gone to plan? Well, the last straw was *Titanic*. Marty wanted to watch it, and Kam had seen more of it than he liked already. He wasn't going to watch it again, no way was he going to sit through it again. He even hid it from Marty, said that he'd let someone at work borrow it, which was a crock because you know how he is about his media, right?"

"Never mind how Kam is about his 'media.' What *happened*?"

"Marty was really reaching a new state. She's been cooped up here for too long and she really did want to see her parents and her sisters and show off the baby and go into the city and maybe get a break from everything, right? So she's been moping and there's nothing that will get Kam broken down faster than watching his wife want something she can't have."

He made it sound like he kept me on a shorter, stricter leash and that this was a forgivable failing in his too-soft friend. "Ha! Go on."

"Finally, Kam decides that he's going to 'find' the copy of *Titanic* downstairs, like he left it in the car or something. But we're also going to see whether we can get the car out of the garage and try getting her out somewhere, anywhere, because the place was just getting too small for us, you know?"

Kamil and Mariam and their daughter Sophia live in a brownstone on Beacon Hill. It has four bedrooms, two parlors as well as a den, a dining room, and a kitchen as large as many studio apartments. There are four bathrooms and a basement that is still an evolving space. The roof has a garden with one of the most enviable views in Boston.

So, no, I didn't know about it getting too small.

Brian had been talking the whole time. "—and we go downstairs and we can't get out, but maybe we'll go for a walk later, and while Kam is digging out the DVD, I realize that he's got all his old gym stuff downstairs. A treadmill, some weights. Plenty of floor space, covered in mats. And a heavy bag."

I began to see where this was going. "Keep talking."

"So I took a couple of jabs at the bag. It felt pretty good, so that by the time Kam dug out the DVD—he'd hidden it in the wine cellar, behind the Austrian stuff, where Marty would never think to look—I'd got some rhythm going and a little footwork. So he saw me just as I was throwing hooks.

He was pretty surprised; he'd never seen me do that before."

"I can imagine." Brian's flirtation with exercise was a new phenomenon, and he'd started taking Krav Maga after I got into it, long after he and Kam had been roommates in graduate school. A surfer and skateboarder in his youth, more recently Brian hadn't much bestirred himself to physical exertion unless it involved the beach, or maybe some yard work. The occasional set of sixteen-ounce elbow bends, usually with imported beer.

"So he gives me some gloves and he pulls on some gloves and we were just going to go at it easy—"

I finished. "Except you boys got all wound up and competitive and then it started going a little harder, and then everyone's primitive male instincts came screaming to the surface and . . ."

"Well, yeah."

"Okay, *well yeah*, and then what happened?"

Another pause. "And . . . did you know that classically trained boxers don't really expect to be kicked?"

I closed my eyes. "Oh. My. God."

"I guess I kinda took Kam by surprise when I got him with a nice round kick to the ribs. Okay, actually I was getting a little heated and I forgot how good he'd been at university, and that boxing isn't the same as Krav. Jeez, was he steamed! I realized what I did and was about to apologize, and I dropped my guard just in time for the Shah express to come barreling through, final stop, my nose. Next thing I know, I'm lying on the floor, blood everywhere. It was *awesome*."

This is not the man I married, I thought. How do they get like this? They're a race of aliens. "Probably not the word I would have chosen. And your nose isn't broken?"

"Well, I felt it, and it's sore as hell but it doesn't feel broken, and we put some ice on it and the swelling's gone down. And Kam didn't think it was broken either."

"You know, I'd be more convinced if the initials after both your names were M and D rather than Ph and D."

But Brian knew himself to be on safer ground now. "Kam saw enough broken noses when he was boxing regularly in the bad old days. He knows one when he sees one. And I'd think I'd know if my nose was busted. It feels a lot better now, but it is still tender, and I swear I'll be smelling leather for the next month."

"And Marty . . . ?"

"Marty came downstairs just in time to see Kam pop me. You should have heard the wailing."

"Oh, sure, hon, but I'm sure it hurt like hell. It's okay if you cried, too, you know."

"Not me, *her*. She walked in just in time to see me kick him and him belt me back, but good. Man, I don't think he's lost anything of his punch since undergrad."

"Yeah, great, I'm glad for him. How's Marty doing now?"

"Actually, she's fine. Once she realized that we weren't really trying to kill each other, that it was just a little overexcitement, she got into it."

I took another deep breath. "You mean there was more?"

"Well, Kam wasn't going to let me get away without getting back on the horse. And showing him how to kick. And he's helping me get more power into my punches. So we ended up having a pretty good time. And Marty thought it was pretty interesting too, watching us work out, and so we haven't had to watch any more damned tearjerkers since then. Kam got some boxing on the pay-per-view, and we've all been getting an education."

"And?"

"And what?"

Again the nervous hesitation, so I knew I was on the right track. "And how is Kam doing?"

There was a kind of nervous giggle. "Oh, we're pretty sure I didn't break any ribs. But we put some red electrical tape on his side and on my nose, so if we get . . . overexcited again . . . it will be a little flag to calm it down. Or at least, not to hit those particular spots."

"You could lay off for a while." Reason was always an option, but not one I expected to be taken seriously.

"Yeah," he said, "but it's so cool that we're both doing this. Me and Kam, I mean. And it's fun."

"Okay, well just be careful, okay? And don't get any bad habits that Nolan will have to train out of you."

"Oh, no," Brian said quickly; he believed he was out of the woods now, as far as I was concerned. "Kam's been real careful to ask what Nolan does and how he does it. He gets all, you know, serious and professorial about this kind of thing, so I doubt I'll get into any trouble."

"And it would be nice to offer to clean up the blood off the floor when you're done."

"Yeah. But it was really neat, for a while there."

"You're both brutes and I get all warm and tingly thinking about you big he-men going at it like animals. So just take it easy, slugger, and save some of that energy for when I get home. And you can tell Kam that if he hurts you again, he'll have me to deal with."

"Thanks, pork chop! You're the greatest! Any man would be proud to have you emasculate him in front of his friends."

"You know what I mean. Now, be good."

We made our goodbyes and I turned around to see that Chris and Sue were there.

Sue suddenly became engrossed in her schedule. Chris was holding his head in his hand, massively hung over by all appearances. He was on the phone, checking in with home. Or at least I hoped he was, because I was starting to hear things that disturbed me.

"Whatever you do, make sure you clean out the tub before I get back. Last time I ended up picking chopped pickles out of my butt."

He met my glance before I could duck out, and I waved halfheartedly. "It's Nell, Em. Nell says hi."

"Hi, Nell."

"Okay, kiss the kids for me . . . all right, wash them first, then kiss them. I miss you all . . . no, not enough to come back. Love you, bye." He disconnected and turned to Sue. "Sorry, I had to take it. Nell's making sure I'm not having too much fun."

I looked at him; his eyes looked like roadmaps and his shirt was buttoned wrong. He saw my glance. "Last night was great. I'm not having too much fun now."

"Do I dare ask?" I said.

"About what?"

"Uh, pickles?"

"Oh, I asked what she had planned for tonight. After the kids are in bed, she's going to get a Monster Burger—extra cheese, extra onions, extra pickles—from the joint down the street, pour a glass of wine, and get into the tub and soak for an hour."

"Everyone's got their idea of paradise," Sue said.

Chris shrugged. "Yeah, well, that's fine, and I don't begrudge her anything, but steam doesn't help you keep a burger that big intact. It gets messy."

"As you've apparently learned," I said.

"Oh, yeah, with all the boats and ducks and shit the kids have in there, you don't notice the stray pickles until it's too late. Not as bad as sitting on a Lego, though. How's Brian?" he asked. "I'm assuming that was Brian."

"He's good. Got punched in the nose, bled all over the place."

"He's okay?"

"Strutting like a peacock."

"Good for him." Chris nodded approvingly.

"He's bleeding, and that's good?" Sue said, dropping all pretense of not listening.

"Oh, he's stopped bleeding," I assured her. "He was just messing around with a friend."

"Some friend!" She looked put out with Kam, and outraged with me for not being more indignant on Brian's behalf. "And you're all right with this?"

I shrugged. "I'm not psyched he got hit, but what are you going to do?"

"Teach him to duck," Chris suggested.

"Well, there's that."

Sue shook her head and told Chris she'd see him later.

"Sue seem out of it to you?" Chris said, watching her practically run across the lobby.

"Maybe it's still the fallout from yesterday," I said. Or maybe she was still freaked out with me, for whatever reason, I thought. I was going to have to corner her, and ask her, ASAP.

He glanced over at me. "I'm surprised you're okay with it. You aren't usually this laid-back."

I shrugged. "Hey, if Brian's fine with me in contact sports, I owe him the same thing. Just gotta pray his reflexes get faster, that's all."

But he knew I was dodging his question. "Actually, I meant with Sue so on edge with you, but the thing with Brian too."

"Where you off to?" I changed the subject and thumbed through the marked-up program. As always, I'd made many plans of where to be when, and then missed about half of what I wanted.

"I've got to get to the—hey, Kenny!" he greeted a guy I knew by sight, but not by site, if you will. "Emma, can you give me a minute—?"

I waved him off. "I'll let you get going. See you later."

Chris turned to speak animatedly with Kenny, and I moved off to consult my schedule. It was at that moment that I was targeted by the entirely too eager Mr. Widmark.

Standing on point, his face lit up in recognition, and waving enthusiastically, he practically loped toward me. Abandoning all pretense to cordiality, I did an abrupt about-face and slipped into the darkened ballroom closest to me.

I closed the door gently, and relying on instinct until my eyes could adapt, I hugged the wall and followed it around until I found an empty seat on the aisle. Actually, there were a lot of empty seats, and I didn't recognize anyone else around me. I slid down into my seat, hoping that even if Widmark had the lack of grace to follow me, he wouldn't struggle too hard to find me in the dark. I ducked down and buried my face in the schedule.

This was a session on farmsteads, something I ordinarily wouldn't have bothered with. Just too far off my radar and usually conflicted with the sessions I needed to see. Now I found myself prepared to be riveted by it.

When after a few minutes I wasn't presented with that smiling face and villainous breath, I began to relax and take in a bit of the paper.

There was one thing, however, that gave me a quick jab in the memory, when the reader was talking about work done in northern New York State by an amateur, Josiah Miller, in the nineteenth century. A recently discovered copy of Miller's work was shedding new light on the material in the area. I usually have a good brain for this sort of thing—references and the like—and kept thinking about it. I got nothing, so then I tried the trick of changing contexts. If you meet someone on the street whose face you remember knowing but whose name isn't coming, you try envisioning them behind a counter or in running clothes, to see if you know them from the lunch place or from the gym or something like that. It usually works pretty well. With references, it's a little different. You try and remember if it was a paper you read—and if so, was it in the library, online, or at home? What color was the cover, what was the font?—or was it something that someone was asking or telling you about? Etcetera.

It vexed me so much that I dropped the slender thread of concentration I had reserved for the paper and devoted it to chasing it down in my mind. I had it narrowed down to something I knew from the distant past of undergraduate rather than graduate school or my present work and eventually gave up, half thinking about the paper as it wandered on and on and on and on . . .

I felt my head nod again, but snapped it back up as soon as I realized I was falling asleep. For about thirty seconds, I was alert again, determined not to drift off, but then the conversation that was being whispered somewhere behind me was more than enough to keep me awake.

"—and typical of him, he never bothered showing. I mean, if he wasn't going to bother, he should have called and let me know, right?"

"He wasn't usually like that about private meetings, he was always happier with them. It's the more public stuff he was shy of."

They—two men—were talking about Garrison. I tried to ease myself into a more comfortable position, the better to hear, without drawing attention to myself. I drew out a notebook and began to doodle.

"Shy? Him?"

"Pathologically. Poor guy, he was really troubled by it—"

Maybe they weren't talking about Garrison after all; shyness never seemed to be one of his many personal shortcomings . . .

"—I guess I had better luck. He showed up right on time to meet me."

"What time was that?"

"About ten, in the hospitality suite. What time was yours?"

"Close to midnight. Jules said he didn't mind, as he didn't sleep much anymore."

Jules? Right, Julius Garrison. I kept thinking of him as

being an entity defined by his last name only. So they were talking about him.

"Huh. Figures. Maybe he did fall asleep."

Now there was hesitation. "Possibly."

"You're not going to tell me what happened, are you?"

"I'm just trying to be discreet. You understand."

"Maybe. I guess I would too, in *your* position. Fortunately, I'm not that hard up."

"It's not as bad as people make out" came the curt reply. The voice was familiar, but the strain in it was disguising it from me still.

A few people angrily shushed them. I wished they hadn't because I wanted to hear more of the two men's conversation.

Then there was a creak of chair, and someone struggling to get out in a hurry and more protesting shhh's. I turned around to see who it was, but when I saw Widmark's shiny suit at the side of the room, I snapped my head around forward again and lost my man.

I waited until the end of the paper and then eased my way out of my seat. Just as I turned around, I realized I was facing Widmark, who was also leaving. Dang.

"Hi, I was wondering whether you had a moment now?"

I hated lying to him, but I couldn't face his questions just now. "I really don't. What if we decide that we'll chat at the reception before the business meeting?"

"Uh, great. If you're really in a rush now—?"

"I really am." I craned my neck around, but my quarry, the second whisperer, had gotten away already. "I'll catch you later."

Even though I joined the leaving throng as quickly as I could, I lost whoever it was who might have been sitting behind me in the shuffle out the door. I only felt marginally sorry for the next person presenting; I consoled myself that there was an equally steady stream of folks fighting their way into the room as we were leaving.

I ran into Duncan, Jay, and Scott in the hallway.

"Didn't expect to see you in that session, Emma," Duncan said. "What was the draw in there?"

I shook my head and looked down the hall as I answered. "Nothing in particular. Why do you ask?"

His voice sharpened, causing me to face him. "What are you being so bitchy about?"

At that point, Jay and Scott exchanged uncomfortable looks, excused themselves hastily, and moved off to the side.

"Me, bitchy?" I hadn't been really, not this time, so there was something else on his mind.

"Or is it that you resent that I spoke up on your behalf with Mark Church last night?"

There it was, that little half-smile that couldn't be completely smothered by his serious expression. It always happened, when he was probing someone's Achilles' heel.

I crossed my arms over my chest. "Perhaps I missed exactly what you think it was you were doing for me."

"I guess I think that putting in a good word for you with the cops is significant, like I might have been saving you some trouble."

That was the word, right there. "Saving. You think you were saving me from them. Just what is it that you think I was doing that meant I needed saving from? I was talking to the cops, but I don't have anything to hide, so why should I need saving?" Especially by you.

He pressed his lips together, the way that he always did when he was digging in, but didn't want to look as though he'd been put out by anything. He looked me straight in the eye, and let the corner of his mouth turn up ever so slightly. "Emma, everyone's got something to hide, haven't they?"

I flinched, but recovered quickly. It was another old trick, I reminded myself. "Yeah, well. It is a truism, but it doesn't mean that whatever one wants hidden is illegal or anything else." And trust you to pick up on that small bit of universal human frailty and exploit it.

He saw that he'd struck close to the bull's eye, that time. "You're right, but to tell the truth, Emma, I think you've got more going on with you right now than you're willing to admit."

I felt my face fix, the way it had a long time ago when I'd been at Penitence Point and had a gun pointed at me: don't give him anything to react to, don't rise to the bait, wait your time. And suddenly it occurred to me that this was just like what Nolan was teaching me about self-defense and game faces and watching your opponent's moves. Duncan had mastered the art of getting in close to his opponent to make the most of his own power while keeping them off balance, years before I knew such a thing could be applied in purely social situations. I relaxed, let him bring it to me, let him think he still had it over me.

"You're right, Duncan." I shrugged a little and nodded. I realized how tight my shoulders were. He wasn't worth that, he wasn't worth my anger, not anymore. I took a deep breath and tried to make my face relax; I was rewarded by seeing him narrow his eyes as he did when he was wary or disconcerted. "You're right."

If you're going to make a move, you have to be willing to back it up, so I went out on a limb and tried to make human conversation. "I hadn't told you that I was sorry to hear about Garrison," I said. Mostly because it was another one of those polite, humanizing fictions. "I know he meant a lot to you."

"You were never his biggest fan," Duncan said uncertainly after a moment. "So thanks."

We both nodded. A silence ballooned between us and I realized that part of not giving in to my baser instincts and being snappish or storming off meant that I'd again be faced with instances just like this one, the same way they turn up in ordinary conversation.

Damn.

"You know," he said, rushing in as though he'd read my mind, "I didn't mean anything back there. With Mark," he said, and I thought he seemed a little too eager about explaining—what happened to his composure? Or is he just reiterating something because it's untrue? "I honestly thought I was helping, that it wouldn't hurt to have a little, uh, you know, backup or support or a kind word in the right ear, or whatever."

"I get that now, I was just a little flustered back there," I said. That's okay: I know how much you like getting those words into those ears, how much both parties appreciate it and think well of you later. "You knew him growing up?"

"Yeah, since grade school. Really nice guy, does a good job. We get together every once in a while, when I'm visiting Mom. Usually hometown friendships don't make it through college."

I nodded again. This was better, seemed more neutral. And it didn't actually hurt me, this gesture, and I might even discover that he had no other ulterior motive in being nice to me, much as I doubted it. Better this way, I decided; I shake it off, he keeps wondering what's up. I groped about for something to keep this going, just another moment or two, to seal the deal of me being the bigger person.

"Actually, that reminds me of something. I heard a reference to Josiah Miller, and something about it is familiar. I just can't place it." I rifled through my bag to retrieve my schedule and find out where I was supposed to be heading next. "It's nothing too recent, and I figure it was something I ran across back in undergraduate. Does it ring any bells for you?"

I looked up, and saw that Duncan had gone positively ashen under his winter tan. "What do you mean?"

"I don't mean anything. I'm just asking whether a nineteenth-century amateur named Josiah Miller means anything to you." A little temper resurfaced now that things were suddenly turning weird.

"Okay." His face was still whiter than white, but he was angry now, like I'd never really seen before; he was always too slick for that. "Okay, what is it you want?"

"Duncan. It was a simple question." I felt my hackles raising in response, all pretense at politeness gone.

"Well. At least we know where we really stand," he said at last. Jay and Scott hovered on the periphery of our discussion. "We'll talk about this later."

He joined the other two, and they stood together in a tight little knot.

That's what you get for trying to be adult and letting bygones be bygones, said the snarky little part of me that is usually against these things. Sometimes those immature parts of us aren't entirely wrong. Sometimes they're there for a good, self-defensive reason.

"Do you have a minute?"

I turned around, exasperated, wishing Widmark would just go away. But to my surprise, it was Church. "Just wanted to see how you were doing this morning. No more notes, no noises in the night, or anything?"

I took a deep breath, trying to regain my composure after my run-in with Duncan. The guys had moved off down the hallway. "No, nothing strange."

"Good to hear," he said. "Just wanted to let you know that I'm keeping an eye on you, that's all."

And although his smile was as beguiling as ever, it really sounded like he was less concerned for me than suspicious.

Chapter 9

CHURCH LEFT AS QUICKLY AS HE'D APPEARED, AND I decided that if I hustled, I could actually see some of the session I'd originally planned to see. Discussions of identifying early earthenware were soothing, and soon I was lost in the discussion of paste, inclusions, glazes, and surface decorations, so much of which you can see with the naked eye. And there's something about the curve of whole pots that is incredibly sexy. Finding fragments of dull red earthenware—essentially the same material as a plain flowerpot—is exciting because not only can you imagine what vessel it was—and once you know the shape, you know the vessel, and from there you can get into use, trade, the whole world from a potsherd—but sometimes there are marks on the pottery that have nothing to do with its manufacture. Fingerprints are wonderful, and while there have been some attempts to link prints with a particular potter, I'm happy just to make the connection that these were manufactured by hand, that a person was responsible for this coming into being. Paw prints, too, are common enough, and it is so easy to imagine a dog running across a floor where a milk pan, fresh off the wheel, had been set for a moment. Blades of grass in the bottom of a vessel, burned away by the kiln, also reveal a pause in the potter's day, the space between finishing work and setting it to dry to leather hardness before its introduction into the kiln. All of these things remind me of the people involved, maybe not named, but individuals who lived in the past. It's too easy to talk about "back then" and lump everyone all together. It's more fun to think of someone yelling at some dumb mutt causing chaos outside of the shed where the wheel sits, chickens squawking and hustling out of the way, feathers ruffled, than it is to think of a faceless entity responsible for a kiln site designated with numbers and letters.

So the pottery session was exactly what the doctor ordered, and two hours later, nerves calmed and spirit refreshed, I decided to reward myself with a trip to the book room. I'd actually remembered to make a shopping list and bring it with me this time, and though I seldom needed assistance in buying books, this expedited things nicely. My credit card got whipped through so many readers so fast that I could smell scorched plastic, and in no time at all I was basking in the afterglow, a cross between the warm, secure feeling of having met my legitimate professional needs and the triumph a hunter must feel coming back with the kill.

After I spoke with the publisher's rep from the press that was handling my artifact book, I was lingering over a gorgeously illustrated volume of late medieval glassware from Venice that I didn't really need. Someday, I argued with myself, I might be working on a site that was high enough status and early enough to have such a thing and anyway, wouldn't it be good to brush up on glass-fabricating techniques?

A stray thought occurred to me. I put the yummy volume down, much to the chagrin of the bookseller, who'd been hoping not to have to carry the heavy thing home with him, and went over to the table that had been the scene of the other thefts.

There was still a display there, and it had been obviously rearranged to accommodate the missing pieces. What was left of the display, which had been a mockup of an underwater site, was some broken pottery and the sand and aquatic weeds that had been arranged to resemble an underwater site.

"Too bad you didn't see it before," the guy behind the table said to me. "It was really gorgeous."

I gestured toward the case. "Are you in charge of this table?"

"No, I'm just watching it while the other dealer takes a break. It's been nutty here."

"Yeah?"

"People buying Garrison's books like crazy, even more than before he died. And plus, everyone's all, I don't know, bleh, because the cops won't tell them anything about what's going on. Shots fired, dead keynote speakers . . . people want books to comfort them." He rubbed his hands together. "You gotta love it."

I nodded. "What was it like before? The display, I mean."

"Nice, real nice. It had a couple of replica pots—you know, based on the fragments that were found—and some nice gold coins and a gold chain. I guess it was meant to be a shipwreck that was found off the Carolinas, but I don't know for sure. Everything was fake, of course, except for a few of the actual sherds themselves, but it's a shame that someone had to go and ruin all the guy's hard work, you know?"

"Yeah. When'd it happen?"

"At night, Wednesday night, before everything got started. The cops found the door was forced open, but nothing else was taken. We're not stupid enough to leave anything valuable in here, that's the funny thing. Someone went to a lot of trouble for about ten bucks worth of costume jewelry and some pots they could have found at any tourist shop."

"Pity. Thanks," I said, turning to leave.

"Hey, you don't want to check out my table?" He held his hands out invitingly. "Got some great stuff here . . ."

I looked over at the table full of display models of metal detectors and catalogues, and shook my head.

"Come on," he cajoled. "There are plenty of legitimate archaeologists who use these, to good effect."

I kept shaking my head. "No, thanks. I know, but it's kind of a personal thing with me. Those things give me the willies. Take it easy."

I left the dealer with a puzzled look on his face, and went out to the lobby to find my lunch.

After I bought my boxed lunch, I noticed a backlit, built-in display case with a collection of blue-and-white ceramics in the lobby. I slowed down to check it out. Bait for historical archaeologists. There were five shelves of plates, saucers, cups, and service ware, like platters and a teapot; a card said that it had belonged to one of the families who'd owned the tavern. I glanced at it for a moment, and thought about how an archaeologist moves from a tiny sherd of one cup, something that may be part of an entire set, to thinking about how a person incorporated that item into everyday rituals, fraught with meaning. There was more to drinking tea than satisfying thirst, there were political and social and economic realities at play, and we had to get at all that culture from a collection of broken sherds. After another moment, I frowned briefly, and then turned when I heard my name.

"Emma, over here!" Chris was calling me. He, Lissa, Lissa's friend Gennette Welles, Sue, Carla, and Jay had snagged chairs around an ottoman near a large planter and were eating their lunches. "Jay's got a question for you."

"Shoot." I squeezed in between Chris and Lissa.

"I just saw you looking at the collection over there," Jay said. "What'd you notice about it?"

"Uh, not much. Why?"

"Just humor me. What did you see?"

"Well, most of it was pretty ordinary blue-and-white whiteware, Staffordshire, most was a little earlier than mid-nineteenth-century. There was one piece of Chinese export porcelain in there, a cup, which might have been a present or something—it was a lot nicer, higher style than the rest of it and the pattern was different, of course. The Staffordshire material was imitating the Asian export porcelain patterns."

"Okay, what else?"

I looked at Jay. "Why don't you tell me what you're looking for, and maybe that would help."

"We've got a little derby going, seeing how many observations each of our colleagues made walking by there," he explained.

"Fine, whatever. What else? Um, there was an odd number of cups to saucers, and there were fewer of them than plates. There was one piece where the pattern was messed up—the piece of inked paper that was set down onto the un-fired clay must have wrinkled. There was an odd-sized plate in there, looks like a later addition to the collection, or it might have been one left over from a complete set of smaller plates."

"Nothing else?" Jay was disappointed. "Duncan Thayer got one more."

I couldn't tell whether that was just a simple statement of fact or a goad. "One of the cups had a repaired handle."

"Duncan didn't get that," Jay said, "but he did notice that one of the plates was a different pattern."

"Right, most of them were a pastoral scene—cows, pastures, shepherdesses, whathaveyou—and there was one of a Gothic architecture scene. Later in period. I said there was a later one."

"But you only mentioned the pattern after I mentioned that Duncan saw it," Jay said, shaking his head. He turned to Chris. "Sorry, man. Pay up."

"Hang on a second," Chris said, smiling. "Emma, why didn't you mention the pattern?"

"Because that style of ware, well, it belonged to a middle-class family, right? If a piece was broken or lost, they just replaced it. In those days, it didn't matter that it was a different pattern, it mattered that it was blue."

"See, Jay? *You* pay up. She saw the difference and added one factoid to the pile."

"Man." Jay looked like he was about to protest, caught my eye, and reached for his wallet. "I was set up. It just ain't fair."

I stuck out my tongue at him. Serves him right for betting on . . . against me.

"It would be more fair if you started betting on the sure things, and left the flashy long-shots alone," Chris said as he pocketed his money. "It's like taking candy from a baby." He smiled at me. "I believe I owe you a drink, m'dear."

"I'll take you up on that later. I just want my lunch now."

It was strange to see so many of my friends together again, I thought, as I dug into my boxed lunch. Usually we scattered to the four corners of any conference after the first night.

"Before you got here, we were talking about the latest 'live like the old days' reality television," Lissa said. She bit into her sandwich with gusto.

It was then that I understood why they were all still together. Taking bets and eating and talking about television kept you from thinking about death and gunshots. It had to do with the same reasons that conversations were muted in the hallways, and other people were moving around in small herds too. Everyone was looking for comfort, for answers, and if they couldn't get them, then they'd make do with physical closeness.

"What I can't get is that people think that they're actually going to live like people in the seventeenth century," Carla said. "Like they're suddenly going to be possessed of the historical spirit and fall into 'thee's' and 'thou's' and not notice any difference. No cards either, Jay. No basketball, no Vegas. Wouldn't that be a pisser?"

"They don't think, that's the problem." Jay ignored Carla. "They just want to be on television."

"Whatever for?" I asked. "I can't imagine anything less appealing."

"People think they're famous if they're on television."

"Um, yum, erm!" Lissa was waving her hand, chewing furiously.

"Lissa, calm the hell down," Gennette said. She was a willowy dark-skinned woman with close-cropped hair and big brown eyes. "You're going to choke, and then I'll laugh."

Lissa finally swallowed. "That will be the day! You're too darn serious as it is. I was going to say those guys on TV think they'll find a simpler life!"

Gennette made a face. "Give me a break. I mean, even without the bland diet, the back-breaking work, the religious restrictions—"

"They're surprised at having to go to the bathroom outside, or in a bucket," Chris said, shaking his head. "Talk about forgetting the essentials!"

"Not everyone is into inflicting the past on themselves like you and Nell are," Carla said. "Reenacting? I don't get it."

"I know, and Nell knows, and you all know, that we're not actually living eighteenth-century military life, any more than those guys on television," Chris said. "Dental care, diet, disease—our immune systems probably couldn't handle a fraction of the parasites that they did two hundred years ago."

"Excuse me! Eating, here," Carla said disgustedly.

I looked at my shrimp salad sandwich doubtfully. The bitten ends of the little shrimp were just too suggestive. Ah well, it was just words. I took another big bite. Not bad, for bugs.

"You know what I mean," Chris said. "The physical differences aside, let's not forget the fact that culturally speaking, we're from different worlds. Same language, maybe, but different outlooks altogether."

"Two cultures separated by a common language," Sue said.

"Look at the differences between Americans and Canadians," Carla said.

"Well, Canadians are just funny Americans," Jay added. Carla kicked at his ankle; he dodged her foot but sloshed his drink all over his lap.

"You know, you're right," she said. "That was pretty funny."

"Nell and I don't imagine that we're becoming people from the seventeen sixties," Chris continued doggedly. "But we are learning about some of the things that make us different, learning how people would have had to think. Gives some insight into what we find in the field."

"I think those shows are much better as laboratory cases of how twenty-first-century people adapt to adverse conditions," I said. "But I still don't get the desire to be on television."

"Why not?" Lissa said.

"For a start, I don't like the idea of losing my privacy like that. As much as I really don't want to see other people having hissy-fits on television, I don't want my own aired either."

"The Puritans would have asked you what you have to hide, if you want that much privacy," Lissa said.

"Sure. If you're not doing something you shouldn't, there's no reason to want to be alone. Fortunately, I live in a time where people are aware that rats, stressed out and overcrowded, will go bonky and eat their young or each other. So I'll take my locked doors and drawn curtains and no neighbors, thanks all the same."

"Hey, don't knock the Puritans. They slept a dozen to a bed, so they weren't all bad," Lissa said. "But seriously, Emma, the Puritans were your people. So what have you got to hide behind all those curtains?" There was an edge to the way she spoke, like she was trying to drum up anything that would be a distraction. "And why do you scorn the light of the media?"

I was growing annoyed with her. "They weren't my people, Lissa. And I haven't got anything to hide."

"Oh, come on," she persisted. "Everyone does."

"Where you off to next, Emma?" Jay interrupted. He seemed as frustrated with Lissa's persistence as I.

"Session on immigration," I said, grateful for the cover he provided me. "One of my students is presenting."

"Cool, I'll go with you."

"Me too," said Scott. "But I got to run to my room first. You guys come with me."

"Fine, as long as I can use your bathroom," I said.

We went up to Scott's room on the fourth floor. He was about halfway down the hallway, and when we went in, I was hit with a strong scent of locker room. And it wasn't a locker room that had been cleaned any time recently.

"Jeez, Scott!" I said. "This place reeks!"

He looked around. "It's not that bad."

"Trust me." I spotted the problem. "You've got underwear on the radiator?"

He looked sheepish. "I didn't think they'd dry fast enough, hanging in the bathroom."

I realized that he said that he still had no luggage with

him. Based on the implications of this, I decided that the conversation needed to stop right here.

Jay, however, wasn't so discreet. "So you're freeballing today?"

"Jay!" Scott turned scarlet, and whipped around to look at me. I shrugged; I'd heard of men's body parts *and* what happened when all the laundry was in the hamper. "What do you want, man? It was either go commando while these things dry or get a case of the itch. It's not like you never got into a jam and—"

That was too much reality for me. "Excuse me, I need to be out of here," I said, heading for the bathroom. "Scott, you could at least get them off the radiator."

"It's not the shorts, Em. It's the rest of my clothes smelling up the place while I'm in bed. The heat doesn't help, and my deodorant was in my suitcase."

I shut the door as Jay informed Scott that he should raid the sundries shop in the lobby. I tried not to listen as Scott said he didn't want to spend the extra money when his stuff might show up at any moment, and when did Jay, borrowing Chris's money, last I saw, suddenly become so willing to spend money? I sighed, finished up quickly, and returned to the room before their tempers could fray any further.

With as little stuff as Scott had of his own things, the place was a tip. Housekeeping hadn't been in yet—always a hazard with the irregular schedule of a conference—and there were three trays with leftovers adding to the smell.

"What, did you have a party after the cops were done with you all?" Jay asked, looking around with interest. Then his expression changed to hurt. "You didn't get another game going and not invite me, did you?"

"No, course not. A couple of us ordered snacks last night. I guess we weren't as hungry as we thought," he answered, trying in vain to cover up a half-eaten burger that was not aging well in the warm room.

"You know, you can put this stuff outside, and they'll come and get it," I said.

"I meant to, but I got out of bed because of Garrison and had no time."

"Who'd you have up here, anyway?" Jay asked, interestedly. "We coulda got a game going."

"Just some guys," Scott said, coloring. "I gotta go to the head."

Jay and I looked for places to sit and wait, when Scott yelled, "I'm going to be in here for a while."

"For Christ's sake," Jay muttered. He hollered to Scott, "I'm going to run down the hall to my room. I'll be back in a minute."

He left, and I tried not to think about what kind of orgy had been going on here. A couple of guys, let off the leash, come back after partying hard. Order some room service, are too drunk to eat, all the while, Scott's lingerie was drying into a husk on the radiator. But Scott hadn't admitted who was up here . . . and one of the glasses had lipstick on it.

The phone rang. "You want me to get it?" I shouted.

"Yeah, would you?"

"Scott Tomberg's room," I said.

"Who the hell is this?" said an irate female voice.

"This is Emma Fielding. Scott can't come to the phone now."

She calmed down right away. "Hey, Em, it's Cathy."

I knew Scott's wife from way back. "Hey, Cath. Scott's going to be a minute. You want to call back?"

"No, I can hang on. How's it going?"

"Uh . . . everyone's a little stir crazy. What with the weather and all."

"I meant, since they found out about Garrison."

"Okay, I guess. People are pretty sad, which is kind of a surprise to me."

Cathy laughed, and it was an ugly sound. "Surprise to me

too. Maybe they're just sorry that they didn't get to him first."

I shrugged, and then realized that she couldn't see me. "I thought I was in the minority, as far as the disliking Garrison camp is going."

"Oh, hell, everyone gets ennobled when they're dead, didn't you know that? Everyone forgets all the bad stuff and gets all sentimental and all that crap. It's just like listening to a presidential funeral. Remember Nixon? You'd have thought Watergate never happened. I'm just glad for Scott's sake that the old bastard's dead."

But Scott had seemed as distressed as anyone by Garrison's death. "I got the impression that Scott had put a lot of his experiences with Garrison behind him. He's never spoken a word against him."

"That's men for you. Trying to make like it never happened, like it wasn't as bad as it was. Typical. Man, I was just dating him at the time, but he and that other guy he's friends with—actually, you might know Duncan Thayer— they used to talk up some serious violence. Bad craziness, like what you could do to someone with woodworking tools." She laughed. "It was like a game, with them, almost. Killing Garrison inventively was like a sport. Get him good and toasted sometime, and ask him about Plan B, the one with the c-clamps and the auger."

"Uh, maybe I'll give that a miss." I heard water running in the bathroom. "Okay, I think he's coming now. Scott, phone!"

He took the handset. "Hey, hon. Yeah, I was in the can. I'm running late, can I call you later? Greatloveyoubye." He turned to me. "Let's go get Jay and get this show on the road."

We walked down the hall, and Scott began to bang on the door to room four-twelve. "Open up, Jay. Let's get moving."

Jay opened the door, looking annoyed as he finished a

phone call: "Yeah, Salt Lake, by sixteen. Gotta go, man." He glared at Scott. "Like I'm the one who's been holding us up?"

"What can I say? You gotta go, you gotta go." Suddenly, Scott pushed his way into the room. "Hey, you got that paper you promised me? Can I get it now, while we're both sober and thinking of it?"

"We're running behind," Jay said.

"Then stop arguing and get moving, asshole."

"Hang on." Jay sorted through a bunch of papers, colorful flyers from the book room advertising books that were available at a discount, and the usual collection of coupons for local establishments that we couldn't visit until the snow had been plowed away.

Jay's room was better than Scott's, but only by degree. It wasn't underwear, but pants and socks on the radiator, and a single tray was on the desk with the papers. A few more personal items—after all, Jay had his suitcase—but most of these were stashed away. One drawer was closed on a pair of underpants, tidy-whiteys. What one did learn from visiting one's friends' rooms, I thought. Mostly more than I wanted to know.

"I saw you hit the casinos in Connecticut on your way up," Scott said, jerking his chin toward a couple of plastic bags with exuberant logos sitting under the desk.

"Oh, sure," I said before Jay could answer. "There's a really impressive museum and research center focusing on Native American culture associated with one of them. I stopped by myself, last time I visited my mother. It's worth the trip."

Scott laughed at me. "Yeah, that's why *Jay* stopped at the casino, Em. For the museum."

"Here." Jay thrust a stapled sheaf of paper into Scott's hand. "Now let's get going, can we?"

The session we walked into was on migration and the effect it might have on the archaeological record. Meg was tackling it in the broadest sense, examining the politics of the period in which the Chandlers had moved to Massachusetts and comparing it with the situation in Matthew Chandler's hometown of Woodbroke, near Norwich. She was attempting to build a correlation between a political fracas there, the Chandlers' hasty marriage and departure, and what appeared to be a slight dip in their fortunes, based on the artifacts from the earliest strata of their house site in Stone Harbor, Massachusetts.

I was interested to see what Meg was going to do with this paper, as I knew she was nervous about it. Meg was developing her professional persona. She'd presented papers before, but in much less formal circumstances, and while there was no other limit I knew to Meg's confidence and aggression, public speaking was the one thing I knew she was not comfortable with. That would come with time, I thought. Meg had the ability to overcome many things, including herself.

She'd dressed up for this, I was surprised to see; usually there was little difference between Meg in the field and Meg in class and Meg at a prom, for all I knew. But instead of baggy army surplus fatigues, a T-shirt, and boots, she was wearing wool dress pants, a silk shirt, and shoes: flat-heeled lace-ups, to be sure, but shoes nonetheless. It made me wonder what her wedding gown—if any—and the whole ceremony would look like.

Meg was all business from the get-go: curt nod of thanks to the moderator, a brief "lights, please," and then she was off.

She was discussing an aspect of the Chandler house excavation that had particularly interested her, Justice Matthew Chandler's reasons for leaving England to come to Massachusetts in the 1720s, a drastic decision for anyone, much less for someone with the means and family connections that he would have had. Meg, as far as I knew, had been corresponding with an archive in England, and they had sent her a copy of a letter that seemed to confirm her hypothesis:

Matthew Chandler had left England because of county political controversies.

I never bought into this theory for several reasons. The first was that, having studied his wife Margaret's journal, I never saw any indication that this was the case. She was an extraordinarily canny woman, and my brief introduction to her world, two hundred years and more after her death, led me to believe that she would have written something about this. The second was my sense that Margaret wrote about her husband with respect and growing affection. While she wasn't happy with being forced to live in the Massachusetts wilderness—indeed, she'd come within a hair's breadth of having been executed for murder—she never blamed Matthew for her situation. My impression was simply that there would have been more blame, or at least some reference to their plight, had they been forced to flee their home for the reasons that Meg was suggesting. Another was that I could find no indication that Matthew had been a part of the tempest in the local teapot. Not solidly conclusive reasons, just instinct.

Meg gave the overview of our two seasons in the field, with some of the gorgeous shots of the brick house that overlooked Stone Harbor itself. She included a couple of good shots of the crew working, and one of them goofing off, which was nice, and then some of the tastier artifacts we'd recovered. She loitered over the chatelaine that we'd found season one, a particular prize of mine because my sister Bucky had found it. And then she wound up her introduction with a description of the politics she believed caused the Chandlers to relocate.

"What I had originally decided was that it had become socially and economically prudent for Matthew Chandler both to marry into the Chase fortune—Margaret's father was a successful merchant who married into a minor branch of nobility—and to leave London quickly thereafter, as the news of the corruption scandal from Woodbroke was just reaching Norwich and London at that point. It turns out I was wrong."

I blinked; I hadn't heard this part.

She took a deep breath. "I received an email just three days ago, from Professor Merton-Twigg, whose work focuses on the documentary history of Norwich in the early modern period. It turns out, however, that although the name Chandler is prominently mentioned in the city records of the time, it is not our Chandlers. I don't even know if they are related, but it certainly wasn't Matthew who was involved. The reason we can confirm this is twofold: The first is that a diarist of the time mentions that Matthew was already in London, having quit Woodbroke for Oxford some years before. The second was that Professor Merton-Twigg realized that the transcription of the document I hoped would prove my point was incomplete. A footnote that had been described as 'illegible' was in fact a remark that Matthew had served with good faith his family and their interests at Woodbroke, and that he never would have let this happen."

Meg took another deep breath and smiled ruefully. "There goes chapter three of my dissertation."

There was a shocked pause, some "awws," and some laughter. I sucked my teeth, knowing what a blow it was to Meg.

She finished up smartly enough, discussing where she could go from here, what else remained to be done, and what were the other options for her research.

I ducked out of that session, went to another couple papers on osteology, and then snuck back in for the wrap-up, a rather dreary report on numbers of immigrants to a small town outside of Hartford during the late nineteenth century. After the question period, Meg was collecting her slide tray—she was still unable to afford more impressive computer hardware and display software—and I sidled up behind her. The lights were up, showing the dull gold wallpaper to no good advantage.

"That's a pain, huh?" I said.

"What are you going to do?" She screwed up her face. "The email came a couple of days ago, and a copy of the letter came right as I was leaving for here. It just nailed down the lid on the coffin."

"And is it really a whole chapter in your dissertation?"

She shrugged. "It would have been fun and interesting, but it's really just a smallish part. I can revise it easily enough, make what I've got part of the family history, then get to the site itself. No biggie."

"I have to say, you're taking this remarkably well. I know you thought you had a hot lead there, that it would have been a nice, juicy scandal to work with. But you might be able to work it into an essay on historiography, or something."

Meg frowned, darting a sideways glance at me, as she worked her carousel box into her backpack. "Well, what am I supposed to do? I'm not about to sit down and cry just because history didn't go the way I wanted. It would be nice to shape the past anyway I want, but I'm not going to screw with the data we do have to suit my own prurient interests."

Neal came up then. "So, how'd it go?"

"Good. Got it over with. Onward and upward. Or downward, as the case may be."

"I'm taking it worse than she is," I added. "Bummer."

"Oh, well, there was some serious pissing and moaning at home, and on the ride up here, and for a while as she was rewriting," Neal offered.

"Thanks, chum," Meg said to her fiancé. "Way to get my back."

"Oh, come on." Neal squished her in a big overblown hug, guaranteed to wrinkle her shirt and rumple her serious demeanor. Meg was smiling by the time she wriggled free. "You're fine now. Emma understands."

"Do I ever," I said.

"Sympathy just makes it worse," Meg said. "Direction and goading, that's what I need."

"Okay, how about this?" I said. "You get me your revised outline in two weeks."

"Yeah, that's more like it," she said, slinging her backpack over her shoulder. It rutched up her shirt so that her bra showed through straining fabric. A little more adventurous than I would have expected. Meg might have mastered lingerie, but she still hadn't come to grips with what wearing dress clothes—however casual—might require.

Then she turned and saw my face. "You're serious."

"Like a lightning strike. You're ready for it. You said you wanted direction."

"Well." She looked surprised by this, but undaunted. "Shit. Okay."

"You can always tell the Caldwell crowd," a voice said from behind us. "It's like pets and their owners. The students and professors start to look alike."

We turned around. "Oh? Hey, Scott."

"Short hair, neatly dressed but not too formal—no suits here—" .

"And just last year my hair was long and I was wearing suits," I retorted. "What do you make of that?"

"That's right, and didn't I see you decked out in pearl earrings and stilettos last year?" he asked Neal.

Neal gave Scott a questioning look. "Emma, I've got to run. Excuse me."

He and Meg took off, and I turned to Scott, whose humor had utterly vanished.

"What's up? News about Garrison? People are really wigging out about the cops here. But I guess they have to treat the investigation as a potential homicide because Garrison's death was sudden and suspicious and possibly violent."

Scott shook his head, surprised that I should have these

facts at my fingertips. "Uh, no. Emma, I need to talk to you about what you said to Duncan earlier."

My shoulders slumped. "What *did* I say to Duncan? I try to say as little as possible to him."

"But what you do say is *choice*. What is it you're after?"

His words were cold, like nothing I'd ever heard from him, and I looked at him in shock.

"I have *no* idea of what you are talking about."

"Let's cut the shit, shall we? You were asking about Josiah Miller. Why's that?"

"Because I heard it in a paper and it rang a bell with me, and for some reason I thought it was something that he might remember." I tried not to think of how scary Scott suddenly seemed to me, as big and angry as he was.

"I don't like you playing Dunk for a fool." He was disgusted now. "If you've got something to say to him, you should just get it out in the open. I thought better of you, Emma."

Now I was really pissed. "Look, for the hundredth time, I have no idea of what you're talking about. And if Duncan is worried that I'm saying something to him—about what, I can't for the life of me guess—then you tell *him* to get *his* cowardly and overimaginative ass out here and ask *me* in person. I don't do threats and hints. Got it?"

I didn't wait to hear what he had to say to that, I didn't care. I was so mad, I could have hit him. He was my friend, and now, for some reason, he could barely look at me. And apparently I had Duncan Thayer to thank for it.

Chapter 10

As I stormed off away from the ballrooms, I saw Petra sitting with some of the older folks, people who'd been doing historical archaeology before there was such a thing. I hadn't been over to see them yet, but I knew I would have to eventually. I usually had to juggle finding as many of them together as possible, avoiding Garrison, and my own schedule. Plus, there was a whole pile of inert reluctance that I had to overcome in order to do it, and it weighed on me like an anchor. Overcoming yourself in order to do the right thing seems doubly hard.

"Evening, folks," I said to the table in general.

"Evening, Emma."

"How are you, Emma?"

"Well, now, Dr. Fielding."

Rob Wilson was sitting over there with them, and I thought that might make it easier. "Hey, Emma!"

"Hey, Rob." He got up and I gave him a kiss on the cheek. "Missed you at the card game."

"Sorry, I got hung up. You know how it is."

"Sure."

A good friend to me years ago, and once a more active member of our set, Rob had only ever played two or three years with us. Ever since then, he "got hung up." It was a yearly exchange on both our parts, and it saddened me.

"Don't I get a kiss?" Roche said.

Exactly what I'd been hoping to avoid, especially after his egregious sucking-up to Garrison during the plenary session. "Didn't know you'd want one," I said, smiling as best I could. I leaned over and bussed him on the cheek and felt a rasp of stiff whiskers against my face. Thomas had missed a couple of places.

"Known her all these years and I still have to ask for a kiss," he groused to the rest of the table.

"Oh, well . . ." I began tentatively. There was no good response.

"I knew her back before she was in high school. Knew her before she got too big for her britches—"

"You've known your wife even longer, and she still waits for you to ask her for a kiss too," Dr. Lawrence said. There was some laughter, and then someone came up to ask Roche a question. I felt a surge of relief.

Petra was still talking with someone and Rob had turned away to speak to someone else, but Lawrence—Larry, as I knew him—turned to me, offering a hand.

"How've you been, Emma?"

I shook his hand and leaned in to kiss him. "Pretty well, Larry. Busy, you know."

"I do know. You'd think emeritus would be a break, but now I'm only doing everything I didn't have time for when I was working full-time. Congratulations on your tenure, by the way. I was very pleased to hear about that. No one deserves it more."

"Thanks. I thought things would ease up a little, but I feel busier than ever."

Larry laughed. "And how is Brian?"

We chatted for a few minutes, until I saw that Petra was getting up to leave. I excused myself from Larry and followed her.

"Thomas Roche is an ass," she said, when she noticed me. "He's been an ass for years."

"He's not my favorite person. But I have known him a long time."

"It doesn't give him the right to presume. Your relationship with Oscar saddled you with a lot you didn't ask for."

I looked at Petra quickly, then just nodded.

"You shouldn't be so surprised," she continued. "I know something about it."

"Oh?"

"Think about my name. Not a lot of seventy-year-old women wandering around called Petra, are there?"

"No."

"Not a lot of seventy-year-old women historical archaeologists either, are there?"

"Nope. Not as many as there will be, soon enough."

"My father was a biblical scholar. We traveled a lot. I got my interest in archaeology from those trips with him. My mother hated it, she hated being out of the country, but what could she do? The one place she really liked was Petra, in Jordan. Maybe because it was fixed in one place."

I was struggling, not understanding what she was getting at. "I always thought it was a gorgeous name."

"Imagine explaining what it meant in the nineteen-forties. I didn't just get a passion for the past from him, I got a damned odd name. I also got an entrée into the field through his colleagues, which made things a little easier for me, I'm sure, in those days." She glanced at me. "And a little tougher too."

I nodded again, saving this all for later to think about. Working with Oscar had been lots of fun, but at the same time . . . "I was wondering whether I could talk to you about Garrison."

Suddenly, Petra's sympathy evaporated. "What about Garrison?" she asked sharply.

"How he was, before he died."

"He was a cantankerous old bastard before he died," she said evenly, after a pause. "Much the same as he'd been for decades before that event."

"No, I mean . . . had he been having trouble with people, getting into altercations? Trouble with drinking, with his medications? I'm only asking because I've heard conflicting stories," I said, rushing along before she could protest. "And I thought that if I just came out and asked you, it might simplify things."

"Hmmm." She glanced at me. "What have you heard?"

At least she hadn't just told me to take a hike, I thought. "That he was drinking, and he shouldn't have been, with whatever he was taking. That he was suffering mood swings."

"More mood swings than usual?" she asked lightly, but it was an act. "How could anyone tell?"

I shrugged. "You could. You were married to him."

"Yes, I was married to him. We've remained close, so I can tell you unequivocally, not that it's any of your business: Garrison was taking his medications—nothing fancy, just anticoagulants—and he was not drinking, not as far as I knew."

Was there just a tinge of defensiveness in her voice? I wondered.

"And he was no more moody than usual. Garrison died by accident, because he was a stubborn old ass and wanted his walk. He died from sulking, if you want to find a reason for it."

"But . . . what about the—?"

"Emma, Garrison died by accident." Her words became louder, more insistent. "He went outside, he fell, he cracked his head. Let's not make anything more of it than that. It was an accident. Excuse me."

She swept past me toward the elevator banks. Had she

been squashing me with practical truths, or had she been denying something? I could not tell, and I was still left with the unease of having been pressing her beyond decent limits in her grief.

"Hey, Emma, come over here!"

I turned around and saw Lissa and Sue. Lissa was waving excitedly; Sue had her hand on Lissa's arm, like she had been trying to keep Lissa from calling me.

"I saw the ghost! The hotel's ghost!"

"Bull," I said.

"I'm telling you, I did." Lissa was so excited that she could barely keep her feet on the ground. She hooked her blond hair over one ear. "And get this, she was wandering by Garrison's room."

"Well, if she was, she was lost," I said. "Isn't Garrison's room in the new wing?"

"Yeah, but—"

"Then why would the ghost have been there? Shouldn't she be waiting for her husband in the old part of the hotel?"

"Why should she be tied down?" Lissa asked happily. "By this time, she should have the run of the whole place. I tell you, I saw her."

"Lissa, just how faced were you?"

She shrugged, and waved her hand airily. "No worse than usual."

"Which is to say, you were pretty well hammered. And your contacts?"

"I'd taken them out, but I was wearing my glasses."

"Same glasses that are around your neck now?" I picked them up, and we could all see the heavy layer of greasy smudges over both lenses.

"So I need to clean them. Ask Sue, she was with me. She saw."

I turned to Sue, who looked as if she would have happily melted through the floor to get away from me, if she could have. "I was walking Lissa back to her room. I didn't see a ghost. I saw a woman in a bathrobe. She was trying to get into her room. She had the wrong one, at first, I guess, because she had to try a couple of doors, a couple of times."

Lissa would not be put off. "She vanished when you turned around. Besides, you can ask Laurel Fairchild. She was there too!"

"When I found your room key, I turned around, yes, and she was gone. And yes, she was near Garrison's room, but I'm assuming she finally got into her room. And Laurel was gone just as quickly, and she's not a ghost."

"I'm so excited," Lissa said. "I've always wanted to start a rumor or a path, and now I'll get my chance! Come on, Sue, we need to go to the bar and tell people!"

Sue was all too happy to go. I turned, and almost bumped into Laurel.

"You've been hearing about the 'ghost,' huh?" she said.

"Oh, yeah. Made Lissa's year, near as I can tell."

"Well, don't get too excited about it. I saw the ghost and it wasn't one at all. It was Petra Williams."

"What!"

"She went into Garrison's room that night. I saw her." She paused significantly. "In her nightgown."

"But he . . . when was this?"

"About midnight, half past."

"Shoot." So did that mean she'd gone into his room, and he was there, or that she went into his room when he wasn't there? I chewed my bottom lip. So that makes Petra and whoever was sitting behind me at the session earlier, at least, who saw Garrison after he was supposed to be in bed. The man seems to have done more business after bedtime than most hookers. And while Petra might like to insist that he died by accident, the cops are certainly treating it as a suspicious death, and I would be willing to bet that there were no hunters out there when those gunshots were fired.

My head was already spinning, and that was before you added ghosts and the thefts of Bea's artifacts and the replicas from the book room.

The door to one of the offices opened, and I saw Widmark, the one person who absolutely did not belong here, ashen-faced, being led out by Church, whose face was grim.

"Laurel, will you excuse . . . ?" I didn't wait for her answer, but was already walking away.

Widmark looked around, dodged over to the elevators, and was away before I could blink. Then Church signaled to me.

"We've been looking for a friend of yours," he said.

"Oh?"

"A Professor . . . Bradford DuBois. You wouldn't happen to know—?"

It took me a minute to realize that he was talking about Brad the Boy. "Actually, I haven't seen him since last night," I said. "He was feeling poorly, and went to bed early."

"We'll contact him there, then." He paused. "So. You're not in any records we've got in New Hampshire. You don't show up on the radar as a crazy or a criminal. And one of our guys talked to the state police crime guys, and they've actually heard of Stuart Feldman down in Massachusetts. We haven't had a chance to talk to him yet, but you know, it's interesting that you know his name."

I looked at him hopefully. "What does that mean?"

"It means we haven't found that you've been lying to us. Yet."

"I haven't been lying. And I think that the fact that you were talking to me when the shots were fired outside might indicate that I'm not any more involved in this than I've said."

"But people we've been talking to say that you have an

unusual degree of interest in what's been going on. That you've been asking a lot of questions—"

"I would be willing to bet that everyone's been asking a lot of questions: You haven't told us anything. People get upset and worried when they think something dangerous is going on and they can't put a name to it."

"Fair enough. So, what have you been finding out?"

I looked at him, and knew that he wasn't offering to trade me what he knew for what I knew. But if I really did think that my curiosity would help, then I owed it to him to tell him about the late-night visits that so many people had had with Garrison. So I did, and his face remained impassive the entire time.

But I noticed that he wrote everything down.

"Have you found out what was going on with the gunshots?"

"I'm not at liberty to say."

"But it wasn't hunters, was it?"

"I'm not at liberty to say."

"Is there any news about Garrison's death? Was it murder?"

"We're still waiting for the autopsy, it's not as quick as you see on television. We have to treat it as a suspicious death. I will say that all of the wounds were on the back of his head—a pretty nasty laceration—and it didn't look as if he walked out onto the ice only to fall over backward."

That was news. "And what about—?"

His patience finally wore out. "Look, Dr. Fielding, there's a lot going on here that you don't know about—"

"And so if you would just tell me—"

"—and it's better to keep it that way. There's the safety of my officers to be considered."

"What were you talking to Widmark about? He's someone I've never seen before, and I don't really like his story, he doesn't feel right to me—"

"We'll do the asking, thanks." He leaned in closer. "And if you do interfere, it will go on your permanent record." He was acting as if he was teasing, but I could feel it to my bones that he meant it. "Good evening, Dr. Fielding."

I almost went after him, but my fatigue was not bad enough to keep me from doing something so terribly silly. Casting about for something I could do, I realized that I was grinding my teeth. I couldn't make him tell me anything to do with Garrison's death, I couldn't make Scott say what he was after, I couldn't do anything.

I spied Meg. She looked like hell. If nothing else, I was willing to bet I could fix that.

After she greeted me, I asked, "When was the last time you ate?"

"Oh, about an hour ago. I grabbed a Pop-Tart up in the room."

"Uh-huh. And when before that?"

"Umm, I dunno. Breakfast, maybe."

"Okay, we're getting dinner now. Bring your friends, if you want, but be warned: If they come, they'll all get an ear-ful of my conference survival strategies."

It wasn't hard to round up enough to get a table to ourselves. Meg was popular and there were others from Caldwell there—Neal and Katie, for example, though one of my other students, Dian Kosnick, had said hello to me yesterday and I hadn't seen her since—so there were eight of us squeezed in around the table in the big restaurant.

Meg made the introductions. I shook hands. "Okay, take your name tags off."

Confused glances were exchanged around the table, but everyone reluctantly did as I told them. "I thought the point of these things was to get to know people," a young woman said. I recognized her as the Gypsy-clad woman from the opening reception dance. Jordan.

"Yep, and now we all know each other. You need to turn

off the conference thing for a little while every day. And," I added, as I removed my own badge, "if you take your name tags off when you leave the site in a big city, you're no longer marked as a tourist and a potentially easy mark for muggers."

There were a few nods and some shrugs. They'd learn how useful this was in the years to come.

The waiter began filling up water glasses, and someone else arrived with a basket of bread. This was handed around and emptied before you could blink.

"Next. It is altogether too easy to forget to eat, or eat whatever happens to be at hand. I always make a point to eat at least one meal a day with real food, not fast food: real chairs—not stools—and metal flatware. This meal doesn't necessarily need to be dinner; if you get a good breakfast in, with lots of fruit and some protein, that works too. And just as important, if you can remember to keep drinking water—these conference hotels will dehydrate you faster than the Mojave Desert—that's half the trick to keep from getting headaches on whatever cold is going around."

"You sound like my mom," said Kyle, who was baby-faced and prematurely balding. He didn't seem to be complaining, though.

"Well, she's right, on this score. Again, the idea is to take care of yourself, especially if you have to do the grab-stuff-and-run thing." I looked at them, calculating how many were probably in a room together. "Or foraging snacks at the receptions or eating in your rooms, and I don't mean room service."

There were some grins at that last. I'd done my share of eating peanut butter crackers and dried apricots, washed down with tap water, and didn't miss those days. I did miss the energy I had then, though.

After we placed our orders, I said, "Next, go to the gym if you can swing it."

"But we're here to work. We're spending money to work," spoke Alex, a heavyset lad with a pierced lower lip.

I tried not to stare at the stud in his lip, but it just looked so damned uncomfortable. I nodded and put the wine list aside. "You are, and if you're going to get the most out of it, you need to relax. There's no point in exhausting yourself if you're not going to retain all of your contacts, paper citations, books, etcetera. And if you don't work out, or you don't have time, at least try to get some fresh air. The worst times I've had at conferences were the ones where we were snowed in, like now, and everyone started getting bug-eyed and stir crazy. The fresh air will help on a lot of levels, clear your head, kill cold germs, refocus your eyes. Who knows? You might even find someone you're trying to meet out there doing the same thing."

"Like smoking," Jordan said.

"Not my choice, but sure. You may have noticed a big clot of folks clustered around the front door? That's the Canadian Club," I said. "Not just because they are always outside in the snow or drink cheap whiskey, but because sometimes they bring the good cigars to us benighted folk in the lower forty-eight. Just don't accost people in the bathroom. They might want a moment to pee in privacy."

Suddenly I felt two hands on my shoulders. The scent of lilacs reassured me, however, and I patted one of the hands and looked up at Michelle. "Need a place to sit, my darling?"

"Not a bit of it, cupcake. I'm over there with my fellow science freaks. I just wanted say good evening."

"So thoughtful," I said.

She smiled and drifted over to the other table.

"What was that about?" Alex muttered.

"That was Michelle Lima. Does good work for the park service, down in Delaware. We met about fifteen years ago."

"You guys must be really good friends," said Alex pointedly.

I ignored the implication. "Oh, you know. There were supposed to be five of us giving papers. One person was delayed, another canceled, and another never showed. Since
they were the headliners, virtually no one showed up to hear
us present, so since then, we decided if no one else loved us,
we would always be there for each other."

I saw them exchanging looks. "Oh, come on. You guys
haven't got a sense of humor? Never do anything silly? Ah,
get over it." Our drinks arrived.

"Where were we? Right, one last thing. Don't forget to
empty out your bags or notebooks regularly. If you tidy up
all the flyers and books and business cards and little notes
and lagniappes every so often, you'll keep track of what you
got and what you need, you'll remind yourself of things to
do, and you'll save your back a lot of wear and tear."

"What's a lagniappe?" Katie said.

"It's pronounced 'lan-yap.' It means a gimme, something
you get with a sale or as a premium. Conference swag. It's
from the Spanish via Cajun French. Great word, isn't it? And
there's one other thing. Very important. Something Oscar
didn't ever tell me, and I sometimes wonder whether he even
knew about it himself."

There were some whispered conversations when Jordan
explained to Alex who my grandfather Oscar was. They all
leaned forward, breath bated.

"Moisturizer. Trust me."

They still looked disappointed.

"I'm serious. It's almost as important as a sense of humor," I added. "Here endeth the lesson."

"Evening, everyone!"

I looked up. Duncan had swanned in, and it was as if we'd
never had that last discussion. "Emma, are all these yours?"

I could feel my face freeze. "No, just a handful."

"Aren't you going to introduce me?"

Duncan, what the hell are you up to? Why the sudden

change? "Sure." I went around the table and was horrified to
see everyone looking at Duncan with something like worshipful adoration. Except Katie, who was staring glumly
into her lap. Holy Gilderoy Lockhart.

"Well, I just wanted to say hello. I'll catch you later, Em?"

Only if I get caught in a bear trap, Dunk. "Later."

Katie looked better as soon as he left, I was relieved to
see. I took a big sip of wine and was delighted when the food
showed up shortly thereafter.

There wasn't much talk for a few moments, while we
tucked into the food, which was a good step above what you
got in the café. My salmon was nice, but I thought that the
sauce wasn't very good, compared to Brian's. I sat back and
listened to the students chatting.

And complaining—apparently Hedia, an attractively
dressed woman who'd been quietly observing until now, was
a "mirror hog" by Meg's lights.

"I like to make sure I'm put together," Hedia replied, "and
it's not as if you were late for your paper."

They went back and forth for a while, with no real heat,
and the conversation drifted off to other subjects. I got a
good feel for most of the folks who were new to me and answered the questions that they had about archaeology books
or my own work. I wasn't one of them, and it is an im-
mensely complicated and difficult thing to try and be someone's friend when you have so much control over their
future, so I was happy to let them do most of the talking. Of
course, discussions of beer and travel and movies weren't
too personal, and I had no qualms about chipping in here and
there. About an hour later, I felt relaxed, smug about taking
my own good advice, and pleased to see color in Meg's
cheeks again.

During dessert, I picked up the bill and settled it. There
were a few protests, but I waved them off.

"My treat. And besides, you all gave me a good excuse

not to sneak back to my room and work on an overdue article." Which wasn't true, but it let them off the hook too.

"Well, thanks again, Emma," Hedia said as we all got up, stretched, and collected our bags.

"My pleasure." And it really was, because I felt better for having done something constructive. It was also like I was getting to pay back all the folks who'd sprung for drinks or meals when I couldn't afford it, who gave me advice when I was ready for it, and who'd generally treated me like a human when others weren't so concerned about the direction a twenty-something might take.

My buzz evaporated. I saw Noreen out of the corner of my eye, waiting for the elevator, just where I was heading. And damn if she didn't turn around and see me. Drat, there was no avoiding her now.

She gave me the once-over, and flipped her hair. "What, are you running for office or something?"

"What do you mean?" Good God, with the dangling belt, dangling earrings, dangling pendant, she might as well be a fishing lure.

"Soliciting the underage vote?"

"Just giving some survival pointers to some of the coming generation, that's all."

"Half of them won't be here in five years. Doesn't stop you from always trying to find an audience." She said the words almost to herself, but it was too blatant for me to let go. There was a lot of pent-up anger here.

"Noreen, what is your problem? You seem to have a real attitude about something, about *me,* and I'd really appreciate it if you'd just tell me to my face."

She looked up, surprised by this. "What?"

"You keep muttering things, just out of my hearing, that I'm supposed to overhear. Why don't you come out with it?"

The car arrived and she got in. I followed her; she paused there, staring at the bank of buttons in the elevator before she hit the button for the fourth floor. Then she turned around to me, amazingly bitter. "You're never happy with what you've got, are you?"

This was so stupid. I laughed. "Is anyone?"

"You know what I mean. It's always got to be the center of attention for you, doesn't it?"

I reached over and stabbed the button for my floor. "And how do you reach this conclusion?"

"Oh, please."

There was nowhere for her to run to, we were trapped between the mirrored walls and the posters showing views of the restaurant and business center, so I forced the issue. "No, I'm serious. I have no idea what you're talking about and now's your chance to tell me."

She had been gearing up for this apparently. I imagined her counting over her grievances like a miser for years. "You get everything in the world and you're never happy. You get your way paved for you in archaeology with your grandfather and his cronies. You get these awards for your dissertation, like the fix wasn't in there too—"

"You're kidding, right?" Unless that was a fox that Noreen had been nursing? Had she been up for the ASAA dissertation prize that year too? I couldn't remember.

"The special secret card games that everyone in the world knows about—"

"I don't believe this."

She raised a hand. "Save the outraged modesty."

"Did it ever occur to you that Oscar has been dead for years now? Or that perhaps by dint of having started in this field, oh, ten years before everyone else, I might have had a little more experience, had a better idea of how to go about things? Sure, I got more experience because of Oscar, but I also put in maybe twice as much time as everyone else. So don't you ever let me hear you suggest that I might have gotten that prize for something other than my hard work, because any suggestion otherwise is jealous bullshit."

The door opened at the second-floor mezzanine, but there was no one there. It took an eternity for the doors to slide shut again.

"Hard work, like you got the Caldwell job?" Noreen spat. "And the Westlake chair?"

"*Exactly* like that. A friend of mine died, that's how that chair was created. You know, I used to worry that I got where I did because of connections too. And let's say they got me in the door. Then what? People don't bother with you, unless you've got something else going on. And since I don't have the clout that I might possibly if Oscar was still alive—and if you ever heard about how he drove his students, you should have seen how he drove *me*—then I think it might be fair to consider that I've got something else on the ball besides family connections."

She looked as shocked as I felt. I never did this sort of thing, never stood up for myself like this, not even with myself. Duncan was right: I was no longer the person I used to be.

The door opened on the third floor, and I stepped across the threshold, keeping the door from shutting.

This new, more aggressive me, seemed like a trade up. Strange, but good.

"Whatever," she said. "It just makes me sick, that's all. You bustling around with the cops, making a scene about Garrison. You didn't even like him. And now you're using him, after he's dead, to promote yourself or something. It's sick."

"I'm not using him. And you're right, I didn't like him—"

"Why on earth not?" And for the first time, I sensed genuine distress in her voice. "How could you not like him, after what he did for the field?"

"I have nothing against what he did for the field. It's what he did to me, personally, that is why I don't like him. Just personal stuff, even if I happen to think his reputation was overblown."

"Straight party line, just like your grandfather."

"Tell me again what this has got to do with Oscar?"

"Everyone knows that Oscar was always badmouthing Garrison. That he was jealous of him, and whenever Garrison tried to do his job, Oscar took it personally. Not very professional, if you ask me."

"You can say whatever you like, Noreen, but it all sounds like sour grapes to me." Suddenly I was tired. I stepped out onto the floor. "You might try working for something, rather than running your mouth off and complaining all the time. It will make a nice change for the rest of us."

"Don't even bother, Emma. You make me—"

And the doors slid shut before she could finish telling me again how sick I made her.

"Whatever," I muttered, and gave the English two-fingered salute to the closed elevator doors. Two fingers always seemed to have so much more violence than that one, solitary finger.

I found my way back to my room without incident; the incidents started when I had the door safely locked behind me. I picked up a folded piece of paper I found shoved under my door at the same time I saw the red message light flashing on the phone on the desk. I flipped the sheet open as I crossed to the desk. "You were warned. If you're not worried about yourself, then think about the kids."

I didn't do anything, I thought wildly. I didn't talk to the cops, I didn't do anything! What does this person mean?

I stared at the paper a moment longer, then dialed in to the answering service. It was Meg's worried voice I heard. "It's me. When we got back to our room from dinner, the door was open. I don't know how it happened, but someone got in and tore our stuff apart. Jordan's pissed, Katie's in hysterics, but other than that, no one was hurt."

There was a pause before she continued. "There was a message on the mirror, written in lipstick. It said, "Ask Emma." Emma, what's going on here?"

Chapter 11

THERE WAS SO MUCH THAT I REGRETTED IN MY LIFE that sometimes it felt like I was choking. And this weekend was the catalyst for bringing those regrets all to the surface, not even counting whatever I was getting myself into at the moment.

The students' room was a mess, but while some toiletries had been spilt and scattered about—mascaras stepped on, lipstick on the mirror, shampoo dumped out and all—very little else was damaged. Whoever had done it, the police said, had been in too much of a hurry to really do any damage.

Any damage was too much, I thought, but at the same time, I couldn't figure out what it was I was supposed to have done that would bring the note-writer's wrath down on the students' heads. If I didn't know what the rules were, how could I obey them, even if I wanted to?

I handed the note from my room to the uniformed officer who was there. He looked at me, surprised, when he saw that it was in a plastic bag. "Artifact bag," I said. "I had a bunch of them in my briefcase. I didn't touch it too much, if you want to check for prints."

"This doesn't seem to be the same as the other break-ins," he said. "Nothing was taken, you say?"

"We don't have anything *worth* taking," Meg said. "No, not as far as we can tell. What other break-ins?"

"There've been a few thefts, from other guests' rooms," he said. "But it was nothing like this. Just what you seem to get with any big convention."

After explaining to the officer about the last note, and that I didn't have the faintest idea of what I'd done, we sorted the students out. There were no other rooms for them, but apparently it didn't matter: Hedia was leaving. The roads were nominally cleared now, and she wasn't willing to stay any longer.

"Nothing personal, Dr. Fielding, but there's no way I'm sticking around here."

"I don't blame you a bit," I said. "I'm sorry this happened, and as soon as I know why, I'll let you know."

Neither Katie, Dian, nor Meg took me up on my offer to share my room. I decided that Meg was happier squeezing in with her fiancé, and that Dian was always happier when there were wall-to-wall men anyway. And after Katie had calmed down, she found a bed with a friend from another school. Nothing personal.

After the officer departed and the night manager had been up offering apologies, I realized I was just in the way and returned to my room to brood.

I chewed over what the note might have meant, but I couldn't figure out what I might have done. I had seen Church, or rather, he'd seen me, but that had lasted no more than two minutes and was about as innocuous a conversation as one could imagine. I hadn't done anything I wouldn't do at any other conference, I thought.

Unless it had something to do with the strange way Duncan and Scott had been acting toward me. They were right there too, the last time I saw Church. But Duncan had been perversely pleasant, at dinner. Was he covering up the break-in? Was he trying to distract me from it? Was he—or Scott—capable of doing such a thing? Why were such strong threats directed at me? And why involve the students?

I had to give some serious thought to Duncan and my reactions to him. I didn't want to, but if I did, not only might I come up with a possible motive for his behavior, but maybe I'd banish a few ghosts of my own too.

Where to start? At the beginning, of course: the visit to Penitence Point and Fort Providence on Wednesday. That had brought up a lot of emotional turmoil. Going out to the site was hard. I'd been out there since Pauline's murder, of course, but not to have her there was particularly hard. Maybe because I would have liked for her to have seen the interest in her site, maybe because I would have liked my friend to see me putting on the show, so grown up . . .

Knock it off, I told myself. Pauline knew you as an adult, she saw you as a professional.

I missed her. I missed her awfully, still. I knew I wasn't the reason she died, but I still felt as though I drew the attention to her. And as much as I wanted to remember her, it killed me to see her name painted on the door of my office every day I went into work.

She would have died eventually. The bequest still would have been in place. The name would have still been on my door, somewhere, probably.

Anyway. And as for Oscar . . . for some reason, he was haunting me this weekend. Or rather, I was haunting him. I knew he wasn't perfect, I knew that when I was growing up. Petra was right, as much as Oscar might have done for me, he took it out of my hide. I worked like a dog, and I loved every minute of it, of working with him. He drove me, I was happy to be driven, it served us both. Made us both proud.

But he didn't save me from Duncan.

No, he didn't. Should he have?

Maybe he could have. He defined the world for me in a lot

of ways and didn't do a whole lot to show me that his was just one opinion. He didn't see Duncan for what he was, any more than I did, and he should have been able to. He was older, supposedly wiser.

Maybe he wasn't paying as much attention as I thought or hoped. Maybe he was as susceptible to praise and flattery as anyone else. Maybe Duncan wasn't quite as fully formed a demon at the tender age of twenty-three as I seemed to be remembering, and that's why Oscar didn't pick up on it. Maybe Oscar wasn't God.

Yeah, I knew, I got that. I lost out, maybe, in not getting to know Garrison outside of that context.

That's part of growing up, and everyone's background affects how they come to see something. And maybe I wouldn't have liked Garrison much anyway. He wasn't a nice guy. But he wasn't the devil either.

What would have happened if I hadn't had Pauline in my life? Pain and all, at the end?

Unthinkable.

Did I not have the coolest grandfather on the face of the planet? Was he not the world to me?

I did. He was a curmudgeon and a tyrant and a bully and I was a brat and his trophy and the apple of his eye, and I loved him and he loved me. I wouldn't trade that for anything in the world, not even the hurt I felt when I realized that love didn't always look like hero worship.

And Duncan?

What about him?

It was just an affair, passionate and selfish, and people are allowed to have entanglements that aren't the grand passions of their lives and still hold their heads up. It was over ages ago—

And I never let myself get over it, even when I had the emotional tools to deal with it. And then it got buried under the rest of my life. Until now.

So?

I don't need to feel embarrassed. I can let myself off the hook for being young and maybe a little blind and a whole lot of egotistical. My feelings for him are long gone, but the hurt I felt about the way he did it . . . it's like a tooth that's hurt so long that when it's finally pulled, you don't even realize that the pain's stopped. Just empty. No big deal.

But Duncan was still a tool. Still a climber, still out for himself.

No doubt about that whatsoever. The questions now were: What did he want from me? What was it that he thought I was threatening him with? And could he be responsible for such disturbing and misdirected vandalism?

I realized that I was a bundle of nervous energy, aching for something to do. I had too many questions; I needed too many answers.

It seemed to me, based on the conversations I'd overheard in the farmstead session and what Scott and the cops had said, that the last place that Garrison had been seen alive, by someone other than his murderer, was in the hospitality suite on the second floor. I decided that if the place hadn't been blocked off by the cops, that I might have a look around there myself. And if the destruction of the girls' room hadn't been connected with Duncan, then maybe it was related to the questions the cops had asked me about Garrison.

The kids were squared away, safe, for the moment. As for me, I decided that I might as well be hanged for a sheep as for a lamb.

There was no indication that I shouldn't go into the hospitality suite—no police tapes, no guard, no signage—but the door was locked. It wasn't a good enough reason to keep me out, and it wasn't a good enough door to keep me out: Anything that an assistant professor—who is heading into her late thirties and is a card-carrying nerd—can break into can't properly be called a lock. And if the card I was carrying—an expired museum membership—was one that I didn't mind getting dinged up, well, that was just my good luck. So in my book, this closed door didn't count.

I fiddled with it for less than ten seconds before I figured it out, a combination of pulling the door forward and poking the card just a little harder. I am consistently amazed by how well violent force works. I slipped in and let the door shut quietly, then turned on the light, which turned out to be a single table lamp. The main switch for the overheads was on the other side of the room. I decided that the dim yellowish light of the table lamp, as melancholy as it was, would be enough for me to see by without attracting any undue attention.

There had been nothing particularly hospitable about the hospitality suite during the day, as it had the same collection of tea water and coffee urns that populated the tables outside the ballrooms. There was the addition of bottled water, most of which was usually room temperature, and there were rumors of cookies at one point, but these were long gone by the time the report got around to me. I saw by the pink crumbs that there may well have been Italian cookies. Not my favorites, but, hey, I would try any cookie at a conference.

I looked around and saw absolutely nothing. Less than nothing, for the room was so anonymous a hotel suite that I was willing to bet that it even drained the personality out of those who loitered there too long. The prints were the same Federal-style architectural elements as the ones in the rooms, the couches were a nondescript floral in shades of brown and tan, and the lighting fixtures were nearly colonial revival—make it colonial revile, and you'd be closer to the mark. The only thing that distinguished it from the other guest rooms was the lack of a bed and a slightly wider floor plan. There were two extra windows, both of which were also laced with snow and freezing rain that struck the pane like BBs against the glass. It smelled like synthetic fabrics, burnt coffee, and perspiration.

There was nothing on the end tables save for the lamp, and nothing on the folding table but the urns and crumbs. A few napkins, none of which were used, though one had a coffee spot on it. I even shook them out, in case someone had left a note written on one of them, as I often did, but there was no luck there.

The bathroom off to the side was equally bare. It made me depressed to see how blank a space it was. I went back into the main room and sat, in one of the two single chairs, trying to think of what to do next.

I blame what happened next on dressing up. Because I was wearing my grown-up go-to-conference trousers with the acetate lining, instead of my usual jeans or chinos, my good, going-to-meetings pen slid right out of the pocket. It was a recent acquisition, a fancy, jewelry-grade ballpoint Waterman that had been a gift from my father for getting tenure; although it was about the last thing I needed, I was touched that he understood that getting tenure was a big deal and should be marked as such. Most of the time, he either ignored or pretended not to understand the ways of academia, possibly as a reaction to his father, the uber-professorial Oscar. His real estate interests were about as far away from academic life as you could get.

I felt the weight of the pen slide out of my pocket and looked down at the seat beside me: The pen had vanished between the cushion and the side of the chair. I reached in tentatively, just knowing I would find stale crumbs, and instead got the corner of a piece of thin cardboard jammed under my nail. I pulled it out, cursed and sucked my finger, then reached back and retrieved my pen. When I glanced down at the paper, I realized that it was a business card. To my shock, it was printed with Sue Ayer's name; on the reverse was cramped writing that, in the dim light in the room, was too difficult to read.

Before finding the card, I had decided I would leave the room as quickly and unobtrusively as I had entered it. Now, instead, I was rooting through all the sofa and chair cushions, looking for other such clues. There was nothing apart from a few buttons, another, cheaper pen that was marked with a technology logo that was all sound and style but gave no clue as to what the company did. More crumbs.

I sagged into a chair and blew a wet, tired raspberry. I was going to try and decode the hieroglyphics on the card when I heard a rattling. I looked over to the door, which was now moving back and forth. Someone was jiggling it. That same someone was using a knife to try and get the lock open.

Suddenly, the knife withdrew. I heard another, very faint, metallic noise that was different from the first. This one sounded less like someone trying to pick a lock and more distinctly like someone slotting a bullet into the chamber of a gun.

I froze for just a second, and then decided that I was not willing to wait and find out whether I was right. My hindbrain was already reacting, reminded of the sounds that it had learned when Meg had taught me about handling firearms, a couple of years ago, after that night at Penitence Point. There really wasn't much mistake to be made here. I looked for someplace to hide, and unless I thought the shower curtain in the bathroom was going to shield me, I was out of luck. I tried the door that was at the back, the one that presumably joined with the room next door to form a larger suite, but it was locked tighter than the door from the hallway. Shit.

I grabbed my phone and called nine-one-one. I tried to whisper, stopped and realized that the person coming in *should* hear that I was calling the cops. I spoke up.

There was a pause, but then a renewed banging at the doors.

I had to get out of here.

I hung up, stuffed my phone into my pocket, and looked at the first two windows: They were painted solidly shut. As quickly as I could, I went to the one at the end, and the lock was stuck, the window was swollen with moisture, but not painted over. The wind belted another flock of icy pellets against the glass, and I realized . . . Emma, get used to it: In a moment, you're going to be on the receiving end of all nature's fury. Still a better option than a gun.

By now, my armed friend outside had realized that the butter knife was no good, and had moved on to credit cards. Luckily, he or she was as concerned as I had been with keeping quiet, and so I gained a few more precious moments as the intruder tried to figure out how to open the door silently.

I reevaluated the risk of climbing out onto an icy ledge during a blizzard: the building was old, but the roof of the porte cochere would surely hold me; I was only on the second floor and the twenty feet or so I could possibly fall probably wouldn't kill me. There were my dubious abilities in disarming someone; I'd done okay in my Krav Maga classes, but my instructor Nolan had gotten a fake gun up to my head often enough to make me doubt my chances. Although I doubted that whoever had that gun would want to risk the noise in firing a shot, *I* couldn't risk that he might also have brought a silencer.

I had already started bashing the lock on the window.

The lock gave. With a little effort, I hoisted the window up. I couldn't believe I was going to do this, but I was more interested in saving my life than I was at being embarrassed, at this point. A blast of cold air and hard sleet roared through the window and I had second thoughts about going out there. Surely it would be better to try and hide or try and get the gun away from whoever was out there while I waited for the cops . . .

No. Guns require a drastic response.

Any thoughts I might have had about trying to shut the window after me were immediately banished. The wind whipped so hard that I could barely keep myself stuck to the wall and keep my feet under me.

There was no sound behind me, at least, nothing I could hear over the wind, the ice, and the blood pounding in my ears. Then a shot seemed to come from below me—I felt a thud next to me and brick chips flew up at me—but it must have been a trick of the wind. I couldn't stay put, in any case, and wait for the cops to show up.

As I shuffled along the narrow, level part of the porch roof, the only thing keeping me from sliding right off the icy masonry was the elaborate system of spikes to prevent pigeons from nesting on the building. I crushed some, and felt a couple getting ready to pierce the leather sole of my shoe as I moved my feet, but that was preferable to bullet ventilation and extreme lead poisoning. At least they provided some traction against the ice.

My fingers were numb and, suddenly, I was measuring happiness by the millimeters of gap between the surface of the mortar and the edge of the bricks. Every second I was losing my sense of touch.

I tried to yell, maybe get the attention of those in the next room. The wind howled around me and drowned my calls for help: I would have to get closer to the window before I had any chance at all of being heard. I would have to get to the window before I froze to death, which felt like it would be in about three minutes on a night like this.

With all of my concentration on the natural forces working against me, I'd nearly forgotten what had compelled me out there in the first place. Another bullet whined past me just as I slipped on a particularly slippery patch. I could literally feel myself being peeled off the face of the building when a contrary blast of wind knocked me back into the wall. Not daring to look above me, with the side of my face slammed into the cold brick, I shot my hand up over my head in a blind attempt to find a hand hold on a decorative course of brick that jutted out slightly. The first time I did nothing but jam my fingertips into the underside of it, knocking loose a small volley of icicles down onto me. And yet, the next instant I found a purchase again. The only thing I had on my side was that whoever was following me would increase the risk of detection every time the gun was fired. I scraped along the wall as quickly as I dared and prayed that the shooter's visibility was no better than my own, blurred by snow, tears burning like acid down my cheeks.

Moments that felt like hours had passed, and my strength had almost run out, when I heard my name. I risked turning my head back to the window I'd left—was it really still so close?—and saw Church cupping his hands to his mouth. He was pointing ahead of me. There was a light, now, in the next room, and I could see uniformed officers moving in there. I held on for dear life.

They got their window open, and hollered for me to move to them; I took a few more shuffling, clinging steps and felt a strong hand grab on to the waistband of my trousers. I inched forward, looked down, and saw a bedspread being passed around me, and someone grabbed its other end. With this support I felt like I could try to ease my way down and through the open window, into the room. Too quick: I slid back. But the bedspread was there, barely, and I could hear the shouts and curses of those inside as they struggled to hang on to me. I grabbed the bottom of the raised window frame and slid in.

Chapter 12

"**W**HAT IN GOD'S NAME WERE YOU DOING OUT there?" Church demanded. Apparently when he heard that there was more excitement at the General Bartlett, he decided that it was time to visit in person. He looked exhausted, as well as angry.

"Well, there was someone trying to get into the hospitality suite," I said, "and I heard what sounded like a gun."

I'd finally stopped shivering, shaking hard enough to feel my brains rattle in my skull. I could feel my fingers and toes, though, and had managed to thank the guys who'd hauled me inside.

"And what were you doing in there in the first place?" The scowl on his face was outclassed by the anger in his eyes.

I gave him a quick rundown of the events, but when I got to the part about finding the card, I realized I hadn't thought everything through. I'd meant to give myself enough time to look at the card more closely, before I told anyone else about it.

"Let's see it" was all he said.

I hesitated. Then, realizing that I really did need to help

find Garrison's killer, no matter who it might be, I reached into my pocket and pulled out the card. As soon as I saw it, in the brighter light of the room, my heart dropped away. I now recognized that the cramped writing was Sue's spelling out Garrison's name and appointment time.

It doesn't mean anything, I told myself, it could be anything, it could be . . .

"This is very interesting," Church said, getting up. "This fits in with a lot of the information we've assembled." He spoke briefly into his radio.

My stomach rolled. "It isn't necessarily . . . it doesn't have to be interesting." But as soon as I said the words, the thought that it was Sue's card came rushing back to me. Sue's reaction to Garrison's speech was understandable, but then there was her reaction when I told her of my potential career changes. There was her late arrival to our card game. There was her early absence from the bar. There was the public humiliation.

There was too much.

"You don't have to worry." Church was pleased now. "We won't tell Dr. Ayers where we got the card."

But I'll know. "I don't want someone who might be innocent—"

"Neither do we, of course. This is just *one* part of the investigation."

I realized that he was trying to be kind to me, but I couldn't stop myself protesting. "It's just that . . . Sue's had a real bad time lately. I wouldn't want something unnecessary to make things worse or . . ." But every time a word left my mouth, I knew I wasn't doing Sue any favors.

"What about the shots?" I said. "I could have sworn that some of them at least were coming from below me."

"They probably were," he said. "I think this would be an excellent time for you to leave yourself out of all of this. Didn't you just receive another threatening note, this time followed up with tangible repercussions? Even before you went exploring?" He shook his head. "And there are things going on here that have even less to do with you than you already imagine."

Afterward, I took a long shower. Dressed in my more formal clothes—I placed the more casual stuff I'd been wearing on the radiator to dry out—I went and sat down on a bench near the railing of the mezzanine. People on their way to parties were quieter than I ever remembered. A few waved to me, but didn't ask me to join them; I was just as happy that they didn't. I didn't want to be alone, but I didn't want to be with anyone else either. I assumed that they hadn't even heard the shots. Between the parties, the weather, and what I assumed was a silencer, the most they might have had to react to was the continued, sometimes increased police presence. That was, of course, until news about the students' room got around.

An hour later, Sue walked out of the elevator. She was staring like a zombie and moved as if she'd just gotten a new pair of knees and hadn't quite gotten the hang of them yet. And for some reason, despite her earlier antipathy, she homed in on me.

She sat next to me, but it was more like her new knees just buckled and she happened to land on the bench by accident.

"Jesus, Em, the cops were questioning me. Just now." Sue was shaking like a leaf, as badly as I had been a couple of hours before. "It's like they think I killed Garrison, or something."

"What happened?"

"They were banging on the door when I was in the shower. I didn't hear them, until they got really loud. Scary loud." She shivered. "I got the impression if I hadn't gotten out right then, they would have busted the door down or something."

They probably would have just got the manager to let them in, I thought uneasily.

"Anyway, they gave me a minute to get dressed, but I kinda got the impression that they were scoping the place. They wanted to know if I had a gun. What the hell would I do with a gun?"

It was at that precise moment that I knew more people than I realized who had guns. Meg had a handgun, Chris had shotgun, I knew that Lissa went hunting on occasion—not that they would necessarily have guns with them, of course—and who knew who else? I shook myself, suddenly scared again.

"Maybe they were wondering about those shots we heard the night they announced Garrison's death," I said. "And . . . Sue." I watched her face carefully. "Someone shot at me too."

"What?" Sue began to cry, and I realized that she wasn't really tuned into anything I was saying. "Emma, what's happening here? And why are they asking me about it?"

"I guess they—"

"I know, I mean, they told me that I had reason to kill Garrison. I thought he was a miserable old prick, but I wouldn't—who would? I'd already made my decision to go, I told you that, when was it? You should tell them that, if you get a chance." She put her head down and sobbed. I handed her a tissue, hating myself, hating everything about this.

"Sue. If they haven't arrested you, then there's no problem, right? If they're . . . just asking questions, that's not so bad, right? You haven't done anything wrong, have you?" I meant it to come out as reassuring, but I didn't do a very good job. Sue still didn't notice.

"I know, this is just messed up. Logic will kick in, in a minute. After I've done crying." She snuffled and looked at me. "But Emma. I was supposed to meet Garrison, the night he was killed. They say it was right about the time he went outside, maybe, from what they heard from other folks."

"Did you meet him?"

"No. I . . . what was the point? I was going to try and ask him to reconsider, but it was already too late, wasn't it? He'd already made his recommendation. I just went up to bed, like you saw."

"Right, and that's what you told the cops, right?" Jesus, Emma, how can you pretend to be her friend, when you're the one responsible for all this? No, not all of it. Maybe telling the police about her card, but as for the rest of it, there's Garrison and Sue herself and possibly others . . .

Telling the cops something, after someone's tried to kill you, doesn't make you a bad person. If she didn't do anything, she's in no different a situation than the rest of us.

Not thanks to you, she isn't.

She snuffled again, not done crying. "Yes, that's what I told them. Exactly."

"Well, you're okay, then. As long as you keep telling the truth, right?" I stood up. "I hate to leave, but I'm still feeling shook up. From earlier."

"Emma, you were shot at *tonight*?"

She stared at me, her eyes glazed with tears, and I couldn't believe that Sue had anything to do with any of this. "And you're letting me go on like this? Damn, I feel like such an idiot!"

"Oh, God, please don't, Sue!" I closed my eyes and tried to find my way out. "I should have said something, but I wasn't sure how, if you see what I mean. I'm fine, well, not fine, kind of on autopilot, if you know what I . . . and I just want to check in with home, you know?"

"Go, please. I'm fine, I'm good, I'm done crying for now."

I left and headed back to my room. I kicked off my shoes, my feet ached to be flat on the warm carpeted floor. It was even better when I went into the bathroom; the cool tiles eased the ache further, and I congratulated myself on my recent decision to stop wearing high heels all the time to conferences. It just wasn't worth it. But now my flats were soaked, maybe ruined.

I rolled my head around gently and heard the cracks that were getting louder and more numerous as the weekend continued.

I got out my phone and then dialed.

My sister picked up after the first ring. "Yeah?"

"It's me."

"What's wrong?"

I told her about what had happened tonight, ending with my conversation with Sue.

"You're okay?"

"Fine, pretty much. I'm glad I had my phone with me."

"Amen to that. Hang on—it's in the drawer! Yes it is! Well, look underneath—aha! See, I ain't completely senile yet. I'll just be a minute." The phone was muffled for a minute. "Sorry. Joel couldn't find the ice cream scoop."

"Since when do you have an ice cream scoop?" Last time I knew, my sister's idea of domestic implements went as far as a can opener, a big knife, and a hammer.

"Since Joel thinks I'm a philistine. Now he's moved in, it's Betty-frigging-Crocker rides again. So, you told me you're okay, that the cops came. What's the other problem?"

I thought about avoiding the issue, but that would have been stupid. "I feel guilty."

"What else is new? That's steady state for you."

I ignored her. "The students wouldn't have had to leave, their stuff would still be intact. Sue wouldn't be going through all of this if it wasn't for me."

"And maybe you wouldn't be going through this if it wasn't for Sue. Honest to God, Em, you're such a dork. Haven't you been through this before—hang on."

There was another muffled exchange, and I heard raised voices. Somehow, I didn't think it was about the Ben and Jerry's.

"—she is too! What do you know about it? You are such a pain in the ass. You there?"

That last question was apparently directed to me. "Yes."

Bucky sighed. "Look, I'm sorry."

For a minute I thought she meant the yelling on her end, but then my sister surprised me when she continued. "You're upset—no, not upset. Scared and angry. I can see that. I'm sorry, and I shouldn't be adding on to it. But all I'm saying is that you've been through this before and by the looks of things, you'll probably be through it again, and it will probably suck less and less each time you keep doing it, right? You're not going to stop, so you shouldn't slow yourself down with guilt for something you'd willingly do again."

I could only blink in stunned silence.

"So, to sum up, I'm glad you're not hurt and Meg's not hurt and I hope you'll call Brian and I think you're beating yourself up for no good reason. Which is fine, if you're into that, but all evidence to the contrary, I don't think you're really a masochist, but if you're just flogging yourself for kicks, don't involve me, okay? My ice cream is melting."

"Uh, okay. Thanks. Say hi to—"

But Bucky's newly found, emotional awareness—unexpected and limited as it was—didn't alter her social skills, and she hung up on me.

After I finished getting undressed, I dove into bed and was asleep almost instantly.

I had planned to sleep in, as late as I wanted, Saturday morning, but slamming doors got me out of bed about eight anyway. It was still better than six o'clock, though I was surprised that there was still so much activity that early, on the penultimate day of the conference. I regarded the skirt and shoes I'd put on the night before, draped over the chair, and decided that I couldn't face them. I put on the jeans and boots I'd worn out to the site and that I'd planned to wear on the drive home tomorrow afternoon. The conferees had seen archaeologists in jeans and boots before, and they could deal with it or not.

I found my way to the coffee shop and saw Lissa talking to Gennette Welles, someone I now knew well enough to say hi to, but that was about it. What I heard as I reached for my chair almost made me turn around and leave.

". . . hungry, and you know there's a reason they call them cat head biscuits," Lissa was saying. Enthusing, even. She ran her fingers through her hair as if caught up in the sensuality of the discussion.

I paused, wondering if this was a conversation I wanted to be part of.

"Oh, my grandmother makes the best ones," Gennette said. "Shoot, I could go for a plate now, with gravy."

"Tell me she doesn't use cat-head gravy too," I said, sitting down and hoping I'd heard them both wrongly.

"Huh?"

"I'm going to regret asking this, but—cat's head biscuits? Color me morbid, or maybe it's just the lack of coffee and a desperate misunderstanding, but all I can imagine is the shing-shing of the deli meat slicer." I mimicked moving the blade of the slicer back and forth. "Please tell me I'm wrong."

"That is the most disgusting thing I've ever heard, Emma!" Lissa looked like someone wrung out a diaper near her.

"Excuse me? I'm not the one for whom cat heads are a part of every good breakfast."

"Emma! They're called cat head biscuits because they're the size of cat heads! They're a Southern specialty. Don't be gross!"

"Why do you eat with her?" Gennette asked Lissa, but she was smiling.

"She's usually much better behaved, this time of day," Lissa explained. "Quieter."

"Just because you got to the coffee first," I grumbled, reaching for a mug. "Anyone could have made that mistake."

Gennette had been staring at my name tag. "You know it's never occurred to me before. Fielding's your last name? Married name?"

"No, I kept my birth name," I said, bracing for the inevitable questions about having worked with Oscar.

"We've got some Fieldings in Richmond. I wonder if there's a connection. When did your people come over?"

"Uh, could be . . ." Although it wasn't the question I was expecting, I wasn't a whole lot happier with this one. "I'm not really . . ."

The waitress arrived with the coffee, and I was able to stall. The coffee, however, was just hot and weak. This would not do, I thought. Eleni—where's Eleni? I want her crabbiness and her lack of professionalism and her wonderful, wonderful coffee. I drank what I had anyway, but it really sucked.

Once again, however, Lissa decided that she was not there to protect me or offer any refuge.

"Emma's people came over on the Mayflower," she announced.

"No, they did not!" I said. "They didn't, I promise you."

"Well, if not the Mayflower, then the next boat over," she said, shrugging. "I'm better with the boats coming in to Raleigh."

"Lissa, would you *stop*?"

"You know what I mean," Lissa said, then turned to Gennette confidentially. "Very old family."

"Everyone's family is very old," I said, gulping down more coffee.

"Anyway," Gennette said. "I bet I could find a connection between your family and those in Richmond. They were early too. And speaking of which, I see you're from Caldwell College in Maine."

Her fascination with my name tag was apparently endless. Perhaps we both needed more coffee. "Yes, that's right."

"I spoke with someone there at the art museum about one of the paintings I've been trying to track down. A Dr. Sarkes-Robinson."

I gulped. "Oh, boy. Dora." If she'd been talking to Dora, I knew what was coming next.

Gennette's face soured. "You know her, then? I have to say, Emma, she was not very helpful. In point of fact, she was downright rude."

"That's Dora for you," I said. "She's a bit, um, preoccupied with her own work." Which was the understatement of the year. And since her work was exclusively with the Italian renaissance painters, what the hell was Gennette doing talking to her?

"Apparently she's taking over the role of the head curator while he's on leave," Gennette continued, as if she'd read my mind. "She actually told me that she didn't have any time for, quote, unschooled provincial painters whose only virtue was that they were so untalented, they couldn't fully or accurately represent the obvious ugliness of their parvenu sitters. Unquote." Gennette sat back, and looked at me and Lissa with disbelief. "Can you get over that? I told her that if she was so darned important, what was she doing in a piddly little school like Caldwell, way the heck up in Maine, instead of someplace decent like New York or London."

"Ahem, Gennette," Lissa said.

Gennette's hand flew up to her mouth when she realized her faux pas. "Oh, Lord, Emma, I'm sorry. I didn't mean—"

I waved it aside. "Don't worry about it. Caldwell *is* small. Of course, it's the department that matters."

Gennette nodded quickly.

But I'd often wondered about that myself, why Dora was in our little part of the world, when her attitude was so clearly geared to a larger stage? Truth be told, Dora could be a world-class pain in the neck, but for some reason, we were drawn to each other. It wasn't quite friendship, not quite. More like mutual fascination. "Maybe if you told me what you were looking for, I could check it out for you. Sometimes I can catch Dora when she's in a good mood."

"When's that, when the moon is full and she's just eaten her fill of freshly slaughtered cattle?" Gennette said. Then she shook herself. "I'm sorry. Yes, please, that would be very helpful."

"I'm over there all the time, because there's a small collection of colonial portraits. Nothing great, fine arts–wise, but some really interesting stuff."

She handed me her business card. "Right, that's the collection. It's a picture of a small plantation house . . ." She went on to describe the architecture and landscape and colors. "So if you could just look at it—I think it's in storage— and let me know what you can see in the background, I'd really be forever in your debt. And if it's what I need, I'll tackle Ms. Pert-pants and try to get a slide made up of it. Thanks so much for this."

I nodded, scribbling down the last of her description. "No problem. I have to go down there when I get back anyway, so it will be a piece of cake. If you don't hear from me in two weeks, give me a call or drop me an e to remind me."

Lissa and Gennette got back to their conversation, and I was left mercifully with my hot, brownish water and muffin. I was grateful I had time to get it down—I was really in a hurry now—and finished just as the other two women said goodbye to each other for what seemed like a full five minutes.

"You guys are going to see each other on your panel later, aren't you?" I said, signing my check, after Gennette left.

Lissa got it right away. "Yes, of course. But we like to make sure everyone is fine and happy with everything before we go our separate ways. It's a Southern thing."

"Whatever," I said. "I'll see you later."

And leaving just enough time for Lissa to say "bye," I was gone myself.

I was really running to hide, and was mostly successful. I saw Chris and Scott off in a corner with a few other guys, huddled around a piece of blue plastic tarp spread over the carpet. It was the noise that really drew me over: hard crack of stone on stone, followed by the occasional clink of what sounded like breaking glass. I knew what they were doing without even looking, knapping pieces of flint into tools. With good enough flint, clean with no impurities in the matrix, you got the clear ring of glass as it broke off in regular pieces. Although I really didn't want to be drawn into it, there's something mesmerizing about watching the larger hammer stone in the hands of someone who knew what he was doing, knocking a sharp blade from a core stone and then rotating it for the next strike, almost like watching someone repeatedly removing slices from the round meat of an apple. One of the guys was actually making an arrowhead; he was also saving the waste flakes, or debitage, perhaps to use as a demonstration tool for a class, to show both the waste and the finished product. I figured Chris would be taking his blades and using finer tools of antler or some softer material to shape them into flints for his musket for reenacting. Or maybe he'd use some of the other fragments as a strike-a-light with an iron for making his encampment fire. I just hoped they'd all be careful with the flakes—they were incredibly sharp all on their own. And by the sounds of things, the stone they were working came from somewhere other than coastal Massachusetts, Maine, or New Hampshire for all I knew; usually the stuff around where I lived was pretty rotten to work with—it didn't fracture as nicely as some materials from New York or Vermont.

After that brief distraction, I actually hit a few morning papers. But it felt like I absorbed nothing of them. I was just sitting there, trying to look like an archaeologist, trying to hide in plain sight, trying not to think. Sue had been in the shower when the cops came to ask her questions—there was no saying how long she'd been in there, or whether she might have come back to the hospitality room to clear up any traces of her connection with Garrison.

A shower might have helped clean up any gunpowder residue.

Was there any connection between the shots fired by "hunters" on Thursday evening, and the shots I could have sworn came from outside and below me, when I was out on the porch roof? Even if Sue had been involved, there was no way she could have been in both places at once. And she was certainly not one of the two voices I'd heard whispering behind me at the farmstead session, not that one of them had to be the murderer, but . . .

Laurel Fairchild must have made an unprecedented foray out of the bar, for she caught me wandering toward the dead end of a hallway before I registered that I was nowhere near where I meant to be heading.

"Whoa, there, cowgirl. Nothing you want to see down there, is there?" She took my elbow and led me back down toward the hospitality suite. The door was open, the lights were on, and there were coffee mugs and donuts. I was so grateful that I almost didn't notice how the room got quiet when we went in.

After we loaded up, we found an empty corner by a large fern on the mezzanine. "How you doing?" she said. "You look a little . . . well, honestly, you look like hell."

I stared at her. "Okay."

She nodded. "And I heard you had a little excitement last night."

"Oh?"

"Emma, don't be like that. You know I hear things. Well, right now, rumors are flying thick and fast and everyone's talking. About Garrison, about the gunshots fired the night of Scott's announcement, about student vandalism, and now we hear cops are discussing the crazy bitch out on the roof during the storm—"

"It wasn't the hotel *roof*."

"—and you know, the odds favor the news—in whatever shape—getting around. But I'm not here about that now." Laurel's face was dire. "You know I don't listen for the sake of gossip. I'm not here to dig for juice."

I looked at her tiredly. She was right, and I knew it. "Okay."

"I'm giving you the head's up about a few things. Things you might already know, but if you don't, well, I think you're better off if you do."

"Okay."

"First." She ticked off her points on her fingers, long, tapered, with carefully polished nails. "Noreen McAllister. Never a friend of yours, I know, but she's taking it to a whole new level now. I don't know what happened between you guys, but she's stopped mouthing off about you trying to draw attention to yourself, and she's started saying that the cops are talking to you so much because they have decided you are "a person of interest" in Garrison's death. Which, as we know, is Noreen's way of saying you offed him."

My jaw dropped. "You can't be . . ."

"Yeah, I am. Just when you think you've plumbed the depths of someone's stupidity, they have to go and surprise you. I told her that she should consider whether her words are actionable, whether they could be construed as slanderous, and that shut her up for a while. But you never know."

"Thanks. And thanks for sticking up for me."

Laurel shrugged. "I've never heard anyone bitch so much about so little. It drives me up the wall. Next, news you might also not be too thrilled about. A couple of people I know you have close ties to lied about their movements on the night of Garrison's death. Both of them were seen having words with Garrison, and both of them did not tell the police this."

"Who?"

"Sue Ayers, for one. I understand that they had another interview with her last night."

"She's really in a state," I said. "I'm getting worried about her." And she also told me that she hadn't met Garrison, I thought. Made a point of reminding me that I'd seen her go up to bed, which didn't really count for anything, but it felt like she was trying to snowball me.

"Yeah, well, I heard her talking with Jay Whitaker in the restaurant last night. She went up and saw Garrison, and they had a row. She didn't mean to, but somehow she just lost her head, was how she put it." Laurel's words were loaded with meaning.

"If she saw him, it doesn't mean anything," I said. "No one's said Garrison was killed."

Laurel gave me a pitying look. "Right, they haven't. But there's been gunplay on two separate occasions and enough crazy shit to keep the cops here on an almost twenty-four-hour basis. What do you think, Em?"

"Okay. Still doesn't mean she did anything about it. Who was the other person?"

"Duncan Thayer."

I froze. "I don't have ties to Duncan."

Laurel canted her head and glared at me over her glasses. "Maybe you didn't for a while there, but you sure do now."

"What the hell does that mean?"

"He wants something from you, Emma. That's clear."

"He's going psychotic on me, is clear. First he was trying to be decent, but then he went all paranoid—about what, I don't know—and now he's sucking up."

She tilted her head. "Sounds about right."

"Laurel, what do you know?"

"I don't know anything for sure, but I have my suspicions. One thing is strange: Someone's reviewing some old work of his. Going through the collections, reevaluating his work. That would make anyone edgy, but an egotist like Thayer?" She shook her head.

"Which work?"

"His dissertation work. The stuff out on the western frontier of New York State. The Haslett site, wasn't it?"

I shrugged. "It's been a while; if someone's doing work out there, it would make sense. A lot of sites get reviewed; people come back to the data for all sorts of reasons. It doesn't need to mean anything."

"Maybe." She stood up, shoved her cat glasses back up her nose. "Well, you're looking less like you're going to puke all over someone's new shoes. My work here is done."

I had a sudden inspiration. "Hey, before you leave?"

"What?"

"Duncan started acting weird when I mentioned Josiah Miller. A nineteenth-century amateur, did some work way out in New York State."

"I don't recognize the name. And that's a little far inland for me."

Laurel's work kept her focused on ports and coastal sites. "Oh, I heard it in the farmstead session," I explained. "The guy who was chairing it, I think, was the presenter."

"That was Kevin Leary," she said promptly, and I realized that it was possible that she'd committed the entire program to memory. "He took off right after; had some research to do in Massachusetts while he was out here. I know because I wanted to ask him about a reference and I just barely caught him."

"Shoot." Well, I was sorry to have lost that lead, but I began to wonder about whether Leary had been the one reviewing the Haslett site. Maybe he was the link between Duncan and Josiah Miller—that was it! Relief at having solved that puzzle flooded me.

Then I remembered seeing long ago the manuscript Josiah Miller had written on Duncan's desk. But why should Duncan be so upset now by the mere mention of Miller's name?

Because Leary had described Miller's work as "recently discovered"! If that was the case, then why would I have remembered seeing it in Duncan's possession back before he'd even started his work at the Haslett site? Was that the reason Duncan was so defensive about it now? Holy cow, the implications of all of this were quite . . . breathtakingly serious.

Laurel seemed unaware that I'd checked out, stunned by my realization. "I've got to get back," she said. "People will start to talk if I'm not helping hold the bar down." She looked past my shoulder. "Hey, Gutierrez, wait up!"

Laurel vanished as quickly as she had appeared. I did feel better, even though I had a lot to think about in terms of what might be up with Duncan. At the same time, a tiny sliver of my brain was free to wonder just why Laurel had decided to tell me any of this at all.

I tried to sneak off with a sandwich around lunchtime—I knew a donut wasn't going to keep me—but Lissa and Jay found me. I was getting a little tired of seeing her bouncing all over the place, and although I knew it was just a matter of too much stress in too close quarters, I wished the snow would let up so Lissa could go hit the outlet malls.

"I hate being inside. This weather is for the birds. And why do Yankees leave their Christmas lights up to rot on their houses? I swear, we take ours down on New Year's Day, and that's that."

"Maybe we need the extra light to get us through the long, dark winter," I said. I knew for a fact our department administrator left his on his rented house all year long. He lit them every day too. Chuck liked the pretty colored lights and saw no reason that they should be restricted to Halloween or Christmas.

"Let's tell secrets," Lissa said. "Emma? Come on, spill it. What dirty dark secrets are you hiding?"

I looked at her. "Jesus. I'm not hiding anything. And I'm not in the mood for sleep-over party games. Piss off."

"Oh, come on, Em. Everyone's got something to hide," she said.

"Except you; everyone knows all your dirty laundry," I shot back.

"You'd be surprised at what you don't know about me," she said coyly. "You've been acting strange all weekend, confess, confess."

"Lissa, cut it out. You're being infantile."

"Am not. Jay, you'll play, won't you? Tell us what dark secrets lurk in your past."

"Lissa, for Christ's sake, just grow up. Leave Emma alone!"

We watched with open mouths as Jay stood up and stormed off.

I looked at Lissa, and her eyes were brimming. Maybe it was something about her persistence, but it suddenly occurred to me that someone keeps asking you about something because they probably want you to ask them about it too. "Oh, don't worry about him. Everyone is all screwed up this weekend. What's your secret, Lissa?"

She took a minute to catch her breath and then she smiled. "I'm gonna be a mama."

Of all the things I thought she was going to say, that was about the last. "Holy snappers! Congratulations!"

"Thank you! About a month or two now, I think."

I didn't bother trying to hide my glance at her stomach, which was nowhere near third trimester.

"Matt and I are adopting. We're just really excited."

"That's wonderful! So tell me everything."

And so I got all the details—girl, from China, they'd been trying for a while—and then I had to ask. "So, Lissa. Why couldn't you just come out and say it?"

She shrugged and looked away. "Oh, you know."

"I guess I don't."

"You know how people can be. They all still think of me as the same horny kid I was when we were all just starting out. Matt and I have been married for four years now."

It was my turn to shrug. "You still talk a pretty good game. And you don't mention him all that often."

She ran a hand through her hair. "Hey, I might be on a strict diet, but that doesn't mean I ain't gonna at least look at the menu. And if I don't mention him, it's because none of you know him, and I'm out having fun and catching up with you guys. Shoot, no one but you and Chris ever ask after him. Sometimes Sue. But I'm here at the conference for me, I get to have a break too." She threw her hands up. "Oh, I don't know. I guess I'm still sneaking up on the idea of being a mother myself. Scary, you know? But we're real happy. I just didn't know how to bring it up, not with it happening all of a sudden and everything."

Again I found myself about to open my mouth and let out all sorts of platitudes, but I caught myself. "I know what you mean. My life's . . . been changing lately too. I'm feeling a million miles away from where we started out."

She held up her hand, as if she was testifying in church. "That's the understatement of the year."

I shot a glance at her. "What do you mean?"

"Well, darn it, Emma. Everyone knows there was an "incident" with the window of the hospitality suite last night. Everyone knows, or thinks they know, that you've had some weird damn things happening to you recently—or did you not know that stories were getting around?"

"I guess . . . I figured that if I wasn't saying anything much, the cops—"

"I'm not talking about this weekend, though you should hear what that witch with a "b" Noreen is saying about you." I was surprised to hear Lissa so angry. "I'm talking the past couple of years. You figure that no one would read the papers or hear what the field crews were saying or anything?"

"Well, you know." I looked around at the subdued group around me. "One lives in hope."

"One lives in fairyland, more likely. Sounds like you're avoiding something."

"Not anymore. Not really." I took a drink of my soda. "Just figuring out how to spring the news, now that I'm dealing with it myself. You know how it is."

"I guess I do at that." Lissa smiled. "We get kinda caught up in other people's perceptions of ourselves. Me, the boozing party-girl, you the uptight Yankee—"

"Hey!"

"Okay, how about 'serious scholar from a tony northeastern school'?"

I shuddered. "You make it sound so . . . dire."

"Nah, just a convenient pigeonhole. People are comfortable with them, gets hard to shake them, even when you want to." She looked guilty for a minute, then shrugged it off. "Okay, so spring it on me. Your secret, that is."

"I'm thinking about branching out. Maybe forensics."

"Shoot, is that all?" She looked relieved. "Hey, I can help you with that."

I looked up. "How's that?"

"Emma, my dear idiot, I work on battlefield sites. My Rolodex is absolutely *crawling* with people who would be delighted to talk your ear off." Lissa gave me a look full of guile and innocence. "And, hey, you should talk to Carla. Our very own Bone Lady."

I nodded, but my heart wasn't in it. "I don't know, I'm still kinda shy about it. Wouldn't she think I was moving in on her—oh, shit."

Petra Williams had gone into the bar and was sitting by herself. I wanted to talk with her before anyone else took a seat. And if I brought Lissa, maybe she wouldn't just take off on me.

"What?"

"There's Petra, I need to talk to her. Come with me, just for a second?"

"Sure."

Neither of us was really eating anyway. We bolted over to the bar.

"Hey, Petra, I was wondering if we could join you for a moment?"

She looked past my shoulder, then coldly at me. "What we?"

I looked left, whipped my head to the right: Lissa was nowhere to be seen. I turned to see if she was still behind me, but the crowd was thin enough for me to see her retreating back. "I guess Lissa had to go to the ladies' room." Again. I just couldn't get past the fact that she always baled out on a situation when she was nervous. "May I?"

As much as I didn't like talking to Petra again, I knew I would have to. I had too much I wanted to know.

"I got shot at last night. I'm convinced that Garrison's

death . . . wasn't . . ." I knew as soon as I said the words out loud that it sounded far worse than I ever imagined. ". . . an accident."

She looked at me sharply. "On what do you base this?"

"It's not fair, I know, but until I know for sure, I don't want to tell you, exactly. Too many people might get hurt if I'm wrong."

Her face creased with distaste. "You don't ask much, do you? Why do you keep at me, like this?"

"No, I'm just trying to . . . you knew him better than anyone here, I guess."

"Yes."

"And . . . someone said that they saw you going into his room Wednesday night. Late."

"Yes, of course. I told you I walked him up—"

"No, not then. Really late. In your robe. And you had a key to his room. Were you still friends? I mean, after the divorce? Did you, you know, talk?"

"Yes, of course, we, 'you know,' talked," she snapped back. "We were divorced, and it was painful, but we were better as friends. And, since it's making the rounds, we were still occasionally involved. Not that it's any of your business."

She looked at me, past me, to something behind me. "Or perhaps it is. Are you interested in the Connecticut job too?"

I gaped. What? "No, I—"

"Like so many of your fellows, maybe you wanted Garrison's imprimatur for it? I know Bradford DuBois did. Wouldn't leave poor Julius alone, not even when he told him he couldn't stand him and wouldn't support him if he was the last candidate on earth. I mean, we all know Julius was outspoken, but it took an awful lot for him to explode at Dr. DuBois like that."

Just then, Duncan pulled up to the table, but it didn't stop Petra. "Or perhaps it wasn't the job. Maybe it was something more personal." She darted a glance over at Duncan, whose face was a study in nonchalance; maybe he hadn't heard what she'd said. "How would you like it if someone went poking around in your personal life? Into your past? Or was it one of your reports that Julius was reviewing? He'd been wearing himself out, reading a stack of site reports three feet high; even though he was retired, people still valued his opinions. Maybe you were concerned that he'd have something to say about your work. It wouldn't be the first time that Julius had something to say about work done by a Fielding."

Garrison reviewing site reports? An alarm went off somewhere in memory, but I had to stick to the topic at hand. "You know I'm not doing this for the fun of it, Petra. I was shot at. I want to know why."

"You haven't answered my question."

I looked her straight in the eye. "I believe I could stand his scrutiny or anyone else's, into my work or my past. If it was as important as I think this is."

The same smile I saw on Thursday, when she was needling me about Duncan, was back. "But with all your hints, Dr. Fielding, you're not just asking me whether I was still seeing Julius. You're asking if I might know some reason that he might not have had an accident, as you've so eloquently put it?"

"Uh, yes."

"You're unbelievable. He took too much of his medicine. He'd been drinking. He was a selfish, stubborn idiot who went outside when he shouldn't have, and he had an accident." She swiped at the sudden tears that I was horrified to see running down her cheeks.

Petra had said before that Garrison had not been drinking. Was this denial or a slip-up on her part? "I'm sorry, it's just that you had been speaking so angrily to him before the panel—"

"He was an easy man to get angry at! This isn't your business, and if it is something the police should look into, then leave it to them." She brushed at the last of the tears. "I might ask these same sorts of questions of you."

"What do you mean?" I glanced around.

"Well, there was obviously no love lost between the two of you. Your paper was a marvel of unspoken antagonism paneled over with some factual, occasionally lauding, remarks."

"Huh?"

"You seem to have had some problem with Garrison that you weren't saying—"

"Well, you'd know all about that, wouldn't you?" Once again, I was reduced to a petulant teenager's response.

"I beg your pardon?" she said. "I know nothing of the sort."

"Clearly that's some of the reason that you've disliked me so much over the years." I wished the words away as soon as I said them, cringing inside.

"You might find this hard to believe, but I haven't given you a thought one way or the other. Why should I?"

"I don't know. You were always so distant with me. Curt."

She gave a short barking laugh. "We had nothing to talk about. How should I have been? No, never mind. I think this interview is long past over." She turned to Duncan. "Dr. Thayer? Would you mind?"

He offered her his arm, and she left the room like a queen dismissing an impertinent commoner, which I guess was pretty close to the truth.

I sat back in my seat, free to consider what had triggered the mental alarms while Petra was chewing me out. Duncan. Laurel had said something about someone reviewing Duncan's work; we had both assumed or guessed that it had been Kevin Leary, whose paper was on the amateur Josiah Miller and early research in New York in the session on farmsteads.

What if it hadn't been Leary reviewing Duncan's work? What if it had been Julius Garrison? What if Garrison had made the same connection between a supposedly recently discovered research report and Duncan's dissertation work?

How far would Duncan go to cover up some professional misconduct? Was it possible that he had—

Laurel came in just then and immediately took Petra's empty seat.

"How's it going, Em? You look like you're a million miles away."

"Uh . . . I get the thousand-yard stare about this time every conference." I shook myself; I had to think more about this before I got much older, but not in public and especially not in front of someone as perceptive as Laurel. I now had more suspects than I knew what to do with.

"Can I ask you something?" I said, thinking of Petra's ramrod straight back as she left with Duncan.

Laurel nodded. "You can even ask me something else."

"What did you think of my presentation on Garrison? The one at the plenary?"

She thought about it for a moment. "Careful. Hit all the right notes, but very careful."

"What do you mean?"

"Like you were trying very hard to keep your own feelings out of it. I counted the number of times you said 'I' and it was only about a dozen, tops. Everyone else was closer to hundreds, going for the personal connection with Garrison, naturally enough."

"Huh. I expected to have a hard time writing the paper, but it was a whole lot easier than I thought. I was thinking of it as a nice historical piece, is all."

"Hmm. How much personal stuff could you have put in?"

"A bit," I admitted. "I tried to, tried to keep it light. It just didn't work, so I took it out."

"Like what?"

That was Laurel for you; not only did she pay attention to things like word counts in paper presentations for fun, but she always asked the question you hoped she wouldn't. "Like a photo in the office. You know that riff that Roche went on about? How Garrison's office should be sent to the Smithsonian as a capsule summary of historical archaeology in twentieth-century America?"

"Eeeyuw, yes. Spreading it a bit thick for my taste."

"Well, I was in one of those pictures."

"Impossible." She reclined. "Roche covered every single picture. I counted them. Had slides of them all. I didn't see you in one of them."

If anyone would have noticed, it would have been she.

Laurel wasn't done. "But there was that one of Oscar, wasn't there? If I was going to put money on any of them, it would be that one. Am I right?"

I nodded. "You wouldn't have recognized me. I was right behind Oscar, a bit to the side. I didn't like Garrison much in those days, and liked him even less as time went on. But I'm there."

"Interesting. I'm surprised that Roche didn't mention it."

I was about to explain when Laurel got it on her own. "Ah. Oscar was at the edge of the group. The frame covered you."

I nodded again. "I doubt Garrison would have bothered to cut me out, even. He barely noticed me as it was."

She pointed at me. "But he did something for you to notice him."

"Jeez, Laurel, have you ever thought of taking up therapy, as a profession I mean? You just home in on the jugular!"

She laughed, which made me all the more annoyed. "Well, Emma, if the way her ladyship stormed out of here is any indication, you were doing a little prying yourself."

I sighed. "Yes. You're right. Again. I've been trying to figure out why anyone would want to kill Garrison. Apart from the obvious reasons."

"Hmmm" was all she said to my guilty admission. "So tell me about the photo."

"You know I spent summers with Oscar."

She nodded.

"Garrison was on one of the committees that voted on funding for various projects, including one of Oscar's, up on Cape Mary. One of his visits was captured in that photo. He and Grandpa were violently in disagreement about the interpretation of the site and its dates, that was par for the course, with them. But after Garrison lost Oscar his funding, he never dared to come back to our sites again. They didn't speak after that."

"That makes sense. But what did he do to you?"

"It was before the blow up. It wasn't anything, but it really pissed me off. Like I said, he never paid much attention to me. But once . . ."

"Yes?" Laurel steepled her fingers.

"Once he saw me and for some reason, said that little girls with red hair were thought to be witches in the old days, and did I think I would like burning at the stake."

"What a prick."

"Well, I'm sure it was just generational humor or social disconnect, or whatever, but it really bugged me," I said in a rush. I felt petty just bringing it up. "Oscar was never around when Garrison said something like that, but I told him. He told me to ignore Garrison, who was just 'an old idiot,' or I could tell him to stop, but essentially, it was no big deal and I could take care of myself. But the last time Garrison did it, he pulled on my hair too, so I decided that if he really thought I was a witch I would make a potion for him."

"More and more interesting. How old were you?"

"Nine, maybe. Maybe ten."

"And?"

"And the potion was just booger berries—you know, just the red berries you find on any shrub in New England—mashed up good, some old seaweed that would stink to high heaven when it dried out, and one of those little coffee creamers that had been sitting out in the sun all day. Stuff a ten-year-old would think was nasty. I waited until they were on the other side of the site. Garrison's car windows were left open, of course, so I went to the far side, opened the door, and pulled up the floor mat. Poured just enough to make a good layer, but not so much that it would stink too quickly—I wanted a little distance between me and the event, of course—and replaced the mat. To this day, I don't know what happened. If he knew it was me and told Oscar, I never heard about it."

Laurel laughed and signaled the waiter. "You have unsuspected depths, Emma. I never would have believed you capable of such retribution. Easily done, carefully considered, and yet costly and a righteous pain in the ass. Remind me never to call you a witch. But may I make two potentially unpleasant observations?"

"Who's going to stop you?" I said wearily. Reliving the past was like carrying an anchor around with me, and my shoulders and neck ached.

"You'd be surprised. One—no disrespect intended to the memory of your grandfather, but if he couldn't do more than tell you to ignore a jackass making hurtful remarks to you, young as you were, he wasn't doing his job."

My stomach dropped away, like someone had opened a trap door beneath me. She was right. "And the other?" I said, after a moment.

"If you are thinking that Garrison was murdered, you've just given me all sorts of reasons to suspect you. Professional rivalry with your beloved grandfather, loss of some income and possibly the right to dig on an important site, personal hurt that might have festered over the years. And who knows what you haven't told me? Didn't you both have words at the site on Wednesday? All that careful planning for vengeance, even at that early age—and you get away with it? You sound like a fabulous suspect to me."

Chapter 13

"**M**ARTINI, PLEASE," SHE TOLD THE WAITER. THEN she turned back to me. "That's why the cops might be keeping you so close. Are you having anything?"

"Uh, no. No, thanks," I told the waiter, and he left. "Laurel, you know I didn't have anything to do with Garrison's death."

"You're not my favorite suspect at the moment," she admitted with a rueful little grin.

"Well, I didn't. Just so you know. Damn, Laurel, how can you be so cold-blooded about this?"

She shrugged. "Simple. I don't have any skin in this game."

It was such a perverse thing to say that I got up and left without a word. Soon I found myself on the fourth floor, and I knocked on Chris's door. I heard the television get turned way down; the door opened, and Chris looked bleary-eyed, a beer in one hand.

"Hey, man," I said. "I'm glad I caught you. Where is Brad's room? It's this floor, right?" I didn't just want to call Brad and warn him that I was on my way to see him.

"Uh, yeah, just taking a nap." He rubbed his face, which was red. "He's in four-sixteen."

"Great, thanks. Sorry to disturb you."

The image of the television reflected in the mirror caught my eye, and I quickly looked away. When I take a nap, I like watching professional golf. I find the low murmur of the voices soothing. Apparently when Chris took a nap, he liked to watch naked women washing a truck.

"No problem. See you tonight."

He shut the door hurriedly; I heard the television volume rise, but just a hair. I went down the hall to Brad's room and knocked.

When he opened it, I saw he was fully dressed, and didn't seem sick at all, although his color was not good.

"How you doing?" I asked.

He scratched at his head. "Oh. You know. Okay."

"You had a meeting with Garrison the night he died, didn't you?" I said.

I'd hoped he'd be taken off guard by my directness; I was more than surprised. Brad grabbed my wrist and pulled me into his room. He shut the door behind us.

"What do you know about this?" he hissed.

"You're hurting me," I said as calmly as I could. When he didn't immediately let go, I jerked my wrist toward his thumb, and freed myself.

"How did you know that?" he repeated.

"Petra Williams said that you'd been after him." I glanced around his room; it was immaculate. The only thing out of order was the rumpled bedspread; I noticed family pictures on the nightstand. "What time were you supposed to meet him?"

"I . . . I didn't . . . he never showed up," Brad said.

"You're lying."

His mouth twitched. "I . . . Emma, I think I killed Garrison."

Now if he was trying to shock me, I don't think he could

have succeeded any better. "You . . . think . . . you killed Garrison?"

"I might have, I don't know." He burst into tears.

I was horrified. "Brad, have you spoken to the police?"

"Yuh—yes, and I told them the truth."

"What?" That couldn't be . . .

"I answered their questions truthfully," he insisted. They asked if I'd seen Garrison after eleven o'clock. I hadn't. We were supposed to meet at ten-thirty."

"Oh my God, Brad!" My hand flew up to my mouth.

"But we didn't," he insisted. He snuffled, and managed to pull himself together. "I ran into him earlier in the evening, down by his room, and I spoke to him, asked him if he wanted to chat sooner. You know, so we could both get to bed early."

"And?" I wanted to shake him for the answers, comfort him . . .

"He said no."

"And that was it? Is that when you killed him?"

He recovered enough to look indignant. "I only said I thought I did. I don't know for sure."

"This isn't the time for playing with semantics, Brad!" I said, clutching his arm. "When did you go outside?"

"Outside?" He shook his head, puzzled. "We didn't go outside."

"Brad!" I exploded. "He was found outside, in his winter clothing, on the lake! If you 'think' you killed him, how did you manage to do it without going outside?"

"Well, here's what happened." He paused, wringing his hands. "I'm scared Emma."

"I know, I know. Just tell me."

He took a deep breath. "I went up to him, in the hallway. I said hello. He didn't answer. He was going through his pockets, looking for his key. I spoke a little louder, he turned around. His eyes seemed really unfocused, like he was sleepwalking, or something." Brad paused.

"Yes?"

"So I asked him if we should talk now, rather than waiting until so much later. He mumbled something about not wanting to talk to me at all. I asked if another time would be more convenient. He told me to go to hell." Brad buried his head in his hands; I could barely hear his next words. "Emma, I can't even look at you."

"Tell me what happened." I tried to keep my voice as calm and uninflected as possible.

"I—I never did anything like this before. I grabbed his arm. I didn't want him to just walk off on me like that, like I was nothing, not even worth answering. I didn't mean to . . . but . . . I grabbed his arm . . . just to keep him from going into his room right away. I didn't mean to, I mean, I just wanted him to stop. But he . . . his arm was so thin. I . . . I must have hurt him, I didn't mean to. He cried out. I let go, and he stumbled against the doorjamb."

He took a deep, shuddering breath.

"What happened next? Did he fall?"

"No, the door wasn't open. He just . . . sort of bumped himself against it. He might have hit his head. I don't know. I couldn't tell."

"But . . . you didn't see any blood?"

"No, I don't think so. No, I would have seen it. Maybe . . . he sort of bumped his forehead. Maybe."

"Brad, the cops said that Garrison's wounds were all on the back of his head."

"That's why I didn't think it was important, at first," he said eagerly. Then Brad drooped. "I wondered whether he didn't go out afterward and then fall down. I think that's what happened, Em."

"But then, that would be an accident, Brad, wouldn't it? That's . . . that's not murder."

"But I was so angry. I was so tired of being dismissed. Things . . . things have been really bad lately. I always knew something bad would happen if I ever lost . . . things got out of control."

For Brad, with his planning and schedules . . . "Things have been out of control for a while now?"

He nodded. "Francine is leaving me. No matter how many therapists we see, I don't see how she's going to be happy. I should be grateful she stuck around while I was sick—"

"You were ill?"

"Sick." He swallowed. "Cancer-sick." He could barely bring himself to say the word, much less give me any other details. "She waited until we knew I was out of the woods, then she said she wanted to leave."

"My God." I sagged. "And you never said anything, to any of us?"

"I wanted to make sure, one way or the other. It's been a horrible year. I don't know what to do, I love my kids, I can't live without them." He started to cry again, softly.

I put my hand on his shoulder. "And the Connecticut University job?"

"I hoped a change would be good for us, I thought it would help. She says we're in a rut, I thought if we moved, shook things up a little . . ." He shrugged weakly; he could barely lift his shoulders. "It's not good to feel desperate, Emma. I . . . I can't tell you how awful it is."

I thought about what he was saying. It didn't fit. "But what about the artifacts?"

"What artifacts?"

"Bea's stolen artifacts. The stuff that was taken from the book room."

"I have no idea." His face brightened, but then took on a different degree of puzzlement. "Wait, yes I do. Bea's found her artifacts. She'd left them behind the chair in the bar."

I swore to myself. "Are you *kidding* me? When was this?"

"Yesterday. Friday." He shrugged again, happier to have one answer, at least.

"Jeez, I guess it's not surprising that she wouldn't be as vocal about having found something as having lost it, but you'd think she'd at least tell people so they didn't think there were thieves around."

Brad shook his head. "But there are. There were a few break-ins. And there was the book room, don't forget."

I rubbed at my forehead. "The detective has been trying to tie them in with Garrison, but I don't think they're related."

I thought about the other things I had questions about. Was whoever came after me looking for something that had nothing to do with Garrison? That didn't seem likely. "Where were you yesterday afternoon?" I asked Brad. "We haven't seen you since Thursday night. Now it's Saturday; that's a long time to be out of sight at a conference."

"But there was the session that I was chairing, all afternoon. And then there was a meeting into the evening. Why?"

"There was another incident, last night. I was shot at and the police think the two were connected." I looked at him. "I think the fact that you had a hundred people watching you at the session would be a pretty good alibi."

Brad looked relieved. "Still I think you need to talk to the police," I said. "Maybe they'll be able to tell you that you weren't responsible for Garrison's death, and if by some remote chance you . . . it's as you said, then they'll know and they'll find out it was an accident, and all of this will be over."

At this point my head was spinning, and it wasn't even that I needed to focus on sorting things out; I needed to reboot entirely. I didn't feel safe enough alone in my room, and I was in no mood for the bar any longer. It was that awkward part of the day when you have finished the day's papers but are between cocktail parties, and too early for dinner. My feet, however, knew exactly what my head needed, and they marched me right over to the pinball machine at the side of the lobby.

I had a pile of quarters still in my pocket from my poker winnings, and I set three of them down on the Plexiglas, after I loaded one up. It had been way too long since I'd played pinball, and I spent the first quarter recalling my old skills. I'm not a brilliant player, no one will ever play *Pinball Wizard* when I walk into an arcade, but I play well enough to shut everything else out and keep my brain happily distracted for minutes on end. This was an old-fashioned type of machine, a Wild West motif with the bare minimum of electronic gadgets, for which I was grateful. I barely know what to do with the games I pass in the cinemas or at the mall, the few times I've ventured into that juvenile wonderland.

The tension gradually left my shoulders as I got the feel of the table. If you aimed the ball toward the saloon girl in the fancy red dress, you could bank it off and hit the steer target for double points. I noticed that one of the flippers was a little sticky and learned to compensate for it.

I was racking up a respectable score and had just gotten a free ball, when I noticed Katie Bell hovering just within my peripheral vision. I tried to ignore her, but she wasn't going away; I furrowed my forehead with a feigned concentration, and kept playing. Finally, she inched her way closer and closer, until she was finally standing right alongside the table. She wouldn't be wished away.

She waited until I pulled back on the plunger and had launched my third ball before she started speaking. I didn't have to look at her—I was still trying to get another free play—but she started talking anyway. She was too young to know better, I suppose, having grown up with games that could be paused; and I felt bad, thinking I sounded too much like Noreen with her uncharitable description of "Katie Car

Alarm." But she really shouldn't have waited until I pulled the plunger.

"I feel like that ball in there," she was saying.

"Uh-huh," I answered, whacking the ball with the small flipper at the top of the table. Then realizing that it was actually a pretty nasty way to feel and that I was at least partly responsible for it, I asked: "How's that?"

She looked at the leering card sharp whose mechanical voice was coming from the back of the machine and frowned. "Batted around from here to there, too much noise, too much everything."

"I can see that." There—a bit of luck; rather than going down the chute that led to the place behind the flippers from which no ball returns, the ball actually wavered in my favor and slid back down to where I could flip it back to more targets. I looked at her suddenly. "You haven't been attacked, or burgled, or anything?" I suddenly remembered Duncan had "lost his temper" with her. "No one's been mean to you, have they?"

"No, nothing like that."

I paused, then turned back to the table. "Okay. Who's doing the batting?"

"I am, I guess. It's the conference. I just feel like I want to see everything, and I can't. I can't sleep either, because everyone keeps coming in at all hours. Even before the break-in, it was the same. Meg snores."

I tried not to smile. "You can't do everything. You have to prioritize. If you miss something, you can always follow up with emails after." I was within ten thousand points of another free ball and it was the closest I felt to good all day. "You remember what I said at dinner the other night? There's no rule that says you can't take a break, get a nap, order some real food, get a little fresh air—I noticed it stopped snowing earlier. You'll be sharper if you take care of yourself."

"I suppose." She knew she knew better, but was just over-tired and overexcited and on a low. "That looks complicated."

"It's not really, once you get the hang of it. The trick is to just relax, most of the time. Keep your shoulders from tensing, keep your eye on the ball, and don't react to every bit of the racket. The racket is just a distraction. That's when you lose. Actually, if you just wait for things to come to you, that's the best way. Just chill out and make small moves, wait to pay attention to the really important stuff." Here the ball fortuitously drifted toward my flipper, and I batted it away toward the big bumpers.

I risked a quick look at Katie. "And when you get really familiar with things, you can even tell by sound where the ball is, and you can reorient yourself, if you need to. You buy yourself the time you need, when you learn not to react and overreact." I turned back to the table just in time to grab the ball with the middle flipper and send it away again, just in time to be rewarded with a free ball. "See?"

She shifted her weight. "I guess. I s'pose it works for the conference too."

I smiled. Katie was smart enough to pick up on a metaphor. "I suppose. You know, you've got an hour before dinner. You could grab a nap." I wanted her to go away now; I was just hearing the pinging that meant I could get triple points for the next five seconds. I was about to beat my personal best for the day, and I was only on my second quarter.

"No, I'm too wound up."

"Get someone to go with you, and stick your nose outside, then, while there's still a little light." Please, Katie, I'm not your mother. I was starting to get wound up myself and was missing easy geometry with all the talk, and I had been so close to clearing my head.

I could see her shrug her shoulders. Shit, I lost my ball and was down to my last free play.

"No, that guy just went outside again, and I don't want to run into him."

"What guy is that?" The ball arced up and around the table.

"You know, that weird guy from Northeastern Consulting? He's been popping in and out all day. He's a little sketchy." She struggled with her scrunchie, trying to get it to stay put in her hair. "Do you know he was actually outside the building when the police were questioning everyone? He wasn't supposed to be, none of us were. But I saw him."

It took me a minute to register what she said. "What? You saw him leave the dining room Thursday night? By himself?"

"Yeah and he didn't come back. Hey, be careful! You're going to miss—!"

But I had already turned to her. "How come you saw him?"

"I asked the cop to let me go to the ladies' room. He was just going out the side door when I went in. I don't think he was supposed to," she said unnecessarily.

I caught my breath. "Katie, I've got to go, I'll talk to you later, okay?"

"Don't forget your quarters!" she called.

"Play a couple of games for me," I called over my shoulder as I raced for the side door and outside.

I saw Widmark a couple dozen meters ahead of me, just at the edge of the road. It occurred to me that I could be following Garrison's killer. If he saw me, I figured I'd apologize for ducking out on him last time, and I hurried a little to catch up with him. The snow was still fairly loose and flew up as I walked, not making a lot of noise.

He didn't follow the path I had, but went down a road off to the left: the access road that led down to the lake and the shed with the snowplows, I realized, remembering how Garrison's body had been found by someone going to get equipment. The road was paved, and it was a hell of a lot easier going down here than down the steps I'd taken the other night: It was sanded, and the icy patches were concentrated at the middle of the road. Garrison, if he'd come on his own, would have had only little trouble, especially if the roads had been plowed, as they were now. The streetlights that lined the road were already illuminated, the late afternoon was so overcast.

I ducked behind a tree, my heart racing from more than the exercise. It started to make sense to me: Here was someone that no one had ever seen before, who seemed to have absolutely nothing to do with the field, by his own admission, and who was asking for names of everyone around me. He'd been at the periphery of nearly every event the police were present for, and they'd spent some time talking to him. What was he really up to at the conference, and what was he doing now?

I could find that out, if I kept myself quiet and kept following. I was sweating in spite of the cold.

So far, he seemed to be on exactly the same mission that I was, following the access road down to the shore of the lake. Was it possible that he was going down to make sure he hadn't lost anything at the crime scene? Maybe he was going to recover something that he'd taken from the body?

He began to slow down, and as I did, I realized why I found his motions familiar, the way I did at the Thursday-night opening reception: He moved like my martial arts instructor, Nolan. Quickly, with a graceful economy of movement, on the balls of his feet. This did not fit with the image I'd come to associate with him—middle-aged, overeager, underfed. Bad breath. I moved off the road now and then, when the secondary growth was thin enough to move through easily but still capable of providing some cover for me. Widmark stopped; I stopped.

He pulled out a gun.

I had nothing.

It took me a moment longer than I wanted to force myself to look out from behind the tree that hid me. If he'd seen me, I reasoned, he surely wouldn't be continuing on as he had. He wouldn't have shown the weapon to me, giving me the warning that he was aware of me. There was something else going on here.

My heart was now beating so fast that I could barely draw breath. I watched, counting out a full fifteen seconds before I followed him again. I only moved when I could find the next glacial erratic to dodge behind, or the next tree to shield me, should Widmark suddenly turn around and start emptying out the pistol at me. He got only a little farther ahead of me, mostly because he was being as careful as I was, and there was a clearing to the side of the road that left a virtually open path between us. Well, open save for the trees—the pricker bushes were farther off the road to the left than they had been before.

His caution didn't really fit with my present hypothesis. Something much bigger was going on, and perhaps I needed to get the hell out of here.

It was already too late. Something ahead of us both drew Widmark's attention. He extended a pistol, flashed a badge, and shouted, "FBI. Throw down your weapon!"

An odd muffled bang, followed by a noise like a baseball bat hitting a bag of laundry: whump. The next noise was a scream. It was Widmark. I watched as he looked about and pointed his pistol roughly in the direction of the lake, away from me and to the right. Before he could fire, the dull bang and the whumping noise came again, and he did a clumsy pirouette, slammed himself against the tree and fell down.

Widmark pulled himself over onto his side, and I saw him painstakingly raise his hand again. He was still alive.

I had to help. I began to run, hunched down and stooping toward him, always careful to keep something between me and whoever was out there willing to shoot at an FBI agent.

I still didn't know what was going on, so I hid out behind a boulder and pulled out my cell phone.

The battery was charged and the signal was at maximum. I found myself fumbling for the buttons and tried to focus on the numbers: My vision was playing tricks on me, closing in on the screen. I blinked, just once and quickly, afraid almost that I would fall asleep in a state of denial, to clear my head. I dialed nine-one-one and got the operator almost immediately.

"Emergency response."

"I'm by the General Bartlett Hotel, in Green Bank, New Hampshire," I said, the words stumbling over each other because I was so desperate to get all the information out in a hurry. "There's an access road behind the place, there's been shots fired, someone is hurt, I think he's probably bleeding—I can't see who is out—"

"Okay, ma'am? You stay down, is there somewhere you can be safe?"

"Uh, I'm in the woods," I said, trying to figure out what constituted safe at the moment. "I'm behind a big boulder. It's pretty big." Suddenly, I wasn't so sure.

"Okay, you stay there, try and keep hidden, okay? If you think it's safe, get out of there. We're sending someone right away, hang in there."

"An ambulance too," I said.

"How many people are with you?"

"Me, and this other guy, Widmark, I think he's with the FBI, he said so, and who . . . whoever is shooting."

"Do you have any idea of who it is?"

"No, I don't know, I can't see from where I am . . ."

The voice on the other end of the line continued calmly. "Don't move, okay? You just stay put."

At this point Widmark looked back and saw me. His eyes widened and he gestured vehemently for me to move away.

I shook my head. "He's going to get killed if I don't pull him away from there," I said to myself.

"Ma'am, don't—"

I put the phone, still connected, down on the rock.

By this time, Widmark was hissing at me like all the steam was escaping from him. "Get the hell out of here!"

"I called for help," I said from behind a rock. "I'm going to," I continued as I hurried along, low to the ground. ". . . to get you out of here," I said from behind a stand of trees five feet behind him.

"I don't need help, I'm not badly hurt—sssh!" He fired twice—the noise almost deafening, so close—then there was silence.

I waited for a handful of heartbeats. "I saw you got hit, maybe three times."

"I'm wearing a vest, I—what are you doing!"

I grabbed him by the collar of his jacket, which threatened to rip off, and under one armpit—the one without the gun— and pulled him back a few inches. "I'm getting you to cover," I said, through gritted teeth. My nails ached as I readjusted my grip and pulled again, this time bunching up the fabric in my hand. He weighed a ton, and whatever it was he was wearing under his coat was probably adding some more weight to him. The next try got us another eighteen inches, but he made a noise that people shouldn't make, and my heart almost left me. Two more tries, with Widmark pushing back with his good leg, and I had him behind the comparative cover of the trees. I sat down heavily, sweating as the snow melted under my butt and into my jeans.

"Okay, now get the hell out of here," he gasped. He slapped a fresh clip into his pistol.

"No, I'm going to take you with me. I'll get you out of here, you said you're not hurt badly—"

"I'll be okay if you've called for help. My leg isn't going to get me anywhere, and you can't stay here."

I shook my head. "I can, I'll help keep—"

"I'll shoot you and say you were resisting arrest," he said. "Get the hell out of here."

I didn't think he was really going to shoot me, but in this case, I guess he outranked me, and since he seemed pretty adamant about it, I nodded. There was nothing I could do, really, that wouldn't get in the way, or cause more of a distraction for him. Or maybe get myself hurt or killed as well.

He saw me waver. "Get back up to the hotel. Let them know what's going on—"

"Don't you have a phone?" I said.

"It's what stopped the first bullet," he said calmly, "and you said you called already anyway. Don't go by the road, you're too obvious a target. If you cut diagonally up here," he gestured with a hand to our left, "you should hit the street leading to the hotel pretty quick. If nothing else, there's cover. Now get the hell out, while our friends over there are still trying to figure out what's going on."

I nodded, thought about protesting, thought about asking what was going on, then nodded again. He was right, and as much as I didn't like leaving, the idea of staying scared me even more.

I paused, picking out the route before I started. There was a kind of pathway that led the way he indicated. I must have hesitated too long, because he slapped at my shoulder. "Get going!"

I looked at him a last time, realized there wasn't really anything else I could do, and began to take a deep breath. Another bang was followed by the sound of a bullet splitting wood, and I shot up like a startled animal, running as hard as I could. It was more difficult than I imagined; there were trees, snow-concealed roots, dips in the ground, and flattened bushes. I stumbled a few steps, moved forward until I got my balance back, then kept going on as fast as I could.

As much noise as I knew I was making, I couldn't hear anything but my own breath.

My pace was excruciatingly slow, and I had the nightmare sensation of struggling as hard as I could with little return for my effort. The overgrowth caught at me, tearing my clothes as I staggered past, and suddenly I felt the raw cold as my cheek was slashed by a trailing thorny branch. I kept on, stumbling over a rock, and I rolled my weight over my right ankle the wrong way. Thank God for my boots: If I'd been wearing shoes, I might have broken my ankle. Hell, if I'd been wearing shoes, they have been left behind as I struggled through the snow and roots. A few steps more and I measured my length in the snow. Frigid air rushed over broken skin—I realized I'd scratched my chin raw on the icy crust that had formed over the snow. I hopped up, stumbling as I put too much weight on my ankle, and pelted on as fast as I could, my lungs burning even as I felt my face and fingers going numb with the cold. The pain receded, but I knew I'd pay for it later. My breath left my face damp as I struggled to breathe and run. My only goal was to keep on in the direction that I thought would take me to the main road to the hotel, knowing that if I faltered, it was more than a long trudge back through the woods that I would have waiting for me.

The grade rose gradually more steeply, and I realized that I was coming to the road. My foot slipped on the sodden leaves under the snow and I came down hard on my hands, jarring my whole skeleton nearly out of my skin. My teeth clacked together, and a sharp pain and the taste of warm copper followed; my tongue began to throb, and a small sob escaped me as I struggled up the bank. I grabbed at a branch and it snapped under my weight; I slid and made another grab, successful this time, and hauled myself up another few feet. I dug in again, and this time had enough momentum to see the asphalt beyond the snow as I staggered out of the woods.

The snowbank was compacted by the plows and had the same icy glaze as farther back in the woods, but there were coarse handholds that held my weight as I dragged myself up. I could not hear a pursuer, but I didn't care: I would keep moving until I was either completely safe or I gave out entirely. I rolled down the other side of the snowbank and felt the grit of ice and sand as I slid onto the verge.

I stood up and looked around wildly, trying to orient myself, and staggered into the middle of the street. A blare of a horn made me jump, and as I turned, a big red pickup truck swerved around me, the horn still sounding and the driver an angry blur of reflexive driving and vehement gestures all at once.

I spun around again, not sure which way I should go to avoid the danger that was now already past, when I saw that the truck had stopped a few meters ahead of me. Bracing myself against the driver's anger, I realized that not only was he *not* extracting himself from the cab, but also that I recognized the hat that was visible through the rear windshield. A colorful Andean knitted hat with a jaunty peak and earflaps with strings dangling was just about visible past the driver's headrest, and I realized that it was Meg Garrity who was driving. She was shouting at me, though I couldn't make out what she was saying for the blood pounding in my ears. All I know was that the familiar TRK GRRL license plate meant my salvation was at hand, and I ran for it.

Meg opened her door and almost got out, but I screamed, "No, don't! Just get us out of here!" I flung myself at the back of the truck, my feet now feeling leaden and my muscles resisting every demand that I made on them.

Sliding on the ice where there was no salt, and rolling forward on the coarse grains where they were, I threw myself up and over the drop door of the truck, getting a facefull of plastic woven sacks full of sand. My feet still dangling outside the bed, I slapped at the rear panel, and the truck lurched away.

"Go! Go!" My grip was less sure than I imagined, and I slid back, almost falling off the truck altogether, my elbows slamming into the drop door and saving me, even as one foot dropped off the bumper and bounced the toe of my boot along the pavement as Meg sped away. The cold metallic tang of the truck bed, the industrial feel of the sand bags, and the exhaust of the truck were the most reassuring smells I could have imagined at this point.

Meg swerved to miss potholes, but then hit a couple of doozies that knocked the wind from me. Praying that my upper body strength was not as depleted as I feared, I hauled myself up and finally over the back of the truck, coming to rest on the lumpy sacks. I rolled over, watched the gloomy sky fly past overhead, and tried to catch my breath, my chest heaving and my body soaked in sweat that I now could feel running in rivulets down every part of me. The cold seemed to catch up with me, now, and I was shaking.

I heard something that sounded like a human voice, and realized that Meg had slid the rear window back and was shouting at me. I shinnied down the bed as quickly as I could without actually getting up, and caught her last words:

"—going on? What should I do?"

"Drive anywhere, fast," I shouted. "Anywhere there's people. Fast!"

I didn't hear her response, but saw her nod and heard the window slide shut. I let my head sink down onto my uncomfortable nest once again, feeling the cold follow the warmth of the sweat congealing on my body. I was glad to think that the aches I knew were awaiting me were going to come, that I was going to live to clean out the cuts and to ice the strains and curse my bitten tongue. There are some times when pain is as welcome as a hug and a cup of tea.

Chapter 14

"**W**HAT THE HELL IS GOING ON?" MEG SAID AFTER she pulled over in the parking lot of the hotel. "What are you doing out here, with no jacket! And"—her eyes widened—"you're bleeding!"

"It's not bad," I said automatically, though I was now trembling violently. She took off her coat immediately and put it around my shoulders. "You got a phone?" I said through chattering teeth. "I left mine down the road."

"Yep." She tossed it to me, and I dialed information for the hotel. I was lucky, and I got the manager right away. I told him to get the cops who were here down the road, there was a shoot-out, there was an FBI officer down.

Meg kept the rest of her questions to herself until I was done, and then handed me a water bottle from the cab of the truck. Even as I had finished the call, the aches and chills I was feeling were making themselves known. Then I was swarmed by uniformed officers. Okay, there were only two of them, but they were big enough, or seemed so to me, at any rate. I was still seeing with tunnel vision. I heard more sirens in the distance and hoped that Widmark was still alive.

I was still sweating and shaking more than a half hour later, sitting in the driver's seat of the truck with the heat on high, as I repeated for what seemed like the millionth time the details of what I saw to Church. Church, with his red cheeks and turned-up nose, looked like he'd just come in from sledding. The smudges under his eyes told another story.

The racket from the radios eventually confirmed that the massive team that had descended upon the service road had found Widmark alive, and had gotten him into an ambulance and off to a hospital. So far, however, it seemed that they'd found nothing but footprints in the snow down the road, and empty cartridge casings. Whoever had been down there had found a way out and away.

There was a last batch of indecipherable crackling and jargon, and one of the officers looked at me. "The only look that Widmark got of the shooters—there were two of them—was when they rushed across the road, chasing after the crazy broad who dragged him to safety and then took off screaming through the woods."

I was not screaming, I thought. I was far too busy breathing. And I guess that was about as much of a thank-you as I would get. A second later, I felt sick. I never dreamed they were behind me. Were coming after me. Had seen me. Who the hell were they? "I was lucky that Meg went by when she did."

"Yes, you were. But the team followed their footprints off to the road. They had a car pointing away from the hotel, and they made themselves scarce pretty quick." Then Church did a double take: Maybe I looked as ill as I felt. "Thing was, they veered off a ways from where you were," he admitted. "They moved a lot farther south of where you were, so it seems they were more interested in getting to their car than they were in finding you."

I nodded; it was about all I was able to do. I wasn't actually freezing anymore, but every part of me was stiffening up and throbbing. Even places where I wasn't scratched felt scraped raw from the cold.

We went over what I'd seen, or rather, what I hadn't seen, up until the point that I'd taken off, and I realized that I was only paying about half attention to my answers. Maybe it was stress and denial, maybe it was cussed curiosity, but I found myself thinking more about the questions I was being asked as a way of determining what the police knew. There were no cars missing from the lot that had been registered by guests; nearly everyone save Meg and me was at the banquet or accounted for in their rooms or at the bar. It seemed the police believed that whoever shot Widmark was an outsider, not a part of the archaeology conference.

"But what is he doing here in the first place?" I said. "I mean, what was he looking for? He might not have been shot by an archaeologist, but apparently we're what brought him here in the first place. And what does this have to do with Garrison?"

"It looks like Garrison—" one guy said.

That was a bit too much for Church and he broke in. "That's not something we can discuss with you right now. Suffice it to say, Special Agent Widmark was working on a case and you wandered into the middle of it. Why was that again?"

"Same as I said before," I said with a sigh. "I wanted to know why he was outside when everyone else was being kept in the ballroom. I thought he might have something to do with Garrison's death."

"And you didn't call us because . . . ?"

"Because he might have just been going for a walk! Because it might have had nothing to do with anything here! And if I hadn't followed him, he might be dead now. What was he doing out there anyway? Was he following someone?"

"He was working on a case and I'm not at liberty to discuss it with you," repeated Detective Church.

"Okay, I'm sorry," I said, taking a deep breath. "I'm sorry I snapped. I'm tired and I feel like . . . I don't feel so great. I think you know I wasn't the one responsible for his shooting—can you at least tell me if they might be coming after *me* again?"

"I'm sure you'll be fine if you stay inside the hotel. We're working on it and we've got some valuable leads now. I wish I could tell you more, but I'm not—" He stopped at the familiar phrase and shrugged.

I nodded wearily. "I know. Look, like I said, I'm not feeling so hot, and I'm afraid Meg is losing out on her dinner because she stopped to help me. Is it okay if I go now?"

I sounded pathetic, perhaps even as bad as I was starting to feel. Meg did her best to look hungry and waiflike—she was surprisingly good at it—and we were eventually given permission to leave.

We went into the hotel lobby, and it was nearly empty. We could hear the sounds from the banquet taking place in the ballrooms that had been opened up on the second floor.

"What were you doing out there anyway?" I asked Meg. "Not that I'm not grateful. Thanks for being out there."

She held up a large paper bag. "Liquor store. You've seen what they're charging at the bar."

As I fumbled getting my key out of my pocket, I looked down at my trembling hands. They were a mess. I could feel that there was a pretty good scratch on my left cheek, and a bunch of scrapes on my chin. My jeans were torn where I'd fallen. They and my boots were soaked through.

Meg was okay. She probably wanted to talk. I guess I wanted to talk too. I was reluctant to bring Meg any further into this, but I owed her something, though I wasn't sure what it was, outside of thanking her for helping me. Again. She'd acted quickly, not asking questions until she saw that whatever was going on was behind us. She was good in a bad spot.

That was it: I kept being in the right place to get insider information. Meg kept being in the places near me, and had stuck her neck out—literally and figuratively—on more than one occasion to help me. Maybe it didn't strictly follow, but suddenly I had the notion that if I expected to be accepted as a source of help—professional or not, bystander, insider or whatever—then maybe I should afford Meg the same opportunity.

Besides, it wasn't as though anyone else was going to tell me about what rumors were flying around, about Garrison, about the conference, about me. Meg would.

"Okay, we've missed most of the banquet anyway, and so thanks to me, you've missed dinner. Come up to my room and we'll order food and talk. No one will miss us for an hour or so, not any more than they might have already."

"Sounds good."

We got up to my room and, suddenly, I was limping and exhausted. I couldn't decide what to do first. I stood there, then moved to the phone, then thought of the bathroom and a hot shower, then of cleaning my scratched hands, then moved back toward the phone as my stomach rumbled.

"Why don't you go clean up and I'll order the food. Get warmed up," Meg suggested. I'd almost forgotten she was there, but she was already digging out the room-service menu.

I nodded and turned for the bathroom; she called after me, "What do you want?"

"There's a steak salad. Blue cheese dressing on the side. A big bottle of water. A glass of red wine, whatever cabernet they have."

"I'll have a glass too. Want to get a bottle?"

"Why not?"

"Unless you'd rather have something harder?" She nodded to the bag from the State Liquor Store.

"No thanks. You bought that for the troops; I'm not going to steal it. Wine is fine."

The scratch wasn't deep, but there were some other abrasions that I hadn't noticed, until now. There was also a good scratch on my left cheek that I remembered getting on the way through—rather than around—a sticker bush. I cleaned them out good.

I looked in the mirror. My hair was standing out at angles, sweat plastering it off my face, which was red with exposure and exertion. The scratch gave me a vaguely roguish look that I might have enjoyed any other day. Now I just felt beat up.

It took me a while to peel off my clothing, stuck to me with sweat, slush, and, here and there, a bit of drying blood. I got into the shower, then got back out, and pulled my bathrobe on. I retched over the toilet, as quietly as I could, wiped off my face, and then got back into the shower, shaking as if my arms and legs would come off. Eventually, by adding more and more hot water, I felt warm enough to get out and dry off. I'd stopped shivering so much, but now just felt weak as I put antibiotic ointment on my cuts and scrapes. I tried not to think about the fact that Church had said there were two shooters, tried not to think about the shots coming at me from below the porch roof Friday night. Last night.

"So what are we doing?" Meg asked as I returned. She had the chair by the desk, so I sat on the bed, leaning on the headboard, my feet stuck under the covers. I was still in my robe, a towel wrapped around my head. Apart from my skirt and heels, everything else I had was either dirty, drying, or lying soaking wet in the tub until I had the energy to hang them up.

"We eat, we talk. But here's the deal," I said. "I'm not real comfortable talking about what I *do* know, never mind figuring out what the hell Widmark got me into. I don't like talking about people who you might know, and airing what may or may not be their dirty laundry when it all might be completely innocent. On the other hand, if I don't tell you, now that you've been seen with me and talking to the cops, you might be in trouble too."

She shook her head, palms upraised. "That's my business."

"I'm not sure I wouldn't feel responsible." And more than simply involving another person, I had to keep in mind that Meg was still my student. Until she graduated or left the program, that would complicate our relationship and I had to be aware of it.

Meg shrugged, and pursed her lips. "Too late, Emma. I'm in it. So let's talk."

She was right; she was in it as soon as she picked me up. And I owed her. "What I'll do is give them names to discuss them by," I said finally, staring at the television cabinet opposite the bed. "If we think we find something incontrovertible, I'll tell you who it is then. Otherwise . . . I guess I hope I'm not messing with innocent people too badly."

"Emma, you got to fish or cut bait," Meg said. "Either you're in this, or you aren't, and you can't afford to worry about other people. Especially when you might be in danger. Besides, they won't know you're talking about them."

I closed my eyes and tried not to scream at Meg, but she was right.

"Okay, let's take them one by one." I paused, saw the dessert menu advertising pie. "We'll start with Apple."

She looked at me.

"What? You want vegetables? We'll throw some vegetables in there too."

Meg picked up the hotel notepad from beside the phone and marked down APPLE.

"Apple," I began, thinking of Sue, "like everyone I'm going to mention, either had reason to fear, hate, or want something from Garrison. In this case, Garrison had put the kibosh on a major project of Apple's. That would be fine, Garrison has done this to a lot of people, including yours truly, but—"

Meg looked up sharply.

I shook my head. "Only by association, but Garrison had his finger in *every* pie. Apple's project had taken up several years and a lot of energy; it was something to expand a career with. Additionally, Apple was also not where his or her original statement said. Apple was seen arguing with Garrison when Apple claimed not to have met with him that night."

Meg nodded. "Any way of finding out what Apple was up to when Garrison died?"

I shrugged. "I don't think so."

"What about . . . what would the benefit be to killing Garrison after the project was quashed?"

"None, I guess. Call it a crime of passion. Revenge. Apple also stopped talking to me about the same time I mentioned that I was looking into formalizing my role with the investigators. Seeing how I can parley my archaeological skills into some form of forensic investigation."

Meg's mouth dropped open.

"Sorry, I forgot that I hadn't said anything about it to you."

"What! But . . . you're going to keep teaching? Right?"

The alarm in her voice shook me. "Oh, yeah. No doubt about it. Just . . . going to see . . . what's what, that's all. A sideline." I realized that people relied on me to keep teaching, and I had to be careful about making them think that I was opting out entirely. "But with regards to this other thing, I wondered whether Apple wasn't worried that I might find out something and pass it along to the police."

Meg wrote that down too, and since I was not going to talk any longer about my bombshell, continued. "Okay, what about Banana?"

"Banana," I said, moving onto Brad, "Banana is a little more tricky. Banana is interested in applying for a job at a place where Garrison had strong connections. Banana claims to have no problem with Garrison, but I've discovered that there was no way that Garrison would have allowed Banana to get said job."

"That doesn't seem like much of a motive," Meg said, doubtful.

"No, but if Banana was desperate to get this job, well, you know exactly how many opportunities there are in this field. You know how rare they are. If it meant the world to you . . . ?"

"Maybe." She looked doubtful. "Aren't there safeguards against that kind of thing, though?"

"Yeah, sure, but they don't always work," I said. "Banana was also supposed to be in bed at the time they think Garrison went outside, but again, this was proven false. And Banana admits to having physically confronted Garrison, though claims he was alive at the end of the encounter."

Meg looked up from her notes, horrified. "Shit, Em!"

I shook my head, even though I remembered what Brad said about losing so much, feeling so desperate. "I don't know. It still doesn't feel right to me. Carrot is tricky too." I thought about Duncan and was surprised at how easy it was to imagine him acting impulsively, violently, even. Nothing I saw this weekend indicated to me that much had changed in him. Laurel had said that someone was reviewing his work, and Petra had told me that Garrison had been asked to review some site reports. "I have reason to believe that Carrot might have had material being reviewed by Garrison. Perhaps there was something that he didn't want discovered. If that was the case, and Garrison made it known, it could ruin Carrot's career." I sighed heavily; did I really think Duncan was capable of killing Garrison? This seemed like the best motive of anything I'd come up with so far. "Okay. What's a *D* fruit?"

"Durian? Daikon?" Meg offered.

I looked at her askance.

"A durian is a stinky, spiky pear," she explained. "A daikon's a radish. Not really a fruit."

I tried to think of what I could say about Scott. "Well, Durian has just been acting oddly around me. I understand that Garrison heaped plenty of abuse on him years ago, but Durian claims to have gotten past it. I also discovered that Durian is not as over Garrison's treatment of him as I was led to believe."

"Em, that's not much to go on. Even less than the last one."

"You're right." A thought struck me, the connection between the Haslett site—Duncan's dissertation site—and the nineteenth-century exploration of the site by Josiah Miller. I was beginning to suspect that Duncan had used the Miller data in his research and not cited it. Leary, the presenter at the session I'd been hiding in, had mentioned that the Miller report was recently discovered, but that was impossible if I'd seen the report on Duncan's desk all those years ago. If Garrison had discovered that Duncan had used a work and not cited it, it could be disastrous for Duncan's career. Was Scott covering up for Duncan, afraid that I would expose him?

"It's also possible," I said slowly, still tasting the idea, "that Durian is covering up something for Carrot and may be complicit." I wracked my brain. "I'm not doing a very good job of this; I don't want to go into details that might have nothing to do with the case." I could also be mistaken about having seen the Miller report, but I didn't think so. "That's why I feel funny talking to the cops about this."

"That's why you should formalize your role with them," Meg said practically. "That way, the way you make your decisions is more clearly defined."

Again, I wasn't thrilled with how close Meg cut to the problem. "Yeah, you're right."

"And maybe it's time for another session with me and Sally down at the shooting range? If you're going to be hanging out with cops?"

Sally was Meg's Heckler & Koch. "Meg, the whole point

is that I would be amply protected by being in the midst of the establishment."

"Suit yourself." She shrugged. "You seemed to have fun, last time, and you caught on quick. It's just paper punching."

I hate guns. I hate how people treat them casually, like toys, and seem to forget what they are made for. I hate the noise they make, even when you're wearing ear protection. I hate how they fascinate, cleverly contrived mechanisms with a heft that is damnably, seductively appealing. I hate that I enjoyed the target practice, and I hate that I was good at it.

I turned back to the television cabinet. "We'll see. Anyway, that's all I got for now. Problem is, I don't know whether it has something to do with the thefts of reproductions from the book room. Who'd want reproductions?"

"Someone who didn't know they weren't real."

I nodded. "And I don't know how any of these might tie in with Widmark, and why the FBI is involved in all of this. I might be missing lots of important things." Like whether there were other reasons besides friendship that Petra might have had for going to his room that night, or whether it was possible that she concealed that fact for more than discretion. Like what any of this might have to do with Widmark's investigation.

Room service came up about then, probably speeded up by the fact that dinner was mostly over for ninety percent of the rest of the hotel's denizens at the banquet. I signed for the food and Meg moved her chair over to the other side of the cart. As soon as she took the covers off the food, hunger and thirst overtook me. I sat down, poured a glassful of water, chugged it down, then tore into the salad, spearing a big forkful of steak and blue cheese into my mouth. For the sake of a balanced diet, I swilled down more water, then a mouthful of lettuce. The salad tasted so good that I went for another big mouthful of meat and cheese, and this time chased it down with a big sip of wine: Meg had thoughtfully poured me out a glass.

When I realized that I'd been head-down in my food for several minutes, I looked up and saw that Meg was eating, but more slowly. She was also regarding me with a mixture of worry, awe, and amusement.

I wiped my mouth and swallowed a too-big mouthful. "Sorry, I'm behaving like a pig."

"No, please. Day you've had, I say go for the gusto."

"More wine?" I picked up the bottle and gestured.

"Sure. I saw Professor Fairchild ordering this one night, so I figured it must be okay."

"It's pretty good, isn't it?" I finished topping Meg up and looked at the label. I'd have to run the name past Bucky and see if she'd heard it. She was the oenophile in the family.

"Yeah, I guess." She took another cautious sip, shrugged, and drank more deeply. Booze was booze, as far as she was concerned. "So, I wanted to ask you something."

"Shoot." Although I'd slowed down eating, I was still making steady progress through my food. Good thing the hotel plates were sturdy; they were taking a beating tonight.

Very businesslike: "You have a problem with me and Neal?"

I shook my head, trying to finish my mouthful and reassure her all at once. "No, Meg, I honestly really don't. God, no. Like I said, I think you guys are great together."

"Then why . . . you seemed hesitant, when we were out at the site, when I told you. Something more than surprise."

I sighed, then sat back with my glass of wine. "It's an old reaction, Meg, that's all. I tend to think that it's problematic when people in the same department get involved. It's me, my own baggage. Nothing at all to do with you guys. I swear to you."

She nodded, drinking thoughtfully. I think she finally believed me. "So, was it someone I know?"

"Damn, Meg, I don't know if I want to go—"

"Because I heard something about you and Duncan Thayer."

Oh shit—but I caught myself. I had to stop treating this like it mattered, like it was a state secret. It was neither material nor secret. "Who's so stuck in the past that they told you this?"

"Oh, it wasn't anyone here. It was before I transferred to Caldwell, I was trying to find out about you. It came up. I can't remember who told me. Someone older, someone senior."

"And how did it affect your decision?"

"It wasn't pertinent." She looked at me, curious. "So was it?"

I sighed. "Yes. A million years ago. I fell hard, and then he dumped me, out of nowhere, as far as I could see. It hurt like hell." I shrugged and leaned over to work on the salad again. "I didn't understand then that it wasn't anything personal, it was just that Duncan always tries to trade up. Girlfriends, colleges, jobs . . . we met when he transferred to Boston in our junior year. Collided, exploded might have been a better word. But he's always had one eye open for the next best thing."

Meg nodded.

I continued. "I hadn't seen him for ages, actually; out on the site on Wednesday was the first time in a long time."

Comprehension lit her face. "I thought you looked edgy."

I nodded. "And the time before—a long time ago—it wasn't pretty."

"And now?" she said. "Does it bother you?"

I fished a bread roll out and began to butter it. "I think it's more that I suddenly remember the emotions, remember things that I haven't thought about in years," I said. And I *hadn't* thought about them in years, I realized. "It's kind of like going back to your hometown, after you've been away for ages and things have changed. Buildings go up, buildings come down, new houses and roads are built and there's suddenly a new mall where there used to be a farm stand and a field. But even though none of it seems even vaguely recognizable, you kinda know your way around, and that's surprising. And then you remember things, and emotions, and you're surprised by the fact that they're still there. I'm startled, I guess," I corrected, trying to keep myself on track, "that they're still there. And it's not even nostalgia, just . . ."

"Muscle memory. Reflex."

"That's it. Habit. You wonder why you feel nothing or you remember something suddenly and why it's still there and how it's all connected. It's a bit existential, I guess," I said apologetically.

"No, I get it. It's cool."

"I'm just surprised, that's all, that the memories are still there, that they're as strong as they are. I guess I've been sitting on them for a long time."

She nodded. "And now that you're looking at them?"

"Curiosity, I guess. It's a little startling—another life. I can live with it because it really has nothing to do with me now."

"I can see how it would put you off the notion of intradepartmental romance." She nodded slowly, then looked at me unblinkingly, the way she did when she was challenging herself. "I'm worried about getting married."

Holy snappers. Well, I'd brought it on myself, I thought. "Is it just the usual stuff, or something specific?"

"I'm not sure what usual is, but I'm just not sure that I know *how*," she said. "To be married."

"You guys have been living together for how long now? Couple of years, right?"

"Since that first season at Penitence Point. Almost four years."

"And how's that been?"

"Fine. Good, even. I mean, Neal's great, but where there

are two personalities, there's bound to be friction, occasionally. And while I've lived with men before—I mean, my brothers and my dad—sometimes, it's like living with another species, you know?"

I thought about Brian's blood all over Kam's basement. "Oh, yeah. So what's the problem?"

She chewed her bottom lip. "I just don't know . . . I'm worried we'll end up getting divorced."

"It's a possibility."

Meg looked at me liked I slapped her.

I shrugged. "No, it is a possibility, a remote one, maybe, but it exists in the universe of things that could happen. I had the same worry. When my folks divorced, well, it wasn't like they weren't better off, but it made me wonder if I was built for marriage. Whether anyone was. I decided Brian was worth giving it a shot. Don't let the past dictate your future."

"Yeah, but I'm worried that I'll change. Or that I won't change. Or that we won't be friends anymore."

It was interesting to see Meg so overtly anxious about anything, but I suspected that everyone who was part of a couple had fears of permanent stasis or of spiraling out of control or leaving their partner behind. "Look, nothing's going to change. Or rather, it will, but you'll probably be able to sort it out together. You'll grow, but you'll also continue being best friends. Only with sex and joint taxes."

"Hell, Emma, I didn't know you were such a freaking romantic." But she looked happier now, and that was fine with me.

"I am. It's just not in the fluffy kittens-and-paper-lace hearts mold. Let's go downstairs and get dessert with the others."

I got dressed, feeling hugely restored by the shower, food, and rest, and we went downstairs. The banquet was over, but people were still gathered at their tables, talking and laughing loudly. I urged Meg to go join up with the others—I was fine now, thanks to her—but asked her not to say anything about where she might have been.

She gave me a dirty look for insulting her intelligence and then left.

It took me a moment to notice a couple of things. The first was that I realized I was trying to get an idea of who was here, and who wasn't. Impossible of course, but I just wanted to see whether there were any obvious absences. Sure the cops had said I'd be safe inside the hotel, but that wasn't going to stop me from trying to improve my odds. I also noticed that as I neared some tables, people tended to clam up when they saw me. At first, I just figured they were wondering about the scratch, and then I realized that Lissa was right: People had been talking, and this weekend had focused a lot of that gossip on me.

I saw a group clustered around one table, each examining the label of a wine bottle minutely. It was the same group who brought their own wine with them every year.

"Hey, that's a pretty nice merlot," I exclaimed to the ring-leader, Hank.

"You bet your ass, it is," one of them said, head back, eyes closed in worshipful ecstasy. Hank tilted his chair back onto two legs and opened his eyes. "Emma! *Quelle surprise*. I had you down as one of the beer-swilling barbarians."

I smiled. "You say that like it's a bad thing."

"Well, like I said"—he exchanged glances with the rest of the party, who all suddenly became engrossed in their glasses—"just a surprise, that's all," he finished weakly.

I nodded; I got it. "See you."

As I moved on, I heard a roar across the room. A crowd at another table was intent on Duncan, no surprise there, but apparently he and Chris were engaged in a monumental contest of drinking and storytelling. At one point, Chris climbed on top of his chair and beat his chest.

As I shook my head, I bumped into someone. I recognized

the fringe of blond hair and the awful Captain America tie right away; he'd been wearing the damn thing for years, as both a protest and a sop to formality. "Hey, Mickey." I gave him a buss.

"Emma! Haven't seen you all weekend!" He gave me a big kiss on the cheek. "Every time I see you, your hair gets shorter. You look completely different, really great."

I didn't ask if that meant he thought I didn't look great before; I knew what he meant. "Oh, it's not so big a change."

"Sure it is. Short, jazzy hair. All buffed out."

"It's *not* that different."

"See? Even standing up for yourself more."

"I did before," I said, a little more forcefully. I guess I was tired, no surprise.

"What did I tell you?"

"Huh. I still don't think I'm all that different. Maybe it's tenure. Maybe all the racing around has made me a little tougher."

Mickey shook his head. "Don't think so. This is more recent."

"Whatever." Just let it go, man.

"I'm not saying it's a bad thing. It's damn sexy, when you think about it."

I looked at him sideways. "Jeez, tell me that wasn't a pass."

He cocked his head. "Well, it could be. Would that be so bad?"

"We're friends. I like that a lot. I don't go in for the other stuff."

"Wouldn't friendly sex be better than the alternative?"

"It's just not an option. You're a friend, and so I'm going to forget this conversation ever took place."

"See what I mean?" He nodded, satisfied he was right. "Year or two ago, you would have stammered, then run away."

"Whatever. My answer still would have been no, thank you."

As I turned to walk away, he called after me, "Just like I said. Different. No more bullshit."

"What the hell is going on here?" I muttered.

"The world is going crazy, of course," Laurel said, appearing at my side. She had a glass of wine in her hand and was brushing the crumbs off her black turtleneck. "You didn't miss much of a meal."

"You noticed I wasn't here?"

"Everyone did. Walk and talk with me, Em. I need to get up to my room, for a moment."

Laurel's room was nicer than mine, of course, a corner room with a great view out onto the forested area around the lake. Her heat worked. She had a work area with an extra desk. And that wasn't all that she had. As soon as she walked into the room, she hit a switch on a small, technical-looking cube in black matte and silver plastic; clear music came out. It was jazz; not one of my favorite genres, but it changed the whole feel of the space.

She plugged in her phone and PDA. "First things first," she said. "Ever notice that where once it was animals you had to feed and bed down at the end of the day, now it's the electronics you have to attend to?"

Laurel then brought a small leather travel case, just smaller than a shoebox, into the bathroom with her. Candles were on the nightstand, and I thought about the pretty light they would have cast lit, in the dark with the snow outside. She also had a small refrigerator; she pulled a bottle from it and returned to the bathroom.

"Okay, now I know you didn't get that into carryon," I said.

"Pardon?" she called back to me.

"How come you got a fridge?"

"I asked for it. You can usually rent them cheap. Makes life easier."

Life? At a conference? "The music and candles too?"

"Oh. You never know who you're going to run into."

She was teasing—she and Emily had been together for ages—but it struck me that Laurel worked hard at maintaining her quality of life. "So how come you didn't go to Chicago last year? For the nationals?"

"Didn't feel like it." She returned with a martini glass.

"No, really. And where'd you get the glass?"

"I brought it with me, nice little travel kit. I'd offer you one, but I didn't think you liked vodka. I could do you up a cosmo, if you like. There's cranberry in the fridge."

"No thanks. I already had some wine with dinner, and I'm beat."

"Suit yourself. I happen to believe that martinis are the new tea parties. Rather than balancing hot tea in fragile porcelain cups to show how poised and knowledgeable you are about social rituals, now you have to be able to stand, talk, and not slosh your drink. You have to show you can hold your liquor, literally and figuratively."

"Interesting," I said, and I thought of Jay spilling her drink. I was still waiting for her answer.

She shrugged. "And as for Chicago, there's no point in running up your Visa bill and risking athlete's foot at a second-rate hotel, if you're not also going to get a kick out of it. I'd just been to Chicago for another gig, and since I wasn't giving a paper, and there was no one I wanted to meet, I blew it off. I personally am in it for the intellectual thrills, and it makes it tough if you are the most interesting person there."

I made a snooty face at her, and she shrugged. "I'm getting too old for posturing, Emma. I can't be bothered and it wastes my time. I fix up my room the way I like because I see no harm in traveling comfortably."

She mixed up her drink, and as she did so, she said, "Those cuts on your hand and face look nasty. You clean them up good?"

"Yep."

"You should be caught up on your tetanus shots anyway, working in the field like you do."

"Yes, Mother."

She sat back on the bed with her drink, no trace of anger on her face. "You can be pissy if you want, Em, be my guest. But the sooner you get used to me helping you, the better company you'll be for me too."

"Sorry. I'm just fed up. Everyone is strange, what with the thing with Garrison and everything."

"Everyone is strange." It could have been agreement on a question.

"Either they're exactly the same as they've always been or they're totally different. I don't know what's going on. I'm irritated with everyone."

"Your own experiences are probably coloring that."

"Whatever. The thing with Garrison, I don't know. I'm worried. I'm worried about who might have been out there today. Shooting at me." I explained the day's events to her; she took it all in without a word.

Laurel looked thoughtful. "Huh. Who didn't you see, when you came into the banquet?"

"I didn't see Sue. I didn't see Brad. I didn't see Scott. I didn't see you, at first."

"And yet here you are, telling me all about it." Laurel was looking out the window now, her face momentarily obscured by her glass. "Why is that?"

"Uh." I thought about it. "You were in dry clothes; your face wasn't red or anything, from exertion and cold. And people would have missed you, if you hadn't been at the center of the party."

"Interesting." She set her glass down. "The thing you need

to worry about now, Emma, telling the wrong things to the wrong people. I don't know if you realize that you won't necessarily be able to speak to people the same way again, if indeed, they'll feel comfortable with you at all."

"What's that supposed to mean?"

"Just what I say. People might find your choices ghoulish. They might decide that they trust you as a friend, but as a cop—"

I shook my head violently. "I'm not going to be a cop. Far from it—"

"They'll see you as right next door and they might decide that they have things they don't want that close to the law. Or they might just think you've flipped your wig." She picked up her glass, sipped her drink, and made an approving face.

"It's not as bad as that."

"People don't like change. You're leaving the fold—in their eyes, even if not in fact—you're throwing their decisions to stay in their faces. You've got the brass ring, what with tenure and all, and you seem to be saying it's not enough. It's not appreciated."

"It has nothing to do with anyone else."

"And yet, see how you bridled when I told you I didn't bother with conferences that didn't interest me. Same thing."

"Laurel?"

"Yes, Emma?"

"I'd like that drink now, if you don't mind."

Chapter 15

AN HOUR LATER, I WAS DRAGGING MYSELF TO MY room, worn to a frazzle. The hallway was deserted, and as I fit my key into the door, I felt as though I couldn't get into bed fast enough. The thought that the cops were still bustling down in the lobby made me very happy indeed. The knob turned readily enough, and I stepped just inside, stooping to pick up the fallen room-service request. Then I felt a tremendous blow on my back, and it sent me sprawling forward.

As I hit the floor, the light from the hallway went out. The door to my room swung shut on its security hinge, and I was engulfed in darkness.

I wasn't alone. I could hear heavy breathing behind me, and I shook off my denial that I'd been attacked: No, it wasn't an accident, no, I wasn't dreaming, no, it wasn't Nolan at the gym. I'd been attacked, and whoever it was had followed me into my room. This was for real, and if I didn't move fast . . .

I rolled over as soon as I hit the carpet, bringing my foot up to kick whatever got near me. My head was right at the foot of the bed, so I'd have to shift before I could get to my feet. I couldn't see anything but blurred shadows—the snow stuck to the window helped block out some of the light from the outside—but I could follow motion pretty well. My attacker moved toward me, lunged, and I kicked out, catching a leg, just above the knee, by the feel of it. I was rewarded with a muffled exclamation inspired by pain and surprise. My shoe got snagged in the trouser fabric and was pulled off as he—it was a man, from the size of him—backed away. I kicked off the other shoe, scooched over, and got up—nice, clean, and technical, swinging my leg around my hand, which was firmly planted on the floor—just in time to realize that my opponent was swinging at the left side of my head.

I muffed the block—I didn't bring my arm up fast enough—and got caught on the cheekbone with his fist.

Several things happened then.

The blow hurt like hell, but not as badly as I'd feared. I'd had my head tucked behind my shoulder, too. My assailant was wearing gloves.

I took the punch and kept going, loading up my counter. I launched a sweet right cross and caught him square on the side of the head. I felt skin give. If I could have seen better, I might have landed it right on the nose, but was pleased as, well, punch, to land anything at all. I heard another curse, and he backed off a step.

At the same time, I realized that not only was I not hurt so much as I was mad—and I was truly pissed—but also that the guy wasn't expecting me to fight back. And I was fighting, I understood, with a shock. I had actually blocked a punch, against someone who meant to hurt me. He wasn't even very good at this, and if I could keep my act together for a few minutes—

He was still between me and the doorway, and with the back of my legs brushing the bedspread, I had no choice but to follow up, bring the fight to him.

He threw another wild roundhouse, and I slipped it. I tried a quick jab, but he was out of range, so I hauled back and let loose with a front kick that connected solidly with his stomach.

With nothing but nylon stockings on my feet, I lost my purchase on the carpeting as I connected with him, and I hit the ground. He went back, hard, slamming into the door, making a sick wheezing sound.

The noise of him hitting the door brought an angry protest and knocking on the wall from the occupant of the room next to mine. This reminded me that there were other people nearby, and as I was getting up again, I did what I should have done in the first place.

I screamed. Long, loud, and unladylike.

My assailant was fumbling with the door at this point. I tripped over my shoes, landing against the bathroom door just as he slid out into the hallway. I regained my footing, screamed again, putting every bit of my outrage and pain into it, and scrambled to follow.

Maybe I wouldn't actually attack him again, but I sure as hell wanted to see who it was, if I could.

"What the hell is going on out here?" A woman I recognized but couldn't name immediately was clutching a parka over her pajamas. She stepped in my way.

"I was attacked!" It was all I could do to keep from shoving her aside. "I have to—"

She put her hand on my arm, restraining me. "Omigod, you mean it's happened again!"

I shook her off, more vigorously than I meant. "I have to—"

I got past her and across the hall, to where the door to the stairs was. I stuck my head in and listened: nothing, not a sound except for the blood pounding in my own ears. Both the elevators were moving, too, and so I was out of luck there. I looked up and down the hall, but the doors that were opened framed other sleepy or drunken archaeologists, in various stages of undress. There were no parties on this floor, that I could hear, so I was pretty sure I'd lost my man.

I had to turn and, once again, saw the curious glances following me.

The woman didn't seem to notice that I'd shaken her off so rudely, as she kept talking the whole time I was looking for my quarry. ". . . and now . . . were you broken into, too? Are you hurt?"

"What? No. No, I don't think so." But even as I spoke, I reached up and felt my sore cheek. It burned, and I knew from experience that there was an abrasion on top of what would be a pretty good bruise, if I didn't ice it up in a hurry. "I'm fine."

Her face froze as she realized . . . "But you . . . you've been hit! Omigod, are you okay?"

"I'm fine, don't worry about it." I looked at the concern and fear in her face, creased and puffy with sleep, and realized that wasn't the answer she was expecting. No normal person would make that answer. "I was hit, yes, but I get hit worse than this all the time when I'm working out. I box." It seemed simpler than trying to explain Krav to her, and I didn't want to be out here all night. "And he was wearing gloves, so it could have been a lot worse."

Even as I said it, I knew it was a fact. My attacker was dressed for inside, except he was wearing thin gloves. They didn't feel like leather, they weren't knitted wool, they reminded me of the sort of gloves that some weight lifters use to keep a good grip. Driving gloves, maybe, I decided.

"I'm going to call the front desk and the police," the woman finally said.

"Don't worry about it," I said. "I'll stop down there now and tell them what happened."

"No," she said firmly. "I'm going to call them myself."

I could read it in her face: Maybe *I* was the one responsible for all this. Maybe *I* had brought this all on myself. Maybe *I* was the dangerous one.

I nodded. "You're right, maybe they'll be able to catch him if you call. But they'll find me down at the desk. Thanks for your help."

She paused at her doorway, still viewing me with suspicion.

I stepped forward, very calmly. "I mean it. Thank you for coming out and seeing what was wrong when I screamed. Not everyone would do that."

She blushed, and her face softened a little. "It's okay. I'm sure other people called the desk too. I just happened to be closest, that's all."

"I'm Emma." I stuck out my hand. It might be a little late for a formal introduction, but it was never too late to convince someone that I wasn't a mental case.

"Becky Goldschmidt." She shook my hand and then suddenly turned shy. "Well, I'd better . . ." She gestured to the inside of her room.

"Yeah. Thanks again."

I looked down the hallway. People were moving back into their rooms, some were looking at me oddly, some were too drunk or sleepy to care. One person down the hall didn't move, just stood there and stared at me.

Duncan.

He was shirtless and barefoot, and it looked like he was wearing—jeans? Blue pajama bottoms? He never wore the tops to his pajamas, I remembered suddenly. Why do I remember something like that, after all these years? Why that, and not more important things, like bibliographies and phone numbers, things I truly cared about?

I'd worn the tops a number of times, when we were together. Who's wearing your pajama tops these days, Duncan?

Why on earth did that pop into my head?

Almost as if my question had called him, he started walking down the hallway toward me. I couldn't very well flee back into my room, and besides, there was no need to, I told myself sternly. I'm on my way down to the desk to report the attack.

"Are you all right?" he asked. His concern looked genuine. More than that, he didn't look as though he'd just attacked me. He was a little flushed, but that looked more like the color that follows eating and drinking than hard physical exertion. There were no marks on his face. And he'd been in the ballroom, when I got in there. I didn't think he could have been one of the shooters in the woods, if that was the case.

Didn't mean he couldn't have killed Garrison.

"I'm fine." I finally registered jeans. And chest hair. Familiar and yet a million miles away. I was having a hard time keeping my thoughts on track.

"What happened?"

I shrugged. "Someone followed me into my room. I guess he came from the stairwell. He rushed me. I have no idea what it was about."

"And you don't think it has anything to do with Garrison, or you talking to the cops, or anything?" He crossed his arms across his chest, one eyebrow raised.

I was annoyed that he should think that I was taking this lightly. "I'm sure it does. I just don't know why."

"I see." His eyes widened when he saw the graze and swelling on my face. I pulled away from his hand as he reached out to touch me.

"You should put something on that. Do you have any alcohol or bacitracin or something?"

"Yeah, I'll take care of it in a minute."

"Of course you do. *Semper paratus,* that's our Emma."

I looked at him sharply, but again, there was no trace of sarcasm. Maybe just a few molecules of fondness, on his part.

I started trembling, and I thought, oh no, not now. But it's what happens after a fight, it's inevitable. All that adrenaline, all that energy; once it's no longer needed, it has to leave your system somehow, and this was the second time today. My stomach roiled, and I swallowed, trying to keep my mind off how sick I suddenly felt. I tried to keep my hands from shaking too noticeably, but Duncan saw, damn his eyes. He always saw everything.

"Emma, I know you probably haven't got anything to drink in your room. That's not your style, not at conferences anyway. Or it wasn't. I've got some good whiskey, come have a drink. You've been attacked."

I shook my head. "It's nothing, it's just a reaction. Happens all the time."

He shrugged, maybe it did happen all the time. "Okay, but you've been shaken up, you could use something to calm you down."

"I'm fine, Duncan. I don't want to bother you." I don't want to interrupt you, was what I was about to say, but that would have smacked of too much cattiness or, worse, interest. It was just an easy assumption.

"It's no bother, I was just reading. I find I need to settle down a little before I sleep, these days. Remember when we didn't need sleep? Times change. Come on."

He turned, assuming I would follow him. I was tempted, even, to see if I could do it, have a drink with him. Be better than him, find out what was going on with him. I almost said yes.

"I can't, Duncan. I have to go down to the desk, call the cops, that sort of thing." Then the words slipped out before I could stop them. "Another time maybe."

"Another time, then. I'll hold you to that. Good night, Emma."

"Night."

I had turned to the elevators when I heard him say, "Call me. If you need anything," and it wasn't arch and it wasn't a pass and it wasn't anything but human concern. I began to wonder if it was possible, and if so, why now?

I went downstairs and discovered that my neighbor Becky had done as she'd promised, or threatened. The night manager was waiting there as if he expected me. He came around from the desk immediately.

"I've called the police. Someone will be here right away."

"Thanks."

He put his hand to my elbow and led me to one of the conversation areas, insisting I sit. "Can I get you anything? Are you okay?"

I realized, I wasn't really, but shoved it aside for the moment. "No, thanks. I'm just a little shaken up. I'll be fine in a minute." I sat down, a little heavier than I meant; my legs still felt like they'd buckle under me if I asked much more of them. So much for being safer inside the hotel, I thought bitterly.

He frowned. This wasn't the response he was looking for.

"A little freaked out, too, if you want to know the truth," I added, but I didn't want to know the truth myself, not until I had a moment to sit and think about what it really meant to me, by myself. I couldn't afford to think of it now, or I'd lose it. My stomach was still not entirely convinced it was going to stay put, and it lurched ominously.

He nodded. "How did it happen?"

"This guy came out of nowhere," I said. "I should have been more alert when I opened my door. I usually know better."

The night manager said ruefully, "While we always recommend caution, we don't usually expect our guests will have to be alert." His jaw tightened, and then he shook himself. "This is not something for you to blame yourself about. We consider this to be a very fine establishment, and the thought that one of our guests has been attacked is an indication that something is profoundly wrong. It's not as though you're in a war zone and have to be aware of what's behind every door. We're doing everything in our power to make it right, and I hope that you'll come back someday, as our guest, when this has all been cleared up."

"Uh, of course. I appreciate that." He's right, Em, I told myself. No matter what you might think of how you handled things, this isn't about scoring yourself in some game you've challenged yourself to. You were attacked, and it doesn't matter whether you were capable of fighting back. Don't forget that: None of this is your fault, your doing. You were attacked.

"Thank you," he said. "What happened?"

"Right. He shoved me into my room—"

"He shoved you in?" He looked at me sharply. "He wasn't already inside?"

"What do you mean?"

"There have been several other . . . incidents. Rooms have been broken into, and there have been some thefts—"

I recalled suddenly that my down-the-hall neighbor Becky had said, "It's happened again!" It's as if I had too much information at the moment and had shut down some reactions, just to deal with the trauma of being attacked.

"—but no one was ever attacked or hurt. People were either asleep or out of their rooms. And you say that he shoved you *in*?"

"Yes. Definitely. So I don't think this is related."

"I know it isn't. We arrested the thieves who've been breaking in during the banquet."

I looked at him. "What?"

"Nightcrawlers. One of every hotelier's nightmares. Thieves who come in and try the rooms until they find one that isn't locked—you'd be surprised at how easy it can be for them. Anyway, they were caught during the banquet, emptying someone's room."

I thought about the odd phone message I'd had, about "crawling," and that made a lot more sense now. But it didn't seem to have anything to do with the graduate students' room being vandalized. "And they were responsible for the book room theft too, right?"

"Yes."

I finished, "Because they stole the things that looked valuable—the replicas—and left the things we would think of as valuable, the actual broken artifacts."

"I think that's right," he said, nodding.

"So my attacker wasn't one of them." He didn't have a gun either, so perhaps the people who shot at Widmark— and me—weren't the same as whoever murdered Garrison? I didn't think there could be two significant, unrelated crimes at the conference, though.

"Is that supposed to make me feel better?" At least there was a wry grin on his face this time.

"I guess not. Anyway, he wasn't that good, and I managed to chase him off pretty quick. That's when the racket—"

"Your screams." He wasn't about to let me get away with anything; I didn't like it, I wasn't sure I liked him, but he was right. And I did appreciate where he was coming from.

"—woke up my neighbors. And they called you."

"Yes. The police said that they'd get their man down here to talk to you, just as soon as they finish checking out your room and the floor. My assistant is with them with the keys."

I blinked. "They're already here?"

"Yes, there's been someone here since this afternoon. Although they weren't too happy about sparing someone during the snow emergency, they admitted it was probably necessary."

"Ah."

He looked past me. "Here we go."

The officer came over, told me there'd been nothing to see upstairs, that I was probably right to assume that someone had come out of the stairwell, though the possibility of someone coming in from another room couldn't be ruled out. I told my story and mentioned that maybe someone had peeked out, and seen where he'd gone.

There wasn't much else to do, but the officer did walk me back up to my room and looked through it with me, and then even walked me down to the ice machine to fill my bucket, before I let him out. I promised to file a report in the morning.

By the time my door was shut, locked, and dead-bolted, most of my shaking had stopped. The nausea persisted, though, and I became acutely aware of it as I shoved a chair in front of my door. I set the two thick glass water tumblers on top of it, right next to each other, so that they would clink together if anyone tried to open the door.

I sighed and went into the bathroom with my bucket of ice. I washed my face, noticing a couple of reddish rug burns on my hands. When I examined my face, I saw that on my left cheek there was the merest graze on top of a far more interesting lump in addition to the earlier scratch and the scrape on my chin. I put a little antiseptic on it, wincing, then found the little cardboard envelope with the plastic shower cap. I filled the cap with ice, twisting the elasticized opening as closely shut as I could to keep the melting ice inside, and sat down on the lowered toilet seat. I fiddled with the ice and a facecloth, and was finally able to rest the pack gingerly on my cheek. Glancing over in the mirror, I could see that on my left side, I looked, well, not exactly okay, but not as bad as I thought I might. The thorn scratch, of course. I had bags and lines under my eyes. The skin of my face was drawn and a little grayish under the unflattering lights and around my eyes was puffy and reddish: just about normal for the Saturday night, the fourth day of a five-day conference. The things that were really worrying me were all on the inside.

This had nothing to do with the other break-ins, I told myself. You know that. The M.O. was completely different and the cops already caught them.

This was because you've been talking to people. You've brought this on yourself. The manager is correct; you shouldn't have to be worried about being attacked in the hotel under normal circumstances. But you are changing your circumstances, doing it willingly. And that invites trouble, no matter how undeserved.

I know.

And are you prepared to continue with this, just as willingly? How much does this mean to you? What does it mean to you?

I'm changing. I think this is all part of it. Tonight was bad, but not impossible. I was as ready for it as anyone might be.

Anyone who isn't a professional, perhaps. You could cause more trouble by helping, you know.

I know. That's part of what I need to think about.

Yes, you need to think about it, the tired face in the mirror reprimanded me. And you need to think about it hard, and soon.

Later, when I've had some sleep. I promise.

After another five minutes, I dumped the ice out into the sink and carefully dried off the shower cap and set it aside on the sink. The swelling had gone down a bit, but I didn't want to take any aspirin on top of the drinks I'd had. I had taken a couple of antacids, but my stomach was already calming down, though I didn't feel I could sleep yet.

There was a knock at the door. Warily, I looked through the peephole.

It was Duncan.

I sagged, but curiosity got the better of me. What mood would he be in now? I took a deep breath, moved the chair away, and opened the door a crack. "What's up?"

"Got time for that drink now?" he said. "I was keeping an eye out for you."

"Uh, sure."

Feeling a little like I was going to a firing squad, but determined to make the most of any effort I could to finally put this all behind me, I let him in. I wondered what he'd say to me, whether he'd mention Josiah Miller or Garrison.

Besides, he had a bottle of single malt and two glasses of ice. Not that I was willing to drink with him.

"At least you brought the good stuff," I said.

"Need something to end a day right," he answered automatically.

"You used to say just the same thing in college," I said. It was the first time I'd made any reference to our shared past that wasn't couched in accusations, and I felt like I was sidling onto a pond that had only looked frozen.

"Did I? I guess so. Still a good way to put the aches of fieldwork behind you." He poured two drinks and took a good swig of his own. "Not so much of that these days, eh, Em? All paperwork and bureaucracy and meetings." He glanced at me. "How about you?"

"No, I still get out into the field pretty regularly. Got more work than is good for me, sometimes."

"Well, good for you. I always knew you would be the one who'd keep the faith."

The way he was talking to me was more like some kind of interview or something. There was a level of patronizing, avuncular pride that I found particularly annoying, like he'd always known how brilliant I was. And maybe he had, but he'd also thrown it away without a second thought.

I decided to poke him, see what was going on. "Yeah. Making some changes soon, though, I guess."

He stiffened, ever so slightly, a microscopic hesitation before he recovered. "Oh, yeah? Time to start a family?"

"Hell, Duncan. Like that's the only sort of change that I

could possibly be contemplating." He'd put ice in my drink too, but I'd gotten in the habit of drinking it neat ages ago. I fished out the cubes on my way into the bathroom and threw them into the sink.

He shrugged. "No? I always thought you would, one day. You'd make a great mother."

Again with the patronizing crap. It was bordering on proprietary nostalgia this time, and that sickened me. "Who knows? But what I'm talking about is professional—"

"I didn't get a chance to congratulate you on getting tenure, by the way," he broke in quickly. "Good job, that. Good thing, too, the job market being what it is. It's really tight out there."

"Yeah, thanks, it was a massive relief to get that over with," I said. I understood one thing: He wanted something, was definitely trying to pull the conversation around to broach that. I was equally determined to keep it going my way, at least for a few more minutes. "But I've been thinking about branching out a bit."

Again, he stiffened, as though getting ready to start a fight. "You're not thinking of leaving Caldwell?"

I saw that there was real fear in his eyes. "Not at all. I'm looking into studying what I can do in forensics."

He actually laughed, he was so relieved. "Good God, Emma. Why on earth?"

"Just seems like the next natural step."

He took a big drink. "Well, I suppose there is a kind of boom in that right now, what with all the television interest in the scientific aspect of criminal investigation or whatever. Lots of dramas specializing in it, not to mention all the documentaries, regular series on the science channels and what all. Could be a lucrative sideline, I guess. I don't know whether it would be the best thing for you, in terms of career advancement, though. It might be a little late for you to start breaking into the scientific subdisciplines. You're much better off in this tidy little niche you've created for yourself."

"What little niche is that?" I said. I could feel my jaw tightening.

"You know, you practically dominate the early contact stuff in the Northeast. And the feminist stuff too, for other periods. You're becoming the go-to girl for a lot, and I think you might be better off staying where you're established. Consolidating your position, if you like."

"I don't think of it that way," I said.

"No? Not building off Oscar's foundation? Not building your own little Fielding empire?"

I frowned. "Really not. My interests have always been varied, and now I'm in a position to follow through on more of them, is all. And if I've been working in the field for longer than most people our age, that's not calculation or empire-building, or anything else. It's interest, passion, a vocation. You're bound to rack up some pubs, some data, some information after twenty years or so."

"Suit yourself. But I think this forensics thing is probably more of a fad. You're better off staying out of it."

I felt myself stiffen and felt an attack of Yankee-grade iciness coming on. What Brian called my "arctic front." "I wasn't asking for your advice, Duncan. I was telling you of my plans. And it has nothing to do with fads or advancement. It's what I can do with my skills. How I can put them to good use."

He was looking around the room. "Whatever, Em. Why would you want to, though? Doesn't quite seem your suit."

"My suit might have changed since you knew me last, don't you think?"

"I think people stay fundamentally the same," he said.

I found myself losing my temper with his comfortable arrogance, but decided I would find out what he wanted and then kick him out. No point in making things worse when I was trying to make them better, especially now that I was pretty sure that he couldn't have been the one to attack me.

"Well, then maybe there was some germ of this in me earlier on, and it's just coming out now."

He shrugged and poured himself another drink, ignoring my raised eyebrow. "Well, I'm thinking of making changes too."

"What, are you pregnant?"

"Very funny. No, I'm thinking that I've gone just as far as I can go with the stuff here in New Hampshire. I'm looking into the Connecticut job."

At last. "Really." So that was what was behind all of this.

"Really. I think it might be fun to shake things up a little."

Get your hands on some of that new funding, I thought to myself. Get a piece of a high-profile department. Another upgrade. No wonder he was worried; he was thinking that I might be going for it myself, perhaps, with the leverage my recent promotion had brought me.

Funny, I didn't have all these thoughts when I was talking to Brad, but then, I was convinced he was in it for the work and not the exposure. But was either reason more or less the right one?

"I think the competition won't be much of a problem," he continued. "I was just hoping that I might get a letter of recommendation from you."

It came out, just as smooth as that, and suddenly I understood just how naïve I really was. He had less interest in mending fences with me for its own sake, for the sake of maturity, than he wanted my support. How typical. How traditional, if you like, of him. I almost laughed.

"Do you mind?" I said, holding out my glass. He rushed to top up my untouched drink, and for a moment, I hated myself. It was just the same sort of manipulative shit Duncan would have pulled himself. So I put an end to it quickly.

"Sorry, Duncan. You asked too late."

"Why?" I was surprised that he seemed more curious than

hostile or resentful. "Because of . . . because of what happened between us?"

"No. That's done. It's because I've already been asked to write a letter. I wouldn't feel comfortable, it wouldn't be ethical to do a second."

"Oh, yeah?" He drank, unconcerned. "Who's it for?"

"I don't know if that's any of your business. I don't know if it matters. But good luck anyway."

"Well, certainly you can change your mind."

The utter audacity of it made me blink, and I almost couldn't believe that he said it, almost went into denial that anyone would be so presumptuous. That's why he wasn't more upset; he didn't believe I would refuse him.

"I certainly could. I choose not to."

He sighed, annoyed. "I have to say, I'm disappointed in you, Em. I expected more imagination from you."

"You're not the first person to tell me that," I conceded, thinking about the site at Penitence Point. I had braced myself, fully expecting to be crushed by his words. He was always good with words, and I'd gotten used to feeling their effect. I even kept myself in the habit, by remembering that effect over the years, and that was my own fault.

But once again, there was nothing, just the lost-tooth feeling. I probed it a little deeper and nodded and smiled.

I could tell Duncan was surprised by that, because even though his face was totally blank, he still had the habit of running his finger along the beard at the bottom of his chin when he didn't know what to think. Old habits do die hard.

"You can't be serious. I mean, the job description was practically written with me in mind—"

"Then you probably don't need my help as much as you think. A point of curiosity, Duncan: Did you ask Garrison to write you a letter? He was your dissertation director, after all, and Connecticut was his first significant position."

Duncan's expression was unreadable. "Emma, Garrison's dead."

A shiver ran down my spine. "I know, but—"

"And besides," he continued, "you'll look silly backing someone else."

"Possibly. Probably. I can live with it. I think you'd better go now. I handed my glass back to him."

He stood up. "I'm very sorry about this, Emma. I can't tell you how disappointed I am."

"I'm sorry too. Good night."

I shut the door behind him, reset my alarm system. I think he was waiting out there by the time I was done, but I didn't bother looking. It didn't matter.

I was probably already more than half asleep by the time I crawled under the covers, just aware enough to enjoy the dry crisp rasp of the sheets against my feet, and I slept as soon as I laid my head down.

I didn't dream at all that night.

Chapter 16

IT WAS THE PAIN THAT WOKE ME SUNDAY MORNING. The radio alarm was playing, my watch alarm was beeping doggedly, and I still wouldn't have heard any of it if I hadn't rolled over onto my left hand. A sharp pain jarred me awake, and I sat up suddenly, swearing. I hadn't fallen on a run; I hadn't wrenched it doing fieldwork—

I'd been attacked.

The memories came rushing back to me, and I realized just how good it had been to be asleep, undreaming, unremembering.

I flexed my wrist, testing it, and the pain came again, just as sharply as it had before. Nothing broken, as far as I could tell, and it would be fine in just a few days. I should have put the ice on it last night, but it wasn't bothering me then. I hadn't noticed it through the adrenaline and endorphins.

Not so different from how I often felt after a tough bout with Nolan. Even then, I realized, I had wraps and boxing gloves, and so did he. This was for real, and truth be told, I'd done okay.

I hauled myself out of bed, and stretched; my ankle hurt,

and I realized that I must have aggravated the earlier wrench when I slid on the carpet last night. Apart from that, and my hand, I didn't feel too bad. My cheek was tender, but I'd blocked a much worse blow, and the ice and sleep had done most of the work of bringing the lump down. The other little scratch was already healing, nothing more to remind me of what had happened. I applied a little concealer, and looked almost normal.

I showered, stretched out, and dressed—now in my dried dress pants and my still-damp boots, as my ankle wasn't up to heels—then hustled downstairs. It wasn't until I was actually in the elevator that I understood that I was ridiculously cheerful for the hour and my battered state. I finally identified the sense of accomplishment that buoyed me along.

Not many people were up yet, being as late as it was in the course of the conference, and I myself wouldn't have been up except for my hand. And I also needed coffee above and beyond what was in that smelly little sachet in the room that had so ineffectually darkened the hot water.

There was Scott, sitting in the lobby with his coffee. I got some from the urn, and he nodded coolly when I sat down with him. He looked like he'd never been to bed at all. He looked worse than he should have, and I thought about the message I'd taken from his wife, and wondered just how much of this he hid on a regular basis, and how okay he really was. Denial could be a good thing, once you were over a rough patch in your life, but not if it kept you from really dealing with what happened.

"I've got to talk with you, Em," he said gruffly. "It's important."

"Okay. Shoot." Please, I thought, don't let this be what I think it is. Please don't let this be about—

He stared at the carpet, just a minute, then looked me straight in the eye. "It's about Duncan."

"What is it?" Crap, I knew it, I knew it, I knew it . . .

"You've got to leave him alone. One way or the other."

I felt my mouth drop open with the surprise. "What!"

"Em, I know . . . I've heard . . . that you probably have reason not to be . . . Duncan's best friend. But you've got to let the past stay dead. You've got to leave him alone."

"Leave him alone? Scott, I guess you didn't get the memo, but Duncan's already spoken to me about everything! He's trying the suck-up approach, so now I think it would be a good idea for you to back off playing the heavy. And a little advice from a friend? Let him clean up after himself. He's not worth you taking his part."

"I didn't know you could be like this," Scott said. I'd never seen him really angry before, and it changed his whole face into something unrecognizable. It was dreamlike, the way that someone you know, you think you know, metamorphoses into someone you've never seen before. I'd never seen Scott use his size to intimidate me before. "I didn't know you could be so vindictive," he said. "So ugly."

"Whoa, hold on here! Just what is it you think I'm being ugly about?"

He gave me a look of such pure impatience and disgust that I was more convinced than ever that I was dreaming. I pinched the skin on the back of my hand, felt the sharp pain of fingernails.

He took a deep breath, he couldn't get enough oxygen. He opened his mouth to try, then failed, tried again. "It's about the Haslett farm material," he finally said.

"What about it?"

"Leave him alone about it," Scott said. "It was a long time ago, Emma, it . . . it doesn't really matter anymore. Not really. Can't you just let it be?"

"Scott, spell it out for me: What you are talking about?"

His face was a study in disgust, betrayal, and maybe, a little doubt. "You're telling me that you weren't . . . threatening him about the Josiah Miller report?"

I'd been on the right track, I realized. "Me threaten Duncan? You're confused, Scott, you've got the wrong girl."

"You didn't ask him about Josiah Miller and the Haslett farm site the other day? Out of the blue?"

"What? No! I mean, yes, I asked him about Josiah Miller, something that I heard in a paper. It reminded me of something, I thought he could tell me what. It was only later that I figured out he'd actually seen this supposedly recently discovered report."

"And so you were taunting him with it," he said doggedly.

"Damn it, Scott, I don't taunt people. You know me, you know that."

I wasn't sure that he believed me yet, but at least now he looked uncertain, which was an improvement over what I'd seen on his face before.

"There must be some mistake," he finally muttered.

"Damn straight, there is. Now why don't you tell me exactly what was going on there?"

"I . . . don't think that would be a good idea." He was backing off, retreating physically as well.

"You don't get to do that! You don't get to make all sorts of wild-assed accusations to me, and then tell me to buzz off."

"Emma, it's not my . . . it's up to Duncan. It's not my business to tell."

"But it's your business to say all sorts of hateful things to me? I thought we were friends. Goddamn."

"We are, but Duncan and I . . ." He groped for the distinction. "He was there during some hard times, Em. I owe him a lot. You should ask him, if you want to know."

I stood up, frightening myself with how angry I was now. "How about this? How about I ask everyone *but* Duncan if they know what this is all about. I bet I'll get some answers that way, one way or another. I'll contact Kevin Leary, and find out from him." Scott was willing to do something hard, awful for Duncan, to throw away our friendship, and then just toss that fact aside? And he thought I'd take it?

He sighed deeply, and wouldn't look at me. When he began to speak, it was in a monotone, as if the story was coming from somewhere else far away. I sat down again.

"You know the Haslett farm is the site on which Duncan based a lot of his dissertation data. Lately, some other folks—Kevin Leary's team—have been reexamining the site, going back to compare it with other work that's been going on in New York. They found a copy of a report by Josiah Miller, who'd done some work on the Haslett site long ago. He actually did a pretty good job, even by our standards, though he died before he was able to bring the work to its full completion. Although he wanted to, he never published the data; it was his first time trying archaeology, and he was doing it on his own. He and a man he hired from the village nearby. They didn't publicize it, because they were concerned about the site being looted."

"Go on." I had the horrid feeling I knew exactly where this was going.

"Duncan found one set of the notes. He talked to the owner of the house of the property now, and there they were, up in the attic. He took them. He used them."

"He used them as his own," I said.

"It's not like that. I mean, it is, but it isn't. They didn't dig in the same areas. Duncan, well, he used them, in his dissertation, yes, and he didn't cite them. But he didn't falsify the data, he just sort of . . . think *Cliff's Notes*. His conclusions were extrapolations of . . ."

"Of what *Josiah Miller* had written."

Scott ignored me. "And when you mentioned it to him, and that other work is being done now, he just thought—"

"He thought I was threatening him." I took it to the worst extent. "He thought I was blackmailing him."

Scott looked relieved: I hadn't made him say it. "Well, what does it look like to you?"

"Hey, don't try to make this my fault! I was asking an honest question, it was his guilty conscience that made it into something else." I looked at Scott, and to my horror, I could feel my eyes filling. "And you believed him. You . . . you're acting as his intermediary."

He shifted his weight uncomfortably. "Duncan's my friend. He made a mistake. I was trying to help him."

"You were trying to help him cover it up. You're my friend too, Scott. And now, now . . . you're treating me like I did something disgusting, and I didn't and you're using the excuse of friendship to blame me for something I didn't do. You're overlooking an awful lot here, chum."

"You have reasons to want to hurt Duncan. He told me. You'd be happy to see him go down."

"I'm so over him it isn't even funny." I stood up. "And he even had the gall to come to me and ask for a . . . I don't believe this." I stood up. "You know, that doesn't surprise me. What really hurts is that you were so willing to believe whatever he told you, even though you say you're my friend, and take up his part, just like that. Even when you know how . . . unreliable he can be. No, not just unreliable. Downright dishonest."

"Duncan's done a lot of good for the field, Em. It's not worth throwing all that away, just over something stupid he did when he was young. It wasn't like he was falsifying data, or anything."

"He was cheating, Scott, and then he was trying to cover it up. Don't talk to me anymore. Don't ever talk to me again."

"You don't mean that, Emma. You can't."

"Maybe not forever, but I sure as hell mean it right now."

"Come on." He was pleading, groping.

I stood up and winced.

Scott noticed. "What the hell happened to you? What's wrong with your foot?"

"Got into a scuffle last night."

"Bullshit." He tried a half-smile, trying to disbelieve me.

"Not a bit." I didn't really want to talk about it, not with him. "You should see the other guy."

"Damn it, Emma, that's not funny." Scott ran his hand through his hair.

Almost at the same time that the heavy white restaurant mug hit the scuffed veneer of the table, the realization struck me. "No, it's not funny. Scott, I've got to go."

"Aren't you going to tell me what happened?"

"I will when I get back."

"Like I'll be sitting here waiting for you." Tough guy, again.

"I'll find you; we're not done talking yet. Not by a long shot."

I headed for the coffee shop, then stopped myself. The coffee shop didn't make any sense; if the guy bore any marks from our fight, then he wouldn't be showing his face so readily. Maybe he was even ordering room service, hiding out.

Think, Emma, think.

I couldn't very well ask who was ordering room service.

But the police could.

I stood a moment, chewing on a hangnail. There was something else, a thought that was still half formed, but not completely half baked. Duncan came out of the elevator, as I stared blankly. As I'd noticed last night, he didn't have any marks on his face aside from evidence that he still hadn't gotten out of the habit of shaving too quickly. He'd nicked himself on his neck, an angry red cut showed up just below his chin.

That was it. I nodded. Okay, I know it wasn't Duncan who'd attacked me, but he had inadvertently pointed me in the right direction. Another memory, nothing to do with him, but a high school episode that I never would have remembered otherwise, when my then-boyfriend's best friend had appealed to me for help with an illicit hickey. You've got to help me, Emma, he'd said. Do you have any makeup I can borrow?

I thought of my own scratch, and what I'd done about it. I turned and went into the sundries shop.

I always case the sundries shop, trying to assess what might be there in case of an emergency—whether they'd have candy bars or water, in case of missed meals, or pantyhose.

The clerk looked bored and tired, but carefully put his paper away when I entered. "Can I help you?"

"My husband," I said, thinking quickly, "I asked him to pick up some more concealer for me. He's obviously gotten lost on his way back to the room—"

"There's a breakfast reception at the Manchester ballroom this morning," the helpful clerk added. Then he got a closer look at my face, and his features darkened with suspicion. "You okay?"

"Oh, I'm fine. I took a header out in the parking lot. My husband probably found a friend and started chin-wagging. Can you tell me whether he actually stopped by, or did he forget?"

"I just got on shift. There's been no one in here, since I came on. We don't carry concealer, but we do have a couple of foundations, right over there." He pointed to the wall.

"Thanks." I examined the wall of toiletries. The supply of condoms was running low, I noticed, and so was aspirin and Tums, but not much else. There were two colors of foundation, one for dark skin and one for fair. There was a space where someone had taken the first off the rack, for fair skin. That didn't really tell me anything much, though.

I stood there, about to tell the clerk that I'd seek out my fictional husband and his fictional errands elsewhere, when I got my first nice surprise of the morning.

"Looks like he stopped by, though," the clerk announced, looking at a computer printed sheet. "Inventory. Vic sold one last night. That's good for you."

"Huh?"

"I mean, you don't want to have to buy two things of foundation. Stuff is expensive."

"Uh, right."

"I know it drives my girlfriend crazy when I get the wrong kind, or the wrong color. Beige, taupe, warm peach, pleasant peach, plum peachy, I don't know how the hell you girls can tell the difference. It's all light brown to me. And what's with sanitary pads and things? I mean, I swear she asked me to get her a package of half-caff, double-wide, with wings or some damn thing the other day."

I shrugged unhelpfully. "Can't help you with that one. But he must have remembered to pick it up for me last night, stuck it in his pocket and promptly forgot about it." Improv on demand. I was figuring out what to do next.

He'd kept keying through computer screens, however. "Yeah, here you go. Room four-thirty-two. That's yours, right?"

"What!"

He looked alarmed. "That's your room number, right? Four-thirty-two?"

I suspected at least three people who had a room on the fourth floor. "Yeah, sorry, I was . . . spacing out there."

He nodded sympathetically. "Early, yet."

"Well, thanks for your help. I'll, uh, go find him."

I left the shop, speeding toward the elevators, when I caught myself. This is where we start doing the smart thing, I said, as I redirected myself straight over to the desk. I told the day manager everything, and she immediately called the police. I didn't have to be told twice to stay where I was, and I settled into one of the overstuffed and poorly designed chairs. Too low to be comfortable, too deep in the seat to be sit-able. Yet another hazard of conference hotels was the price you paid in tormented backs.

I grinned to myself: Already I was in denial about what I'd just done, about what might be happening. I couldn't quite believe it. I was excited, I was nervous, I was doing things by the rules. Well, the rules as far as I knew them. I sat, barely able to contain my excitement, which was part fear, part thrill, part fatigue.

"Hey, Jay-Bird!" I'd looked up just in time to see my friend heading out for the parking lot with a small bag.

He was out of hearing range, but I couldn't just sit there, I was too excited, I needed to talk to someone. I trotted out after him and was delighted to see sun and blue sky. "Hey, Jay! Over here!"

The parking lot was mostly cleared by now, but the individual cars still needed digging out. Jay fumbled with his keys at the icy lock and managed to pry the trunk open. He tossed the bag inside, slammed the trunk, dropped his keys, then swore.

I caught up to him as he dug in the snow for his keys. "Hey, you heading out?"

He was still engrossed in trying to find his keys. "Yeah, gotta make an early start. I said goodbye to everyone else last night."

"Well, I'm glad I caught you."

He looked up sharply, and that's when I saw it. My smile freezing on my face had nothing to do with the cold. Jay looked as though he had a tan on just one side of his face. Not a bit of the usual variation of human skin coloration, and it stopped abruptly at his chin and temple. Unblended, it looked like a mask.

No. Please, God, no.

"I . . . uh, I mean, I'm glad I got to say goodbye," I said hastily, swallowing and closing my gaping mouth. I began to rub my arms as if trying to keep warm. Maybe he didn't realize I knew, now, but I wanted him to get used to my arms moving, get him thinking all my movements would be this innocent. "Got time for a quick cup of joe before you leave?" I said as I backed off a couple of steps, jerking my head as if I was heading back to the hotel and he should follow.

"Not really," he said, bending over his keys. "I gotta hit the road. Shit."

He'd dropped his keys again, and got tangled up in his coat as he tried to dig them out. When I saw what he was doing, saw that there was in fact a gun he was fumbling for in his pocket, I screamed as loud as I could and shoved him into the side of the car.

He wasn't expecting it, though he should have known by now that I would fight back. Jay didn't drop the pistol, however, and I knew that my first goal was to keep him from pointing it at me. I couldn't believe that I was doing what I was doing, but I stepped in closer to Jay, to his side, stumbling in the compacted snow. At the same time, I grabbed his wrist and the gun by the barrel and jerked both toward him with a sharp movement. He had no choice but to let go. Suddenly I had the pistol.

I backed away, a careful step at a time, trying not to get tripped up by the snowplowed berms, and tried to put some distance between us, so that if he tried anything, I'd have time to react. Despite the fact that I'd followed Jay out of the hotel with no coat, I was sweating. Again came the delayed response of an adrenaline flood, and I began to tremble.

Jay saw this and made as if to get to his feet.

"Don't even think about it," I said. I swallowed again, trying to moisten the inside of my mouth, which was suddenly and desperately dry. I hate guns, I've always hated the damned things, but if it came to a choice, I knew what end I wanted to be on. It was heavy in my hand, and I could see that the point was wobbling crazily. I still had it trained on Jay, and he could see how badly it was jumping around;

maybe that would keep him scared enough to stay put, until some kind of help came for me or we both froze to death or I decided what to do next.

I guess the wildly shaking pistol didn't intimidate Jay as much as I'd hoped. "You don't know how to use that, Emma. You're far more likely to blow your own head off. Why don't we talk about this?"

"I know enough to keep from blowing my own head off. I know that this is the trigger, this is the safety, and this"—I pulled back the slide and did a press check—"means there's a round in the chamber." Thank you, Meg, thank you, thank you . . .

The metallic noise was wrong out there, under that broad blue sky filled with strong winter sun, where there should have been nothing but the sound of bright, biting wind through snow-laden boughs and birds whistling in flight. Jay got that too.

"I don't know what you think is going on, Emma," he was pleading, "but I just want to leave. I don't want to hurt you—"

"Shut up, shut up!" I said, my voice sounding shrill even to me. "Stop talking. I know what's going on, I know it was you, you attacked me in my room."

"I didn't want to hurt you," he said, and it worried me that he was so calm about this. I didn't want him to be calm, I wanted him to be worried what I would do. What I was capable of. He sounded too confident and I didn't like it.

I was unable to suppress a nervous laugh. "Why else would you—?"

"I saw you talking to Widmark. I just . . . wanted to distract you from him. From me."

"You were the one in the woods," I said, not wanting to believe it.

"*No!*" He shook his head vehemently, raised his hands in denial. I watched him carefully. "This has nothing to do with you, Emma. I just want to get out of here."

"No," I said.

"After all these years?" he asked sadly. "You can't do this one little thing for me?"

"What? Give you back the gun?" I felt so sick now . . .

He shook his head vigorously; he thought he was making inroads. "Keep it. A girl can always use a little protection, am I right? It's not mine, it's not registered. I got it from . . . friends. My friends in the woods. Just let me get in the car and go."

I stared at him, marveling. "You must think I'm an idiot."

"I don't!" He backpedaled rapidly. "These friends can get you whatever you want! Name it, name anything!"

"These are the same friends you got the gun from?" I asked slowly.

"Yes! They're very powerful people."

"Powerful enough to be willing to shoot an FBI agent. Powerful enough to get you to attack me, and you still have the balls to call me on our friendship? You son of a bitch."

At that moment, I heard a disembodied voice booming toward us. "You are surrounded. Put the gun down!"

It was Church.

"No, you have to cuff him first!" I surprised myself, but there was no way I was doing anything until I knew that Jay was no longer a threat.

"We've got it under control, Emma." But Church sounded a little nervous. "I have my officers in place. They're very close to you, and they're going to show themselves now. Put the gun down."

Suddenly I saw the heads of three very burly New Hampshire State Police officers emerge from behind various cars nearby. I lowered the pistol a mite; the more I lowered it, the closer they edged to Jay. My hand was still shaking hard. I took a couple of deep breaths, focusing on relaxing, not even on opening, my hand. Finally, my fingers relaxed enough, and I was able to put the weapon down, carefully as I could.

They cuffed Jay the instant the pistol hit the snowbank and skidded to the plowed asphalt.

Then one of them turned to me, grabbing me by the upper arm and walking me well away from the other officers.

"I hate guns," I was saying. "I just hate them."

"You seem pretty comfortable with them, for hating them so much."

"A friend of mine was trying to help me understand them. She thought I'd be less nervous around them." I thought back about Meg's carefully reasoned instruction—carefully reasoned and utterly specious, if you ask me—and shuddered. "Now I just understand in detail why I hate them so much. I don't think understanding the mechanics of how something kills makes it any less deadly, though I suppose that knowing how they work can help you out in a pinch, you know, if you know what's going on, you're that much better prepared, and I guess, safer . . ."

I trailed off, realizing that I was babbling. The state trooper just stood there, just as impassive as one of those guards outside Buckingham Palace.

"Let me guess," he said after a minute. "You're from Massachusetts, aren't you?"

Before I could say anything, Church came over. "I'd like to have a word with Dr. Fielding, if that's okay, Hill." He turned to me. "So why are you out here anyway?"

"I was saying goodbye to a friend of mine." I sighed. You will not cry now, you will not. Not now. "That's all I was going to do."

He nodded, eliciting again. "And things just got bad from there?"

"It was just that I saw the makeup on his face." I was almost pleading now. "I'd tried to pretend that I didn't notice, but I guess he saw. He tried to pull the gun on me."

"And how did you end up with it?"

"I took it away from him."

Church laughed nervously. "Mother of—are you out of your *mind*?"

"No. I saw a chance and I took it. It was dangerous, I know—"

"Dangerous? *Dangerous?*"

"—but it would have been so much worse if I hadn't. I did what I had to do to protect myself. If I'd thought I was going to get into any trouble, I would have told you, just like I did all the other times."

"All the other times you got into trouble? All those times—"

"Were purely accidental. I was always on my way to do something else. It just happened . . . it was just . . . that I knew what else was going on. I had a few more pieces of the puzzle, that's all." It's not my fault, I thought fiercely. I've done everything right this time, as far as I could. "Like I told you about the room service and how whoever attacked me last night probably would be trying to hide his injuries. You were tracking that down, when I found Jay. I was just saying goodbye to a friend."

Chapter 17

THERE WAS THE USUAL HULLABALOO AFTER THAT, statements and all, but I didn't even need the information I weaseled out of Church about the autopsy to get most of the story: Jay started singing right away. He'd already given away too much to me to claim that his murder of Garrison was purely a personal matter, because of Garrison's review of Jay's site reports. Jay's gambling debts had become an issue, it seemed, and he got involved with people who were all too happy to make the most of that. As odd as it sounded, an archaeologist in one's back pocket for the right contractor is a useful thing; he has the power to move ahead with large civic and urban projects, as long as the state signs off on it. As long as no one was paying too close attention to what Jay was finding and what he was actually reporting, he had the power to greenlight any number of projects that might have been held up by archaeological reconnaissance. I'm sure that was the least of the debt he owed his "friends."

He confessed that he'd followed Garrison out of the hotel and walked with him down the access road to the lake, trying to talk him out of what he knew Garrison would inevitably do:

Expose Jay's falsification of data to the state. I was left with an image of Jay half-dragging Garrison as far from the hotel as he could, then knocking him over, smashing the back of his head against the ice that had formed over the shallows of the lake. The anticoagulants that Garrison was taking probably contributed to the speed with which a subdural hematoma formed, keeping Garrison unconscious while he froze to death. Realizing that the chances of Garrison recovering, or making it back to the hotel, where he was imagined to be in bed, were slim, Jay had simply walked away, leaving it to look like an accident. It was one of the few good bets that Jay had made, apparently. I'd even seen him on his way back, I remembered later, hoping he hadn't seen me with Duncan in the slide room.

At first I was just angry with Jay—angry with what he'd tried to do to me, tried to do with our friendship, angry with his lack of self-control when it came to gambling and the thought of the sites and information that he'd cost the world forever. Then I started to think about what he must have been going through, how afraid he must have been to be willing to compromise so much, and what threats must have been hanging over him.

Of course, that didn't stop him from alerting his "friends" to the presence of Special Agent Widmark with pictures from his cell phone at the reception. Widmark, who'd been trying to unearth the connection between him, Garrison, and the mob. They'd been out there, the night Garrison's death was announced, shooting at Widmark, and they tried again when I'd followed him into the woods. It didn't stop him from shooting at me that night I went to investigate the hospitality suite, or letting his associates know that I was outside, so they could take a shot at me, a sitting duck.

It was the fact that he actually made me feel outrage and pity for an old man I disliked so heartily that let anger win in the end. The notion of Garrison's fear, in his last conscious moments, the image of his beret soaked in blood on the ice, was what finally tipped the scales for me.

I was left sorting through this unpleasant collection of emotions and memories as I headed for my room when Duncan hurried up alongside me.

"Got a minute?"

Considering I'd only recently dismissed him as a killer, that I'd just been in a struggle over a gun with someone I counted as a friend, that he'd turned another friend against me, and that I'd learned that he'd fudged the conclusions on his dissertation, I thought I was remarkably gracious.

"What?"

"Look, can we go in? Just for a second?" he said hastily, still unsure of where he was and where I was.

I held the door open and he followed me in quickly.

"Super, thanks," he said, when the door had shut behind us. It was just the two of us, him turning it on and me with my arms across my chest, again. He looked around, and suddenly realized what seemed unfamiliar to him. "Wow, it's clean in here."

"Yeah, thanks. Housekeeping came while I was talking to the cops."

"No, I mean, no piles of your crap everywhere. Books, clothes, that's what I remember. This Brian must really be having an effect on you."

Suddenly, I felt my blood boiling: He doesn't get to talk about Brian, not after what I found out about him. "I just don't think the housekeepers should have to suffer because I'm a slob, that's all."

"Whoa, hey, no harm meant." Duncan realized that he wasn't starting off on the right foot. "I'm sure I gave the wrong impression last night. It's just that I'm so interested in this job. I was tired, then, I was probably one or two over my limit, I came off too strong. I'd like to apologize for that."

"Great." I was convinced that he had to have known there

was a chance that Scott had spoken to me about the Haslett data, but there was no sign of that in his nervousness. In fact, he relaxed as soon as I answered him.

"So, I'd like to ask you again, if you'd reconsider writing a letter for me. I'm sure it would be a big help, and I'd really appreciate it."

The phrase "really appreciate it" was heavily freighted with promise.

"You never give up, do you," I said. The thought flitted through my head that if I said yes, he'd be out of my hair forever. I thought about what I'd be willing to pay for that, a little closure, if there were promises being made, and shivered at the possibility. "You just . . . . don't. Ever give up."

He mistook my tired smile for affection, and he unleashed a twenty-gigawatt smile right back at me. "That's me. Stubborn as hell."

"Yeah, I know." I wanted to slap the stupid grin off his face, I wanted to batter him into an unrecognizable paste. I wanted to eradicate him from the planet, from my past, from memory. I'd tried denial, I'd tried being human, but nothing seemed to work.

And I don't believe in closure.

Funny thing was, something Nolan was always drumming into my head chose this moment to appear. He was always saying, if you miss hitting your opponent in one place, go for something else, but keep at it. If you miss swinging with your right hand, kick with the opposite leg. If you're already moving in one direction, go with it. Make it work for you. If someone pushes you, react, and make it strong. Go for the fight-ending blow to start, but if it doesn't work, keep eroding your opponent's will to continue.

And so this time, instead of merely reacting out of a habit of anger or shame or anything else, I reacted tactically. I found my fighting stance, so to speak, got grounded and analyzed the situation. It didn't take long, really, because I already had all of the information I needed. Some of it was from a couple of decades ago, some of it was from the past four days. And now I knew what to do with it.

I looked at Duncan, really gave him a careful going over. He didn't seemed fazed by that; he was used to people looking at him and enjoyed the sensation. Needed it, really. He'd aged better than some, that was for sure. And I could see past the slight slackening in the facial skin— something I just knew would turn into interesting Redford-style crags someday—where it wasn't hidden by his beard. The receding hairline that was showing gray in some lights. But it was still Duncan, and he was still good-looking. His mother was right; had we had children, our kids would have had red hair and they would have been gorgeous.

It wasn't the signs of aging that made him change for me. He wasn't so much different from when we were together, and that was the problem. In fact, it suddenly occurred to me that he was even more like the old Duncan than I could have believed possible, and that was because he wanted something from me. I recognized that now, for what it was. Sure, everyone wants something from the one they love, even if it's just plain old desire. But with Duncan, it was all that and something else as well. I had something he wanted.

A million years ago, maybe it had been sex or a study partner or maybe, and I was going to admit it to myself for the first time, maybe it was Oscar and what Duncan believed a connection with Oscar would do for him. Maybe he genuinely loved me and just was too chicken to commit to an adult relationship, as he claimed. Even if he had, I now knew that eventually he would have come to believe that he could do better, for whatever reason, because for Duncan, there was no end. There wasn't a place that he could choose to say, okay, this is what I want, how can I make it better, how can I share it, how can I take a rest? For Duncan, there would always be another goal, one more hill to climb, and then he would receive the ultimate prize.

Only there was no grand prize, not as he imagined it. And even if there had been, he wouldn't have been happy with it.

I saw in him something of what I had been attracted to all those years ago, a lifetime ago. I saw the ambition and the brains and the charisma, and they were still appealing. I also saw how much of that was attractive because it mirrored what I was like in those days, when life was merely a set of hurdles to sail over, and obstacles were simple problems that could be removed by dint of hard work, enthusiasm, determination, and bravura.

Those were still useful attributes, but they weren't the only ones. These days, I found that I tired out quicker, and so found other ways instead of brute strength, instead of bashing my head against the wall of accomplishing my goals. I let Brian help, I compromised, I changed my mind, changed my goals, when they weren't enough to justify their pursuit, because life is too short to waste time. I learned that life is not a zero-sum game, that just because someone else got something, it didn't mean that I had lost something. I learned that I wasn't even the most important thing in the world, though I made a hell of a lot more difference to those around me if I took care of myself as if I was. Compromise has all sorts of cheap, tacky connotations. If, however, one thought of it more as finding a scenario where everyone could win most of their objectives and no one was miserable, then that was a pretty good thing.

"Can you help me out, Em?" he repeated.

I took a deep breath. "Not the way you want. I'm sorry."

"Yeah, I am too." His words were heavy with sarcasm. "So much for acting like adults."

I laughed. "Get out of here, Duncan."

"Don't worry." He reached for the handle of the door. "Oh, by the way, I need to pass something along to you."

"Oh?" I waited, figuring he was going to lay some heavy riposte on me, some big exit line. I could live with it, if he needed to cover his ego.

"Billy Griggs says hello."

He hadn't even moved the door open another inch before I was on him. I slammed the door shut, and before Duncan knew what was happening, I'd shoved him as hard as I could against the opposite wall.

"Billy Griggs? What the fuck do you mean by that? You have no business—none—even *thinking* about *anything* to do with—"

"Holy shit, Emma!" Duncan was scared. He tried to move along the wall, away from me, but I blocked his way with my elbow, sticking my finger in his face. There was no way he was going anywhere, as far as I was concerned. "What the hell is wrong with you?"

"You tell me! What the hell do you know about Billy Griggs, and what makes you think you have any right to mention him to me?"

"Goddamn it, Emma, I met him out in Chicago, last year. This guy came up to me in one of the bars outside the hotel where a couple of us historical types were hanging out. He said he knew you, wanted me to say hello, that's all." Duncan didn't make any effort to get away from me; he seemed too afraid to try.

"Don't lie to me, Duncan! Billy Griggs is *dead*! I watched his murder, years ago, back at Penitence Point. Billy is *dead*."

Duncan looked shaken by my violent response. "Well, then, maybe I've got the wrong guy. He was older, maybe in his early sixties? Dark hair, clean shaven. Weather-beaten, been in the field a while, I figured, but well dressed."

I shook my head. "Doesn't sound like anyone I know." I backed off slowly. Maybe Duncan had only made a horrible mistake. If it was a practical joke, an attempt to get under my skin, he'd be very, very sorry he'd ever tried. "And you're sure that was the name he gave you?"

"Yeah, I'm sure. He came up to me at the bar, asked if I was Duncan Thayer. When I said yes, he said he was glad he caught me, said that we'd met years ago and he asked after you. I was surprised, because that . . . was a long time ago. Said he'd been hoping you'd be at that conference, that he'd have a chance to run into you. Then he said, 'Do me a favor, tell Emma Billy Griggs sends his regards, and that I'll catch up with her some time next year. Next time I'm in Massachusetts.'"

A horrible icy knot began to form at the pit of my stomach. "What did he sound like? Did he have an accent?"

"I dunno, kinda Southern, I guess. I couldn't tell where from."

Dear God. "Duncan, are you sure you're telling me everything?"

"Yeah, positive." He looked at me and swallowed, another old habit he had when he was scared and not going to admit it. "Emma, what's this about?"

I started to shake, my head aching like it was in a vise. I stepped away from him.

It had to be Tony Markham. It was just sick enough. Maybe he'd dyed his hair . . . and as a former colleague of mine, a Mesoamericanist, the historical archaeologists wouldn't be so likely to recognize him. The authorities had said he must be dead, but I never believed this, not the way he looked when he killed Billy Griggs while I watched—he was just too evil to let a little thing like a hurricane get him . . .

"Emma, what's your damage?"

I shook my head, trying to think of something logical to say, something that would make this all go away. Finally, I sat down. It had to be Tony.

"Emma?"

"Just something I thought was over with. Don't worry about it, Duncan. I know you'll find this hard to believe, but it has nothing to do with you."

It couldn't be, I thought. Christ, it never ends, nothing ever ends, can't I ever be done with something? What was it that Faulkner said? The past is never dead; it's not even past.

An hour later, I'd recovered myself, convinced myself that it was a practical joke, on Duncan's part or someone else's. Had to be. Maybe it was sick, but people at conferences do sick things, sometimes, in the name of humor.

Carla caught me on the way to the bar for lunch. "Good conference, Em?"

"Yeah, sure. Pretty busy," I said automatically, wondering whether I was capable of eating. The menu was far too familiar to tempt me.

"You must not have noticed that my sarcasm needle was pinning the irony meter," she said. "I hardly saw you after the first night or so. I don't think you went to any of the usual papers you go to, and I saw you not only talking with cops, but also sitting in on the papers where it's usually just us osteological ghouls hanging out."

I struggled to figure out what to say, what she was saying to me.

"Ah, forget it. Lissa told me. You might have told me yourself."

I felt myself flushing, guilty.

"Hell, Carla, I—"

"I know, I know, it was a busy weekend for you—I've been hearing rumors. And sometime I'd like to know all the details. But in the meantime . . ." She dug into her bag, once filled with cigars and cards and flyers for her program, and now filled with new books. She handed me a battered forensic anthropology text. "I just picked up the new edition. It's not going to do you any good with the legalities south of the border here," she said, "but it should provide some good references to get you started."

"Carla, I don't know what to say."

"That's good, because I haven't got the time to listen; I'm out of here." She handed me one more thing from her bag. The battered deck of Chippendale cards. "Here. Lissa's going to be around for a while, and Chris, if he isn't too hung over, said he wouldn't mind a game. So give them back to me next year, okay?"

"Thanks, Carla, I owe you."

"Boy, do you ever." She gave me a hug. "Don't take any shit from these jokers, Em. Stay in touch."

"You too."

Later on, I found Meg. I owed it to her to tell her what I knew. She'd been out there, that night at Penitence Point years ago, and she'd saved me, truth be told. She deserved to know, so I told her everything, excepting what I'd learned from Scott about Duncan. That would come out all on its own, I figured, and he was his own punishment.

I also told her what he'd said about Billy Griggs. She needed to know that, if anyone did. Just in case.

She listened gravely, her brow furrowing deeper and deeper. Finally she shook her head.

"I don't buy it. I think that was the last salvo he had, and it blew up in his face."

"But Duncan seemed so surprised by my reaction." I still really wanted to believe her, desperately wanted her to be right.

She wasn't bothered. "I'd be surprised too, if you reacted like that to anything I said! Face it, Emma, and I say this as a friend . . ." She looked at me, anxious that she wasn't assuming anything.

I nodded. "Go ahead."

"If he's always been able to play you, use what he knew about you to get what he wanted, then why couldn't this be the same thing?"

I considered it, hoping. "You mean, he'd found out about Billy and Tony and everything, and was just trying to play with my head?" I frowned. "It's possible."

"But he wasn't expecting you to bite back, this time." Her face cracked open in a smile of purely malicious glee. "I would have given money to see that."

"I'm glad you didn't, but thanks. And that other stuff"—I shook my head—"feels like it happened in someone else's lifetime."

"It did. Like you said: another life."

I was quiet for a moment, then decided I was done with those thoughts for the moment. "And speaking of other lives . . ."

"Yeah?"

"I notice a bunch of you young'uns aren't leaving until later tonight."

She nodded. "We've got a couple of hours until we have to drive people to Manchester and Portland, to the airports. We're camping out in the bar, until then."

"You guys got any money?"

She snorted. "Are you kidding me? We're graduate students. The ranks of the eternally impoverished."

"Thing is, I've got a deck of cards and two friends who are dying to give me more of their hard-earned cash. I was thinking, what's the point of having graduate students near at hand if you can't exploit their labor *and* take away their drinking money?"

"You think you can beat me at cards?" She threw back her head and laughed. It was fabulous to hear, an epic laugh. "Emma, you know I spent most of my early life traveling between military bases. Poker was an integral part of my early childhood training."

"Gosh, I'd think you'd have nothing to worry about, then. But if you're scared . . ."

"Ha! Are you kidding me? You're giving me a chance to take your money away from you, wipe the floor with you in front of *my* friends, in front of *your* friends, and you think I'm going to pass that up?" She laughed again. "When and where?"

"My room, I've got it until late. For some reason, the hotel is being very, very accommodating with me. Say three o'clock?"

"You got it." She suddenly turned shy, in that stubborn way of hers; she might hesitate, she might be uncomfortable, but Meg would never back away from what she felt she had to do. "And Emma?"

"Yeah?"

"Thanks."

Epilogue

MONDAY MORNING, I WOKE UP AT HOME, IN MY own bed, to a marvelous quiet. Brian had left for work hours ago, and I'd fallen right back to sleep after he left. There was no hum of traffic or the inner working of hotels, no feet padding along carpeting outside my door, no slam of doors down distant hallways, and no omnipresent throb of climate control and plumbing that isn't mine. No rumble of cocktail parties that grows into a roar as one draws near, no restaurant racket, muted voices, or discreet clink of cutlery. I luxuriated in the silence, the lack of things demanding memory or attention or anything of me at all.

That lasted about five minutes. Minnie the cat hopped up and marched across my head several times until she was satisfied that I was awake and aware of her presence, whereupon she betook herself to the far side of the bed and began to wash. I listened to the tranquil repetition of rasping tongue on fur, but when she got to making a production of chewing on her hind claws, teasing off the old shells, I relinquished the bed to her. I got dressed and went downstairs, loving the fact that I would not have needed to get dressed if

I didn't want, if it wasn't for the fact that it was just below freezing outside. As the coffee dripped, I watched Quasimado licking his considerable belly—apparently it was bath time for all the Fielding-Chang felines—and he leaned back with a catty sort of sigh, his tongue still half stuck out. I didn't blame him; it was an awful lot of cat he had to wash with that small tongue, and lounging like that, he resembled a beached killer whale. A furry killer whale, with a potbelly. He caught me looking at him sympathetically, and gave me a dirty look.

Tant pis, cat, I thought.

Quasi hauled himself up, and strode off to continue his ablutions elsewhere. If he still wasn't my best friend in the world, then at least, considering he now had to compete with Minnie—for my attention, body heat, or ability to disburse cat food—he was a lot mellower toward me.

I found a note by the coffeepot: Brian knew where to go to register on my radar. It said: "Babe, last night you were talking about how you loved me for all of the small things I did and knew and that Duncan might have been good at grand gestures but didn't know what love really takes. I know what you meant, but I'm afraid the words 'small' and 'little' just didn't sit right—guys don't like those words, ever—not when you were making comparisons with a former boyfriend. I don't care how long ago you broke up."

Suddenly, my heart went icy. I continued to read, one hand clutching the countertop.

"So look at the other side of this paper, and let's not ever have any talk of little/small ever again. I'm very glad you're home. All love, Brian."

I flipped the sheet over: The note had been written on the back of a computer printout. It was an online travel itinerary. Brian had booked us a trip to Hawaii.

In pencil was scrawled, "That BIG enough for you?" Below that, in smaller print: "We were talking of going to San

Diego to see my folks anyway. Don't worry, I checked your summer calendar."

A real vacation? Brian! I could exorcise every ghost haunting me, I thought, so long as I'm married to this man.

After a leisurely two cups of coffee, I went upstairs and flipped through my email. It was early, yet, to be getting any follow-up correspondence from the conference, and for a change, my mailbox was relatively empty, as almost everyone I knew had been in New Hampshire. I did, however, send an email to Brian, with "Message Received," in the subject heading. The text of the message was just the URL for the bathing suit section at Eddie Bauer.

Enjoying lack of immediate demands, my glance fell on my Rolodex. I thought for a moment, then pulled it to me, and flipped through until I found the card I wanted. It had dirt creased into it from having ridden around in my pocket a couple of summers ago and it read: Stuart Feldman, Massachusetts State Police, Crime Scene Service Officer. Even if it wasn't today, or next week, I knew I would call him eventually. Once upon a time, out at the Chandler site, he'd suggested I put my archaeological skills to official use, and offered to help me out. Now, I realized I would do it, though not today. I'd made the decision, I got through the conference, but the day after was always a holiday.

Back downstairs, I pulled on my boots and my parka and took my coffee mug with me to check the mailbox. Gravel crunched underfoot and I paused to remove a piece that got stuck in the tread of my boot. The snowbanks on either side were little glaciers, dirty and compact, dead grass and gravel entombed in icy piles at the side of the drive. The flag was up and it was with a knowing contentment that I hastened down the way to retrieve whatever happily ordinary deliveries there were.

Electric bill, oil bill, car payment. Catalogue for used historical books, catalogue for lingerie that was addressed to me but always ended up in Brian's pile—it was a discreet fiction that my name was on their mailing list. The usual stuff. But a blank postcard, the sort you buy at the post office, had slid all the way to the back, and my nails scrabbled against the cold galvanized zinc surface before I could raise an edge.

I glanced at it, assuming that it was something local as it was handprinted with my name and address and had no return address. Something was scribbled on the message side, but it was the postmark that caught my attention. It said Caldwell, Maine, which made me think of work and quite possibly recalled library books, but my heart began pounding painfully fast before I consciously realized that I recognized the handwriting of the address. Distantly I heard a flutter of paper and the sharp crack of my mug breaking as it hit the gritty asphalt. My head began to spin.

Black ink, bad handwriting, letters cramped from years of fieldwork, arrogant slants with wide spacing between the words. A smudge of a dirty fingerprint that I didn't need a police lab to identify for me, though I had no training in reading such things. I would have bet the Funny Farm that if one went through the field notes and artifact logs at the anthropology department's Mayan collections at Caldwell, there would be a thousand copies of this same mark. Only one word, four letters, was written in the message section. Enough to make my mouth go dry.

"Soon."

PERENNIAL DARK ALLEY

Get Shorty: Elmore Leonard takes a mobster to Hollywood—where the women are gorgeous, the men are corrupt, and making it big isn't all that different from making your bones.
0-06-077709-5

Be Cool: Elmore Leonard takes Chili Palmer into the world of rock stars, pop divas, and hip-hop gangsters—all the stuff that makes big box office.
0-06-077706-0

Eye of the Needle: For the first time in trade paperback, comes one of legendary suspense author Ken Follett's most compelling classics.
0-06-074815-X

More Than They Could Chew: Rob Roberge tells the story of Nick Ray, a man whose addictions (alcohol, kinky sex, questionable friends) might only be cured by weaning him from oxygen.
0-06-074280-1

Men from Boys: A short story collection featuring some of the true masters of crime fiction, including Dennis Lehane, Lawrence Block, and Michael Connelly. These stories examine what it means to be a man amid cardsharks, revolvers, and shallow graves.
0-06-076285-3

Fender Benders: From Bill Fitzhugh comes the story of three people planning on making a "killing" on Nashville's music row.
0-06-081523-X

Cross Dressing: It'll take nothing short of a miracle to get Dan Steele, counterfeit cleric, out of a sinfully funny jam in this wickedly good tale from Bill Fitzhugh.
0-06-081524-8

PERENNIAL
DARK ALLEY

An Imprint of HarperCollinsPublishers
www.harpercollins.com

DKA 0305

Investigate the Hottest New Mysteries!

Sign up for the FREE HarperCollins monthly mystery newsletter,

The Scene of the Crime,

and get to know your favorite authors, win free books, and be the first to learn about the best new mysteries going on sale.

To register, simply go to www.HarperCollins.com, visit our mystery channel page, and at the bottom of the page, enter your email address where it states "Sign up for our mystery newsletter." Then you can tap into monthly Hot Reads, check out our award nominees, sneak a peek at upcoming titles, and discover the best whodunits each and every month.

Get to know the magnificent mystery authors of HarperCollins and sign up today!

MYN 0205